TH[ ]

SHORE

Siobhan Dunmoore Book 9

Eric Thomson

Published in Canada
By Sanddiver Books Inc.
ISBN: 978-1-998167-03-6

Sanddiver
Books Inc

— One —

Sara Lauzier had achieved her life's ambition thanks to Judy Chu's timely death from a heart attack. As of fifteen minutes ago, after a final Senate vote that came on the heels of long, acrimonious debates, she'd become the youngest Secretary General in the Commonwealth's history.

Lauzier, tall, slender, with elegantly coiffed long dark hair, entered the immense SecGen's office on the Palace of the Stars' top floor. She stopped just beyond the threshold, feeling her heart swell with pride. Lauzier knew the space well, her father having been SecGen for two full terms, but she now perceived it in an entirely new light because it was hers. She was the head of a government ruling countless star systems — in effect, the most powerful human being alive — and she would fundamentally transform the Commonwealth.

Her first act would be appointing a totally new cabinet made up of people she owned, loyal people willing to sacrifice anything for her vision. Those secretaries, in turn, would appoint the same sort to the key positions in their various departments, ensuring the government marched in lockstep under her orders.

There was one fly in the ointment, however. Among Judy Chu's last acts as SecGen before she passed away was naming Kathryn Kowalski as Grand Admiral and commander-in-chief of humanity's Armed Forces. Kowalski was no friend of Lauzier's Centralist creed, and the power wielded by the Grand Admiral was second only to hers.

Lauzier couldn't remove Kowalski except for cause — surprisingly and contrary to past practice, her tenure as Grand Admiral was 'during good behavior' the same as that of federal judges. Of course, she could always arrange for Kowalski to suffer from a heart attack, just like Judy Chu, but it was a much riskier proposition, one with immeasurable consequences. Grand Admirals enjoyed greater protection than SecGens because they commanded the most powerful military forces in the known galaxy.

No, she'd just have to live with Kowalski for the duration of the latter's term, then arrange to have someone more amenable named as her successor. That, in itself, might become a challenge. The four-star admirals and generals wouldn't accept an open Centralist as their leader.

A shame she couldn't simply make the appointees of the previous administration commit seppuku. It would be much cleaner and more effective.

Lauzier strolled to the tall windows overlooking a choppy Lake Geneva under a leaden sky. Winter wasn't her favorite season. The bare trees, the short days, and the biting icy wind howling down the mountainsides all made it highly unappealing. Perhaps she should move the capital to somewhere tropical, Brasilia, for instance, or Lagos, or maybe even Brisbane.

A knock on the door jamb broke through Lauzier's reverie, and she turned.

"Madame Secretary General." The gray-haired man wearing a charcoal business suit bowed his head. "It's a pleasure to welcome you to your new office."

"Thank you, Johan."

Lauzier smiled at her executive assistant, Johan Holden. He came with the job, having been her father's EA before becoming Judy Chu's. Her father thought highly of him, and she'd already decided to keep him on. She needed someone who knew where all the old skeletons were kept, and who better to fill that role than the EA to four successive SecGens?

"Shall I summon the cabinet secretaries?"

"No. They're all dismissed, effective immediately. I will provide you with the list of their replacements so you can prepare the appointment notifications."

"Very well, Madame."

If Holden felt surprise at her wholesale clean-out of the cabinet, he concealed it well. Usually, most secretaries were kept on, at least for a bit, while a new Secretary General settled in. Getting rid of all upon assuming office was unusual.

"I've taken the liberty of transferring the computer accounts over from the late Madame Chu," he continued. "You have access to everything. Will you be attending her memorial service?"

"Yes. I suppose I have no choice. Am I correct in assuming they sent Judy's remains back to her homeworld?"

"Indeed, Madame. Will you be keeping Mister Favreaux as chief of staff?"

Pierre Favreaux was another civil service member, like Holden, assigned to the SecGen's office rather than a political appointee, and she nodded.

"For now, at least. I'm only dismissing the cabinet, not the permanent staff."

"They'll be glad to hear it, Madame. We eagerly anticipate serving you.

"Good. While I have you here, when will Grand Admiral Lowell hand over to Grand Admiral designate Kowalski?"

"Tomorrow, as a matter of fact. There will be a ceremony at Joint Base Geneva in the morning."

She made a moue. "And they didn't invite the SecGen."

"Madame, the Fleet hasn't invited SecGens to change of commands since the Shrehari War. It's a little gesture to reinforce their independence from the political realm. Not even the Secretary of Defense has been invited."

"We'll see if we can change that when Kowalski hands over to her successor. Book her for a meeting with me the day after tomorrow. I might as well establish our relationship sooner rather than later."

"Yes, Madame. Was there anything else you'd like right away?"

"No. I'll go through Judy's to-do list."

"In that case, let me raise something that came up in the last hour." When Lauzier made a go-ahead hand gesture, Holden said, "The Shrehari ambassador has brought a request from his *Kho'sahra* to our attention. A significant anniversary of the war's end is coming up on the Shrehari calendar, and Brakal plans to mark the occasion with a ceremony on Ulufan, where the treaty was signed. He has invited a delegation from the Commonwealth to join him."

"Well, I'm certainly not making a trip that long so early in my term as SecGen." Lauzier frowned. "But we should send someone senior, preferably an admiral since the Shrehari are militaristic. Let me see. Not Kowalski. She needs to stay on Earth for the foreseeable future."

"I had assumed as much, Madame. May I propose Admiral Dunmoore, who commands the 3rd Fleet? She and Brakal go back to the war when they clashed a few times. They also met during the signing of the armistice on Aquilonia Station."

"Make it so. But pass the invitation and my instruction that Dunmoore will attend via Kowalski once she takes over tomorrow."

"Yes, Madame."

"If that was everything, you may prepare the appointment notifications for my cabinet. I'll transmit the names right now."

***

"Congratulations, Admiral." Ezekiel Holt stuck out his hand.

Grand Admiral Kathryn Kowalski took it, beaming.

"Thanks, Zeke. And congratulations yourself."

Holt glanced at his uniform sleeve, which displayed the brand-new stripes of a vice admiral, and grinned back at her.

"I never figured I'd rise beyond captain, yet here I am, in command of the Armed Forces Security Branch, thanks to you."

Kowalski waved away his words.

"Your work as head of counterintelligence got you the promotion and the job."

Both stood at the center of the hangar, which had been converted into a reception space, now filling with the spectators who'd attended the change of command ceremony under a blustery yet sunny sky. The outgoing Grand Admiral, Zebulon Lowell, walked up to them.

"Zeke, Kathryn. Splendid parade, wasn't it?"

"It sure was," Kowalski replied.

"Excellent speech you made, sir. Timely and prescient."

Lowell grimaced. "And one I could only make at the very end of my time in command. I'm afraid things will come to a head now that Sara Lauzier is SecGen. Part of me is glad my term's over, and you're now at the helm, Kathryn. The upcoming battle will be more in your wheelhouse than it would have been in mine."

"Where are you off to now, sir?"

A faint smile appeared on Lowell's lips. "You mean Kathryn hasn't shared it with her closest confidant? I'm shocked."

"I thought I'd keep it quiet until you were no longer in uniform." Kowalski turned to Holt. "We're starting a new tradition. Since Caledonia is now the de facto Fleet homeworld, we will appoint outgoing Grand Admirals as governors general, beginning with Zeb."

"How did you ever get that past the government?"

Kowalski put on a mischievous air. "You mean the Colonial Office since Caledonia has the status of a federal colony?"

Holt's handsome face lit up with understanding. "Ah. Of course. Silly me. We still have friends in high places in the Colonial Office, such as Mikhail Forenza."

"Indeed, Zeke. And since he's now director general of their Intelligence Service, he sits at the head table alongside the permanent undersecretary, who has the actual power when it comes to governor general appointments rather than the secretary herself. I quietly arranged it with him a few months ago."

"Congratulations, Governor General Lowell. And will you settle on Caledonia afterward?"

"Yes. There's nothing for me back on Marengo. The Fleet is my family now, and what better place to retire than the family's very own homeworld? That way I can maintain contact, maybe even instruct the occasional class at the War College or the Academy, that kind of thing. Besides, it seems like most senior flag officers — Ben Sampaio, Jado Doxiadis, Raoul Espinoza, and many more — have recently retired there. I'll be in good company."

"I certainly will join you eventually." Holt turned back to Kowalski. "Before I forget, one of my contacts in the SecGen's office told me that you should expect an interesting directive from Madame Lauzier this afternoon."

"Oh? And what would that be?"

"Brakal is holding some sort of anniversary ceremony marking the end of the war on Ulufan in a few weeks and has invited a Commonwealth representative. The SecGen has decided that would be our Siobhan."

Kowalski's eyebrows shot up. "Really? How appropriate."

"She is the closest four-star to the Shrehari Empire."

"Thanks for the warning. Siobhan will be delighted to attend — her last act as Commander, 3rd Fleet."

"Where is she going after Ulufan?"

A smile lit up Kowalski's face. "Here. She's the next Chief of Naval Operations."

Holt chuckled. "Figures you'd bring her on as your number three. Speaking of which, your number two is headed this way."

General Avi Nagato, Commandant of the Marine Corps and the Fleet's second in command drew himself to attention in front of Kowalski. He was stocky, with short black hair, impassive brown eyes, and a face hewn from granite.

"Congratulations, Admiral."

"Thank you, Avi."

"And where are you off to now?" Nagato asked Lowell.

"Caledonia."

"You as well, eh? It seems to have become the destination of choice for the old boys and girls after they hang up their uniforms."

"Except that I'll be spending a few years as governor general, remaking the star system's administration into something more attuned to the Fleet's needs."

"That's excellent. Do enjoy."

"I certainly will."

"If you'll excuse me." Nagato nodded at Kowalski and headed for a cluster of Marine generals forming to one side.

"And me as well," Holt said. "I see a lineup of people wanting to wish both of you good luck."

"I'll speak with you later, Zeke."

"Of that, I have no doubt."

— Two —

Siobhan Dunmoore sat back after reading the message from her new boss, Grand Admiral Kathryn Kowalski. She was to be the next Chief of Naval Operations. The professional head of the Commonwealth Navy, the most powerful force in the known galaxy. Although the Shrehari might dispute that.

How her career had changed in the last ten years. From a captain passed over for promotion one last time to CNO. The only downside of the appointment was relocating to Earth. She'd avoided humanity's capital her entire career since graduating from the Academy, but no more.

Still, she had one last duty as Commander, 3rd Fleet — attending the anniversary of the end of the Shrehari War on Ulufan, an imperial world in a border star system. She had never visited because she had been dispatched to the War College on Caledonia before the treaty negotiations actually began. And since there was little contact between both naval forces, she hadn't entered the imperial sphere since her famous raid on the Shrehari Prime star system which ended the war.

Dunmoore touched a control embedded in her desktop, and her aide's voice came on immediately.

"Yes, sir?"

"Call the senior leadership together in my office in fifteen minutes. I believe they're free this morning."

"Will do."

Fifteen minutes later, Vice Admiral Oliver Harmel, the 3rd Fleet deputy commander, Rear Admiral Fernando Juarez, the chief of staff - operations, Rear Admiral Gregor Pushkin, the chief of staff - administration, and Command Chief Petty Officer Kurt Guthren trooped into her office as one and took the chairs in front of her desk. The four had expectant airs — Dunmoore rarely summoned them at such short notice.

"The Dunmoore era at 3rd Fleet is almost over, folks. I've just received notification from Grand Admiral Kowalski that I'm leaving for Earth in two months on what will likely be my final assignment before retiring."

"As what, sir?" Pushkin asked.

A smile broke through Dunmoore's stern countenance.

"Chief of Naval Operations."

Pushkin pumped a fist in the air. "Yes!"

"Congratulations, sir," Harmel and Juarez said almost in unison, both grinning.

"Who's replacing you?" The former asked.

"You are, Oliver. Congratulations on your nomination as the next commander of 3rd Fleet."

Harmel's grin threatened to overtake his face. "My word!"

"Gregor, you're coming with me to Earth as one of my assistant chiefs of operations. It's a vice admiral's billet. And Fernando, you're stepping into Oliver's shoes as the next 3rd Fleet deputy commander, so congratulations to both of you as well."

The two vice admiral designates looked at each other, delighted by the news.

She turned to Guthren. "And I'm taking you with me as Chief Petty Officer of the Navy. In the meantime, I have one last task before I leave."

She briefly explained her upcoming visit to Ulufan.

"You'll be traveling aboard *Salamanca*, I presume?" Juarez asked, naming the 3rd Fleet's flagship, a Reconquista class cruiser.

"Yes. And I'll take a frigate as escort. If *Jan Sobieski* is available, so much the better."

"She is, sir."

"It's a shame *Iolanthe* is in space dock," Pushkin said. "She'd have made an even more impressive sight, returning to Shrehari space in triumph all these years later."

"Perhaps, but since the 101st Battle Group isn't part of 3rd Fleet, it's a moot point."

Juarez shrugged. "I'm sure Admiral Devall would gladly have lent her to you. However, *Salamanca* and *Jan Sobieski* it is. Let's call it Task Group 3.10. I'll take care of drafting the deployment orders. Any news about who's replacing Gregor and me?"

"No, not yet." Dunmoore looked at each of them in turn. "That was it. Congratulations once again, and let's get cracking on the transitions. Two months may seem like a long time, but it'll be over quickly. Gregor, Chief, if you could stay a few minutes."

"Certainly, sir."

Juarez and Harmel left, closing the office door behind them.

"Kathryn Kowalski probably engineered our appointments to Fleet HQ, meaning whatever she's been working on for the last decade is coming to a head, especially now that Sara Lauzier has become SecGen. You and I will be at a severe disadvantage for the first few months there since none of us have ever served on Earth and experienced the political swamp firsthand."

Pushkin grimaced. "You're right about that. But we'll be okay, I'm sure. We stared down the Shrehari Deep Space Fleet and gave the various bad guys in the Protectorate terminal heartburn."

"Aye, that we did," Guthren said in his deep, rumbling voice.

"Still, I'm sure Kathryn has more in mind for us than simply running the Navy, and she's assigned you to join me because she figures I'll need your help."

Pushkin's grimace turned into a faint smile. "I will always have your back because I owe you more than I could ever repay. Without you, I'd have become a washed-up lieutenant commander forced into retirement shortly after the end of the war, not a vice admiral designate."

Dunmoore snorted.

"You'd have enjoyed a long career whether or not we had met all these years ago because you're a superb officer who had one turn of bad luck under a lousy captain. And we're not arguing about this," she added. "By the way, would the both of you like to come with me to Ulufan? You have almost as much history with Brakal as I do."

Pushkin cocked an eyebrow at her. "Sure."

"Of course, Admiral. Where you go, I go."

"Good. I'll be glad for the company. Otherwise, I'd end up alone in *Salamanca*'s flag quarters with nothing to distract me. At least Gregor and I can play endless games of chess."

"Oh, lord. It's been a long time, but I remember you turning it into a blood sport."

Dunmoore laughed with delight. "It'll be fun."

"If you say so."

***

The bosun's pipes trilled as Admiral Dunmoore stepped aboard *Salamanca*, the ship looking a little more tired than she had when Dunmoore first boarded her years earlier. The cruiser was docked at Starbase 30, her main airlock attached to one of the arms that sprouted from the orbital station like spokes on a wheel. Meanwhile, the frigate *Jan Sobieski*, a veteran of the war and Gregor Pushkin's first command, had already left the base and was trailing it by a few kilometers as both orbited Dordogne.

Captain Won Haneul, *Salamanca*'s commanding officer, stepped forward and raised his hand in salute, a gesture Dunmoore, trailed by Pushkin and Guthren, returned.

"Welcome aboard, Admiral."

"Thank you, Captain. It's always good to be in the 3rd Fleet's flagship." They shook hands while the bosun and his four mates tramped away in a single file, vanishing down the main starboard corridor. Dunmoore added, in a lower tone, "And thanks for respecting my desire to be received with minimal fuss."

Haneul, of middling height with short black hair and angular features, chuckled.

"I wouldn't dare impose unwished ceremonial on you, sir."

"Would that everyone understood I mean it."

He turned to Pushkin and Guthren. "Welcome, Admiral, Chief."

They shook hands as well, and then Haneul said, "Yours, Admiral Pushkin's and Chief Guthren's quarters are ready, but per your orders, we have not activated the flag CIC. However, it will repeat everything from the ship's bridge and CIC, should you wish to observe maneuvers in private. If you'll come with me."

Followed by their aides — in Dunmoore's case, her senior one — who pushed floats loaded with luggage, they headed deeper into the ship to the officer's accommodation section, where several cabins, including a large suite, were set aside for her and her staff.

Dunmoore still vividly remembered the first time she came aboard, as a captain heading Readiness Evaluation Division Team One. She'd been given the flag suite then and had used the flag bridge as her control center while putting the ship, her captain, and her crew through the most rigorous evaluation known to the Fleet, including a no-win scenario at the very end.

Once in her cabin, Dunmoore unpacked and carefully hung up her dress uniform, complete with sword. The gold braid on the cuffs — a full admiral's large stripe and three narrower ones topped by the executive curl — still left her a bit in awe even after several years as Commander, 3rd Fleet. The braid reached almost to her elbow.

She rarely wore the dress uniform and even less often with her impressive rack of full-sized medals, now pinned to the tunic's left breast, beneath her pilot wings. But Dunmoore had to admit she cut a fine figure in it.

Just then, the public address system came on, warning the crew of *Salamanca*'s imminent undocking and departure, and Dunmoore figured she'd watch from the flag combat information center. Pushkin and Guthren had the same idea because she met them in the corridor, and they headed forward to take the stairs up two decks.

"How are your quarters?" Dunmoore asked Pushkin.

"Nicer than the cabin they gave me when we were aboard as RED One, but still not as spacious as yours."

"Stands to reason. She is *my* flagship, after all."

"True."

"And you, Chief?"

"The same quarters I had last time we were in her."

The door to the flag CIC opened silently at their approach, and they saw their aides already seated at a pair of consoles. The primary and secondary displays were live with exterior views repeated from the ship's bridge. Dunmoore took the throne-like command chair in the center while Pushkin settled at the workstation to her right, and Guthren took the operations chief's console.

They could hear the communications between the ship and the starbase over the bridge speakers. Dunmoore was pleased to note that they were calm and professional, as expected from a cruiser commanded by a veteran officer such as Captain Haneul.

Soon, the outside visual aspects began to change as the docking arm released *Salamanca,* and she used her thrusters to move away from the station. Then, she accelerated and peeled out of orbit directly, followed by *Jan Sobieski,* and both starships headed for the hyperlimit in the general direction of the Shrehari Empire.

"That was nicely executed, with no fuss." Dunmoore stood and glanced at Pushkin. "Did you want to head for the wardroom now and beat the rush?"

"What? You intend to slum with the hoi polloi instead of enjoying meal service in your quarters?"

"We're passengers, Gregor. If I weren't wearing four stars, we'd be on an aviso where quarters are tight and stewards nonexistent."

— Three —

Brakal, *Kho'sahra* of the Shrehari Empire, wasn't in a good mood. But that seemed normal nowadays whenever he had to deal with an emperor bound and determined to have his say in governing. Tumek refused to acknowledge that emperors had been mere figureheads for generations and would stay so, especially when the actual power was in the *Kho'sahra*'s hands.

The emperor hadn't been a problem during his minority, but as soon as he reached the Age of the Warrior, when males were considered grown up, he'd begun trying to interfere in Brakal's running of the Empire. And every meeting with him since then had given Brakal a massive headache.

He'd tried to limit his interactions with Tumek, but when the latter summoned the *Kho'sahra*, he had no choice but to obey. And this time had been more contentious than any other occasion in recent memory. Yet it was over a trifle in the grand scheme of the Empire.

Tumek wanted to go to Ulufan for the memorial ceremonies to mark the sacrifice of those who'd died during the war with the humans, despite the fact emperors never left the homeworld. Under the state religion, they were bound to the soil and could not be parted from it. When confronted with that restriction, he declared he would hold those ceremonies on Shrehari Prime. However, it had been a tradition since time immemorial to hold the Act of Remembrance at the spot where the war ended, or near it. Ulufan was the closest star system to the human Aquilonia Station. Moreover, it had been the site of the negotiations that turned the armistice into a lasting peace.

They had argued for two hours behind closed doors, with Brakal's blood pressure rising steadily while the emperor worked himself into a frenzy of rage, threatening to summon the Kraal and ask it to remove Brakal as *Kho'sahra*. All the while, Brakal remained outwardly calm, respectful, and unyielding. He knew the senior nobles who formed the Kraal would almost universally back him, as they had the day he became the Shrehari Empire's military dictator. They considered themselves the guardians of tradition, even against a willful emperor, and Tumek was bucking many customs to the consternation of those nobles.

"Sire." Brakal finally stood. "This discussion is futile. You cannot attend the Act of Remembrance. No emperor in recorded history has attended any of them since we stopped fighting on this world. And I must now return to my other duties."

Without waiting for permission, Brakal left Tumek's office and hastened down the corridor leading to the outside, worried the emperor might follow and keep berating him, but this time in public. Tumek wasn't doing his dynasty any favors by constantly struggling against the *Kho'sahra*. The clashes had become common knowledge, even though Brakal carefully avoided criticism of his master.

Unfortunately, Tumek had a coterie of younger nobles with whom he shared too much, despite Brakal's warnings. And they spoke out of turn, trying to blacken his reputation. Not that it worked. People didn't consider the emperor's friends as serious warriors. Still, one of these days, he would have to do something about them, and that could result in various complications.

He reached the back door to the imperial residence and climbed aboard his waiting car, driven by the loyal Toralk, whose skull ridges were getting leathery with age. It whisked him across the Forbidden Quarter under a lowering sky to his smaller, less opulent official palace, where he worked and lived. Once he was behind his desk, ready to deal with the next in a never-ending series of issues, his aide appeared at the open office door.

"Lord, we have news from our ambassador on Earth. The Commonwealth will send a small delegation to Ulufan for the Act of Remembrance. Admiral of the Second Rank Dunmoore will head it."

The aide thoroughly massacred Dunmoore's name, but Brakal recognized it nonetheless and felt an unaccustomed surge of pleasure. His old foe, the flame-haired she-wolf. How thoroughly appropriate. And she was an admiral of the second rank, too. A well-deserved series of promotions. The last time they'd met on Aquilonia, she'd been an admiral of the fifth rank. If he recalled the human order of battle correctly, they only had one admiral of the first rank, their commander-in-chief.

"Apparently," the aide continued, "she commands the humans' 3rd Fleet, which is responsible for the entire sector adjoining the Empire and the Protectorate."

"A worthy choice, then. I approve."

"And Regar begs for a moment of your time."

"Has he stated why?"

"No."

The head of the *Tai Zohl*, the Empire's outward-looking intelligence agency, rarely sought an audience with Brakal beyond their normally scheduled meetings.

"Tell him he may see me now."

"Lord." The aide bowed his head and vanished.

Shortly after that — the *Tai Zohl* headquarters were around the corner from the *Kho'sahra*'s palace — Regar appeared in Brakal's office doorway. When Brakal looked up, he bowed his head.

"Lord. Thank you for seeing me."

Brakal gestured at a heavy wood chair, its legs covered in intricate carvings. "Sit."

"A few things have cropped up that I thought you should know about right now rather than wait until our next regular meeting."

"Go ahead."

"Your aide told you Dunmoore will be the human representative at the Act of Remembrance. But he was unaware she would be appointed commander of the entire human navy when she returns home."

Brakal grunted in surprise.

"Well, well. It seems my old foe is doing even better than I thought."

"Next, the humans have a new leader. She is the daughter of the human who led them at the time of the armistice and who you met on Aquilonia. And apparently, she intends to bring greater central control over the human star systems, which will put her in conflict with Dunmoore and the new commander-in-chief of all human Armed Forces who do not favor greater centralization."

"Hmm. How did you find out about this?"

A fierce smile appeared on Regar's face. "That's for me to know, Lord."

Brakal's eyes narrowed as he contemplated ordering his spymaster to reveal his sources, then thought better of it.

"Watching the contest between the military and civilian supreme leaders will be interesting."

Regar's smile widened, revealing wickedly pointed teeth. "That it should be, Lord. Finally, there have been new rumblings in the Protectorate Zone. It appears that the Confederacy of the Howling Stars is significantly expanding its activities and taking on the lesser criminal organizations with the goal of either absorbing or eliminating them. It will be another contest worth watching."

"What is it with the humans and the Protectorate Zone? They have so many renegades there, it might as well belong to their Commonwealth."

Regar made a dismissive gesture. "I think it is because humans are fundamentally anarchic, and the ones who cannot control those impulses flee into the Zone where no one rules."

"Perhaps." Brakal ran a massive hand through his warrior-style crest of stiff, black head fur. "Or maybe the humans are encouraging settlers to head for the Zone so they can annex it at some point."

"That could also be true, but it would take a longer view of history than human leaders, save for a few, usually have."

— Four —

"Grand Admiral Kowalski is here, Madame." Johan Holden stood in the open doorway to the SecGen's office, a solemn expression on his face.

Since she was aware that Kowalski was in the antechamber, not the outer office, and therefore couldn't see nor hear Holden, Lauzier could make her wait in the old bureaucratic game of asserting power. But she considered herself above such obvious maneuvers. Besides Kowalski would know precisely what she was doing and occupy herself by working on other items while she waited.

"Please show her in, Johan."

"Yes, Madame."

He disappeared again to return a few moments later and usher Grand Admiral Kowalski into the office. Lauzier stood to receive her visitor but remained behind the desk rather than come out and shake hands. They were acquainted with each other from frequently crossing paths in and around Geneva over the years. More importantly, both knew about the vast gulf between their respective political views on the Commonwealth and its future.

Kowalski stopped in front of Lauzier's desk. Since she wasn't wearing her beret — on purpose — she didn't salute.

"Madame Secretary General."

"Grand Admiral. Please." Lauzier gestured at the chairs facing her, then took her own.

"Thank you."

Kowalski sat, understanding that Lauzier could have invited her to take a more comfortable seat if she'd moved to the settee group on one side of the office so they could hold their discussion less formally. Instead, Lauzier left the wide expanse of the desk between them, asserting her superiority. Kowalski understood everything she needed to from the coldness in her gaze.

"I'll be completely frank with you, Admiral. You're not my choice as commander-in-chief of the Armed Forces. Had Judy Chu passed away before naming you to the position, you would have faced retirement at the end of your tour as Commander, 1st Fleet."

"Thank you for your candor, Madame. It certainly lets me know where I stand with respect to your administration."

"Since you were appointed during good behavior, I'm stuck with you unless you engage in egregious conduct that would warrant dismissal."

A cold smile briefly lit up Kowalski's face.

"I will ensure that nothing happens, nor will I allow it to be portrayed as if I am guilty of misconduct."

"No doubt," Lauzier replied in a dry tone. "So, I propose we stay out of each other's way as much as possible. You run the Fleet and don't indulge in politics, and I'll leave you alone. Step out of your lane, and I'll make your life impossible."

"What do you consider stepping out of my lane, Madame?"

Kowalski saw a flash of irritation in Lauzier's eyes.

"Let's not be coy, Admiral. I'm a Centralist who believes in enhancing Earth's power over the star systems as the best course of action for the Commonwealth's future. You, on the other hand, are a supporter of the sovereign star systems principle. That makes us diametrically opposed. Make any pronouncement that contradicts my administration's views, or worse yet, take any action against me, and I will retaliate."

"How? By shortening my tenure just like that of the late Madame Chu?"

Lauzier's face hardened as the irritation in her eyes turned to fury.

"I don't like the insinuations you're making, Admiral. Take great care in choosing your words."

Kowalski cocked a mocking eyebrow at her.

"My apologies, Madame. I did not intend to insinuate anything."

Lauzier didn't immediately reply, stunned by the blatant lack of servility in Kowalski's words and behavior. She'd become used to the fawning respect of her subordinates and considered the Grand Admiral among them. Kowalski, obviously, did not.

"Just stay in your lanes, Admiral, and we'll both be happier. Once your term is up, I'll gleefully replace you with someone more suitable for the position."

"Just make sure my replacement suits the four-star admirals and generals in the Fleet. Otherwise, he or she will not be accepted."

Kowalski and Lauzier locked eyes in silence for a few heartbeats, then the latter said, "That's another thing which will change, the four stars having a say in who the five star will be."

"Good luck with that, Madame. The Fleet has entrenched the practice since the end of the war, which started disastrously due to politicians meddling in military matters. Like imposing unsuitable top appointments on the Navy—people incapable of leading us."

"You really have no respect for me, do you?" Lauzier asked with a clenched jaw.

"Not you personally, Madame, I don't. But I respect the office you hold and will carry out any lawful order you give me, provided said order does not interfere with my running the Fleet."

"Why do you have no respect for me, Admiral?" Her tone held an edge of danger.

"Because you're a scheming Centralist who would set back relations between the OutWorlds and Earth to how they were in the time before the Second Migration War. And I will not see the Commonwealth self-destruct in a third one. Especially not with the Shrehari still smarting from their losses. *Kho'sahra* Brakal might not want a resumption of hostilities, but there are plenty of revanchists in the Empire."

Lauzier scoffed. "*You* will not see? Presumptuous, pompous even, Admiral. But I'm glad we've cleared the air between us. I will be SecGen long after you've faded into obscurity. You can be sure of that."

"If you believe so. Still, a lot can happen during the next few years."

"Such as?"

Kowalski shrugged.

"Any number of things that might derail your push to centralize power on Earth. For instance, I don't think you have the requisite number of votes in the Senate to enact the necessary laws. Even some of the Home Worlds are leery of your vision. Fail to push it through often enough, and you won't get a second term as SecGen."

"We shall see. In any case, this meeting is over. Take heed of my warning, Admiral. Keep to strictly military matters, and your term as commander-in-chief will go smoothly."

Kowalski climbed to her feet. "Madame. It was a pleasure."

Then she turned on her heels and left a thoughtful Sara Lauzier to stare at her receding back.

***

"Come on in, Zeke." Kowalski waved Vice Admiral Holt through the door and into her spacious office, indicating the settee group to one side, where she joined him. "Thanks for taking the time."

"For you, I always have time. I presume you'd like some advice after your meeting with Lauzier?"

"Yes." She went on to describe her conversation with the SecGen almost verbatim.

"Let me guess, you'd like to know whether Lauzier might be daft enough to try having you assassinated by her SSB goons?"

Kowalski nodded.

"Well." Holt sat back, elbows on the chair's arms, fingertips pressed together. "That's an interesting question. There's no doubt in my mind she's capable of doing so. Lauzier is a highly controlled psychopath, someone without a shred of empathy who'll do anything to further her ambitions. But would she do it? No Grand Admiral has died in office, ever. If you — healthy, fit, relatively young — were to pass away unexpectedly, there would be serious questions in the Fleet and among the OutWorld senators. And because everyone in this town knows that you and Lauzier have completely different political views, and they can't remove you unless you're guilty of malfeasance, eyes would naturally turn to her. She probably doesn't want that because not all Home World senators are convinced she's on the right track."

"Well, that's a relief. I'd rather not follow Judy Chu into an early grave."

"I think it's much more likely she'll try drumming up a scandal involving you, something to trigger a judicial review of your appointment, leading to dismissal for cause. But even that's unlikely, considering the thorough vetting you underwent throughout your career. Besides, Lauzier must be aware that she won't have a Centralist appointed as your successor. The four-star flag officers simply will not allow it. Of course, it doesn't mean she won't have a Henry the Second moment."

Kowalski frowned, trying to place the reference and gave Holt a questioning look.

"English king, twelfth century. He famously said *will no one rid me of this turbulent priest* about Thomas Becket, the Archbishop of Canterbury. He did not express it as an order, more as a complaint, but upon hearing of it, four knights traveled to Canterbury and killed Becket. It's possible Leila Gherson or one of her SSB minions might hear the boss complain about you and act on it."

"Would you mind making Gherson aware that if she takes it out on me, it could lead to the downfall of the SSB?"

"Certainly." Holt gave Kowalski a sly look. "Although the SSB's days are numbered in any case."

"Maybe, but there's no need for her to discover that."

***

Holt, wearing a dapper civilian suit, dropped into a chair across the corner table from Leila Gherson, Director General of the Special Security Bureau. They were in the *Genfer Ratskeller*, a restaurant in the basement of the old town hall that counted as among Geneva's best. But its ambiance — stone walls and floor, heavy blackened ceiling beams, subdued lighting, and wooden furnishings — made it memorable. It was going on twenty-hundred hours and Gherson was waiting for her dinner companion.

"Leila."

Holt gave Gherson a mocking smile, knowing of her distaste at people she considered inferior using her first name. And she certainly considered vice admirals beneath her, even the head of Fleet Security.

Gherson gave him a haughty stare. "What do you want, Holt? I'm expecting someone."

"Yes, I know. Axel Renouf, man about town and permanent undersecretary for the Department of Public Safety. Playing it pretty close to the nest, aren't you? Best be careful you don't foul it."

"My private life is none of your concern. How about you get up and walk out of here before I turn nasty?"

"Oh, please do, Leila. I haven't experienced your nastiness yet." Holt winked at her suggestively. "But this will only take a few moments. You remember the truce between the SSB and the Fleet, the one imposed by Jado Doxiadis? Yes? Well, I'd like to remind you of it now that we both have bosses who just as soon kill each other than share a glass of wine. Make sure Grand Admiral Kowalski comes to no harm because some idiot working for you decides that Sara Lauzier complaining about her constitutes an execution order. I'd rather Kowalski not end up like Thomas Becket."

"Or what?"

"The SSB gets wiped out, period. You and your senior people will not survive. Nor will most of your field agents."

When she seemed unimpressed, Holt asked, "Do you know what I am now?"

"You're the head of the Armed Forces Security Branch."

Holt nodded. "And that means I have a bead on your entire organization. Take me seriously, Leila. Your life depends on it. Keep your people away from Grand Admiral Kowalski and every other senior officer in the Fleet."

When he saw a man headed toward the table, he stood. "Enjoy the rest of your evening."

As he and the man crossed paths, Holt smiled at him and said, "Strange choice of girlfriends, Axel."

— Five —

Task Group 3.10 emerged from FTL at the Ulufan system's heliopause, and *Salamanca* immediately began broadcasting their identity and destination in Shrehari on the latter's emergency channel, hoping the Ulufan Strike Group was expecting them. After less than an hour, they received a single Anglic word in reply — welcome.

Dunmoore and Captain Haneul glanced at each other, and the latter said, "Terse, aren't they?"

"It's the Shrehari way. They use as few words as possible to get their meaning across." She smiled. "Besides, they're not very good at Anglic and tend to keep it short. Let's jump inward, seeing as your navigator found Ulufan."

With that, she, Pushkin, and Guthren left the bridge to return to the accommodations deck. It would be approximately twelve hours before they emerged at the planet's hyperlimit. Once they were alone in her cabin, Guthren drew three mugs of coffee from the small urn that was always kept fresh and handed them out.

"Feeling a bit of trepidation starting, Admiral?" Pushkin asked over the rim of his cup before taking a sip.

"Perhaps. I've never set foot on a Shrehari world before. I know they're oxygen-nitrogen breathers like we are. Their ale is perfectly digestible by humans and even favored by many. Beyond that?" She shrugged. "You?"

"Oh, I'm getting the old nerve vibes, faint but present. How about you, Chief?"

Guthren made a face.

"I got nothing going on."

Pushkin grinned at him.

"Stolid as usual."

"When you have a good thing, you stick with it." Guthren took a big gulp of his coffee, then sighed contentedly. "You know, it's fitting that we meet Brakal at this juncture."

"How so?" Pushkin asked.

"We'll head off to Earth soon for our final assignments before retiring. Saying a last goodbye to the old rogue seems like a fine thing, considering how often our paths crossed during the war."

"True. Especially when you realize we, or more precisely Admiral Dunmoore, are responsible for Brakal becoming *Kho'sahra* and ending the war. After all, it was *Iolanthe* that destroyed Brakal's forward operating base, forcing his superiors to send him home as surplus to requirements, where he then set about to overthrow the ruling council which had started the war." Pushkin raised his mug at Dunmoore. "The raid on the Shrehari home system was merely the icing on the cake."

The thirty-second jump klaxon sounded, and all three took seats to better weather the momentary nausea, as they'd done countless times since their first FTL jump from their homeworlds heading to basic training long ago.

"It never gets easier," Guthren said once *Salamanca* was in hyperspace and the nausea dissipated.

"We still have plenty of jumps to make before finding a place to settle and establish deep enough roots that we'll never depart from the surface again, Chief."

Guthren let out a grunt.

"Aye. But there's an end in sight, and then it'll be Caledonia for me, alongside the rest of the old chief petty officers who only have the Navy as a family."

"You and me both, Chief." Pushkin turned to Dunmoore. "How about you?"

"Considering I haven't been home in over thirty years, Caledonia seems like a good place to retire among other Fleet personnel."

They finished their coffees, and then Dunmoore shooed them out.

"Since I plan on being awake when we emerge at Ulufan's hyperlimit, I'm going to bed now."

"Good idea."

***

"The human ships are inbound, Lord," Brakal's aide reported once the *Kho'sahra* waved him into his temporary office. It lay in the governor's palace at the heart of the Forbidden Quarter of Ulufan's capital, Kordar. He and his small retinue — the aide, Toralk, and a detachment of bodyguards — had taken over a wing of the palace reserved for high-status visitors. "Two of them, one the equivalent of a *Tol*, the other of a *Ptar*."

Brakal grunted his thanks.

"Let me know when they're within reach of instantaneous communications. I would speak with Admiral of the Second Rank Dunmoore."

When the aide expressed surprise, Brakal gave him a predatory smile. "She and I go back to a time long before you were considered fit for the Deep Space Fleet."

And with that, he dismissed him. His inviting humans to the Act of Remembrance for the war against them did not thrill everyone. None dared say so to his face, but the loyal Toralk had kept an ear to the ground and heard enough. There was a groundswell of opposition to Dunmoore's presence, especially once word got out that she'd led the raid on the home system, precipitating what most saw as the Empire's surrender rather than a simple cessation of hostilities. Returning the star systems taken from the humans still angered many even now, at the time of the Act of Remembrance after the prescribed number of years had passed since the war's end.

He couldn't do anything about those sentiments, however. Only ensure Dunmoore and her delegation were received with due honor, stood in silence beside him during the Act, and then left again.

It was a long trip for a brief ceremony, but ancient tradition demanded it be done. Inviting a former foe was also part of that tradition, even though for the first time, she would be human. And that bothered the detractors because many remained bitter. Still, Dunmoore was here at the *Kho'sahra*'s invitation, which should prevent any unpleasantness.

***

Dunmoore, Pushkin, and Guthren, along with the two aides, were back in the flag CIC shortly before the warning that *Salamanca* would return to normal space in thirty seconds. The wrenching nausea came and went in a split second, and the planet appeared on the primary display, surrounded by four small moons. The display zoomed in on Ulufan itself, revealing a strange-looking orbital station with mysterious markings on it, as well as starships, both naval *Tols* and *Ptars* and civilian vessels.

Moments later, the speakers came to life with a rough Shrehari voice issuing an incomprehensible order. Or at least incomprehensible to everyone but Dunmoore.

"We're being told to enter orbit at the same altitude as the station, approximately ten kilometers behind it," she said, translating for the bridge crew's benefit.

"Where they can keep both an eye and their big guns on us," Captain Haneul's disembodied voice said. "Thanks for that, sir. We will comply."

Pushkin cocked an eyebrow at Dunmoore. "No words of welcome for us?"

She shrugged. "It's the Shrehari way."

"What if we didn't have someone who speaks the language aboard?"

"Wait for it." A few seconds passed, then she smiled as a text message appeared on a side display. It was essentially the same order they'd received verbally, but this time in broken Anglic. "And there you go. They have someone who can translate as well. Not surprising, really. After almost twenty years of peace, a good amount of trade flows across the border, meaning more Shrehari can speak Anglic, and more humans can speak Shrehari."

"I wonder — will Brakal provide us with a translator during the ceremony?"

"Maybe, but I'm sure he remembers I understand and speak his language."

"Feels strange, doesn't it, though," Guthren said. "Us heading toward a Shrehari world with weapons tight and shields down. The last time we were in their space was with guns roaring."

"That it does, but I'd rather this way than how we did things the last time."

"Amen," Pushkin said. "How long do you figure we'll be sitting in orbit?"

"No idea. I believe they will invite us for the ceremony and nothing more. Which is a shame because I wouldn't have minded walking around Kordar, but I understand they usually confine human traders to the spaceport district, so we would stand out." Dunmoore climbed to her feet. "There's no point in hanging around the CIC now that we've had our very brief introduction to Ulufan traffic control."

Just then, the bridge called.

"Admiral, we're receiving a transmission from the surface. If I understand correctly, it's *Kho'sahra* Brakal, and he wants to speak with you."

Dunmoore retook the command chair, eyebrows raised in surprise as she glanced at Pushkin. "By all means, put him through."

Moments later, the primary display showed Brakal's face, and Dunmoore was transported back to the ruined bridge of the

Victoria Regina, more than twenty-five years earlier, when she had first seen him. But he appeared visibly older, his skull ridges more leathery and his skin darker, though the ruff of fur on the top of his head was as black as ever.

"Dunmoore. Welcome to Ulufan."

She hadn't used her Shrehari for years and needed time to process her reply. When it finally came out, it was halting, her tongue rusty.

"*Kho'sahra*, thank you for your greetings."

"It is good to see you again after so long. You have prospered."

"I have indeed, and yes, it is good to see you too."

"Your superiors could not have chosen a better representative for the Act of Remembrance, Dunmoore." He gazed at her with his unnerving eyes, which revealed nothing a human could interpret.

"I am thrilled to be here and eagerly await the ceremony. When are you planning to hold it?"

"Now that you have arrived, tomorrow in the evening. I shall expect your shuttle to land just before sunset at the Kordar spaceport, and I will personally meet you there."

He named the hour in Shrehari, something Dunmoore memorized, to be deciphered later and calculated using the local time, which wouldn't be easy, considering they operated on a totally different system.

"I am honored." Dunmoore bowed her head.

A fierce smile twisted Brakal's mouth. "Then let us make our reunion one to remember for all ages."

"Yes, let us."

"Until then, Dunmoore." Brakal's image vanished, leaving her to feel a little overwhelmed.

"That was — interesting," she finally said.

— Six —

A few minutes after Dunmoore's shuttle cleared *Salamanca*'s hangar deck, just before they began a slow descent, six sleek Shrehari sublight fighters appeared and boxed it in. A voice on the Shrehari emergency channel announced itself as the commander of their escort to the surface.

Dunmoore, Pushkin, and Guthren, all wearing full-dress uniforms with ceremonial swords, exchanged glances. Guthren said, "Escort? More like seeing we don't deviate from the agreed upon route to the Kordar spaceport."

She chuckled.

"Probably, but since I'm a guest of honor, they phrased it honorably." Then, to the pilot, she said, "Make sure you follow the leader, PO."

"Yes, sir," the petty officer first class replied. "Wouldn't want a missile up our six, considering one of the fighters aft just pinged us."

"Bloody cheek!" Pushkin shook his head as he cocked an eyebrow at Dunmoore. "Fighter pilots are the same all over the galaxy."

She winked at him. "Some of us do grow up and become responsible adults."

They soon entered the upper atmosphere, and the shuttle yawed a bit as the thin air buffeted it. But it quickly stabilized, and they spiraled toward the southern edge of the large, globe-spanning, single continent covering thirty percent of the planet. The center of the supercontinent seemed to be an enormous desert, reminding Dunmoore of Earth's Pangaea. She could see lights on the darkened eastern shores, but they were widely spread apart, probably due to a sparse population.

Daylight still bathed Kordar, and Dunmoore studied the city on the shuttle passenger compartment's primary display, seeing row upon row of gray low-rise buildings in an orderly grid with a large plaza at its center and the spaceport to one side. The plaza already teemed with tiny figures, and she guessed it was the site where the Act of Remembrance would be held.

Then, it seemed as if only seconds had passed, and they were already making their final approach to the spaceport. The tarmac, wide, constructed of a substance that allowed no weeds to poke through cracks, was bordered by countless structures with broad openings. The spaceport terminal itself, a single-story building with glass windows and doors, had flagpoles on the roof bearing banners snapping in the breeze. All of it seemed to glow under a darkening sky, reddish beyond what was usual on human worlds.

A ground handler signaled the shuttle to land in front of the terminal's middle door, and once the thrusters had spooled down, the pilot dropped the aft ramp. Dunmoore, Pushkin, and Guthren stood, adjusted their uniforms and swords, and then walked down the ramp toward the door, which opened at that moment, allowing Brakal, surrounded by four bodyguards, to come through.

Both groups stopped in front of each other, the humans saluting as Brakal raised his fist to his chest in the Shrehari equivalent.

"Dunmoore!" He said, baring his teeth in what could only have been a smile. "Well met."

"*Kho'sahra*, thank you for honoring us in this manner. You haven't formally met them, but they were with me during the war and remember you well. Admiral of the Fourth Rank Gregor Pushkin and Senior Underofficer of the First Degree Kurt Guthren."

Brakal turned to them. "Pushkin, Guthren, you are as welcome as Dunmoore."

Neither of them understood the words, but both bowed their heads politely, and that seemed to suffice for the Shrehari leader.

"Come."

Brakal turned and led them through the door and into the terminal, a dimly lit, cavernous space with few adornments other than banners hanging from the high ceiling. They exited on the other side, where a large ground vehicle, armored by all appearances, waited, doors open. The bodyguards ushered them in, Dunmoore sitting beside Brakal facing forward, Pushkin and Guthren facing them. Then, once the doors were closed, two entered the front compartment while the other two climbed into an aft compartment.

The car set into motion smoothly and silently, and soon, they were headed down a broad boulevard bordered by flat-roofed three-story structures clad in gray granite, some bearing subdued signs with undecipherable images and script.

Close up, Brakal exuded a faintly musky scent, not unpleasant to Dunmoore's nose, and she forced herself to relax, even though she was in the company of a military dictator who ruled over a polity as large as the Commonwealth, if not larger. Even after all this time, no human really knew. And he was someone she once considered a mortal enemy, someone she'd fought on many occasions. But that now seemed a lifetime ago.

Yet Dunmoore felt a tad overwhelmed by the strangeness of the situation, especially with Brakal remarking in his guttural tongue on the parts of the city through which they were passing.

"Ah, the plaza is in sight," he said as they turned onto an even wider avenue. "You and your companions simply stay behind me, salute when I do so, bow your head as I bow mine, and follow me always."

"Very well, *Kho'sahra*."

The people she'd seen from above now stood in orderly rows, uniformed on one side, civilians on the other, with an altar in the middle, attended by a dozen elderly Shrehari wearing flowing black robes.

"Priests," Brakal said when he noticed her observing them. "A necessary part of any religious function."

The car entered the plaza, and the military personnel raised their fists to their chest in a general salute. They kept it there while the car drove halfway to the altar, stopped, and disgorged its passengers.

Brakal, facing the troops, also raised his fist, after which a command rang out, and they resumed the attention position. He then turned toward the altar and saluted it, bowing his head, a gesture returned by the twelve priests.

"We will now begin the Act of Remembrance," Brakal said in a loud voice that echoed off the walls of the buildings bordering the plaza, "to commemorate those who died during our war with the humans, whose representatives are here with us, in peace, so they too can honor our dead."

The priests began a low chant that gradually increased in volume as they slowly walked around the altar, which Dunmoore now saw was engraved at the four corners with representations of Shrehari military personnel. Shrehari writing was on the side facing her, and she thought it represented dates, perhaps the years of the war.

When the priests' chant died away after almost five minutes, Brakal barked a command as he raised his fist in salute, followed by everyone, military and civilian. Dunmoore and her two companions lifted their hands to their brows in the human version. Silence fell over the plaza, and Dunmoore felt as if the entire city held its breath because she heard nothing more than the soft sigh of a faint breeze.

After a few minutes, one of the priests intoned what sounded suspiciously like a prayer, even though she couldn't quite understand the archaic Shrehari. A flash lit up the plaza for a brief moment, followed by another and another until she counted thirty instances, convinced it was artillery firing plasma rounds over the city and out to sea. A thirty-gun salute.

Brakal let out another bark of command, and the Shrehari fists dropped, as did the human hands. Then Brakal spoke again.

"Let the dead rest easy, for we will remember them, always."

A lament began, produced by an unseen instrument. It floated over the assembled troops and civilians, all remaining at attention. The music was oddly dissonant to human ears yet sent shivers down Dunmoore's spine. After a minute, many other instruments joined it, and the dissonance grew, as did the volume, but the shivers didn't stop.

Then, as one, the Shrehari sang a slow dirge, their deep voices joining the music in a way Dunmoore would remember for the rest of her days.

The song spoke of honor, of glory, and of death. And of remembrance. Then, the voices faded until only one remained — Brakal's. He sang one last verse and fell silent as well. A trio of fighters appeared overhead, tearing through the sky at low altitude before raising their noses almost vertically and climbing hard toward space on brilliant columns of light. Once the noise had abated, Brakal bowed toward the priests again.

"It is done."

They bowed back. "And the spirits of the dead are now at rest."

Brakal's ground car slowly re-entered the plaza and stopped behind them. He turned toward the massed military personnel, who raised their fists in salute again, returned it, then climbed aboard the vehicle, followed by the humans. The car turned around and drove off into the darkness.

"What did you think of the ceremony, Dunmoore?"

"It was very moving, even though I understood little. The singing at the end was especially remarkable."

"I am happy you found it to be so. Thank you for honoring the dead with your presence. I hope it ensures they will prevent the living from ever engaging humans in war again. We are both evolved species and fare better with honest trade between us." A rumble escaped Brakal's throat. "I believe humans have developed a taste for our ale, judging by the amount we export to your Commonwealth these days. That alone should prevent further hostilities."

Dunmoore smiled at him, showing her teeth in the Shrehari way.

"And a good thing, too, although I have not partaken of your ale in any substantial quantities. I much prefer other forms of alcohol."

Another rumble.

"As do I, but it is good we have at least that in common, Shrehari and humans. You will excuse me for delivering you back to your shuttle and wishing you a good voyage home. The time after an Act of Remembrance is for us to reflect individually, which I will do aboard my flagship. I must return to Shrehari Prime before our beloved emperor does something that will take me months to undo."

"We too have leaders we must prevent from doing things we would rather they avoided," Dunmoore replied, surprised at his candor and responding in kind as well as she could manage in her rusty Shrehari.

"Then we have one more thing in common."

They pulled up to the brightly lit spaceport terminal and exited the car. Brakal gestured toward the door, where his aide stood patiently.

"My shuttle is waiting for me alongside yours." He once again led the way through the terminal, and when they emerged on the tarmac side, a large, boxy Shrehari spacecraft loomed over her smaller one.

"Live well, Dunmoore." Brakal raised his fist in salute.

She and her companions returned the gesture as she said, "Live well, Brakal."

Then, without further ado, he turned on his heels and headed toward his shuttle, followed by his aide and bodyguards. Dunmoore watched him go, knowing he did not expect them to ever meet again. Otherwise, he wouldn't have used the traditional Shrehari farewell.

Fatigue suddenly overcame her, and she gestured at their shuttle. "Let's go home, folks."

— Seven —

Dunmoore was contemplative during the ride back to *Salamanca*, reflecting on the fate that had brought her here to see her old foe become friend one last time. And on the meaning of it in the grand scheme of life and the universe.

Soon, she'd head off to her last assignment as a Navy officer before retiring, yet she still had more than half a lifetime ahead of her should her health and well-being stay as they were. What would happen once she took off her uniform for the last time? Yes, she'd settle on the Fleet's world, Caledonia, but after that? Perhaps teach at the War College or the Academy as a civilian instructor. Or serve in the Caledonian government as a minister or one of the deputy governors general.

Pushkin and Guthren, attuned to her moods after all these years, remained silent throughout, though both burned with a desire to know what she and Brakal had been talking about and what he and the priests had said during the ceremony.

Captain Haneul greeted them on the hangar deck and remarked, "Impressive ceremony, wasn't it, Admiral?"

"You saw it?"

"Yes. The Shrehari transmitted the whole thing on an open channel, and they invited us to watch as well. I got shivers listening to them sing. It's quite amazing we were enemies only twenty years ago."

"Let's hope we remain, if not friends, then at least peaceful neighbors for the foreseeable future." She glanced at Pushkin and Guthren. "That was the major reason Brakal invited humans to the ceremony, by the way. So the spirits of their dead remind the living that trade is better than war. He doesn't want a repeat and will hammer the lesson home every chance he gets."

"Good," Pushkin replied. "Just as long as he keeps a grip on power, we'll be fine. After him, who knows?"

"In my opinion, Brakal will ensure his successor holds the same beliefs as him." She turned to Haneul. "We'll be leaving right away. Oh, and was a *Tol* class ship attached to the station or in orbit near it?"

"Yes, there is. *Tol Vehar* is currently docked."

"That's Brakal's without a doubt. It was his flagship during the latter stages of the war. He's leaving Ulufan right away as well. When I get to my quarters, give me a visual of *Tol Vehar,* will you?"

"Of course, sir."

When Dunmoore entered her cabin, she unbuckled her sword belt, undid her dress tunic's high collar, and unfastened the front, feeling relief. She stepped out of her calf-high boots and trousers and put on her shipboard uniform, after which she stowed the dress getup. Then, Dunmoore switched on the primary display and saw, with satisfaction, that it showed *Tol Vehar* undocking from the station.

"Farewell, my friend," she murmured. "I hope your reign as *Kho'sahra* will be long and fruitful and that you will be successful in eliminating the chance of another war between us."

***

"And that's it." Dunmoore lifted her coffee mug to her lips, having finished telling Pushkin and Guthren everything that transpired in Shrehari during their brief visit.

"Interesting. And you couldn't understand the priests?" Pushkin asked.

"No. I almost did, but their language seemed just archaic enough to defeat my admittedly limited Shrehari."

"You know, it's the first we hear of the Shrehari religion, let alone witness their priests in action. I wonder why and what it's about."

Dunmoore shrugged. "I don't have a clue. They've kept it hidden from outsiders. Perhaps their priests are monastic and generally stay out of sight, just like our Order of the Void."

"It's too bad you didn't ask Brakal."

"I doubt I'd have received a reply on that subject."

"Moving on to other things, will Estrada have finished planning the 3rd Fleet change of command ceremony when we arrive, Chief?"

Guthren nodded. Command Chief Petty Officer Gwen Estrada was his replacement as Fleet chief.

"That she will, Admiral. Gwen is one of the best in the business. It's unlikely that either of us will find any faults in her preparations. Mind you, Admiral Harmel will have vetted everything before we see it anyhow."

"Good. I'd rather get it over with sooner rather than later so I can enjoy some time off between assignments. Plus, I need to sell my house, furnishings, and car before I leave for Earth."

"Going to travel light again?"

"The habits of a lifetime, Gregor. Once I'm retired, I'll have plenty of time to acquire stuff.

"I hear you. I'll also be traveling light, except I don't have a house to sell. Tell me we can easily find furnished apartments in Geneva."

"No idea. I have an official residence on the base as CNO, and so does Mister Guthren as Chief Petty Officer of the Navy. I believe they come furnished. There may be something for vice admirals, too."

Pushkin gave her a crooked grin.

"I'm still not accustomed to considering myself a vice admiral designate."

"Do you believe I have fully grasped the concept of becoming the professional leader of the largest space navy in the explored galaxy? Of course not." She jerked her chin at Guthren. "Only the Chief is handling his new appointment with ease."

"And you'd be wrong about that, sir," the latter said. "I never expected to become a command chief in the first place. Oh, I just remembered something we'll need to arrange beforehand. You know that by tradition, the Navy, Marine Corps, and Army commanders get a guard of honor of their choosing, which ceremonially protects them during the change of command.

Something company-sized that hails back to an important point in their careers."

"No, I wasn't aware. Or if I was, I've forgotten." Dunmoore frowned, lost in reflection. "Does it have to be a Navy guard for the CNO?"

Guthren shook his head.

"They can come from any branch of the Service."

A slow smile spread across her face. "Well, then, I believe I'll call on the Army to provide my guard of honor."

Guthren and Pushkin glanced at each other, and the latter asked, "Do you have any idea what she's talking about?"

"I figure I do, sir. You weren't with us during our time in *Iolanthe*, but you might recall her embarked Marines were actually soldiers. E Company, 3rd Battalion, Scandia Regiment, Commonwealth Army." Guthren turned to Dunmoore. "That's who you want, right?"

Dunmoore pointed at him and winked.

"Got it in one, Chief. I know none of the originals from twenty years ago remain in E Company. However, they still wear an anchor on their left breast pocket to commemorate the company's service as *Iolanthe*'s embarked ground troops during the war."

"It'll be nice to hear the Hakkapeliittain Marssi sung on parade again, sir."

"The what now?" Pushkin asked.

"The march of the 3rd Battalion, Scandia Regiment, Gregor," Dunmoore answered. "Apparently, it dates back to the Thirty Years War, fought in the first half of the seventeenth century, making it one of the oldest military marches still in use. The

Hakkapeliitta were highly effective Finnish light cavalry at the time who specialized in skirmishing, raiding, and reconnaissance, besides being deadly in battle. In fact, their name comes from their battle cry, hakkaa päälle, which means cut them down."

"I see. It seems like an excellent idea to invite E Company as your guard of honor."

"They'll be thrilled, I'm sure," Guthren said. "The few times Admiral Dunmoore has been to Scandia since the end of the war, they were keen on having her visit the 3rd Battalion's garrison and spend time with E Company. The originals might be gone, but a painting of Tatiana Salminen, who commanded the company at the time, with *Iolanthe* in the background, hangs in a special place at regimental HQ. She's the Regiment's commanding officer now."

Dunmoore nodded.

"Which means we must invite her to the ceremony on Earth as a special guest of the incoming CNO."

"Noted. Because of the travel time between Scandia and Earth, we'd better get the word out when we're back on Dordogne, sir, so they can prepare the company."

***

"How's 3rd Fleet been during my absence, Oliver?" Dunmoore breezed into Vice Admiral Harmel's office the morning after her return to Dordogne.

"Same old. The 31st Battle Group pursued a wolf pack into the Protectorate a week ago. They destroyed two of them, but the remaining four got away. Other than that, it's been dead quiet.

Chief Estrada finalized the change of command ceremony plans. You'll find them in your queue. From my perspective, she did an admirable job without requiring further input from me.

"Then I'll probably also be satisfied."

She waved at him and left for her office, soon to be his. There, she spent the rest of the day catching up on things. Dunmoore knew her last month as Commander, 3rd Fleet would go by quickly and simultaneously drag on. But the date was now set, and her job was to make sure Oliver Harmel slid into the job without a hitch, just like when she'd taken over from Admiral Hogue.

That evening, she returned home to find a 'for sale' sign on the fence, proof the real estate company she'd hired earlier that day had moved quickly. It didn't stay on the market for long.

By the end of the week, she'd accepted an offer at the asking price, with a closing date the day after the change of command. She would leave the furniture and household items in place since the buyer was a Navy captain moving to Dordogne and joining the 3rd Fleet staff. He, like so many, traveled light as well. On a whim, Dunmoore also sent him a message offering her car. He took it, also at the asking price.

Finally, the day of the change of command dawned, and Dunmoore, who'd been living in the officer's mess for the last few days, donned her dress uniform with full-sized medals and admired herself in the mirror.

"Looking good, Siobhan," she murmured.

Just then, Dunmoore's communicator buzzed for attention — it was her aide saying she was waiting at the officer's mess main entrance with the staff car to take her to the parade ground. After one last look in the mirror, Dunmoore cinched her sword belt around her waist and left the suite. As soon as she stepped out of the mess, her aide came to attention by the open staff car door and saluted.

"Right on time, sir."

Dunmoore returned the salute, and both climbed aboard, she in the back, the aide in the front beside the driver. The drive to the parade ground was brief. She could have walked there in five minutes if that. But she had to arrive by staff car.

Five hundred spacers were lined up in four guards on the parade ground, facing stands filled with spectators, and the moment the staff car appeared, the parade commander, one of the HQ captains, called everyone to attention. The staff car stopped in front of the dais, and the aide hopped out to stand by the rear compartment door, which opened slowly. Dunmoore climbed out, returning her aide's salute, and stepped onto the dais, facing the parade.

The commander called the general salute, present arms, and the band burst into the prescribed four ruffles and flourishes, followed by the Admiral's March. Dunmoore raised her hand to her brow and held it there until the music died away and the commander gave the shoulder arms.

The rest of the ceremony passed in a blur — inspection of the troops along with Oliver Harmel, handing over of the 3rd Fleet Command Chief Petty Officer's cane from Guthren to Estrada, speeches — until the very end, when she and Guthren stood together on the dais and received the salute of the parade marching past in front of them. Then, it was three cheers for Admiral Dunmoore, another bout of ruffles and flourishes, and she stepped off the dais as the staff car returned to pick her and Guthren up. Once it vanished, Admiral Harmel got his first general salute as Commander, 3rd Fleet.

The staff car didn't go far then either, merely back to the mess where a reception would be held in her honor and that of Admiral Harmel.

For the next few weeks, Dunmoore had no functions whatsoever. She no longer commanded 3rd Fleet and wasn't yet Chief of Naval Operations. After a decade of demanding back-to-back appointments, she didn't know how she felt about that.

But she didn't have time to dwell on it. Most of the senior staff officers approached her individually or in groups so they could say their farewells.

— Eight —

"We received a note from the Shrehari ambassador, Madame SecGen," the Secretary for Interstellar Affairs said when his turn came to speak at the cabinet table. "On behalf of *Kho'sahra* Brakal, he thanks us for sending Admiral Dunmoore to the Act of Remembrance on Ulufan. She did the Commonwealth and the Empire honor. You could not have chosen a better representative."

"If Brakal is pleased with our delegation, then so much the better," Lauzier replied in a manner that verged on the dismissive. Dunmoore was one of Kowalski's closest allies, which made her dangerous. Besides, she'd not forgiven Dunmoore for destroying her plan to eliminate certain people.

The Secretary for Interstellar Affairs noticed Lauzier's tone and said, "Keeping the *Kho'sahra* happy directly influences trade between us, Madame. And it's still growing by leaps and bounds."

She gave him a brief glare, wondering why she'd appointed the man. He obviously didn't have the intellect to be a cabinet member, even though he was as loyal as a dog could be. But he brought money to the table, the sort she needed — plentiful and well hidden.

"Noted. What else do you have?"

"Nothing, Madame."

She turned to the Secretary of Defense.

"How about you?"

"Grand Admiral Kowalski continues to ignore my directives, Madame. It's becoming rather frustrating. Oh, she doesn't come out and do so openly, but it's always now's not the right time, or we'll study it and get back to you, or some other excuse. As per your plan, I'm trying to bring military procurement under the civilian side of the Defense Department, but Kowalski keeps stalling to the point where I can't expect any movement until the next century."

Removing procurement from military control was one of Lauzier's policies designed to centralize power in her office via the cabinet. It would also help in awarding large sole-source contracts to her supporters. Lauzier's face hardened.

"Find a way, Alan. I want it solved before the end of the year."

"Yes, Madame," Alan Olongo, the SecDef, replied, knowing full well that in a contest of wills, Kowalski would win every time, and she was clearly trying to outlast the SecGen. "But the Grand Admiral is proving to be a quasi-insoluble problem. She doesn't consult with me or my deputy secretaries on anything. In fact, I understand she set up a parallel civilian defense administration on Caledonia a few years ago, one beholden to the military, not the Department, and reporting to the Fleet's Chief of Personnel."

"How the hell can Kowalski do that?" Paul Markus, the Secretary of Public Safety, asked. Tall, blond, with aristocratic features and piercing blue eyes, he was as handsome as he was ruthless. "Legislation clearly mandates a civilian Defense Department separate from the military chain of command."

The SecDef shrugged.

"She simply did it. And since Caledonia is essentially owned by the Fleet, getting a grip on things there will prove rather difficult, if not impossible. Especially since the new governor general is the former Grand Admiral and works hand in glove with his successor."

Markus turned to Lauzier.

"Something needs to be done about Kowalski, Madame. She's overtly flouting civilian control of the Armed Forces."

"Not overtly, at least not yet," the SecDef replied. "She knows exactly where the line is and stays within it. But it's not just Kowalski. Her predecessor was doing things that went beyond the purely military command of the Fleet, as was the Grand Admiral before him, except they were very circumspect about it. I fear we might face a situation that has been quietly brewing for a decade or more, and Kowalski is merely the one to bring it out in the open."

"Well, then, fire her," Markus said.

The SecDef grimaced. "We can't. She was appointed to serve during good behavior.

"What? I always thought that the SecGen could appoint and remove Grand Admirals at will. After all, this isn't a quasi-judicial position, let alone a judicial one."

"Kowalski is the first to be appointed during good behavior. Her predecessor convinced Judy Chu to do so."

"More like Kowalski was acting through her predecessor."

"Be that as it may," Lauzier said to end the debate. "We're stuck with her."

"Unless…" Markus let the word hang over the cabinet table.

Lauzier raised a restraining hand. Her Secretary of Public Safety was a bit too bloodthirsty at times. Thankfully, the head of the Special Security Bureau didn't report to him but to her directly. Otherwise, who knew what he'd have her do?

"Let's not even go there, Paul. Moving on, anything else, Alan?"

"No, Madame."

***

Paul Markus returned to his office in the Palais Wilson, lost in thought. He'd used the underground shuttle that connected all of the government buildings in Geneva, with the Palace of the Stars at its heart, unlike many of his colleagues who enjoyed being driven in private on the surface. Once behind his desk, he swiveled the chair around to face the windows and Lake Geneva across from Quai Wilson Street. It was a brilliantly sunny day, the light reflecting from the lake's choppy surface like a million shards of glass.

He couldn't get over Grand Admiral Kowalski's effrontery and the fact that her job was safe unless she committed gross misconduct. As far as he was concerned, Kowalski represented everything that was wrong with the Commonwealth nowadays — the fractiousness, the willful disregard for the central government, and worst of all, at least in his book, the disrespect shown to the Secretary General. Markus had been a Lauzier loyalist from before she even took a seat in the Senate and would do anything for her. Such as getting rid of Kowalski.

He summoned Axel Renouf, his department's permanent undersecretary, and a man Markus had appointed soon after taking charge. Renouf was another Lauzier loyalist, albeit from her time as a senator, and had switched to the civil service from the political staff after Lauzier's first term.

"Come in, Axel." Marcus waved at the sofas around a low coffee table as he rose from behind his desk when Renouf appeared at the open office door.

"Mister Secretary. What can I do for you?" Renouf and Markus sat facing each other.

"You're cultivating Leila Gherson, aren't you?"

"Yes. You know I believe the SSB should come under your department rather than report directly to the SecGen." A small smile appeared on Renouf's narrow face. "Besides, I find her interesting."

Markus couldn't see why — she was the proverbial gray bureaucrat — but made no comment.

He sat back and said, "Grand Admiral Kowalski is becoming somewhat of a problem for the SecGen."

"I know, sir. It's hardly a secret in this town."

"And I wondered whether Leila might suggest remedies to the situation."

Renouf gave his boss a curious look. "Remedies, sir?"

"Ways of dealing with Kowalski, so to speak."

"I see," Renouf said after a moment's hesitation, during which he parsed Markus' words for their hidden meaning. "Let me ask her when we next meet."

"That would be when?"

"Tomorrow evening. We're dining together."

***

"My boss has a problem." Axel Renouf played with the stem of his glass, swirling the ruby liquid around before taking a sip. The waiter had just removed the empty supper plates, and they were finishing their wine before dessert.

"Oh?" Leila Gherson cocked a questioning eyebrow.

"That problem is a certain Grand Admiral crossing the boundary between military matters and politics. It's getting out of hand. She may even upset a fair part of the SecGen's ambitious reform program through her meddling."

"So I understand," Gherson replied in a dry tone. "Kowalski isn't exactly a Centralist."

"No. Quite the contrary."

"And what does the Honorable Paul Markus want, Axel?"

"He was wondering whether you could suggest a remedy."

Gherson let out a humorless chuckle. "Markus wants the SSB to rid him of this turbulent Grand Admiral."

"Perhaps."

"Sorry, my friend. No can do. The SSB drawing a bead on any admiral or general these days means war with the Fleet, and that's something we can't win."

"I'm sure you can make it seem completely accidental."

"If anything unusual occurs involving Kowalski or any other flag officer, the Fleet will hold us responsible, and it will lead to a war." So, no. The SSB cannot help with your boss' problem,

Axel. And if you're thinking of using other means to get at her, don't. Just don't do it because, as I said, they will blame us. When Renouf seemed skeptical, she said, "Remember when Ezekiel Holt buttonholed me at the *Genfer Ratskeller* a while back and left when you showed up?"

"Sure." Renouf nodded.

"He came to warn me that Kowalski and the rest of the flag officers were out of bounds on pain of termination with extreme prejudice for me and most people in the SSB. I take Holt very seriously, Axel. He plays for keeps and is quickly turning Fleet Security into something that, frankly, scares me. Whenever his name comes up, I feel the icy hand of death running down my spine."

Renouf gave her a strange look. "Come now, Leila. It can't be that bad."

"I'm feeling it now, so let's change the subject. Kowalski is off limits to everyone in the Commonwealth government."

But Renouf remained unconvinced. If the SSB wouldn't do it, then maybe his boss might find someone else.

— Nine —

"This is it, Oliver." Dunmoore thrust out her hand, and they shook.

Admiral Harmel was seeing Dunmoore off personally at the Joint Base Dordogne spaceport, where she, Pushkin, and Guthren were about to board a shuttle taking them to the civilian orbital station. There, they would board the *Homeric*, a passenger ship of the White Star Line, for the trip to Earth, as no naval vessel was heading in that direction for another three weeks, and her new responsibilities awaited.

As a result, all three wore civilian business suits rather than their uniforms. They had already stowed their bags in the shuttle while larger items packed in containers would follow aboard a Navy transport that did the rounds of the principal star systems in a few weeks.

"Fair winds and following seas, Siobhan. Good luck with your appointment as CNO."

She smiled at him. "Thanks. I think."

Harmel turned to Pushkin, and they shook as well. "Good luck as one of Siobhan's assistant CNOs. You'll need it."

"That I will." Pushkin grinned. "She's a hard act to keep up with, and it gets harder the higher she goes."

Finally, Harmel faced Guthren and held out his hand. "Keep an eye on both of them, will you, Chief? The trouble they can get in when they're not adequately supervised chills the blood."

Guthren winked at Harmel. "For sure, sir."

The three of them turned on their heels and marched up the shuttle's aft ramp, which closed moments later. Harmel returned to the terminal, standing outside the door, and watched as the small spacecraft spooled up its thrusters. It lifted off almost vertically on columns of pure light and soon vanished into the low cloud cover. Just then, the first fat raindrops fell, and Harmel hurried in.

He and Dunmoore had finished the war as captains, she without a ship, he bringing his to be mothballed. And now they both wore the four stars of a full admiral. Harmel shook his head, still marveling at the twists of fate that had propelled them to the top of their profession.

Aboard the shuttle, Dunmoore sat in silence, lost in thought as Dordogne's surface faded beneath them. It had been her home for the last ten years, the longest she'd ever stayed on a single world since she left home to report to the Academy, which had been on Earth back then — it was on Caledonia now. And now, ironically, she'd end her career where it had started, on humanity's birthplace.

The shuttle landed on the civilian station's hangar deck and disgorged its passengers along with their luggage piled on individual antigrav sleds they'd bought for the trip. Those sleds had tiny AIs and would follow them around.

The station was almost the same size as Starbase 30 and had much the same configuration — spindle-shaped, with docking arms radiating like the spokes of a wheel, extensive cargo handling and storage facilities, and even defensive weapons. It orbited Dordogne one hundred kilometers aft of the starbase at the same altitude so that both stations would always be within the same distance and see each other.

With trailing antigrav sleds, they made their way to *Homeric's* docking arm, where they were met by a purser's mate on the station end of the arm, standing behind a counter to one side of the opening.

"Good day. Could I please have your names and credentials?"

"Certainly. I'm Admiral Siobhan Dunmoore. This is Vice Admiral Gregor Pushkin," Dunmoore gestured at the latter, "and this is Command Chief Petty Officer Kurt Guthren."

"And you're headed to?"

"Earth."

They passed over their credentials, and the purser's mate confirmed the reservations.

"You're cleared to board." He gave out their cabin assignments and key cards, and Dunmoore was pleased to note they were contiguous in the first-class section of the ship. "Just follow the blue arrows to your quarters."

They walked down the docking arm and entered the *Homeric's* main starboard airlock, where blue arrows suddenly lit up, driven by their key cards. They followed them along several corridors and up a few decks via a lift. The first-class section's hallways were identical to those found in grand hotels, and they could have been on the ground for all they knew rather than aboard a deep space liner.

Dunmoore entered her cabin and found herself in a suite — sitting room, bedroom, and ensuite bathroom — as spacious as the admiral's quarters aboard *Salamanca* but with more luxurious furniture and fixtures. After unpacking the bag that held the clothes she'd wear during their trip, Dunmoore knocked on Pushkin's cabin door.

"Come on in, Admiral," his disembodied voice said, proving there was a video pickup showing people in the corridor.

The door slid open, and she entered a cabin identical to hers.

"Nice, isn't it?" Pushkin asked, smiling as her eyes took in the setup.

"Yes. I have the same thing."

"There's a mini bar with complimentary drinks." He went over to a sideboard and opened a panel. "And we're invited to dine at the captain's table tonight."

"How do you know that?"

Pushkin gestured at the display hovering above a desk set against a bulkhead. "It's in the cabin's message queue. You didn't look at yours, I gather?"

"No. Does that invitation include the chief?"

"Yes, it does. And it specifies formal wear, so we'll have to break out our mess uniforms."

"Darn. I was hoping to spend the entire trip anonymously in mufti."

"You're the next commander of the most powerful navy in the known galaxy. There is no anonymity. Besides, I'm sure Captain Hassan's invitation is to honor you in the best way he knows."

"Hassan is *Homeric*'s skipper, right?"

"Right. And he's a veteran of the war, so we won't be the only ones with miniature medals on our mess uniforms." Before she could say anything, Pushkin pointed at the display again. "I briefly perused his biography. It's publicly available on the ship's net."

"You have been busy."

Another knock on the door — Guthren.

"I figured I'd find both of you here," he said, entering Pushkin's quarters. "So, formal dinner at the captain's table tonight. Nice." He rubbed his hands together. "It's no more than we deserve."

"See, Admiral." Pushkin jerked his thumb at Guthren. "You're the only one who's not happy."

The Chief gave Dunmoore a suspicious look before turning his eyes on Pushkin.

"What's she not happy about, sir?"

"Putting on a uniform and announcing to the world that she's aboard this tub."

"Captain's table, first night out? Can't get a higher honor than that in a civilian ship."

Dunmoore raised both hands.

"All right. I'll put on my mess uniform and my sweetest smile for the evening meal."

Pushkin and Guthren looked at each other with exaggerated airs of alarm.

"Uh-oh. Did she say her sweetest?"

"She sure did, sir."

Both knew from long experience that a sweet smile meant trouble ahead for whoever was on the receiving end.

"Okay. Then, my most pleasant smile. And that's all we'll say on the subject. Cocktails at eighteen hundred in the first-class lounge. Until then, enjoy your descent into utter luxury."

With that, Dunmoore returned to her cabin and pulled her mess uniform from its bag.

Homeric undocked soon afterward and headed out to Dordogne's hyperlimit at a good rate of acceleration. Then, she jumped out to the star system's heliopause on the first leg of the long trip.

Siobhan Dunmoore found herself the center of attention the moment she led Pushkin and Guthren into the first-class lounge. There, Captain Ali Hassan, black-haired, olive-skinned with an aquiline nose framed by brown eyes, greeted them with a broad smile and handshakes. He was resplendent in a high-collared white mess uniform with much gold braid on the sleeves and trouser seams and miniature medals denoting wartime service.

"Good evening, Admiral Dunmoore, and welcome aboard *Homeric*."

"Thank you, Captain."

"And how are you, Admiral Pushkin. Welcome. And you, Command Chief Guthren."

"I'm well, thank you."

"Can I offer you a glass of champagne?"

Dunmoore nodded, aware that many eyes were on her, openly and surreptitiously. She cut a splendid figure in her navy blue mess uniform with the heavy gold braid of a full admiral on the sleeves and a rack of miniature medals that reached across her left breast.

"Certainly."

Hassan gestured at the human waiter who approached with a tray carrying four flutes three-quarters full of straw-colored bubbly. They each took one, and Hassan raised his.

"To the next Chief of Naval Operations."

"Hear, hear," Pushkin said as they raised their glasses and took a sip.

"This is top-notch, Captain."

"Thank you, Admiral. It's the finest Dordogne Grand Cru, a Maison Glière."

Dunmoore inclined her head. "I'm honored."

"It is I who's honored to have such a distinguished passenger aboard my ship, Admiral."

"I see you were in the Navy during the war."

"Yes. I joined up for the duration from the merchant service when I was fifth officer aboard the White Star freighter *Gull Blass,* and the Navy pressed it into service. I spent most of the war in frigates and had just been promoted to lieutenant commander when it ended. My assignment was as the second officer on the cruiser *Hector*. Naturally, I returned to White Star Lines afterward."

"And you've had *Homeric* for how long?"

"Going on five years now. She's my home." Hassan smiled. "I intend to command her until I'm forced into retirement."

Hassan proved to be an excellent raconteur and kept the conversation lively at the table, which stood apart from the others in the first-class dining room. Dunmoore thoroughly enjoyed herself and was still smiling when the party broke up late in the evening and they returned to their cabins.

"I haven't eaten this well in a long time," Guthren said, patting his stomach as they strolled down the corridor.

"Neither have I, Chief. The cook really did Hassan proud. And the wine…" Dunmoore grinned at Guthren. "I'm glad no naval transport was available, and we had to book berths on a luxury liner."

"The Navy probably got a discount on our cabins, though," Pushkin said. "I can't see them spring for full price first class suites. Let's enjoy it while we can. I doubt we'll ever experience this level of pampering again."

Once in her cabin, Dunmoore gratefully peeled off her mess uniform and poured herself a cognac from the minibar. Then she settled on the sofa in the sitting room with one of the books she was reading. As Pushkin had said, she'd better enjoy the calm aboard *Homeric* because once she set foot on Earth, Dunmoore wouldn't see a moment's peace until her term as CNO ended.

— Ten —

"Leila won't do anything, sir," Axel Renouf reported. "She's afraid of starting a war with the Fleet they can't win."

"Damn." Paul Markus clenched a fist in frustration. "But how can the Fleet wage war on the SSB?"

Renouf shrugged.

"Easily, I'd think. They've been positioning themselves for the last few years to become a law unto themselves. Leila is especially wary of Vice Admiral Ezekiel Holt, the Fleet's Chief of Security, who she says has a bead on her and her people and won't hesitate to strike the moment anything happens to Kowalski or other flag officers."

"Then eliminate Holt first."

"I think his deputy is of the same mind as he is, sir. That's the thing with the military — they keep functioning even if their leaders are taken out. The next in line will simply pick things up and carry on. In any case, we can't count on the SSB to take any action against the Fleet."

"Which means we'll have to see if the private sector can't help us."

Renouf frowned at his boss. "Private sector, sir? Do you mean organized crime?"

"Or guns for hire."

"I don't know anyone who could lead us to either."

A wintry smile appeared on Markus' lips.

"As it happens, I do, but I'll need to be extremely careful in contacting someone who can help. Some of those people won't hesitate to use the knowledge I called a hit on Kowalski to further their business interests. They can own me until the day I die, and that just isn't something I can permit, not even for the SecGen."

When Renouf said nothing, Markus laughed.

"Don't look at me like that, Axel. The idea is to operate under the principle of mutually assured destruction. They try to compromise me, and I call the fires of Heaven onto them. It keeps both of us honest. And I know just the man."

"If you say so, sir."

"Leave it with me for now."

A thoughtful Axel Renouf returned to his office, wondering why he wasn't surprised Paul Markus, the Commonwealth Secretary of Public Safety and, therefore, humanity's top law enforcement official, had contacts in the underworld.

***

Two days later, Paul Markus climbed aboard his private aircar just after sixteen hundred hours and headed south to Old Marseille, the largest city on the northern shores of the Mediterranean Sea.

Like the New Marseille on Dordogne, it was a port city but founded 3,100 years earlier, two and a half millennia before the first human set foot on Earth's moon, and still possessed an antique charm. It was also the home of the *Milieu Marseillais*, an organized crime group that had existed since before the era of spaceflight and controlled large swathes of the town and surrounding countryside.

The *Milieu*, in keeping with most OCGs on Earth, was part of an interstellar network joining like-minded organizations in a spiderweb of criminal activity and didn't limit its reach to Marseille.

Markus wore relaxed yet expensive clothing, the mark of a wealthy and influential man out to enjoy himself. His aircar was unremarkable, yet fast, and he reached Marseille in under an hour, landing on the city's outskirts and driving to the old port on the surface, where he parked in an underground garage. The *Vieux Port*, as it was known to the locals, appeared untouched by the centuries, surrounded by buildings predating humanity's escape to the stars and overlooked by the Notre-Dame de la Garde Basilica on its hill. It was as if time had stood still in the heart of Old Marseille.

The weather was splendid, blue skies above, with just a hint of clouds, warm air pushing in from the south, and the ripples of the water's surface reflecting the late afternoon sun like so many shards of light.

Markus knew the man he was looking for liked to sit on the terrace of a particular bistro late on Friday afternoons, one bordering the Quay des Belges called *Les Calanques*.

Leon Pannetier was a big man in the *Milieu*, Marseille's top boss, in fact. Markus had first met him years ago through a corrupt cop who owed him a favor. He'd been looking for contacts with off-world OCGs to set up Sara Lauzier's fake abduction aboard the luxury liner *Athena*. And Leon Pannetier delivered in return for a sizable cash donation to his so-called charitable foundation — *La Fondation de l'Occitant* — which acted as a tax dodge and a way of laundering funds. Markus had used Pannetier a few times since to solve problems Sara Lauzier encountered.

He found the man sitting in the shade of an umbrella at one of *Les Calanques'* outdoor tables with two men, his bodyguards without a doubt. They had that watchfulness about them. Markus approached Pannetier, stopping in front of the table under the gimlet gaze of his people.

Pannetier smiled broadly and stood. He was a heavy-set man in his seventies, with thick silver hair brushed back from a high forehead, a patrician nose, and hooded eyes that seemed dead.

"Paul, my friend. It's been a long time." He offered his hand, and they shook.

"It has, Leon."

"You're now the Commonwealth Secretary of Public Safety under Madame Lauzier, I understand."

"That's correct."

"Please, sit. A pastis?" Pannetier asked, naming the anise-flavored drink most popular in Marseille and the surrounding area.

"Certainly." Markus sat across from Pannetier, who'd raised his hand and pointed at him. Within moments, a glass of clear liquid appeared in front of Markus, and Pannetier gestured at the jug of water on the table.

"Go ahead and serve yourself."

Markus added four parts of water to his drink, turning it a milky white, then raised his glass. "To your health, Leon."

"And to yours." They took a sip, then Pannetier sat back and studied Markus. "What brings a busy man like you to Marseille?"

"I need some help again."

Pannetier's eyebrows crept up.

"You need my help? Whatever for? Oh, and by the way, my personal jammer is on, so we can talk openly."

"Mine is as well. But I prefer we do this in private." He glanced at the two bodyguards."

"All right." Pannetier made a gesture, and both men stood, then walked over to a nearby unoccupied table.

"I require someone to remove a certain individual in a manner that can't be traced back to anyone in Geneva, let alone the administration. A natural death."

"Don't you have the SSB for those sorts of things?"

Markus grimaced.

"I'd rather leave them out of it."

"As it happens, I can arrange for permanent removals with the cause appearing entirely natural. Who is your intended target, if I may ask?"

Markus glanced around, even though the jammers would effectively keep anyone from hearing them.

"Kathryn Kowalski."

This time, his bushy eyebrows shot straight up.

"You're kidding me, *mon ami*. Why ever do you want her removed?"

"Because she's standing in the way of policy changes, and my boss can't fire her."

"I see. It is still a momentous thing to assassinate the commander-in-chief of the Commonwealth Armed Forces."

"Can't be helped, I'm afraid." Markus took another sip of his pastis and set the glass on the table again. "So, are you ready to do it, or point me at someone who will?"

"That, I cannot answer until we take a measure of her and the security arrangements she uses." He shrugged. "My people are good, but there are some targets who'll be beyond them if you want the death to look natural. Blowing up their cars on the highway is much easier." Another shrug. "And it will require a substantial donation to my foundation, of course."

"How much?"

"Let's say one hundred thousand to evaluate the target. Then, if my people find a workable way of doing it, another two and a half million."

"Steep."

Pannetier gave Markus a smile.

"What can I say, *mon ami*? She is one of the most powerful individuals alive, which means she'll be so well protected we may not even find a way of doing it. And before you ask, you will find no one prepared to do the job for less. In fact, many of my colleagues in the *Milieu* would laugh you away — if they don't use the fact you approached them to blackmail you."

Markus cocked an eyebrow at Pannetier.

"And you won't?"

"We have done business before. Besides, I'm a man of honor. Too many of the others are not nowadays."

But Markus knew there was more — he was aware of certain things about Pannetier that could get him in deep trouble with the *Milieu,* and Pannetier was aware of that.

"Very well." Markus stretched out his hand, and they shook. "Agreed. I'll have the one hundred thousand cred donation to your foundation sent immediately."

Thank the Almighty for covert slush funds, Markus thought as he took a healthy swig of his pastis.

"And I shall see that my people begin their evaluation the moment I receive the money."

Pannetier's eyes went over Markus' shoulder, and the latter figured someone else had shown up to speak with the mob boss.

"Thank you, Leon." Markus finished his drink and stood. "Until the next time."

"Goodbye for now." Pannetier raised a hand in farewell.

Markus glanced at the man waiting to speak with the mob boss but didn't recognize him, nor did he see any signs of recognition in his eyes, which was just as well.

He was back in Geneva shortly after eighteen hundred hours and squiring his latest date to a table at the *Restaurant du Lac* less than an hour later, charming her with his wit and courtliness.

— Eleven —

"Doesn't look any different from when I last saw it at age twenty-two, outbound for the Rim Sector and my first assignment." Dunmoore studied the image of Earth on the first-class saloon's primary display. The three wore their everyday uniforms, with rank insignia on the collars.

"Agreed," Pushkin said. "But then, the place is a paean to humanity's history, a museum in planetary form. I doubt they've built anything new on the surface in two hundred years."

"Not that we can see anything beyond the landmasses and clouds," Guthren remarked with an innocent air. "We can't even see Starbase One, let alone any civilian orbitals."

The public address system came on, advising passengers that *Homeric* was docking in thirty minutes and to please get ready.

"It's nice of Captain Hassan to let the shuttle from Joint Base Geneva pick us up on his hangar deck." Pushkin gestured at the saloon's door. "Shall we?"

Guthren grinned at him. "Heck, it's nice to get a Navy shuttle at all. They could just as well have told us to take the civilian run to the Geneva spaceport."

"You really think they'd let the incoming CNO go civilian?" Dunmoore asked. "And there's the matter of security. Having me gad about on one of the commercial stations waiting for a ride would give Zeke's people conniptions."

"I suppose, sir."

They headed back to their quarters to wait for an escort who would show them to *Homeric*'s hangar deck. He appeared not long afterward, informing them the shuttle was arriving before they docked since the station didn't want small craft traffic so close to docking arms.

Trailed by their antigrav pallets, they made their way aft, following the petty officer until they reached the hangar deck control room. There, they watched as the space doors opened and a naval craft nosed its way through the forcefield keeping the air in. It stopped in the center of the deck, turned around, and settled while the space doors closed.

The inner door opened moments later, as did the shuttle's aft ramp, and they were escorted aboard, where a lieutenant waited to seat them. He saluted Dunmoore, then, helped by a petty officer, he stowed their luggage.

Within minutes, the aft ramp and the hangar deck's inner door closed, and the space doors opened again. The shuttle lifted off and cautiously made its way through the force field and into space before peeling off and heading downward.

As the shuttle turned, Dunmoore caught a glimpse of Orbital Three, the commercial station where *Homeric* would dock. It was a slightly smaller version of a starbase with civilian markings instead of naval ones, but very much built on the same pattern.

Soon, they felt the buffeting of the upper atmosphere as the shuttle lost altitude and the blackness faded, replaced by an increasingly blue sky. After a while, their descent slowed as they spotted Geneva on the shores of the lake surrounded by mountains. A look straight down revealed the joint base which housed Fleet HQ.

The shuttle settled in front of the base's passenger terminal, and a small guard formed just outside the doors — a lieutenant and twenty spacers, also in everyday uniform but carrying weapons. Before the ramp dropped, the shuttle pilot emerged from the flight deck.

"Sirs, you just leave your luggage here. We'll see that it gets to the visiting senior officers' quarters. And for you, Command Chief, to the visiting senior non-commissioned officers' quarters."

"Thank you, Lieutenant."

"They'll have a car laid on to bring you to the main HQ building where the outgoing CNO is waiting."

As the ramp dropped, Dunmoore glanced at Pushkin and Guthren. "Let's do this, folks."

They marched down and Dunmoore headed for the guard commander, who ordered the present arms. She returned his salute, then inspected the spacers while her two companions watched from the sidelines. Once that was done, she received another present arm, then led the way through the terminal and a waiting staff car bearing a blue plate with four silver stars on it. The driver ushered them aboard, then took the controls and drove them across the base to the large, fifteen-story building that towered over the base and the surrounding countryside.

82 *Eric Thomson*

"Still as ugly as I remember," Dunmoore murmured.

"Aye, it is that." Pushkin grimaced. "Built for function, not aesthetics. I understand there are several subterranean levels as well."

"Ten of them, one which is entirely devoted to the Fleet's main operations center. A place you'll get to know rather quickly."

Pushkin made a face.

"I suppose I shall."

The car pulled up to the main door where an aide-de-camp, a commander with gold cords dangling from her left shoulder, waited. She snapped to attention as Dunmoore climbed out and saluted.

"Good morning, sir. I'm Liv Botha, the CNO's junior aide."

"Good morning, Commander."

"If you'll please follow me, I'll take you to the Grand Admiral's office, where she and the CNO are waiting for you."

They made their way to the tenth floor, also known as the Executive Floor, where the Grand Admiral and the service chiefs had their offices and through the Grand Admiral's antechamber. The inner door was open, and the aide stepped through.

"Admiral Dunmoore, Vice Admiral Pushkin, and Command Chief Petty Officer Guthren, sir."

She stepped aside to let them by, turned on her heels, and left the office, closing the door behind her.

Kathryn Kowalski stood, beaming, and came around her desk, hand outstretched.

"Siobhan!" After a hearty handshake, she turned to Pushkin. "Gregor. It's so good to see you again after so long." They shook as well. Finally, Kowalski held her hand out to Guthren. "Chief, I'm so glad you stuck around the Fleet to be with us today."

She gestured at the four-star admiral standing in front of her desk.

"You know Piotr Antonescu, I presume."

Dunmoore nodded, sticking out her hand.

"Hi, Piotr. It's been a long time."

"It has indeed, Siobhan. I'm glad you're taking over from me. I couldn't think of a better person for the job."

"Where are you off to after the change of command?"

"Caledonia, of course. I'm taking the position of secretary for external affairs with the star system government."

"Good to hear."

Kowalski gestured at the sofas surrounding a low coffee table to one side of her spacious office. "Shall we sit? And how was your trip from Dordogne?"

"Comfortable. We were in first-class suites, and the captain was a Navy veteran of the war. He gave us bridge privileges, and we dined at his table every evening."

"Nice. Beats sailing in a naval transport."

"Does it ever. And it got me here on time to spend two weeks doing a handover with Piotr."

"Speaking of which," Antonescu said, "a company from the Scandia Regiment showed up the other day, claiming to be your guard of honor, along with the CO of the Regiment. They're lodged in the transient quarters and are enjoying the sights of Earth."

"Excellent. I'm glad they're here. I'd like to meet Colonel Salminen and the company commander as soon as possible."

"I'll have one of my aides, soon to be yours, arrange it. And I've installed a second desk temporarily in my office so we can work together during the handover."

They chatted amiably for fifteen minutes, catching up. Then Kowalski's aide stuck his head through the office door and reminded her she had an upcoming appointment.

"Never a moment's peace," she said, climbing to her feet, imitated by the others. "Siobhan, I'd like to invite you for the evening meal in my quarters tonight, just you and me, say eighteen-thirty."

"I'll be there."

"Once again, welcome. You three are a sight for sore eyes."

They left Kowalski's office, Guthren steering for that of the current Chief Petty Officer of the Navy, Pushkin for the vacant office of the Assistant Chief of Naval Operations for Sustainment, his predecessor having already left, and the two admirals for the CNO's.

That evening, Siobhan Dunmoore, wearing casual civilian clothes, walked up to the Grand Admiral's official residence, a sprawling bungalow on a large treed lot at the center of the joint base's residential quarter. It lay next door to that of the CNO, which would be hers the moment Piotr Antonescu vacated it.

A few streets away was the residence of the Chief Petty Officer of the Navy, a slightly smaller bungalow, which Guthren would occupy. Since Gregor Pushkin wasn't expected to host official functions at home, he'd move into one of the senior officer's apartments in the low-rise complex on one side of the quarter.

The front door opened at her approach, and the moment she stepped through, Kowalski's voice called out, "Good evening,

Siobhan. I'm in the kitchen, trying to get the chicken to behave. Oh, and by the way, it's first names only when we're in private. After all, you were once my captain."

"Hi, Kathryn." Dunmoore poked her head through the archway leading to the kitchen. "Why is the chicken misbehaving?"

"I made a mistake in setting my timing. We'll be eating a little later than expected." When she glanced at Dunmoore and saw the look on her face, Kowalski grinned. "Yes, I'm making it from scratch rather than using the autochef. I find cooking relaxes me, and I sure need it in this job."

Dunmoore shook her head. "I don't think I've ever not used an autochef."

"How about you make us some gin and tonics?" Kowalski nodded at the sideboard groaning under the weight of bottles.

"Sure. How strong do you want yours?"

"Not too strong. I can't afford to be tipsy at any time since I'm never really off duty. And neither are you or at least neither will you be once you formally take over from Piotr."

"Gotcha. Not that I'm a heavy drinker by any means." Dunmoore mixed their drinks, then handed Kowalski a glass before raising hers. "Skoal."

"Here's to us." They took a sip, and then Kowalski said, "We're finally in the right places to do the things we must so we can keep the Commonwealth from spiraling out of control before it's ready to transform into something better."

"Whoa, that's a lot to unpack, Kathryn. You'll need to spell it out for me."

Kowalski chuckled. "That's why we're having supper alone, so I can tell you why you're here and what I expect. The chicken will take about three-quarters of an hour. Why don't we take our ease in the living room?"

Once they sat across from each other, Kowalski studied Dunmoore in silence for a few heartbeats.

"Are you aware the Commonwealth might well see a third Migration War if Sara Lauzier and her ilk aren't contained? The OutWorlds have been seriously unhappy with the Centralists for years, and now Lauzier, the ultimate of that breed, is SecGen."

"I know about it, but rather vaguely. There are precious few Centralists in the Rim Sector, so I didn't get to experience the conflict."

"Lauzier's elevation to SecGen is the culmination of Centralist conniving that started shortly after the end of the war. Successive Grand Admirals have been aware of it and scheming to prevent the Centralists from gaining the upper hand. When I was first posted to Earth, I found myself pulled into those efforts and have since been working to expand them. For the last ten years, I've been plotting myself, putting the right people into place — Zeke Holt as Chief of Security, for instance, you as CNO, and others in senior positions throughout the Fleet. You might say I'm the culmination of the Fleet's scheming, the one to bring it all together. Our job, simply put, is to clip Sara Lauzier's wings and buy the Commonwealth a few decades of civil peace so it can evolve into something different without war."

— Twelve —

Dunmoore sat back and raised her eyebrows. "A tall order. How are we going to do that?"

Kowalski gave Dunmoore a tight smile. "We're going to make the Fleet its own entity, separate from the Commonwealth government, the OutWorlds, and the Home Worlds so that we can't be used by either party to put down the other. We'll be the ultimate neutral arbiter in our part of the galaxy. Of course, Sara Lauzier would rather have the Fleet enforce the Centralists' desires, but we will thwart that."

A light went on in Dunmoore's eyes.

"Ah, I see where this is going. The slow, subtle move of Fleet units to Caledonia, light years away from Earth — the War College, the Academy, Special Operations Command HQ, Readiness Evaluation, and more is part of setting ourselves up as said arbiter."

"Indeed. We're in the process of establishing a Forward Fleet HQ on Caledonia which effectively replicates HQ on Earth. Joint Base Sanctum is growing at an accelerated pace and already has a lot of the infrastructure. For example, a Fleet Operations Center will come online within six months and take over, leaving the one here a mere repeater until we shut it down. And the Chief of the Army and his entire staff moved there a few weeks ago. By the time we're done, we'll run everything from Caledonia. Only 1st Fleet, the 1st Marine Division, and the Terra Regiment will be left in this star system. Nothing else."

Dunmoore stared at her, eyebrows raised, uncertain where to begin, and Kowalski chuckled.

"Wow."

"And the Grand Admiral will be freed from politics because she will be on Caledonia, far from Earth, where she'll concentrate on keeping the peace."

"I get the move to Caledonia, but how will you deal with the principle of military subordination to the civilian administration."

"It'll disappear when we become the fourth branch of government. Oh, the Senate will still have to keep on voting our budget, and the Defense Secretary will set the defense policy, with our input, of course. We will simply ignore anything he tries to put into the policy that goes against the Fleet's neutrality. But the day-to-day running of the Fleet will be out of the politicians' hands entirely."

"I can't see Sara Lauzier going along with that."

"She already isn't. Our current flashpoint is procurement, which she wants turned over entirely to the civilian side of the Defense Department, so she has control over what we receive and who gets the contracts. Considering the Fleet's enormous needs, the potential for political corruption of the entire process is infinite."

Dunmoore nodded knowingly.

"Which is why she wants to push the uniforms out of it. So she can reward her supporters."

Kowalski tapped the side of her nose with an extended index finger.

"Precisely. But with procurement now entirely run from Caledonia, where we control access, she's too late."

"But can't she exercise control via the budget?"

"Ah, yes. The budget. At this point, the Senate would override her attempts to throttle us. There are still enough Home World senators who consider defense a sacred duty."

"But when Lauzier replaces every senator she can with those amenable to her wishes?"

"At that point, I hope to have legislation passed enshrining the Fleet's neutral status, including an obligation to fund it."

"Okay. And what's my role in this? I presume you appointed me as CNO for more than just running the Navy. Most four stars can do the job — it's mainly administrative."

"I need your ruthlessness in dealing with the politicians, Siobhan. You'll be my right hand in carrying out the things I must do. The day-to-day Fleet operations will be run mostly by Avi Nagato, the Marine Corps Commandant, who's the deputy commander-in-chief. And he'll do so from Caledonia once the operations center is active. Your deputy CNO, Ulli Radames, will take care of the day-to-day for the Navy, also from Caledonia. The same goes for the Chief of Naval Intelligence and his deputy. While we carry out our mission, Fleet HQ on Earth will continue to be hollowed out until only a shell remains."

"Why me?" Dunmoore took a sip of her drink. "I know nothing and no one in Geneva. In fact, you might say I'm a babe in the woods when it comes to politics."

"I chose you precisely because of that. You don't have any preconceived notions about how things are done in this town, and our task doesn't demand subtlety. On the contrary. I need you to be my hard-charging executive officer who'll plow anyone opposing me under."

Dunmoore grinned at her. "That, I can do. And Zeke — what's his part in your plan?"

"He's our backstop. His job is to make sure we, all of us involved, survive. It means keeping a close watch on the SSB so his people can outmaneuver them if they decide to act against us. Until that is, he eliminates them entirely."

"I beg your pardon?" Dunmoore frowned. "You mean wipe out the SSB."

Kowalski nodded. "Yes. We can't have them running around for much longer. They answer solely to the SecGen, and we can both imagine to what extent Lauzier will go when she realizes what we're up to."

"How will you do it?"

"That's Zeke's responsibility. I imagine he'll terminate the senior leadership with extreme prejudice, destroy their infrastructure, and salt the earth."

"I see." Dunmoore took on a thoughtful air. "What's to keep the SecGen from reviving it under a different name?"

"Nothing, really, yet we'll have gained breathing space. But I intend to force the government into creating a federal police service, an interstellar constabulary if you like."

"Ambitious. Where will you get the people? From the SSB?"

"No. SSB agents will never be hired by the Constabulary. It'll be a paramilitary police force, and I intend to create it using a big chunk of Fleet Security with Zeke as its first head. And it'll have an internal affairs division which will be empowered to investigate any branch of the Commonwealth government."

"I really can't see Lauzier or the Senate approving that."

"Lauzier, no. The Senate, however, will be a different story. Especially once I present them with a *fait accompli*. I'll simply create the Constabulary using Armed Forces personnel and take the funds from our budget. It'll be the child of the Fleet and just as insulated from politics as we're becoming."

Dunmoore shook her head.

"You're really something, Kathryn. I always knew there was much more behind your inscrutable facade, but I never dreamed it was this much. Still, what chances of success do you give yourself?"

"Plenty. The Fleet has been preparing for twenty years because we can take the long view and develop a winning course of action at the strategic level. Politicians like Lauzier and the esteemed senators can only think in chunks of six years at most — until the end of their current terms — and many can't even do that. They're stuck at the tactical level and unable to climb out of it. The audacity of what we'll be doing over the next few years will take them by surprise, not because they won't know it's coming but because they don't expect us to carry it out since they can only see the universe through their limited perceptions. And believe me, most of that ilk's perceptions are extremely limited compared to ours."

"You mentioned earlier that all this is to gain a few decades of civil peace, so the Commonwealth has a chance of evolving into something new and presumably better. Any ideas on what that might be?"

Kowalski shrugged.

"Not completely. There are too many unknowns. But I foresee a split between the OutWorlds and most of the Home Worlds within the next century. They're drifting apart slowly but surely with no chance of reversing course. Hopefully, the peace we gain by setting the Fleet apart as arbiter will ensure that the split occurs without another ruinous war. Whatever happens afterward, your guess is as good as mine."

Dunmoore drained her glass and placed it on a side table.

"Aren't you afraid of a sociopath like Lauzier calling a hit out on you?"

A nod.

"Oh yes, I am. Zeke put the fear of the Almighty into Leila Gherson, the head of the SSB, so I doubt Sara will be able to call on them. But there are many other organizations outside the government who'd gladly do it for a hefty payment. It means I have guards who are never far from me when I leave the base. Zeke's people have carefully vetted everyone who comes into contact with me, my food, and my drink. I'm as safe as humanly possible. And they're vetting those who'll come into contact with you because you'll be as much of a target as I am once it becomes clear you're working with me on ramming through the reforms."

Dunmoore cocked an eyebrow at her.

"Sounds like what I went through at the beginning of my term as Commander, 3rd Fleet. Paranoia's the operative word, eh?"

"Yup. The next few years will be uncomfortable for us, but what we're doing is so utterly vital. I don't think I'm exaggerating when I say we'll likely save humanity from a third Migration War if we succeed."

"That's a heavy load to bear, Kathryn, I won't deny it. But I'm game."

"Good. I knew you would be." She glanced at an antique clock on a sideboard, one that resembled Dunmoore's prized timepiece, minus the outline of the gaunt knight on its face. "And we should move to the dining room now. Time for appetizers."

Kowalski poured the wine, and while eating, they caught up on how the last twenty years had treated them, with Dunmoore marveling at Kowalski's stellar career while hers had stalled for almost a decade. But since she'd had no ambitions to become the CNO in the first place, let alone a Grand Admiral, Dunmoore considered herself extremely lucky.

"Thank you for a most enlightening evening, Kathryn," Dunmoore said as Kowalski walked her to the door once they'd finished their meal and postprandial coffee. "We have an immense task ahead."

"That we do, yet I think we'll pull it off. Our predecessors have prepared the way for us, and we're a pair of hard chargers who always get where we want to go."

Once out on the sidewalk, heading back to the transient senior officers' quarters, Dunmoore reflected on what she'd heard and could see the sense in Kowalski's scheme, even though it seemed rather difficult, if not impossible, to carry out successfully. Yet she'd planned and executed the raid on the Shrehari home system that brought the enemy to the negotiating table and ended the war, something many in the Fleet had believed to be impossibly risky. So why not?

When she was back in her suite, Dunmoore poured herself a dram of Glen Arcturus and raised the glass in a silent toast to their triumph.

— Thirteen —

"Colonel Tatiana Salminen of the Scandia Regiment is here, sir," Commander Botha announced, standing at the open office door.

Antonescu rose from behind his desk.

"I'll make myself scarce so you can spend time alone with your former embarked troops commander."

"Thanks, Piotr. I appreciate it."

Once Antonescu had left, the aide ushered Salminen in. She wore the Army's rifle green uniform with a colonel's oak leaf wreath and three diamonds at the collar, several rows of ribbons on the chest, and a blue beret with the Scandia Regiment's badge, a loping timber wolf on a snowflake. Salminen had changed little over the years. She was still tall and lean, but the lines on her face were deeper, and her short black hair held strands of silver. Yet her crooked smile was as warm as ever.

Dunmoore came out from behind her desk, hand outstretched as Salminen saluted.

"Tatiana. It's so good to see you again."

"Likewise, Admiral. And it's an honor to be here with my old company."

They shook, then sat on facing sofas, both smiling happily.

"So, how are you, and how goes the Scandia Regiment?"

"I'm doing fine, Admiral, although this unexpected vacation on Earth suits me just now since I can use a break from the day-to-day drudgery of running the Scandias in peacetime. The Regiment is all right, as usual, although everyone is excited by E Company, 3rd Battalion being nominated as your honor guard."

"And where's the company commander, Captain Eklund?"

"He's in Australia, diving the Barrier Reef with his people. I figured there was no need to recall him right away."

"You're entirely correct. So, what have you been up to since we last saw each other? What was it? Four years ago?"

They chatted for almost an hour. At the end, Dunmoore asked, "What are your plans once your term of command is over? Will you transfer to the Scandian National Guard?"

"Perhaps, but probably not."

"Why?"

Salminen shrugged. "I think I'd like to try something other than the military for the second half of my life. Teach, maybe. Or become an entrepreneur."

"Well, whatever you embark on, I'm sure you'll do splendidly."

The senior aide, Captain Josh Malfort, stuck his head through the door at that moment. "Admiral, you have the command meeting in five minutes."

"Right." Dunmoore gave Salminen an apologetic smile. "Sorry, Tatiana, but we'll have to cut this short. My first meeting with my soon-to-be direct reports. How about we have supper together in the officer's mess, say eighteen hundred?"

"Certainly, sir." Both stood, Salminen putting her beret back on her head. "With your permission?"

"Until tonight."

Salminen saluted and did a precise about-turn before marching out of the office. Dunmoore grabbed her tablet from the desk and glanced at Captain Malfort.

"Ready."

***

The morning of the change of command ceremony proved auspicious — bright sunshine, not a cloud in the sky, and not a whisper of wind. Dunmoore had moved into the CNO's residence late the previous day and was still a little disoriented as she found the kitchen and searched for prepared breakfast meal packs. She didn't want to head for the officer's mess. It would mean putting on her regular uniform only to change into full-dress uniform later that morning.

Fortunately, Antonescu had left a stack of meal packs in one of the cupboards. She popped one in the autochef before switching on the old-fashioned coffee machine, and for the first time since leaving her house on Dordogne, she ate alone and in private. It made for a nice change.

At ten, Dunmoore exchanged her pajamas for her full-dress uniform, with the Office of CNO's round starburst and anchor badge on the right breast pocket where 3rd Fleet's watchtower and crossed tridents used to be. If anyone had told her even five years ago she'd end up as the Chief of Naval Operations, Dunmoore would have laughed them out of her office.

At ten twenty-five, a staff car with a blue plate and four silver stars pulled up by her front door. Commander Botha alit and ushered her into the passenger compartment, where she joined Piotr Antonescu, also splendidly garbed in full-dress uniform with sword, sitting across from Captain Malfort.

"This is it," he said, grinning at her. "Your turn to take the helm in half an hour."

"You seem quite pleased by the notion."

"Four years was enough for me. I'm looking forward to civilian life on Caledonia, working for Zebulon Lowell again."

They crossed the base to the parade ground where a five-hundred-strong naval contingent, under a commodore, waited for them in four companies of three ranks. Well over a thousand spectators rose as the car entered the square and stopped in front of the dais.

Both aides jumped out and stood by the back doors, one on either side. As Dunmoore and Antonescu exited, the aides raised their hands in salute. The staff car drove off again, and Antonescu climbed onto the dais while Dunmoore stood on one side while the aides placed themselves on the other. The commodore called the general salute, with the band breaking out in four ruffles and flourishes, followed by the Admirals' March.

Once the commodore gave the shoulder arms, Antonescu stepped off and stood opposite Dunmoore in front of the aides. Moments later, another staff car with a black, blue, and green plate bedecked with five stars appeared and stopped in front of the dais, disgorging Grand Admiral Kowalski.

She, too, received a general salute — five ruffles and flourishes followed by the Grand Admiral's March — then the commodore invited her to inspect the parade, which she did, trailed by Dunmoore and Antonescu. Once that was done, Kowalski made a brief speech, thanking Antonescu for his sterling service and welcoming Dunmoore as the new CNO. Then, a table and three chairs were brought out, and with Kowalski sitting in the middle, they signed the change of command parchments — one for Dunmoore, one for Antonescu, and the third for the archives.

The table and chairs vanished, and Antonescu gave his farewell speech, wishing his successor the best. He then climbed on the dais, and the parade marched past, giving him a final salute. Once they were back in position, the commodore had the officers sheath their swords and then ordered the parade to remove their headdress.

"Three cheers for Admiral Antonescu, hip, hip, hip."

"Hurrah."

The band played the first three bars of Auld Lang Syne.

"Hip, hip, hip."

"Hurrah."

The band played the next three bars. After the final hurrah, the band finished the song, and as the last bar faded away, Antonescu stepped off the dais and took a seat. The parade replaced headdress, and the officers drew swords once more.

"Ladies and gentlemen," the narrator said, his voice carrying far and wide, "please rise for the arrival of Admiral Dunmoore's Guard of Honor, E Company, 3rd Battalion, Scandia Regiment."

Dunmoore climbed onto the dais as she saw movement to her left, beyond the crowd. The bandmaster raised his baton, and they burst into the Hakkapeliittain Marssi. After the opening fanfare, the one hundred and twenty-six lusty voices of E Company resonated over the parade square as they appeared.

On Pohjolan hangissa meill' isänmaa
sen rannalla loimuta lietemme saa
käs' säilöjä käyttäiss' on varttunut siell'
on kunnialle, uskolle hehkunut miel'

The commodore ordered the parade to present arms once again as E Company marched past between them and the dais rendering a salute to Dunmoore.

Kun ratsujamme Nevan vuossa uitettihin
kuin häihin se ui yli Veikselinkin;
Ja kalpamme kostavan Reinille toi
ja Tonavasta Keisarin maljan se joi!

E Company marched to the far end of the parade square, then made a U-turn and came back, halting in front of the dais as the last words of the march wafted away. At an order from Captain Eklund, the company turned to face Dunmoore, and he stepped forward and swept his sword down in salute, a gesture she returned with her hand to her brow.

"Captain Tapani Eklund reporting to the Chief of Naval Operations with one hundred and twenty-five soldiers of the Scandia Regiment, ready to take up post as your guard of honor," he announced in Finnish.

"Please carry on, Captain," Dunmoore replied in the same loud tone and the same language.

Eklund turned to face his soldiers and barked out, still in Finnish, "E Company will take post."

Immediately, drums began to beat as the soldiers peeled off from both ends and marched toward the spectators to the sounds of the Jääkärimarssi, spreading out. They stopped in pairs lined up with the front of the dais, and turned around until only

Eklund, his first sergeant, and the four command sergeants leading the platoons remained. At an order from Eklund, the remainder marched up to the dais and took position, three on either side.

"Admiral Dunmoore will now address the parade and spectators," the narrator intoned.

She was, as usual, short and to the point. Then, she called up the outgoing Chief Petty Officer of the Navy and Chief Guthren front and center and oversaw the passing of the cane of office.

With that done, she returned to the dais, and the parade marched past. Once they'd halted back in their positions, the commodore ordered the general salute, which E Company joined. After he'd given the shoulder arms, Dunmoore stepped off, and Kowalski took her place for an encore of ruffles and flourishes, followed by the Grand Admiral's March.

As soon as the music died away, Kowalski smiled at Dunmoore and Antonescu and invited them to follow her off the parade square and to the hangar, where the reception was held while the spectators remained standing, waiting to follow them. When they'd vanished, the commodore dismantled the parade, and E Company reformed to head for the hangar and stand as a ceremonial guard over the gathering.

That evening, the Navy held a mess dinner to honor Admiral Antonescu and his Chief Petty Officer, with Dunmoore presiding. The formal part of the evening concluded with a particularly lusty version of The Wellerman, a sea shanty that was ancient when humans first reached for the stars but which roused all present to stand and put a foot on their chairs as they raised their glasses.

No one remembered when The Wellerman was first sung at the end of Navy mess dinners. However, it was started by the most junior officers present, as was now tradition, and concluded by everyone, Dunmoore included, who belted it out as loudly as the rest.

Antonescu and Dunmoore made very short remarks afterward, no more than a minute each, then released the attendees to the rest of the celebrations.

A tired Dunmoore, back at home well past midnight, finally removed her mess uniform and slipped gratefully into her bed, intending to sleep in that Sunday morning. With any luck, she'd have the rest of the day to relax before facing a few years of twenty-four-seven on duty.

— Fourteen —

"I think my boss spoke with someone concerning Kowalski." Renouf grimaced at Gherson. "An underworld figure. Sorry."

Her lips compressed into a thin line of annoyance as she stared at him.

"There was nothing I could have done," he continued, half apologetic. "Paul Markus can be a bulldog with a bone when he wants to, and he evidently considers her elimination a sacred mission."

They were enjoying their usual evening out at one of Geneva's fine restaurants, this time in *Le Pied de Cochon*, a dimly lit, wood-paneled, cozy place where the tables were nicely separated and flames flickered in the fireplace. From across the room, Renouf couldn't tell whether they were real or holographic. Of course, they both had their personal jammers on so no one might overhear the conversation.

"Damn him. If he gets her killed, I'll catch it from Holt and his people."

"I told him that, but he obviously considers you expendable."

A faint sneer appeared on Gherson's face. "I can show him a thing or two about that. In fact, if he puts my life and those of my subordinates in danger, I may just do so. Secretaries are eminently replaceable, especially in Sara Lauzier's cabinet, autocrat that she is. Senior SSB officers with thirty or more years of experience, not so much."

Renouf gave her an astonished look. "You wouldn't."

"In a heartbeat, Axel. Perhaps you should tell your boss that if I find out he's hired a mobster to kill Kowalski, I'll terminate him instantly."

"You personally?"

A predatory smile briefly played on Gherson's lips.

"Sure. Why not? I've terminated plenty of my enemies over the years."

"Let me think about it."

"Oh?" She cocked a questioning eyebrow at Renouf. "You're not happy with him?"

He made a face.

"Sometimes. No. Make that often. Deep down, he's a psychopath who hides it well. No empathy, no morality, and no soul."

"Meaning he's like most of Sara Lauzier's cabinet secretaries."

This time, it was Renouf's turn to smile.

"She does like to surround herself with people who don't have a conscience."

"Just like her." Gherson took a sip of wine. "Do you sometimes get the feeling that with Lauzier, we've inherited a government of amoral thugs?"

"Aren't they all amoral? Judy Chu wasn't a warm, empathetic person either. Nor was Lauzier *père*."

"Perhaps. But our current rulers seem much worse than any previous ones."

Renouf shrugged.

"Could be. I simply work on the principle that whoever's on top isn't among the nicest humans."

"Speaking of top dogs, you're aware Siobhan Dunmoore, a close friend of Kowalski, took over as Chief of Naval Operations the other day, right?"

"Yes, what of it?"

"We know Kowalski is a schemer. She's always been one, and now that she surrounded herself with allies, Dunmoore being the latest of them, I think whatever she's planning will come to a head soon."

A frown creased Renouf's forehead.

"What would she be planning?"

"I don't know. Her information security is impeccable. We are trying to find out, although I suspect only those directly involved, like Holt, Dunmoore, and a few others, are aware."

"Care to speculate?"

Gherson wrinkled her nose.

"No. I deal in facts, not fancy."

"Well, I will. I think Kowalski is plotting to upset the political construct which elevates Earth above the other star systems and stop the Centralists. She utterly loathes Centralism as a philosophy and hasn't hidden it."

"Perhaps. But how and what parts of the construct?"

"I don't have a clue. It's unfortunate that those knowledgeable individuals have likely been conditioned to resist interrogation.

"Don't even think about such things." Gherson glowered at him. "We'll just have to use the time-honored practice of waiting for the opposition to slip up. Because they will, eventually."

"And you consider the commander-in-chief of the Commonwealth Armed Forces the opposition?"

"Yes. Don't you?"

***

"And finally, the Commonwealth Day reception at the Palace of the Stars." Grand Admiral Kowalski looked around the conference table. "Siobhan and Avi, you're coming with me. The rest of you get a permanent reprieve."

Dunmoore and the Commandant of the Marine Corps nodded.

"The permanent reprieve," she continued, "is so the government gets used to seeing a lot less of us at various functions because pretty soon, none of us will be around to attend."

Her comment drew grim smiles from everyone, especially the Chief of Personnel, who was leaving for Caledonia with the rest of her staff the following month to join the Chief of Procurement and the Chief of Infrastructure, among others who'd already moved there with their people. That certain parts of Fleet HQ felt a little empty was an understatement.

Kowalski glanced at Dunmoore, who'd never attended a function at the Palace. "Full-dress uniform with medals. We travel in our separate staff cars without our aides."

"Got it."

"If there's nothing else?" Kowalski waited for a few heartbeats. "Thank you."

She stood, imitated by the others, and walked out of the executive conference room. Dunmoore and Holt hung back at the latter's signal.

"Just so you're aware, the SSB has you under surveillance whenever you leave the base," he said. "And I'm not sure they don't have agents on the base either."

"Nice."

"Don't feel overly flattered. They're also watching Kathryn, Avi Nagato, the CNI, and me."

"Those of us who are in on it."

Holt nodded.

"Yep. They figure we're plotting something but don't have a clue what it is."

"How do you know they don't?"

A mischievous smile appeared, and he winked.

"That would be telling. But I have people in some awfully strange and useful places."

"Do I need to be more careful when I leave the base?"

"No more than usual, but I have operatives covering those concerned whenever we're not on official business."

Dunmoore cocked an eyebrow at him.

"Really? I haven't noticed anyone."

"Good. If you notice them, they're not doing it right."

"Are there any important details I should be informed about regarding the reception in the Palace? Like, don't eat or drink anything provided?"

Holt chuckled.

"You'll be fine. They won't try anything funny during an official function, and if Leila Gherson keeps her wits, the SSB won't try anything, period."

"Is there anyone else who might?"

He shook his head.

"No. The SSB is the SecGen's personal hit squad. They're the only ones who would even try to get at a Commonwealth admiral. And I've warned Gherson about what would happen to her personally. Even if the SecGen ordered her to, she wouldn't. Gherson's the sort who's seen SecGens come and go and isn't impressed with them."

"Except Lauzier isn't your run-of-the-mill Secretary General. For one thing, she's a lot more ruthless and less the prevaricating politician."

Holt inclined his head.

"Granted. I must confess I'm still playing catchup where she's concerned. Lauzier isn't turning out to be quite what we expected."

"I'm sure Kathryn isn't what Lauzier expected, either."

Another chuckle.

"Probably not. Tell you what, why don't we go out for supper tonight? The *Genfer Ratskeller* serves good food and excellent wine, and we might run across Leila Gherson. She eats out several times a week, and a little birdie told me today's her day at the *Ratskeller*. I'll pick you up at eighteen-thirty."

"Done. Eating alone in a residence big enough for a family of eight is getting to me. And I won't ask about your little birdie."

"Good, because I wouldn't have answered, anyway. But cheer up. The CNO's residence on Caledonia is a lot less opulent."

That evening, a dapper Ezekiel Holt picked up an elegantly dressed Siobhan Dunmoore and drove to Geneva's old downtown, parking in an underground garage on its periphery and walking the rest of the way.

"I must admit, this town is charming," she said, head on a swivel as they passed centuries-old buildings still in excellent shape. "And would be even more so if it didn't play host to the Commonwealth government."

"Only a relatively small part of it. The various departments have offices all over the planet. In fact, the Fleet is the only federal entity to be concentrated in one spot on Earth. Ah, here we are." They turned the corner and finally saw the old city hall. "It's a thousand years old. Most of it is now a museum except for the *Genfer Ratskeller* in the basement."

Dunmoore snorted indelicately. "Half the bloody planet is a repository for antiquities. It's just as well the Academy moved to Caledonia. Less of a temptation to make cadets endlessly visit museums."

"I gather you were not a fan?"

"After the tenth one in my first year, it got boring. You remember how eighteen-year-olds are."

"I quite enjoyed those visits. They opened up new perspectives on our collective past, which I still find useful when looking at the future."

Dunmoore smirked at him sideways.

"You always were a deep thinker. It makes you the perfect staff officer."

Holt smiled back at her.

"Not everyone can be a hell-for-leather fighting admiral, Siobhan. Some of us have an essential role in doing the tough, demanding, behind-the-scenes work."

"Touché."

They entered the old city hall's main entrance and turned left toward the stairs leading downward beneath a subdued sign announcing the restaurant. At the bottom of the stairs, an elderly maître d'hôtel, wearing a black suit, greeted them with a smile.

"You have reservations, sir, madame?"

"Yes, two under Zeke."

The man glanced at the tablet in his hand and nodded.

"Indeed, sir. If you'll follow me."

He led them to a corner table opposite the wall with the high cellar windows and activated the holographic menus emitted from an unobtrusive pad at the table's center.

"Enjoy your meal."

They sat, eyes crisscrossing the room, and Dunmoore asked, "What's good here?"

"Pretty much everything. I usually go for the steak frites and a nice glass of house red — they serve excellent house wine."

Dunmoore perused the menu and said, "I think I'll go for the schnitzel with fries."

"Also a good choice. They make their schnitzels very thin with shatteringly crisp breading."

They both ordered via the holographic menu — steak frites for Holt, schnitzel for Dunmoore, and a glass of house red each — and resumed watching the room, talking about this and that while waiting. A man wearing a white shirt and black trousers delivered the wine within minutes, and they picked up their glasses.

"What shall we drink to, Zeke?"

"Having survived another day in the Puzzle Palace?"

"Sure."

Both took a sip, and Dunmoore nodded approvingly.

"Nice."

"Ah, there's Leila, right on time." Holt nodded toward the entrance. "And Axel Renouf is at her side."

— Fifteen —

As the maître d'hôtel led them toward their table, Gherson met Holt's gaze, and the latter, smiling, raised his glass in salute at her. She merely glowered back for a moment before turning her eyes away.

"Who's Renouf?"

"The Permanent Undersecretary of Public Safety. He's a long-time political animal who worked for Lauzier before sliding over to the civil service and securing a senior job. Paul Markus, the Secretary of Public Safety, appointed him as his number two the moment he took over the position. Markus is a long-time Lauzier loyalist, by the way, as are all the secretaries."

"Are Gherson and Renouf an item?"

Holt shook his head.

"No. He's not her type. In fact, you'd be more her type than he is. But since they're both in similar lines of business and he believes the SSB should report to his boss, they dine together often and discuss matters of common interest. Mostly at his behest."

Just then, the waiter delivered their meals, Dunmoore's platter overflowing with a breaded cutlet and fries, accompanied by a heavily dressed salad on a separate plate.

"So now that we've seen them and they've seen us, what next?" She asked, cutting into her schnitzel.

"We eat, enjoy, and see what the evening brings," Holt replied, stabbing his steak with a fork, then sawing off a morsel. He popped it in his mouth and made appreciative noises. "Still as good as ever. Leila will be curious why you and I are supping here tonight and might come over to talk with us. If so, I can introduce you."

"And that will serve what purpose?"

A slow grin spread across Holt's face.

"So she can see her most ferocious adversary face-to-face, though she doesn't know it yet. Blayne Hersom, the lovely Leila's late and lamented predecessor — murdered by her, though we don't have proof — was a mere piker in matters opposing the two of you. But Gherson will be an adversary more worthy of your ruthlessness."

Dunmoore gave Holt a wry look.

"You're almost waxing poetic, Zeke."

He shrugged, still smiling.

"Blame it on the wine."

"You only had two sips. Can't handle it anymore?"

"Nope." He cut another piece of steak. "That's my excuse, and I'm not offering any other."

They ate in silence until their plates were empty, savoring every bite.

"That was excellent," Dunmoore declared, wiping her lips with her napkin before emptying her wine glass. "I can honestly say I haven't had a better schnitzel anywhere in the galaxy."

"They have been serving them here for over a century. Yes, this place is old. If you can't get it right during that time, you never will. Dessert?" He raised his eyebrows. "They make a superb pear tart Geneva-style, according to a recipe that predates spaceflight by quite a few years."

"Certainly. I still have a bit of room left after that mound of fries I devoured. And I'll have a coffee."

Holt placed the orders and sat back, eyes on Gherson and Renouf a few tables away from theirs.

"When they finish their main course, I think we'll join them."

The pear tarts and coffees showed up in record time, and Dunmoore savored every bit of her slice. "This is magnificent, especially with the whipped cream."

"Told you." Holt crammed the last piece into his mouth and took a sip of coffee. "And they've finished their main course. Let's go have the rest of our coffee with them."

He quickly waved his payment chip over the table's reader and stood, imitated by Dunmoore. Both picked up their coffee cups, and Holt led them to Gherson's table.

She glanced up at the last minute, but before either could say anything, Holt had dropped into one of the two empty chairs and Dunmoore in the other.

"Hey, Leila. How's business? I see you're still giving Axel the time of day." Holt winked at Renouf. "Lucky man."

"Ezekiel." Gherson's lips compressed into a thin line of annoyance.

"I figured I'd introduce you to my friend Siobhan." Holt nodded at her. "Siobhan, this is Leila Gherson, director general of the SSB, and the reprobate with her is Axel Renouf, Permanent Undersecretary of Public Safety."

"Charmed, I'm sure." Dunmoore let a faintly mocking smile dance on her lips. "Siobhan Dunmoore at your service."

"We know who you are, Admiral," Gherson replied in a dry tone. "I see you have the same questionable manners as Ezekiel. Is it something common to flag officers, or did you spend too much time together during the war?"

Dunmoore allowed her smile to widen just a tad.

"A bit of both."

"Ezekiel here," Gherson said to Renouf, "was Admiral Dunmoore's first officer in two different ships. He lost an eye and a leg — since regrown — when the enemy annihilated the first one. Some say it was at least partly because of the admiral's recklessness when she was a mere lieutenant commander, though a court martial acquitted her. It's a trait she may not have completely lost with time and greater responsibilities."

Gherson turned her attention back on Dunmoore.

"But it tamed organized crime on Dordogne, which put a bit of a crimp in our operations. I gather the accord you forced on the OCG leaders still holds?"

"Oh, yes. And it will hold for a long time yet."

"Pity. Now, what do you want, Ezekiel?"

"Other than have coffee with you and introduce Siobhan? Nothing."

"Well then, drink up and piss off."

The use of profanity by such a bland-looking, emotionless individual struck Dunmoore as peculiar, especially considering her flat tone.

Holt chuckled.

"Leila's clearly miffed at us, Siobhan. She rarely uses salty language, at least in public. I have no idea what she does in private, nor do I want to know if truth be told." He raised his coffee cup and took a sip. "One doesn't simply drink up the *Ratskeller's* fine brew, Leila. One must savor it drop by drop. But while I'm here, I just want to renew my warning that if any admiral or general comes to harm, even though it might appear accidental, I will hold you personally responsible."

"Don't worry. Our truce holds. Barely. And then only because I know you're ruthless enough to carry out your threats."

While Holt and Gherson tossed words at each other, Renouf had been surreptitiously watching Dunmoore, something she felt rather than saw, and wondered why.

"Can I do something for you, Axel, is it?" She asked him.

"You can tell me how someone with your background became Chief of Naval Operations."

She gave him a sweet smile, the one that presaged danger.

"Good looks, charm, and a ruthlessness that makes Zeke look tender and loving by comparison."

Renouf returned the smile.

"Okay. I'll confess I walked into that one, Admiral."

"Siobhan, please, Axel. Aren't we among friends here?"

"Are we?" Renouf glanced at Gherson's severe expression. "I think I know which way Leila's leaning."

Dunmoore turned to her.

"So, not friends then. Well, I tried." She finished her coffee. "It's been a pleasure meeting both of you. I'm sure we'll bump into each other regularly. For all its pretensions at governing human space, Geneva is still a small town."

"Populated by small-minded people," Holt added after draining his cup. "Just as long as we stay civil with each other."

Both stood.

"Enjoy the rest of your meal."

When they were out of earshot, Holt gave Dunmoore a sideways grin.

"I hope we ruined their evening by giving them a case of heartburn. Leila doesn't like me at all. She never has since the day she took over the SSB. Back then, I was a mere commodore and too lowly for her. She refused to have any dealings with me, insisting she would only speak with the CNI or another four-star. Now, I'm the only one in the Fleet who'll talk to her, and she needs to keep lines of communication open with us. That makes her grumpy."

"It makes you giddy, though, I'll bet."

"I confess I enjoy aggravating her. She's not a nice person, and as I said, she murdered Blayne Hersom, presumably on Sara Lauzier's orders, because good old Blayne was getting too comfortable with the Fleet."

They took the stairs back to the ground floor and exited the building.

"So Lauzier was directing the SSB, or at least Gherson, well before she became SecGen? How did that work?"

"She's been giving them orders since the days when she was an adviser to her father, with old Charles' full support. That's the problem when you have a law enforcement agency that answers to only one individual with no checks and balances via the Senate or the judiciary. It becomes a personal police force wholly owned by the SecGen and devoid of any morality or legality. And when the SecGen is a rabid Centralist, watch out."

As they strolled along, inhaling the clean night air, Dunmoore asked, "Aren't you afraid of irritating Gherson once too often and finding yourself or your family not waking up one morning?"

Holt snorted.

"She wouldn't dare because my deputy will hunt her down personally. Besides, Reyka and the kids quietly left for Caledonia, where they'll be safe, a few weeks before you arrived."

"Ah, I was wondering why I hadn't received an invitation to *Chez Holt*."

"I'm now living in a middle-aged bachelor's apartment on base, a one-bedroom unit." They reached the underground parking lot and climbed aboard Holt's car. "What did you think of Leila Gherson?"

"Cold, repressed, no soul behind the eyes but capable of instant fury if provoked sufficiently."

"You can still read people like an open book. Well done. And Renouf?"

"Self-controlled, watchful, slow to anger."

"Yep, that's Axel. He also has a streak of self-interest a parsec wide, which is why he probably jumped from Lauzier's political staff to the civil service early on. Axel must have figured staying with Lauzier might not be good for his continued health. She lost a few staffers over the years to so-called natural causes. Except for one, who was the victim of a grizzly murder. We found no proof it happened at Lauzier's behest, but rumors said he was about to turn whistleblower against her, and she had him killed in such a cruel fashion as a warning for others."

"The more I hear about Sara Lauzier, the more I figure we've got a psychopathic monster at the head of the Commonwealth government."

"And you'd be right. She isn't the first morally bankrupt leader humanity ever had. Far from it. They crop up regularly. Most damage their nations to some degree. A few, like SecGen Helga Fremont, whose venality triggered the Second Migration War, cause so much harm they're remembered forever. What Kathryn wants is to ensure Lauzier and her successors are not among them until humanity replaces our corrupt old Commonwealth with a new construct."

"Yeah, that's pretty much what she told me. I just wonder whether it's achievable."

"Maybe not entirely, but we have to try."

— Sixteen —

Dunmoore, wearing full-dress uniform minus her beret and sword, climbed aboard the black staff car with the blue plates bearing four silver stars. The driver, who'd stood beside the passenger compartment door, saluted her as she exited the CNO's residence. He then slipped behind the controls, put the car into motion, and headed for the base's main gate.

They soon joined a line of opulent official vehicles entering the Palace of the Stars grounds via the Pregny Gate, each stopping in front of the main doors to disgorge formally dressed individuals or couples. She noticed Grand Admiral Kowalski climb out of one identical to hers a few cars ahead. Kowalski, in turn, spotted Dunmoore's by the make and plates and stepped aside to wait for her.

Dunmoore stepped out as soon as the driver pulled to a stop after telling him she'd call for the return trip, not knowing when it would end.

"Hello, Siobhan. Looking spiffy as usual."

"I try not to let the Navy down."

"Fat chance of that." They fell into step beside each other and passed through the open doors, making their way to the *Salle des*

Pas Perdus, or Hall of the Lost Footsteps, where the reception was held.

"No receiving line?" Dunmoore asked as they climbed the stairs to music provided by the Army's Terra Regiment band.

"Not Madame Lauzier. She'll make a grandiose entrance once the most important guests are present."

"A tad pretentious."

"Just a wee bit, yes. But she feels it's her due as the most powerful human alive."

They reached the top of the stairs and snagged a glass of champagne each from a passing waiter carrying a tray before looking around at the faces, searching for friendly ones. Almost immediately, they spotted Avi Nagato, wearing the Marine Corp's silver-trimmed, black full-dress uniform, speaking with an elderly civilian Dunmoore didn't recognize.

"Who's with Avi?" She asked as they headed for him, graciously nodding at the people who acknowledged them along the way.

"Chief Justice of the Commonwealth Supreme Court Chidozie Achebe. He's a good sort and one of the few in this bunch who'll still speak with me. Most of the rest, while polite enough, try to keep their distance lest they incur Madame Lauzier's wrath. It's an open secret she and I don't get along." Then, in a louder tone, "Chief Justice. How are you today?"

"Tolerable, Grand Admiral, tolerable." Achebe's voice was more resonant and compelling than any Dunmoore had ever heard. She had the impression that he must come across as formidable when pronouncing from the bench. "And you?"

"Prospering as always."

Just then, a trumpet fanfare broke over the assembled dignitaries, stilling all conversation, and a set of side doors opened.

"Ladies and gentlemen, the Secretary General of the Commonwealth, Madame Sara Lauzier," a disembodied voice announced.

Everyone turned toward the doors, and a moment later, Lauzier, wearing an elegant and expensive charcoal gown, strode through, smiling. She wore her long dark hair artfully piled on her head, a silver necklace with a pendant, diamond studded earrings that sparkled, and a brooch shaped like the symbol of the Commonwealth.

"Magnificent," Dunmoore muttered for Kowalski's ears only.

"Isn't she? And to ponder that magnificence conceals a heart so black no light can escape," Kowalski replied in the same tone.

The band broke into the traditional 'Hail to the Secretary General' and Lauzier stopped to acknowledge it. When the last notes faded away, she began to shake hands and greet the guests closest to her.

"Cronies of the Lauzier clan," Kowalski said. "They obviously knew where she'd appear. I doubt we'll get the old grip and grin."

Conversations resumed as the band picked up the contemporary airs they'd been playing before Lauzier's appearance.

"Quite the look that Sara has," Chief Justice Achebe commented. "High-class something or other, I think they refer to it."

Dunmoore eyed him with curiosity, wondering whether he'd just made a disparaging comment in disguise. When Achebe winked at her, she knew he had. Not a fan of Lauzier, evidently.

The latter eventually made her way around the hall and stopped in front of Kowalski, Dunmoore, Nagato, and Achebe.

"Chief Justice, Grand Admiral, welcome to the reception. You as well, General. And Admiral Dunmoore, your first Commonwealth Day on Earth, is it? It's been a long time since we last saw each other when you rescued me from those dastardly pirates."

Lauzier, who had intentionally refrained from shaking hands with any of them, locked eyes with Dunmoore, both of them aware that the pirates had been mercenaries hired by Lauzier to aid her in removing individuals she believed would hinder her ascent to the top.

"It has, Madame."

"Well, let me give you another belated thanks for your incredibly effective actions that saved me and my companions. You truly deserve your appointment as Chief of Naval Operations."

Though her melodious alto voice sounded sincere, Lauzier's gaze said quite the opposite, but Dunmoore gave her a faint smile and replied, "Thank you, Madame."

"Enjoy your evening." She turned away and headed for the next cluster of guests, a pair of bodyguards discreetly following her.

"What was that all about, Admiral?" Chief Justice Achebe asked. "I haven't seen Sara this insincere in a long time."

"A little over a decade ago, I rescued Lauzier and her companions from pirates who'd taken them prisoner in the Rim Sector and held them for ransom. But I suspected at the time that Madame Lauzier had arranged the entire operation to get rid of certain well-connected people. Nothing since has changed my opinion on the matter, and she knows it."

"Ah. I see. I seem to remember the events. Wasn't the ship that carried Lauzier named *Athena* or something of the sort?"

"Yes, it was."

"And you're the one who found it. Well done. Though I'm not surprised you believe she orchestrated it. Our dear Sara is capable of anything in the pursuit of power. And now that she holds humanity's supreme office, I much fear for the future." Achebe sighed and shook his head.

"You're not the only one," Kowalski said. "Many of us are afraid her uncompromising Centralism might bring about enough civil unrest in the OutWorlds to trigger another conflict on the scale of the Migration Wars. Yet she refuses to see it, which makes the situation almost untenable."

"And what will you do about it, Grand Admiral?" Achebe asked with a knowing twinkle in his eyes. "Seeing as how your oath is to defend humanity against all enemies, foreign and domestic."

"Surely you're not deeming our esteemed Secretary General a domestic enemy of humanity, Chief Justice," she replied in a faintly playful tone.

"Since she was born on Arcadia, we can hardly call her foreign." Achebe's tone was so dry, Dunmoore could almost visualize the

Sahara Desert. "But be that as it may, I trust your oath will be paramount."

"It is, sir."

"Good. I won't ask any questions, but I assume you have plans within plans already set in motion. You have been on Earth a good long time now."

"And I won't answer any, but I am an inveterate planner, as Avi and Siobhan can attest."

Nagato nodded while Dunmoore smiled at Achebe. "That she is. No need to worry, Chief Justice."

"Then I won't." Something attracted Achebe's eye, and he said, "I think we're about to be graced by Sara's dulcet voice waxing poetic on the meaning of Commonwealth Day."

He nodded toward the small stage at one end of the hall that had been vacant but wasn't any longer. Lauzier had climbed onto it and was waiting for the noise of conversation to subside, which it did rather rapidly. None of the people in attendance wanted to attract her wrath.

"Good evening, my friends, and thank you for coming. Commonwealth Day is always a special occasion for me, and also for you, I'm sure. Today, we celebrate the founding of our Commonwealth, that union of human worlds into a cohesive whole, indivisible, united for all times, and it's my great honor to give the keynote address on this auspicious occasion."

Lauzier spoke at length about vanquishing the ever-present forces that risked fragmenting humanity and how she would renew the bonds between Earth and the Sovereign Star Systems. But Dunmoore recognized the radical Centralist philosophy hidden behind the flowery words and soaring sentences. That

Lauzier herself was the primary force capable of fragmenting humanity was seemingly lost on both the speaker and the audience.

When she finally fell silent, the applause was both prolonged and vigorous from everyone except for the OutWorld senators, the three in military uniform, and the Chief Justice, who gave it no more than polite recognition. Many of those senators standing nearby noticed the lack of enthusiasm shown by the Grand Admiral and her two subordinates and gave them looks of renewed interest as if wondering on whose side they were. That the Grand Admiral planned on taking the Fleet to a side of its own wasn't apparent and wouldn't become so just yet.

With the speech over, service droids carrying trays of finger foods appeared and circulated. Dunmoore intercepted one of them while glancing longingly at the exit, but everyone else had to stay until the SecGen left the reception.

A distinguished-looking older man with thick silver hair, craggy features, and intelligent brown eyes snatched a mini quiche from a passing droid and walked up to them. Dunmoore recognized him as Senator George Bregman of Cascadia, one of the principal OutWorlds. Bregman was also the unofficial leader of the OutWorld faction, and the man Kowalski was counting on to drive the Fleet's agenda in the Senate. He popped the bite-sized pie into his mouth, chewed twice, and swallowed.

"What were your impressions of Madame Lauzier's speech?" He asked as he joined their small group, gazing at each in succession. "I'm George Bregman, by the way, Admiral Dunmoore. We haven't met."

"A pleasure, sir. I know who you are, of course."

She gave him a significant look, and he nodded at her in acknowledgment, then speared Kowalski with his keen gaze as he cocked a thick, dark eyebrow in question.

"So?"

Kowalski shrugged. "She spoke to her base, Senator, and ignored everyone else."

"A polite way of putting it, Grand Admiral. I think she was inflammatory, and I use that word deliberately. If she plans on turning her aspirations into reality, she might see the OutWorlds reconsidering their relationship with the rest of the Commonwealth." His face hardened as his eyes briefly took in a beaming Sara Lauzier surrounded by her sycophants across the hall. "And that can have some rather serious consequences. But she doesn't seem to care."

"It's not that the SecGen doesn't care, Senator," Kowalski said. "It's more that she's convinced she'll win because the OutWorlds won't do anything more than complain for a bit and then live with it. And she may be right."

Bregman harrumphed. "Perhaps. But I'm sure she's as wrong as can be because I'll make it so. Still, it fits with her overweening hubris."

"You know what always accompanies hubris, right, Senator?" Dunmoore asked.

He gave her a tight nod. "Nemesis. Let's hope it comes before she can do too much damage."

— Seventeen —

"Wonderful reception and excellent speech, Madame. It certainly sets the tone for your first term as SecGen." Paul Markus took a seat across from Lauzier's desk the following day after she'd silently pointed at the chair.

"Not everyone agrees with you, Paul. I noted a distinct lack of enthusiasm from certain senators, OutWorlders all, the Chief Justice and his Justices, as well as the three Fleet officers present. Speaking of which, why were only Kowalski, Dunmoore, and Nagato there? In previous years, at least a dozen or more admirals and generals attended."

"I don't know, Madame. But I can find out."

"Please do. I know it's not by chance. Kowalski is up to something, and this reduction in Fleet attendance must be part of whatever she's plotting."

Markus nodded. "She's definitely doing things behind your back, Madame. It would be easier if you gave me the SSB, however."

Lauzier's basilisk stare bored holes through Markus' skull, one of the many things about her that sent a frisson down his spine.

"No. The SSB reports solely to me."

It would be a cold day in hell before she'd surrender absolute control of the agency to anyone. They were her Praetorian Guard since she couldn't rely on the Fleet. If only the SSB's expansion could go a little faster... She needed it to be several times the current size. "And that will not change for as long as I'm SecGen."

He inclined his head.

"Of course, Madame."

Lauzier felt a tinge of irritation at not thinking about using the SSB to find out why only three flag officers attended, but then, some days, she had doubts about Leila Gherson's loyalty. Sure, Lauzier had arranged for Gherson's appointment as director general, mainly because Blayne Hersom needed a replacement who wouldn't be quite as cozy with the Fleet. Gherson had seemed like the best choice to help further her interests.

Yet she appeared wary with the SecGen, secretive, and Lauzier suspected she was beholden more to the SSB's interests than hers. It was something she should have expected, seeing as how Gherson became the SSB's head several years before Lauzier was elected SecGen and had plenty of time to mold the position to her liking.

Perhaps it was time she activated her private assets and sent them on a hunt. But not here on Earth, at least not yet. Let them go after easier prey off-world to prove themselves, someone high up in the Fleet's hierarchy whose death would cause consternation.

She shook off her thoughts, leaving them for another time, and asked Markus about the latest concerning his portfolio.

***

Leila Gherson faced a dilemma. Her operatives reported others watching Grand Admiral Kowalski, unknowns, probably from the private sector. With Fleet Security that made three different organizations discreetly following Kowalski whenever she left the safety of Joint Base Geneva.

She suspected that Paul Markus had hired the newcomers. The slavishly loyal Secretary of Public Safety had carried out many dirty deeds on behalf of Sara Lauzier over the years, the sort that should have seen him in a penal colony on Parth rather than a cabinet member. But Lauzier protected those who compromised their very souls for her, and she had been among the most powerful in the Commonwealth long before she became SecGen.

If Markus had arranged for these third-party people, did he do so at Lauzier's behest, or was he acting on his own? Gherson hadn't mentioned Holt's threats against her and the SSB to the SecGen since the latter hadn't yet put out the order to terminate Kowalski.

It was quite possible she never would, knowing the Fleet's eyes were sure to turn on her, possibly spelling the permanent end of her term as SecGen. The military hadn't overthrown a government in the centuries since humanity spread among the stars. Yet the current flag officers held a vastly different outlook from any of their predecessors and were capable of anything in pursuit of their goals.

For instance, they were much less loyal to governments and more to the ideal of the Commonwealth and its citizens. Gherson doubted the Fleet would obey orders to impose sanctions on wayward star systems or intervene on the government side in disputes about colonial independence. Quite the contrary, in fact. She suspected the military would discretely help colonies achieve sovereign star system status, if only to boost the number of OutWorlds and upset the balance in the Senate.

Ezekiel Holt was emblematic of the newer flag officers — ruthless, direct, and willing to act on his threats. She could remember a time when Fleet personnel weren't in the habit of coercing civilian officials as a matter of unwritten policy. But those days were long gone. And it was in the name of serving a higher purpose, that of preserving humanity from another ruinous civil war.

What should she do about these newcomers? Perhaps it might be best if her operatives removed them from the game and subjected them to interrogation, though they'd probably be conditioned against it. Even the private sector used conditioning nowadays. She couldn't take the risk they might be looking to terminate Kowalski. Or maybe she should inform Holt and let him deal with them.

A faint smile appeared on Gherson's thin lips. Yes, that was the correct answer. It neatly took the problem out of her hands and showed goodwill on the matter of the SSB not targeting flag officers.

***

"A bit unusual, you asking to meet, Leila," Holt said, dropping on the bench beside her. They were sitting near the Skanderbeg statue lookout on the shore of Lake Geneva, in a section of the

Palace of the Stars precinct reserved solely for employees of the Commonwealth government. The sky was blue, dotted here and there with clouds, while the lake's surface, choppy under the brisk breeze, reflected a million suns. "What gives?"

"Thank you for seeing me, Zeke."

Holt's eyebrows shot up.

"Zeke? Are we finally on first-name terms? Fantastic!"

Gherson ignored his flippant comment.

"I've called you on a matter of common interest, that of keeping the Grand Admiral alive."

"Okay. I'm listening."

"You know I have people watching Kowalski, right?"

"Sure. They're pretty good, but not good enough for mine."

"Well, they very recently detected third-party observers covering her."

Holt frowned.

"How recently?"

"Does that mean you aren't aware of them?"

"No."

"I was told yesterday. They were spotted the day before."

"Are your folks sure about this?"

Gherson nodded.

"Yes, they are. The people in question aren't quite as good as yours or mine." She produced a data wafer and held it out to him. "All the details are on there, including appearances, habits, the usual surveillance stuff."

Holt took the memory device and slipped it into his jacket pocket, knowing it was safe to do so. Gherson was conscious of what could happen to her if she played him false. He'd still quarantine it once he got back to the office, of course, and access its contents from a segregated workstation.

"I appreciate your telling me of this, Leila. Do you plan on taking any action?"

"No. I was thinking this is more in your wheelhouse, seeing as how Kowalski's your boss. But I would suggest you take them out. They're likely private sector, perhaps organized crime, and have been hired by someone other than Sara Lauzier. She understands that if Kowalski is terminated, it will be blamed on her, and the Fleet will react badly."

"Got any candidates in mind?"

Gherson hesitated for a fraction of a second, then figured she might as well tell him. After all, she had an interest in Kowalski's continuing welfare.

"My guess would be Paul Markus. Axel Renouf approached me a few weeks ago about him wanting to terminate Kowalski. Markus is fiercely loyal to Lauzier, knows your boss represents a clear and present danger to Lauzier's political program, and has underworld contacts from way back."

"Does he now? How interesting. Any idea who?"

"The Marseille *Milieu*, primarily. They're close at hand, effective, and have contacts throughout the known galaxy. He used them to arrange Lauzier's so-called kidnapping during her father's second term as SecGen. A man called Leon Pannetier, one of the biggest bosses around."

"Ah, thank you for confirming that. We'd always suspected it was the case. Would he arrange a hit on my boss without Sara's knowledge?"

"I think so. He's the most loyal cabinet member she has, perhaps the most loyal follower, period, and would undoubtedly play Hugh de Morville to Lauzier's Henry the Second."

Holt grinned at her.

"Your knowledge of history is improving, Leila."

"Let's just say I'm more concerned with keeping the SSB intact than playing stupid games." She climbed to her feet. "That was it. The ball is in your court now. If you need my assistance to end this threat, just call."

Holt watched her walk away, lost in thought.

"Will wonders never cease," he murmured. "A peace offering from Leila Gherson. She must truly be worried. That's if she's not playing with me."

But Holt was sure she'd been telling the truth. He could sense it even in those as controlled and cold as Gherson. It was a gift, one that had made him a superb counterintelligence officer. He stood and walked off in the other direction, where his car waited to take him back to the base.

Once in a sterile room, using a quarantined workstation, he glanced at the data wafer's contents and saw the dossier was complete and professionally done. It was almost a shame they would have to dismantle the SSB and forbid its members from ever working in law enforcement again at the federal level. Some of them appeared to have their act together. But there was no choice. The SSB was permanently tainted by politics and by being solely under the SecGen's control. It had to go.

Holt summoned Major General Yuan — who was in charge of the Security Branch's Special Operations Division — to the sterile room, where he briefed him on his meeting with Leila Gherson before showing him the dossier.

"They look like pros to me, sir. Private sector, you said?"

"Could be Marseille *Milieu*, Peter. If our esteemed Secretary of Public Safety is behind this, he might have called on them as he did before."

"Yeah, that would fit. Paul Markus is a slippery character." Yuan scratched his square chin. "I figure they could be a recon team, scoping the Big Boss and looking for ways to carry out a hit. Assassins usually operate alone or in pairs, not in sixes, and they don't like spending too much time observing a target beforehand. It makes them more vulnerable to being caught. You want me to bag them?"

"Yes. The sooner, the better. Take them to a safe house, make sure they don't know our people are Fleet Security — let them think we're a rival gang — and find out what they know. All interrogation methods are available."

"And afterward?"

"Let them go so they can report failure. There's no point in termination with extreme prejudice. They're simply doing a job. But I'll see that whoever sent them gets the message the Grand Admiral is off limits."

"Okay. Give my people twenty-four hours."

— Eighteen —

Holt, wearing a civilian suit, walked straight to Leon Pannetier's usual outdoor table and dropped into a chair facing him without waiting for an invitation. The two goons with Pannetier immediately climbed to their feet, scowling, and made to eject him. Holt simply gestured to the four Fleet Security operatives behind him, petty officers who were also wearing civilian clothes, and shook his head.

"Why don't you go for a walk while I speak with your boss?" He said in a neutral tone that nonetheless conveyed a distinct warning.

The goons looked from Holt to the operatives, then to Pannetier. The latter waved his hand.

"Go sit at the next table. I'm sure I'll be fine with this gentleman." Once they'd complied, Pannetier turned his attention on Holt. "To whom do I owe the pleasure, *monsieur?*"

"I'm Vice Admiral Ezekiel Holt, head of the Fleet's Security Branch, and I'm here to speak with you about Paul Markus."

"Oh?" Pannetier's eyebrows crept up. "I'm not sure I know anyone by that name, Admiral."

Yet Holt could see in the man's eyes that he not only knew the Secretary of Public Safety but understood why Fleet Security had suddenly taken an interest in him, and he was glad to have his suspicions confirmed.

"Please don't insult my intelligence, *monsieur*. I know Paul Markus has hired you to assassinate a certain senior officer." This time, Pannetier's eyes tightened, confirming everything. "It would be a splendid idea if you withdrew from the project and told Markus he should look elsewhere."

"And why is that? By the way, would you like a glass of pastis?"

"Never could stand the stuff."

Pannetier inclined his head.

"It is an acquired taste. Perhaps something else?"

"I'm not in the habit of drinking with mobsters."

"You wound me."

"Oh, come off it, Pannetier. You're the most influential *Milieu* boss in Marseille and probably one of the bigger mobsters in this star system. But back to your question of why. It's really quite simple. I run the biggest law enforcement agency in the Commonwealth, and since I'm responsible for national security matters, the usual constraints cops work under don't apply. If anything happens to said senior officer, I will wipe out your entire organization, starting with you. They won't find any bodies to bury."

Holt's casual tone, underlain by a hint of menace, got through to Pannetier, whose forehead was marred by the beginnings of a frown.

"Again, Admiral, I do not know what you're talking about, but making threats will not go over well in this city."

"Let me lay it out for you. We captured the six men you sent to reconnoiter the senior officer in preparation for an assassination. Two died under interrogation. The other four broke and fingered one of your lower-level associates. We all know that killing a Grand Admiral is more than he can handle, meaning you're involved. We'll release the survivors in a few hours, and they can confirm everything to your satisfaction. It's over."

Holt paused as he studied Pannetier for a few moments before continuing in the same conversational tone.

"Anything happens to Kathryn Kowalski, and I will wage war on your organization, a war which I shall win and in which I shall take no prisoners. Just so we're clear, that's not a threat. It's my primary course of action. Do you understand me now? Tell Markus to get lost. Better yet, tell him to give up on assassinating the Grand Admiral."

"Tell him yourself, Admiral. After all, you both live in the same town and are engaged in similar lines of business."

"I'll ask you again. Do you understand? Your involvement in this matter is over."

Pannetier didn't reply immediately, but Holt could see anger in the man's eyes. He'd made a dangerous adversary, but so be it.

"Very well. I will withdraw my services," the man finally said. "Though I suggest you never set foot in Marseille again."

"I have no need nor any intention of doing so." Holt stood. "Enjoy the rest of your day, *monsieur* Pannetier."

He walked away, conscious of Pannetier's eyes boring through his back. Holt would take the warning seriously, although he suspected it came from simple pique in the moment. Pannetier was a businessman first and foremost, even though he traded in criminality, and he was fully aware that putting a hit on the head of Fleet Security was bad for business. As bad as assassinating a Grand Admiral.

***

"Paul Markus. It's about time we had a brief chat." Still wearing the same suit, Holt dropped into a vacant chair at the Secretary of Public Safety's table in the *Torteller Weinstube*, one of Geneva's fine eating establishments. He turned to Markus' female companion, a tall, willowy blond at least twenty years his junior. "And you must be Anita Jules. Could you excuse Paul and me for a few minutes, Anita? The bar will surely serve you another dry martini however you take it, shaken or stirred."

Markus, eyes fixed on Holt, said, "Stay, Anita. Admiral Holt is leaving. Now."

"So, you know who I am. Good. That'll make it easier. Bye-bye, Anita."

Something in Holt's eyes and tone of voice caused Jules to stand and nod apologetically at Markus before heading for the bar on heels higher than Holt had seen in a long time.

"What do you want, Holt?"

"I had a very illuminating conversation with Leon Pannetier on the terrace of *Les Calanques* in Marseille earlier today." Was that fear in Markus' eyes? "He suggested I have a chat with you."

"Well, speak. I'll give you two minutes, just enough time for Anita to get herself another martini."

"Your quest to have Kathryn Kowalski terminated is over, Paul. Leon has pulled out, and you won't find any other OCG in this star system willing to do your bidding. I'll make sure of that."

"What makes you think I want Kowalski terminated, as you put it?" Markus raised his chin in a defiant pose.

"Your buddy Leon confirmed that was the case. After I told him we'd taken in his recon team and interrogated them. Two sadly died, but we released the rest to tell the tale. Not all of those four will ever work in a meaningful way again. Extreme interrogation has a way of turning people into quasi-imbeciles. And you'd be a full imbecile if you kept going after my boss. Capiche?"

"I have no clue what you're talking about."

Holt raised his left hand to his throat, palm facing downward, stuck his thumb out, and ran it from right to left in the unmistakable gesture of someone cutting a throat.

"You're on my sensor grid. Try to be a good boy lest you become the late Paul Markus, something that'll happen if you try anything stupid."

He stood, turned on his heels, and left the restaurant, wondering whether he was getting overly predictable, cornering people at their tables to deliver warnings. But Geneva had so many excellent eateries frequented by those he targeted it seemed inevitable.

When Anita returned to their table with a full martini glass, she found a thoughtful Markus staring at the door.

"What was that about?" She sat and turned an uneasy gaze on him.

"Nothing which needs to concern you, love."

But instead of focusing his attention back on his companion, Markus thought of ways he could avenge himself on Holt and find another means of removing Kowalski. She was simply too inconvenient for Sara, and Holt had become too inconvenient for him.

***

"Making two serious enemies in a single day. Congratulations, Zeke."

Dunmoore put down her glass of gin and tonic and gave him an ironic round of applause once he finished telling her and Kathryn Kowalski about the plot to assassinate the latter. All three were in Kowalski's living room, enjoying drinks while the autochef prepared their evening meal.

"You're getting good at this. Do you think either Pannetier or Markus will take your advice to heart?"

"Pannetier, yes. He's a businessman and knows a losing proposition when he sees one. Markus, a definite no. He's devoted to Lauzier and will look for other private-sector killers. With the OCGs closed to him, it'll be less capable mercenary outfits. But now that we know he's in the game, we'll have no problems catching whoever he hires before they become dangerous."

"You hope." A twinkle in Kowalski's eyes belied her words.

"Hope is not a valid course of action, Kathryn. You know that. If Markus hires someone else, we'll catch them with or without the SSB's help. I have him under surveillance now."

"Ah, yes. The SSB." The twinkle vanished. "I'm leery about Leila Gherson being so helpful all of a sudden."

"I chalk it up to self-preservation. She's more concerned about her agency's future than she is about Lauzier's welfare. SecGens come and go. The SSB is forever. Or so Leila thinks."

"And here I figured Sara had arranged for her appointment," Dunmoore said.

"She did, but Leila is the quintessential bureaucrat whose loyalty is to the institution she leads, not the government of the day. Her sort is why successive SecGens and their administrations have such a hard time effecting transformation at a fundamental level and changing the Commonwealth's direction." Holt took a quick sip of his drink. "Except now, in Sara's case, the SecGen and the bureaucracy's aims are converging. Both want greater centralization of power on Earth. I have no doubt Leila feels conflicted by that. She wants what her fellow bureaucrats want, yet she's also anxious to protect the SSB despite the first SecGen who openly espouses the same goals as the civil service."

Dunmoore chuckled. "It almost sounds as if you feel sorry for her."

"No, not at all." Holt shook his head. "But I understand her motivations, and she gave us Markus because he threatened to upset the truce between us and the SSB that keeps the agency alive and functioning."

"Which we will break when the time is right and eliminate the SSB."

Holt inclined his head.

"Just so. The fact this doesn't disturb me at all makes me wonder whether I'm not a tad sociopathic."

"No, just practical," Kowalski said. "The SSB has to go. We've known that for a long time. Whether its members merge with the Infinite Void depends on their choices. If they choose to fade away into the private sector or other branches of government, then so be it. If, on the other hand, they resist…"

"And many will," Holt said in a somber tone. "Perhaps even Leila. They've considered themselves untouchable for so long that they won't be able to deal with it rationally."

"On a different note, my sources in the SecDef's office have told me he intends to set up a new Procurement Branch." Kowalski smirked. "Something that would take over from the current one and fall fully under his control, not mine."

Dunmoore blew a raspberry.

"Good luck to him. The branch is huge and filled with long-serving people who have millennia of experience between them. And they're on Caledonia by now."

"He's bringing over almost half of the procurement staff from the Public Services Department and will force providers to deal with his branch on new contracts."

"I can see Sara Lauzier's hand behind that. The Secretary for Public Services would never give up his people voluntarily."

After emptying his glass, Holt placed it on the table and said, "There's a hierarchy in the cabinet, and the Secretary of Defense is near the top, right behind the Secretary of Public Safety. On the other hand, the Secretary for Public Services is closer to the bottom of the rankings since his department is merely administrative, not policy-setting. He'd have little to say if Sara takes away half of his procurement staff and gives it to the SecDef."

"She does want military procurement out of our hands and into those who can direct contracts to favored bidders. How are you going to deal with it, Kathryn?"

Kowalski shrugged.

"I'll let him expend the effort and quietly tell potential bidders anything that doesn't go through Fleet Procurement will be rejected. And I'll ensure the Senate doesn't cut our budget to pay for the duplicate."

"Do you think that'll work?"

"We can refuse to take anything into service and not pay for it if it doesn't meet our specs, and the only specs that count are the ones set via our procurement officers. The SecDef still doesn't understand who holds the high cards and that the sacrosanct subordination of the military to the political is over. And with Senator Bregman along with most if not all the other OutWorld senators on our side, the Senate will probably ensure our budget remains as is."

— Nineteen —

Dunmoore sat back in her chair with a sigh, eyes still fixed on the virtual display hovering above her desk. She'd just read two messages from Caledonia, the first announcing that the Fleet Operations Center was up and running and ready to assume control of the Armed Forces from the one on Earth. The second contained less pleasant news.

It advised that her deputy, Vice Admiral Ulli Radames, who'd landed on Caledonia a few weeks earlier to oversee the final preparations for the ops center, had suffered a climbing accident while on weekend leave and was clinging to life in a stasis chamber. Radames' love of mountaineering was well known among his fellow flag officers, and she wasn't surprised he'd tackled a difficult ascent so soon after arriving. At least, she assumed it had been a difficult one. A man with his experience shouldn't have almost killed himself on an easier climb.

Just then, her office communicator chimed — Zeke Holt. She activated it, and his face materialized, floating beside the display.

"What's up?"

"You got the message from Caledonia about Ulli, I presume?"

"Just read it. I expect you received a more detailed explanation, seeing as how Ulli is the second most important officer on the naval staff. What the hell happened?"

Holt grimaced.

"My people on site are treating it as suspicious. Ulli was doing a solo ascent of a short vertical face in the mountains approximately one hundred kilometers west of Sanctum. Nothing he couldn't handle. It was presumably supposed to be a simple welcome to Caledonia climb, his first since arriving. Ulli had left word with his aide about his itinerary, but the aide tried to contact him when he hadn't returned by nightfall, hours after he was supposed to be back. When the aide didn't get any answer, he called the head of security for Joint Base Sanctum, who sent an aircar to the site, where they found him unconscious at the foot of the rock face, tangled in his ropes. They immediately called for an air ambulance equipped with a stasis chamber while making him comfortable. Then, they combed the area and examined his gear but found nothing that could indicate how he fell, and I mean nothing at all, which immediately raised their suspicions to condition red."

"Your people don't believe it was an accident, then." Dunmoore's lips tightened into a thin line.

"Their instincts are telling them there's more to it than a simple mishap, but if it was an assassination attempt by a pro, he or she won't have left any traces. Be that as it may, Ulli is out of commission for a few months, at the very least. You'll have to name a replacement."

Dunmoore didn't need to think for very long.

"Gregor. It's a big step for someone who's been a vice admiral for less than a year, yet I know I can trust him. I'll run it by Kathryn, but I need a deputy on Caledonia as soon as possible. The operations center there is ready to take over."

"I'm sure she won't object. Your other assistant chiefs of naval operations might, seeing as how they've been in their jobs longer, but they won't say anything, considering your reputation."

Dunmoore frowned at him, one eye narrowed.

"My reputation? And what would that be?"

Holt gave her a broad grin.

"You're known to value competence and expediency over length of tenure."

"Bull crap."

"Okay, you intimidate people, and they won't gainsay you once you've made a decision."

"Better." Her frown vanished. "I hope there's an aviso ready to go."

Avisos, the Fleet's courier ships, were the fastest vessels anywhere and could climb into the highest hyperspace bands, well beyond what any others managed. But they were almost literally tiny boxes mounted on oversized hyperdrives, which made for cramped quarters. Those sensitive to such things experienced aviso dreams, bizarre and often frightening when traveling at maximum speed, although that shouldn't be Gregor Pushkin's problem. He was as stoic a man as she'd ever encountered.

"There should be at least one docked to the starbase awaiting your pleasure."

"My pleasure? Whatever for?"

"Didn't you know? Having an aviso ready for anything you, the CNO, might need to have transported fast is SOP."

"I guess that must have slipped by the wayside during my handover briefings." She tapped her fingertips on the edge of her desk. "If there was nothing else, Zeke, I'd better get on with sending Gregor to Caledonia. Please keep me apprised of the investigation into Ulli's perhaps not an accident."

"Will do. Holt, out."

His face vanished, and Dunmoore called Kowalski's office, knowing she'd be put through immediately unless the Grand Admiral was away.

"What's up, Siobhan?"

Dunmoore explained the situation, and Kowalski nodded.

"By all means, appoint Gregor as Acting Deputy Chief of Naval Operations and send him to Caledonia via aviso. We're on a timetable and can't afford much slippage. By the next sitting of the Senate, we must be ready."

"Okay. Gregor, it is."

Dunmoore's next call was to summon Pushkin and her senior aide. The latter ushered the former into her office a few minutes later, and she repeated almost verbatim what she'd told Kowalski.

"So, I need you aboard that aviso today, Gregor."

"A good thing I didn't unpack much. I can be ready with two suitcases in a few hours and leave the rest of my stuff in containers to follow on the regular run between Earth and Caledonia."

Dunmoore turned to her aide.

"Please draft a communique for the staff advising them that because of Admiral Radames' accident and the prognosis he'll be out of action for the foreseeable future, I've appointed Gregor as acting Deputy CNO with duty station on Caledonia, to take effect immediately."

Captain Malfort nodded. "Yes, sir."

"Get whatever aviso is docked ready to leave as soon as Gregor's aboard and see that a shuttle is available to take him to the starbase."

"Will do, sir. By the way, the aviso is named *Agemo*, the most recent of the series currently in use." He glanced at Pushkin. "Although it's no larger nor any more comfortable for that. Sorry, sir."

Pushkin waved his apology away.

"It'll only be for a few days, which I'll spend reading up on my new job."

"You may go work your magic, Josh. I have a few more things to discuss with Admiral Pushkin."

The aide stood.

"Of course, sir."

When they were alone, Dunmoore leaned forward and placed her elbows on the desktop, hands joined.

"You and I both know it's a little early for you to become deputy CNO, Gregor and so will the other assistant CNOs. But if Ulli fell victim to an assassination attempt, I need you out there, not any of your colleagues, because you're mentally better equipped to deal with such things."

"Understood, sir. And don't worry about the inevitable grumbling." A crooked grin appeared. "It'll subside quickly enough when you apportion my work among the remaining assistants. Besides, none of them will want to head for Caledonia without their families in tow. I'm the only one with no attachments and can go at the drop of a hat."

"I won't wish you good luck, Gregor, because I know you're dogged enough to get any job done and done well. Since I don't think Ulli will return to duty within the year, your acting becomes permanent in twelve months, and if everything goes as planned, I should join you on Caledonia in eighteen at the outside."

"Do you really think so?"

Dunmoore nodded.

"We have no choice. The alternative is letting Lauzier and her ilk drive the Commonwealth into another ruinous civil conflict, one that might well be worse than the Second Migration War."

"Maybe. Though I still have difficulty seeing Lauzier do that much damage."

"Believe me, Gregor. She started years ago. You and I simply didn't notice because we were busy protecting the Rim Sector. During my time as Commander, 3rd Fleet, I heard plenty of grumblings from the Dordogne government concerning Earth's growing highhandedness when dealing with sovereign star systems. Our project may stem back to the years immediately following the war, but the Centralists have been at it almost as long. Charles Lauzier didn't openly embrace Centralism but was more than just sympathetic to the cause. His daughter is merely saying out loud what her father and Judy Chu said behind closed doors."

"Well, I won't wish you luck either, Skipper. You make your own wherever you go. And I have to go pack. The ever-efficient Josh must have everything lined up by now, ready to whisk me away." Pushkin stood, drew himself to attention, and asked, "With your permission?"

"Go and finish setting up the parallel naval staff on Caledonia so we can begin evacuating our remaining people from here."

"Aye, aye, sir."

Pushkin turned on his heels and marched out of Dunmoore's office to a future that might be more uncertain than they expected. If Ulli Radames had been targeted by the SSB, then Pushkin would be as well. Except he didn't spend his free time climbing sheer cliffs. Dunmoore knew her old first officer and long-time friend would certainly be cautious.

She returned to her queue and opened the next file screaming for attention. It seemed that only the most urgent matters were ever referred to her, the sort that demanded an immediate decision.

Vice Admiral Gregor Pushkin was aboard *Agemo* in record time, and the aviso had gone FTL for the first outbound leg to Sol's heliopause before the working day in Geneva was over.

— Twenty —

"Ah, Paul. Please sit." Leon Pannetier gestured at the chair across from him. He was indoors for once, the rain falling over Marseille having made his usual outdoor table a bit too wet. *Les Calanques* was half empty at this time of day, but the many floating glowglobes that banished the gray skies and disturbed waters of the harbor beyond the floor-to-ceiling windows brightened its atmosphere. "What can I do for you?"

Markus speared the mob boss with cold eyes.

"Holt told me he busted your recon team and warned you to walk away from the job."

"Vice Admiral Holt is a very persuasive character, *mon ami*. And he has enough people around him to cause me serious trouble. I did indeed agree to pull out. Sorry, but that is how it must be. I am a businessman first, and the job has become a losing proposition."

"Then how about changing the target to Admiral Siobhan Dunmoore, the Chief of Naval Operations?"

Pannetier gave Markus a sad smile.

"The Grand Admiral's best friend? *Hélas, non.* I believe Holt would be equally opposed to her death. You will have to look elsewhere, but since he now knows you are intent on having the Grand Admiral assassinated, I daresay if anything happens to her, you're a dead man. Perhaps you should forget about it."

Markus smirked.

"I'll simply have Holt taken care of at the same time."

"That, as they say, is your funeral. I shall not be involved."

"Can you at least point me toward someone who'd be interested in looking at the job?"

Pannetier eyed Markus speculatively as if weighing the risk of helping him further.

"No one in this star system will touch it," he finally said. "Word gets around relatively fast in certain circles. But you might try a shadowy, nameless organization specializing in one-way missions. Rumor has it that they are currently based on Nabhka."

Markus cocked a questioning eyebrow at Pannetier.

"Shadowy, nameless, and does one-way missions. Sounds more than a little like something from a holodrama."

"Yet it exists. Its members belong to a religious sect that believes dying in the service of their deity is the noblest thing they can do with their lives. Apparently, the sect's creation predates human spaceflight by a thousand years, and they have been with us under various guises for all that time. And ever since the first of them appeared, they have chosen to die by carrying out assassinations and other sorts of operations for hire, with the funds supporting the sect. Not that you would ever hear of it. They are extremely adept at staying off anyone's sensor grid. I am not even sure the Fleet knows about them."

"Yet you do. How come?"

A faintly mysterious smile appeared. "I have used them once before to carry out a killing in another star system. They came recommended to me by an ally, and that is all I shall tell you."

"Can you at least tell me how to contact them?"

"Certainly, but without guarantees they will answer your query. You must send a subspace message to a certain Nabhka address, which I will give you in a moment, saying what you need done."

"Put a message in clear on the subspace net requesting a quote for the assassination of three admirals? A bit unsafe, isn't it? The Fleet has algorithms parsing every damn transmission off Earth for stuff like that."

"Ah, but you do not use your name, their names, ranks, or affiliation, nor the word assassination. You simply call it a job and give them an anonymous address at which you can be reached. If they agree to look at your proposal, someone on Earth will contact you and can discuss the details in complete privacy. Then they will either take it, or you will not hear from the contact again. Are you still interested?"

"Yes."

"Then take note of the following subspace address." Pannetier pulled out his communicator and rattled off an alphanumeric sequence that Markus recorded. "This concludes our business, I believe."

Markus understood the mob boss had dismissed him and stood.

"Thank you, Leon."

"We shall never speak of this again. After all, the people you will attempt to contact do not exist."

"Speak of what?" Markus gave him a tight smile, then turned on his heels and left the restaurant.

Pannetier watched him until he disappeared, wondering what he'd unleashed. Clearly, Markus was showing signs of an obsession with killing Grand Admiral Kowalski, and that couldn't be healthy for one of the most powerful cabinet members in the Commonwealth government.

***

"Ulli Radames, Leila. Does that name ring a bell?" Holt asked the moment Gherson's face appeared on his office display.

"Hello to you too. He's the deputy CNO who suffered a climbing accident on Caledonia, right?"

"That's the one. It wasn't an accident. My people are convinced he barely escaped an assassination attempt. As it is, he's still in a stasis chamber while the doctors decide what to do."

"It wasn't us, Zeke. We're keeping the truce. Yes, I have operatives on Caledonia, which should not surprise you, but their brief is solely intelligence gathering. No kinetic action has been authorized."

Holt studied Gherson's face for a few seconds and decided she was telling the truth.

"Could you have agents going rogue?"

"That's always a possibility, as you well know, but I seriously doubt it in this case. I've sent nothing but my best to Caledonia. People who wouldn't go beyond their mission parameters except to save their own or someone else's lives. Maybe your admiral stepped on the wrong toes and was targeted as a consequence."

"Perhaps, but doubtful. My folks vetted Radames, and he has nothing in his background that would warrant termination. Besides, he's only been on Caledonia a few weeks and hardly left the base. I can't see how he'd offend someone that badly in such a short time. If you're not involved, then there could be another party gunning for senior admirals."

"It would be a logical inference. But who?"

"Ah, now that's the billion-cred question. Who? I can think of at least one person interested in winnowing down the Fleet's flag officers, especially those close to the Grand Admiral and her immediate entourage."

Gherson's eyes lit up with understanding, and she nodded.

"If I'm thinking of the same person as you, she would indeed be a candidate. But it means she has other assets working for her, assets neither of us know about. And that worries me because once she uses them, the temptation to keep using them grows rapidly."

Holt knew precisely what Gherson meant. A sociopath such as Lauzier could well unleash a private and very secret army on anyone, she and him included, if it took her fancy.

"How about we find out, Leila? I suggest we share anything our people uncover."

"Agreed."

That she agreed so rapidly told Holt this fresh development worried her deeply, which meant her relationship with Lauzier wasn't that great. He'd always understood Gherson was appointed at Lauzier's behest, but perhaps they were at odds over certain issues of importance. Gherson certainly didn't seem to trust Lauzier, and the latter, it was said, trusted no one as a matter of principle.

Holt shook his head. How could one make it through life without at least relying on a few kindred spirits?

***

"And lastly, Madame," Gherson, who'd been consulting the tablet in her hand, glanced up at Lauzier, "the deputy CNO, Vice Admiral Ulli Radames, suffered an apparent accident on Caledonia, except Fleet Security are convinced it was an assassination attempt that didn't quite work. He's still alive, barely."

Gherson searched Lauzier's face for a reaction and thought she noted a hint of disappointment quickly cross her eyes. It might have been an illusion, something she saw because she was looking for it.

"A shame."

Did she mean a shame that he's still alive or that someone made an attempt on his life?

"Indeed, Madame. One of Admiral Dunmoore's closest associates, Vice Admiral Gregor Pushkin, is on his way to Caledonia aboard an aviso. He left mere hours after the news reached Earth. He's to be acting Deputy CNO."

"Why is the deputy CNO on Caledonia in the first place?"

"You are aware the Fleet is establishing an alternate headquarters on Caledonia and has moved several commands there, leaving merely liaison staff at HQ, correct?"

"Yes. That started several years ago. Unfortunately, it's too late to stop this nonsense."

"Apparently, they also built a backup Armed Forces operations center in Joint Base Sanctum, and the deputy CNO shifted there to oversee it.

"This Dunmoore ally, Pushkin, how close are they?"

"Very. He was her first officer during the war and afterward when she had a Readiness Evaluation team. Since then, he's followed her up the ranks. I'd say they have each other's backs, no matter what."

"So, sending him to Caledonia weakens Dunmoore."

Gherson inclined her head. "Probably, although it's impossible to measure the extent."

"Good. Every bit that weakens the Kowalski-Dunmoore cabal helps."

It was a rare bit of good news where the latter were concerned. Lauzier felt her control over the Armed Forces slipping away, and there was nothing she could do about it.

"Let me ask you this, Leila. How would you remove both of them and make it seem accidental?"

It was the question Gherson had dreaded.

"I wouldn't."

Lauzier cocked her head to one side, frowning.

"What do you mean?"

"It's much too risky."

That answer confirmed what Lauzier suspected — Gherson wouldn't touch the Fleet's senior officers. The question was why?

"For what reason?"

"Because it wouldn't take Fleet Security long to uncover the SSB as the culprit. They already suspect us of having painted targets on Dunmoore and Kowalski. Should anything happen to two healthy individuals like them, and we'll face a covert war, the SSB will lose. And you will also lose, Madame, because the fingers will be pointed right at you as the originator of the order to terminate them."

"I see." Lauzier eyed Gherson speculatively. "What if I removed you and asked your successor the same question?"

"You'd get the same answer, Madame. The SSB cannot afford a war with the Fleet. It wouldn't survive. Not that terminating Dunmoore and Kowalski would change much. Both have deputies who'd carry on in the same way."

"And what if I ordered you to remove them?"

"I would refuse."

Lauzier allowed herself a look of surprise.

"You'd refuse an order from your direct superior and head of the Commonwealth government?"

"Yes, Madame." Gherson met Lauzier's eyes and hoped her gaze was steely enough to convince the latter that she spoke the truth.

"Well then, I'd better not give it. Let's pass on to other matters."

"That was everything I had."

Lauzier watched Gherson leave the SecGen's office and wondered whether it was time to replace her in the same way she'd arranged to replace Gherson's predecessor. At least she had her private assets now, meaning she could act without the SSB's support or knowledge.

— Twenty-One —

Paul Markus felt nervous, and it wasn't a sensation he enjoyed. After all, he was one of the most influential people on Earth, a senior cabinet member. But waiting for the unnamed contact from the unknown mercenary sect in a city he'd never visited ate at his self-confidence. That the meeting was to happen in a rundown part of old Montreal didn't help. The city had been founded over eight hundred years earlier, and the street he was walking down looked as if it had changed little since.

It was early afternoon, and the area teemed with humans of all descriptions, most of them looking seedy. Markus wore casual clothes and didn't stand out too much, but he still attracted glances from those lounging on benches or front stoops because he didn't look like he belonged. The humidity and oppressive heat under a brooding, cloudy sky made for a thick atmosphere, and that didn't help Markus' nerves.

He'd sent a message to the subspace address Pannetier gave him using a disposable node that would never be traced back. A reply followed a few weeks later — an address in Montreal, along with date and time, and a recognition sentence, nothing else. Since it was a transatlantic crossing from Geneva, Markus took the day off and rode the morning suborbital flight, intending to return via the evening one. He wasn't a well-known figure and traveled in almost complete anonymity, using his personal credentials rather than his official ones.

Markus had taken an automatic taxi from the Dorval spaceport on the western part of Montreal Island to the old city and gotten off a few blocks away from his target, choosing to lose himself among the locals for the last kilometer.

The house at the given address seemed inhabited, if dilapidated, and he quickly went up the short steps to the front door, which opened at his touch. Four apartments occupied the ground floor, while none too clean stairs led up to four more. He looked for unit number three and knocked on the door. After a few moments, it was pulled ajar, and half a face glanced out through the opening.

"*Oui*?"

"I am looking for Henri Toussaint."

The face disappeared, and the door opened wide, admitting Markus into a dingy living room that looked half abandoned. A lean, swarthy man of indeterminate ethnicity and age gestured at a sofa. He had thick, black, curly hair and watchful brown eyes framing a large, hooked nose.

"Please sit," he said with a faint accent Markus couldn't place. "And tell me about your needs."

Markus glanced at the none too clean sofa and lowered himself gingerly on its edge.

"I want three people removed, senior Navy officers."

"We can do that. Who are they?"

"Grand Admiral Kathryn Kowalski, Admiral Siobhan Dunmoore, and Vice Admiral Ezekiel Holt."

The man stared at Markus for a few heartbeats, though nothing showed on his face or in his eyes.

"A tough assignment." When Markus opened his mouth, the man held up a restraining hand. "But we can do it, as long as you accept that their deaths may not be seen as accidental. Three million creds for each."

Markus winced inwardly. That would deplete the slush fund.

"Very well. What are the conditions of payment?"

"The full sum placed into an escrow account within seventy-two hours. Payment to us upon completion of the job."

"Just out of curiosity, what would happen if I decided not to release the funds from escrow after you terminated them?"

The man smiled, revealing white, even teeth.

"That would be most inadvisable. Besides, by the terms of escrow, while you are the only one who can authorize disbursement, we are the only ones who can authorize release of the funds back to you."

"I see." Markus nodded slowly. "I assume the account is an anonymous, numbered one, the sort used by organized crime and other entities who'd rather not divulge their identity?"

"It is. Are you agreeable to the terms?"

"I am. Give me the account coordinates, and I will transfer nine million creds into it by the end of the day tomorrow." Markus pulled out his private communicator, and the man rattled off an alphanumeric sequence.

"You may check the escrow account for its terms before depositing the funds to satisfy yourself that everything is correct."

Markus had intended to do so in any case. Always verify. "Unless you have questions, this concludes our transaction. We will not meet again."

"I have just one. What happens if your people die before they terminate the targets?"

"Then we will send replacements." He stood. "Good day."

Markus found himself on the street moments later, sure the man had gone out the back way and vanished. The conditions of the escrow account would seal the deal. Or not. Markus kept a healthy dose of suspicion when doing business with the underworld, and this death-dealing sect was about as dark as it got.

By the following afternoon, he was convinced they were for real because the escrow account checked out, and he quietly transferred nine million from the departmental slush fund into it. If these mercenaries were as good as Pannetier said, then three of the most significant burdens would merge with the Infinite Void soon enough.

***

"You have a message from Admiral Pushkin in your queue, sir." Commander Botha stuck her head through Dunmoore's open office door. "I figured I should tell you in case it was urgent."

"Thanks, Liv."

Dunmoore opened her queue and found it at the top. She tapped on her virtual display, and Pushkin's smiling face appeared.

"Hello, Skipper. I'm messaging you directly to let you know the Caledonia operations center has passed all the tests and can take over from the primary on Earth the moment you say so. Until then, we'll continue to run in parallel and let the primary make the decisions."

A smile danced on Dunmoore's lips. Another step in freeing the Fleet from the political cesspool of Earth. Activating the Caledonia ops center now meant anything requiring her or Kathryn Kowalski's decision would be delayed by over a day, but that's why Gregor was there. To make those decisions in their stead. Besides, considering the subspace radio time lag between Caledonia and the frontiers, anything immediate had to be done by the commanders on the spot anyway.

But that, of course, was the biggest obstacle she faced as Chief of Naval Operations. Her fleet commanders, except for 1st Fleet, homeported on Earth, were quasi-independent where day-to-day operations were concerned. She set policy, strategy, and precious little else because of the lag time in communications.

As the Commander, 3rd Fleet, she'd profited from her independence as much as she could, running the Rim Sector like a medieval fief in many respects, even though she suffered from communications lag in a lesser form. Yet now that Dunmoore had the Navy's top job, the inability to influence things in real time chafed just a little. She shook her head at the unexpected realization, smiling to herself.

Dunmoore checked Kowalski's schedule and saw she was in her office. Might as well walk down the hall and visit her in person rather than call to confirm the Caledonia ops center could take over.

"Hello, sir," Dunmoore entered Kowalski's office after being passed through by her senior aide without a word spoken.

"Hey, Siobhan. What's up?"

"Gregor just sent me a missive reporting the Caledonia ops center is ready to take over for the Fleet, and I wanted your blessing before I start the transfer of responsibilities and the closure of the one here, knowing there will be at least an additional day in the process if ever our input is required."

"You have it. The Senate resumed sitting yesterday, and it's time we triggered the next phase in the process. Our deputies can handle things from Caledonia while we proceed here."

"In that case, consider the Earth ops center shut down and deactivated. We'll transfer the remaining staff to Caledonia in due course."

With General Avi Nagato having moved to the new Fleet HQ on Caledonia, joining most of the other four stars and civilian equivalents, Dunmoore and Kowalski were among the few senior flag officers left at the short end of a protracted withdrawal. One that had been in process for almost twenty years.

***

Leila Gherson looked up from the daily report, eyes staring at nothing in particular. Fleet HQ had just shut the operations center and transferred the personnel to Caledonia. Whatever Kowalski and company were up to, it was undoubtedly accelerating. Could they be relocating the main HQ entirely? Getting it light years away from Earth and direct political control?

Caledonia was a Fleet fief — and how that had happened with no one noticing until it was too late puzzled her. Still, it meant they controlled who landed there, even if only for a few days. Politicians and the bureaucrats doing their bidding weren't invited to show up unwanted, let alone unannounced.

She was surprised her agents were still at large on Caledonia, but they might simply be under observation by Fleet Security — better the devil you know.

Should she share this information with the SecGen? Lauzier had been increasingly distant in recent times, and Gherson figured her refusal to take care of Kowalski had ruptured their relationship, probably beyond repair. If that was the case, her tenure as the SSB's director general was surely coming to a close. Lauzier didn't tolerate people who disappointed her. Ultimately, she decided to include the item about the ops center in her weekly summary for the SecGen and passed on to the next item.

The sun was already below the top of the Jura Mountains to the west when Gherson left her office and headed home, walking the fifteen minutes it took to reach her apartment building. She always traveled on foot when the weather cooperated. It allowed for a brief but welcome decompression period between her busy professional day and her mostly solitary personal life.

Just as she was about to cross the last street before her building, she felt something sting the back of her neck and instinctively reached up to brush it away. Her fingers encountered a tiny needle, and she suddenly felt sick to her stomach, knowing she had moments left to live. Then, everything went black as she collapsed on the sidewalk.

Leila Gherson died seconds later, her heart stopped by a powerful poison that would dissipate long before any autopsy could detect it. The needle that had delivered it was already dissolving, leaving nothing more than a tiny puncture mark as the sole evidence her death had not been natural.

— Twenty-Two —

"Leila Gherson keeled over after an apparent cardiac arrest on her way home yesterday," Holt announced as he joined Dunmoore and Kowalski for their now daily morning meeting. "She died on the spot, a few dozen meters from her apartment building."

"You said apparent. Does that mean you believe someone assassinated her?"

Holt nodded at Dunmoore.

"Yes. Leila was as healthy as us three and no older than I am. She has no reason to simply collapse during a leisurely stroll."

"But why? And who?" Kowalski asked.

"That, we don't know. The SSB took over the investigation the moment the Geneva Police reported her death. She's scheduled for an autopsy sometime this morning."

"How are you aware of this?" Dunmoore arched an eyebrow in question. "Do you have someone inside the SSB? Someone senior?"

"You know I can't answer that."

"Any idea who'll replace her?"

"That's the other reason her death is suspect — her successor was named moments before I joined you, meaning the SecGen already had someone in mind. Axel Renouf, the permanent undersecretary of Public Safety. A Lauzier loyalist, albeit a quiet one who should be acceptable to the SSB's senior brass. He has proved to be quite effective in his various jobs since he left Lauzier's political staff and joined the civil service.

"Interesting. You think Lauzier is behind Gherson's death?" Dunmoore asked.

"She was behind her predecessor Blayne Hersom's, who also died of cardiac arrest, although we can't prove it. And Blayne had been getting a little too cozy with us for her taste, just like Leila was beginning to."

Kowalski frowned.

"Do you think Renouf will respect the truce between the SSB and the Fleet?"

"Difficult to say. He's not a professional SSB officer like Blayne or Leila, but a politico turned bureaucrat. His loyalty won't be to the agency but to Lauzier. If I had to hazard a guess, I'd say no. He'll have received — or will shortly receive — marching orders from the SecGen, and he will obey them where Leila might not have."

"Do you think the hit came from within the SSB?"

Holt shook his head.

"No. Leila maintained a good grip on her folks and earned their respect. If I had to point the finger at anyone, it would be the same people who almost killed Ulli Radames. Perhaps Lauzier has another asset in her back pocket, a mercenary group that does the sort of dirty deeds the SSB won't touch." He grimaced. "Which brings me to my next subject. None of us will leave the base unless on official business from now on, and we will have two of my operatives each, guarding us at all times."

Kowalski and Dunmoore nodded, agreeing to follow the order even though both outranked Holt. After all, he was responsible for their security, and things had just gotten a lot dicier.

Dunmoore allowed herself a mischievous smile.

"Does this mean you won't be accosting people in restaurants anymore?"

Holt nodded.

"I'm afraid those days are over. You know, it's too bad about Leila. She was thawing just a little — we'd reached a first-name basis relationship, which I never thought would happen."

"That would have made the SSB's elimination that much more difficult for you," Kowalski pointed out.

A shrug.

"On the contrary. We might have been able to negotiate a peaceful dissolution of the agency. With Axel Renouf now in control, that option probably no longer exists."

"True." Kowalski grimaced. "Okay, next order of business. Siobhan's meeting with the vice president for military sales of MacKay-Sankuno this afternoon to warn him about not doing business with the Defense Department's new Procurement Branch."

"Indeed," Dunmoore said. "They're interested in bidding on the naval targeting sensor upgrade and have been informally discussing the matter with the SecDef. This will be a litmus test of our ability to control the process fully. We need the sensor upgrades, and MacKay-Sankuno is one of only three companies capable of delivering, along with Nostromo Incorporated and

Geiger-Cobb. And its solution is the preferred of our technical staff."

"Good luck with that, sir," Holt said. "I know for a fact that MacKay-Sankuno contributed heavily to Lauzier's political funds in the past, albeit through cutouts, so they don't appear directly involved. They'll favor the SecDef's approach, hoping to win this contract and many future ones because of their past contributions."

"Thank you for that. I'll definitely use the information if it's necessary. But should they decide to go with the SecDef, they'll not win this one or any others. Or rather, they might win this one, but we'll not accept their product because either Nostromo or Geiger-Cobb will have received the nod from us. In any case, the people they need to speak with are on Caledonia, not Earth."

"All right. Next item."

***

"Mister Yutani from MacKay-Sankuno is here, sir," Commander Botha announced over the intercom.

Dunmoore sighed and put her tablet away. She had the feeling this wouldn't be a pleasant meeting.

"Send him in."

She stood as Botha ushered in an unsmiling, short, black-haired man with a lean face that betrayed no specific age. He could have been anything between thirty and seventy.

"Waku Yutani, Admiral," he said in a surprisingly mellow voice as he stopped in the middle of the office and briefly bowed at the neck. He did not hold out his hand for the more customary greeting.

"Siobhan Dunmoore, Mister Yutani. Thank you for coming." She gestured at the settee group to one side. "I think we'll be more comfortable there."

They sat across from each other, Yutani watching Dunmoore with impassive eyes that missed little.

"What can I do for you, Admiral?"

"I understand your company plans to bid on the naval targeting sensor upgrade."

He nodded.

"We are. It's a major piece of work, and we're one of the few companies capable of delivering."

"And you've been informally discussing it with the SecDef?"

Yutani's eyes narrowed a fraction of a millimeter, just enough for Dunmoore to notice.

"Yes. If I may ask, Admiral, what is this about?"

"The SecDef no longer has a role in naval procurement."

"That's not what he intimated. In fact, he told me all procurement was now under the Department rather than the Fleet."

"He's not told you the truth."

Yutani's eyebrows crept up, a clear sign of astonishment.

"Why would Alan Olongo lie to me?"

"I don't know. But the Fleet retains control of naval acquisitions. The Defense Department is merely responsible for non-military contracting. Mister Olongo would like to change that state of affairs, but he cannot."

She paused to study Yutani but saw nothing in his eyes or face that betrayed his thoughts.

"The reason I asked you to see me is so you understand that the naval targeting sensor upgrade will go through Fleet Procurement on Caledonia, not the Department's on Earth. Should you bid via the Department and be awarded a contract, I can assure you the Fleet will not accept whatever MacKay-Sankuno offers. We will have gone with one of your competitors."

"This is most irregular, Admiral, and I think I may report you to Mister Olongo."

"Please go ahead. He's no doubt expecting it since he knows you and I are meeting today. But this is the reality. The Defense Department is distinct from the Armed Forces, and the SecDef and Grand Admiral report to the SecGen separately. As such, the Fleet has full authority to conduct contracting activities for naval purposes, while the Department has none whatsoever."

Yutani shook his head.

"That is not what Alan Olongo said."

"Please present your bid to Fleet Procurement on Caledonia, Mister Yutani. Otherwise, it will be considered null and void."

For the first time, she saw something in Yutani's eyes.

"I don't think you can do that, Admiral."

"You have no idea what I can do." Dunmoore gave him her sweet smile, the one that presaged a storm. "I'm pretty sure your company expects many dividends from its political contributions to the current SecGen, including this contract and future ones."

That got Yutani's attention. He reared up.

"I beg your pardon? Your words are borderline slanderous, Admiral."

"Oh, come now, Mister Yutani. We both know MacKay-Sankuno has been assiduously funding Sara Lauzier for years, hoping to reap big contracts, sole-source if you can manage it. Unfortunately for you, the Fleet doesn't operate that way. You actually have to win a contract by presenting the best solution at the best price." Dunmoore tilted her head to one side as she met his eyes. "Mind you, my technical people do like your intended proposal for the naval targeting sensor upgrade, so you stand a decent chance of winning by properly participating in the bidding process."

She could see Yutani's jaw muscles work as he looked away, trying to come up with an appropriate reply.

"Was that everything, Admiral?" He finally asked, glancing back at her once more.

Dunmoore nodded once.

"It was."

Yutani climbed to his feet and bowed his head.

"Enjoy the rest of your day."

Then he turned on his heels and left Dunmoore's office. She stayed on the sofa for a little longer, wondering whether MacKay-Sankuno would play ball with the Fleet or stick to the SecDef's procurement agency. Her comment about the company funding Lauzier in return for guaranteed future contracts certainly struck a nerve.

She stood and returned to her desk and the next file in her queue.

— Twenty-Three —

Axel Renouf was less thrilled than Sara Lauzier thought him to be when she announced his appointment as director general of the SSB. Renouf was aware that the career officers in the agency would rightfully perceive him as an outsider lacking knowledge in policing and counterintelligence. And they were well aware that Lauzier named him because she considered him one of her creatures, even though he had wormed his way into the civil service years before.

But he couldn't refuse, so he'd shown up at the SSB headquarters later that day after hastily turning over his Public Safety files to the senior deputy permanent undersecretary. He didn't even have time to speak with Paul Markus, who was away giving a presentation on the challenges of coordinating police work on an interstellar scale in London. Not that Markus had a clue about the subject, but he'd been well briefed.

Gherson's personal effects had been hastily stripped from the office, which was on the top floor of a four-story modern building just beyond the Palace of the Stars precinct, leaving it impersonal and cold. Renouf didn't bring any of his things to decorate the space, but he'd soon change that.

"Is everything all right, sir?" The chief of staff, who'd greeted Renouf at the front entrance and guided him to his office, asked with an air of concern. He was another gray man, the sort the SSB produced on an assembly line basis who went unnoticed in a crowd.

Renouf quickly put his poker face back on, not having realized that it had slipped.

"Yes. I was simply reflecting on how quickly life changes."

"Indeed, sir. It can change rather rapidly. The active files in Madame Gherson's queue have now been reassigned to you, and your direct reports are standing by for an introductory meeting."

Renouf turned around to gaze at the man.

"How about we do that in the conference room now?"

"Give me five minutes to round them up." He disappeared as if by magic, leaving Renouf alone in his office.

He'd had thirty minutes with the SecGen earlier, and she'd laid out her expectations of him, the main one being to stop Kowalski and her cabal, something she intimated Leila Gherson hadn't been willing to do. And that, in turn, made him wonder about her fatal heart attack during her walk home the previous evening. Based on past experience, he was well aware of the extent to which Sara Lauzier could demonstrate ruthlessness, which added to his ambivalence about the appointment as director general of the SSB.

Just then, his communicator vibrated for attention. He fished it from his pocket and saw the call was on his private address, which few people had, but the caller's identity didn't show. Renouf answered anyway, intrigued.

"Yes?"

"Axel, it's Zeke Holt. Congratulations on your taking over as DG of the SSB. You and I need to talk. The sooner, the better. How about sixteen hundred by the Skanderbeg statue in front of the Palace?"

Holt's rapid-fire words and insistent tone took Renouf aback.

"I don't know—"

"Be there, Axel. It's to your everlasting advantage and that of the agency you now lead. See you then."

Holt cut the link, leaving Renouf to stare at his communicator. He felt a wave of anger course through him. How dare a mere vice admiral order him around? Even one who was the head of the Armed Forces Security Branch, the largest law enforcement agency in human space, albeit limited to enforcing the Commonwealth Armed Forces Regulations and Orders. Yet he sounded so confident that Renouf was willing to reconsider his initial reaction.

His chief of staff's announcement that all his direct reports were waiting in the main conference room adjoining his office suite startled him.

The initial meeting went about as well as he'd expected. Guarded looks, even more guarded words, not much of a welcome, really, the attendees having considered one of their own as Gherson's successor. But they were professional enough to greet their new director general with the sort of wary respect a quick replacement for a mysteriously deceased predecessor demanded. Especially one appointed by the SecGen within twelve hours of Gherson's death.

By the time fifteen-thirty rolled around, he walked over to his office window and stared out at the lake, gray and choppy under a lowering sky, wondering whether he should meet with Holt. The head of the Fleet's Security Branch had a reputation in Geneva as someone you didn't want to mess with. However, Renouf was the director general of an independent agency that reported directly to the SecGen.

It meant he outranked Holt in the capital's unspoken but very real hierarchy. Still, perhaps it would be prudent to see what he wanted. Renouf shrugged on his jacket and, with a wave at the executive assistant sitting outside his office, left the building and headed for the Palace precinct.

Holt hadn't arrived yet when Renouf took a seat on the bench by the Skanderbeg statue, but he was a few minutes early and settled down to wait, eyes on the lake's ever-changing surface. At sixteen hundred, a uniformed Holt appeared out of nowhere and sat beside Renouf.

"Hi, Axel. Good choice in coming. I am aware that you extensively deliberated with yourself — the leader of an autonomous organization reporting to the Secretary General's meeting at the persistent demand of a mere vice admiral."

Renouf glanced at Holt sideways and saw a mocking smile directed at him. That smile irked Renouf intensely for some reason, and he knew it was meant to do so.

"Get on with it, Holt. I don't have all afternoon."

"You may not even have the next hour, Axel. Look at your chest."

Renouf did so and saw a small red spot dead center.

"What the heck?"

"That, my friend, is the targeting laser of a railgun-equipped sniper somewhere across the lake. I am unaware of his current location, but the red dot indicates that he is observing us. At my signal, he will pull the trigger, and a twelve-millimeter railgun slug traveling at two thousand five hundred meters per second will blow open your chest. You won't feel a thing." Holt's smile widened. "Welcome to my world, Axel. This little demonstration serves to show you I'm dead serious about what we'll discuss in a moment. Do I have your undivided attention?"

Renouf grunted.

"Yes."

"For many years now, the Fleet and the SSB have had a truce. I negotiated it with Blayne Hersom, and my former boss brought it to Leila's attention. I'm now informing you since you're new to the agency and are not aware. This truce is quite simple. The SSB doesn't target any Fleet member or civilian employee, and we don't target you. And when I say you, I mean Axel Renouf personally. My branch is larger than your organization, and my people are much more ruthless than yours. We could wipe out the SSB in a single night. Are you with me so far?"

Another grunt.

"Yes."

"Excellent. Will you uphold our truce?"

Renouf nodded.

"Sure."

Holt made a hand gesture, and the red dot on Renouf's chest vanished.

"Look down. You're no longer being targeted, but break the truce, and you won't get any warning. You'll simply die, along with most of your senior people. It's evident that Sara Lauzier harbors a strong desire to remove Grand Admiral Kowalski and potentially Admiral Dunmoore as well. Your continued existence depends on both remaining alive, healthy and at their posts. So if Sara gives you orders to eliminate them, think about it really hard and then turn her down." Holt climbed to his feet. "You may have wondered how I knew to call you a few minutes after you arrived in your office. Let me assure you, it wasn't by chance."

Then he walked away, leaving a slightly confused and somewhat angry Renouf to stare at his receding back.

Who did he think he was, threatening the director general of the SSB? Sure, Fleet Security was larger than his agency, but they were primarily low-level enlisted personnel, not consummate professionals such as the Bureau's agents.

Renouf shook himself and stood. Still, the laser targeting dot on his chest had been a serious enough warning, and that Holt knew he was in his new office within minutes of arrival meant he had Renouf under surveillance. Wonderful. And what would he do now? The SecGen had already told him to find a way of stopping Kowalski and company.

Renouf frowned as he gazed out at the lake, not really seeing it, his mind parsing option after option without finding a solution.

Holt, on the other hand, was merely glad he wouldn't have to meet anyone by the Skanderbeg statue ever again. Renouf was the last because his time on Earth was almost over. Unless Lauzier changed the SSB head prematurely again because the current one refused to do her bidding, but even then, would it be worth warning Renouf's replacement about the truce? Probably not in the time they had left.

— Twenty-Four —

"Does anyone ever refuse to meet you, Zeke?" Dunmoore asked after he related his encounter with Axel Renouf to her and Kowalski the following day.

"Not so far. I guess I'm irresistibly mysterious." He winked at her. "Or they're just curious about what I want. After all, I'm well known in this town for dealing with secretive and underhanded matters."

"I think it's the latter reason," Kowalski said in a dry yet amused tone. "Do you believe he'll keep the truce, or are we to consider ourselves SSB targets from now on?"

"Hard to say. He's been a Lauzier loyalist for years, so her desires will likely win against the SSB's needs. Will they also win against the threat we represent to him personally if he acts against us? I don't know. Should he convince himself that we won't go through with it, which is quite possible, then yes, the truce is over, and we've become targets of the SSB. Which brings me to my question. How soon can both of you move to Caledonia?"

Kowalski grimaced.

"Not for a while. We have a lot to do now that the Senate is sitting again, and we understand how slow they can be, especially when they face unpleasant alternatives. Which brings me to our next point."

When Dunmoore returned to her office, she found Guthren waiting for her.

"I heard you might become an SSB target again after all these years."

"And how did you hear that? I only found out in my meeting with Zeke and Kathryn just now."

Guthren smiled as he tapped the side of his nose with an extended index finger.

"We chiefs have our ways. I would propose taking me with you every time you leave the base. I mean, on top of the two Security operatives watching your back. A sort of close-quarters bodyguard, if you will."

"I'll only be visiting the Palace of the Stars — a direct ride from the base and back. Assassins will have a hard time striking at me there."

"Still, I'd rather be with you. The chief petty officer of the Armed Forces is telling Grand Admiral Kowalski the same thing right now."

Dunmoore gave him a sly smile.

"At your urging, of course."

Guthren grinned back at her.

"Of course. Two big, mean-looking senior chief petty officers silently looming behind both of you will be a treat for the eyes."

The Armed Forces Chief Petty Officer resembled Guthren in that both men were tall slabs of hard muscle, with square, bearded faces. But the former had a dark complexion to Guthren's light one. With the impressive rows of ribbons on their uniforms beneath the special forces eagle and trident badge — they'd served together in special ops during the war — they looked good in a menacing way. That they would be effective close-in bodyguards was beyond dispute. Though aging, both were fit and still had the reflexes of younger men, not to mention those of spec ops warriors.

"All right. You can stick to me alongside my aides whenever I leave the base."

Guthren nodded once.

"Done."

"And your first occasion will be this afternoon. The Senate's Armed Forces and Defense Committee has summoned Kathryn and me so we can account for the transfer of major HQ functions to Caledonia."

"Finally noticed, did they? It's about time."

"Oh, I think Kathryn engineered this appearance via a sympathetic ear on the committee, Senator Bregman from Cascadia, perhaps. He's the co-chair."

"Ah. I see. What time?"

"We leave at thirteen hundred. Service dress uniform."

As usual, Dunmoore and Kowalski traveled in separate cars, using different routes. Two more identical vehicles accompanied each car, making it impossible for any observer to tell which ones they rode. Both were shadowed by their chiefs and senior aides, the latter sitting up front, the former in the back with their admirals.

The two convoys reached the Palace of the Stars almost simultaneously and entered through the Pregny Gate to stop in front of the main doors. Dunmoore, Guthren, and Captain

Malfort emerged from the third vehicle in her column while Kowalski, her chief, and her senior aide, climbed out of the first in hers.

Kowalski in the lead, followed by Dunmoore, the two chiefs, and both aides, they entered the building and headed for the second floor where the Senate committee rooms were located. Government employees moving through the corridors gave the six curious glances. So many uniforms at once on a workday were unusual.

"Ah, here it is."

Kowalski entered the open door to the committee room's antechamber, which held a scattering of comfortable chairs grouped around low tables, a sideboard with coffee and tea urns, and a water dispenser.

A slight, older man sat at a small desk beside the inner door. He stood when they entered and bowed his head politely.

"Grand Admiral. The committee isn't quite ready yet. If you'll please take seats. Feel free to help yourselves." He gestured at the sideboard. "I assume all six of you will enter?"

"Yes, although only Admiral Dunmoore and I will speak. The others can sit behind us."

"Of course."

The man sat again and busied himself at his virtual workstation, a holographic projection that hovered over the desk. After a few moments, he climbed to his feet and slipped through the inner door. He reappeared a minute later and resumed his place behind the desk.

Dunmoore wandered around the room, examining the paintings hanging on the walls. They weren't of any great artistic merit, and she suspected they were reproductions anyway. She glanced at the sideboard and briefly debated pouring herself a cup of coffee, but with her luck, she'd spill some down the front of her uniform seconds before they entered the committee room.

The attendant suddenly stood and turned toward Kowalski, who sat in one of the chairs, studying something on her tablet.

"The committee is ready for you, Grand Admiral."

Kowalski stood, tucked her tablet in her tunic pocket, and nodded.

"Thank you."

He opened the door, and they filed in. The committee room wasn't particularly large, and the table with the twelve members took up half the space. A smaller table with two chairs faced it, while a dozen unoccupied chairs sat behind the latter. The members and principal guests had nameplates in front of them, although Dunmoore was familiar with the senators, as was Kowalski, and they, in turn, recognized both admirals.

"Welcome, Admiral Kowalski, Admiral Dunmoore," Senator Bregman said in a grave tone. "Please be seated."

A small fuss behind them caused Dunmoore to glance back, and she saw five civilians entering to take the spectator seats alongside the chief petty officers and the aides. They wore the somber business suits common among senior officials, and she remembered Holt saying that observers from the SecGen's office and the SSB were sure to be in attendance.

"Thank you for appearing in front of this committee," Bregman continued. Not that they had a choice. Failing to show up for a senatorial committee hearing could entail consequences, including imprisonment. "I believe we are already acquainted and can skip the usual introductions."

Kowalski nodded silently, acknowledging Bregman's words.

"This committee is meeting today so it can delve into the matter of Armed Forces Headquarters' major functions being transferred to Caledonia, an OutWorld."

Dunmoore found Bregman qualifying Caledonia interesting. It was common knowledge that the Fleet's fief belonged to the OutWorlds, which were colonized during humanity's second migratory wave. Why make the point deliberately?

"My first question to you, Grand Admiral, is whether you've been shifting parts of your headquarters to Caledonia."

"Yes, we have, Senator."

"And you intend to move the entire headquarters there in due course?"

"Yes."

"Will you eventually move to Caledonia yourself once the headquarters here are no longer functional?"

"That is the plan."

To Dunmoore's private amusement, the reactions from the other eleven committee members were divided between smug approval from the OutWorlders and alarmed expressions from those representing Home Worlds. One of the latter, Senator Viviane Sholto from Pacifica and the committee's other co-chair, raised a hand, and Bregman nodded at her.

"Why are you doing this, Admiral?" She asked.

"For several reasons, the first and foremost among them being the need to have our HQ closer to the restive areas of the Commonwealth. As you are aware, the communications lag can lead to numerous issues, particularly in urgent circumstances. By relocating closer to the Fleet's main areas of operations, we cut down on that lag."

It was a specious argument. The extra half day gained by being closer to the most active outer sectors wouldn't make a difference, but several senators nodded as if approving of the idea.

"The second reason is to get politics out of the Armed Forces' day-to-day operations once and for all. Relocating to Caledonia will ensure that."

Seeing as how senators were consummate politicians, used to throwing their influence around the corridors of government, the Fleet included, Kowalski's comment drew some angry glares.

"What do you mean get politics out of day-to-day operations? I don't see any interference with the Armed Forces." Sholto drew herself up with an air of self-righteousness.

"You may not see it, Madame, but perhaps you're not looking in the right places. Politics are a bane on the Fleet's business, and that needs to cease."

"If I may," Dunmoore said. "Political interference in Fleet affairs not only led to the last war when the Shrehari perceived our weakness but caused the first few years of it to be disastrous for the Commonwealth. That is a fact beyond dispute. We can never allow ourselves to be placed in such a situation again, yet politics are once more casting a baleful shadow over the Fleet."

Kowalski nodded.

"Just as Admiral Dunmoore said, Madame Sholto. We must be able to operate without external pressures irrelevant to our primary mission, which is to defend and protect humanity against all enemies, alien and human."

"Well, I find that rather questionable. Isolating yourself from Earth and the representatives of that same humanity you're sworn to defend and protect seems counterproductive."

A wintry smile played on Kowalski's lips.

"It's not so much you and your colleagues, Madame."

Sholto's eyebrows shot up.

"Oh, so you mean the administration is the one putting external pressures on the Armed Forces? May I assume your moving Fleet HQ to Caledonia is being done without the government's approval?"

"The administration has no say in the dispositions of the Fleet."

"Not even the SecGen, your ultimate boss?"

"The SecGen may issue directives on defense policy. The day-to-day operations are my prerogative alone, and shifting to Caledonia is operational, not a matter of policy."

"You hold the Fleet to be an entity separate from the government."

"No, Senator. But our mission supersedes the demands of any administration."

And there you had it, Dunmoore thought. The first shots fired openly at Sara Lauzier. Things would get interesting quickly now. She resisted the temptation to glance back at the civilian spectators to gauge their reaction. Lauzier would surely know about Kowalski's words before they left the building.

"I see." An air of disapproval settled over Sholto's doughy features. "Though I'm not sure I approve of your attitude, Admiral."

"Whether or not you approve, Madame, it is a fact. Our mission is paramount."

Bregman held up a hand.

"Does anyone else have questions for either of our guests?"

The senior senator for Scandia leaned forward.

"First, I'd like to say good on you for taking these steps, Grand Admiral. Moving Fleet HQ away from Earth was way overdue." Dunmoore saw Sholto's lips compress in annoyance at his words. "Notwithstanding the opinion of some of my esteemed colleagues. My question is, when do you expect the move to be completed?"

"With the Fleet Operations Center on Caledonia now active and the one on Earth shut, the move is essentially done. We still have important parts of HQ to transfer, but essentially, my deputy and Admiral Dunmoore's are running the day-to-day operations from Caledonia."

That statement brought a few low-key gasps from the committee members.

"We were unaware it was so advanced," Sholto said in an accusatory tone.

"I expect what's left to follow before the end of the year, Senator."

— Twenty-Five —

When they left the committee room, half of the senators were smiling, the other half frowning. The five observers had scurried out ahead of them and vanished down the corridor before they emerged from the antechamber.

"At least one of them is now racing for Sara's office," Dunmoore remarked as they turned right toward the stairs, "with news of our explosive testimony. And another is likely calling the head of the SSB on a secure link. Who did the other three represent? Your guess is as good as mine."

"One of them probably belongs to the SecDef, and perhaps another to Public Safety."

They reached the front doors, where their cars were waiting under the control of the Fleet Security operatives assigned to them, and climbed aboard. As both little convoys headed for the Pregny Gate, the cars shuffled position, leaving Dunmoore in the first of hers and Kowalski in the third of hers.

"I noticed a distinct split between the OutWorlders and the Home World senators," Guthren remarked as they left the Palace behind and headed southwest through Geneva, using a different route from the one they'd taken earlier. "The OutWorlders looked smug as hell, while the rest seemed like they were fighting heartburns."

"That's because the Home Worlders are Centralists and know moving Fleet HQ beyond Earth's grasp will harm their cause immeasurably."

After stopping at an intersection, the cars shuffled places, leaving Dunmoore's in third position, but she hardly noticed, the change being routine by now. Instead, she was reviewing their appearance in front of the committee in her mind, trying to find further evidence Kowalski had engineered the whole thing, including the Scandian senator's remarks. But it was in vain.

They eventually reached Geneva's outskirts and found themselves behind Kowalski's little convoy as they turned onto the sole, albeit short, road leading to the base. Dunmoore glanced up and noted there were now five cars identical to the one she rode in front of her. Then she looked at her tablet again, preparing for her next meeting. The two oncoming vehicles, large and drab, didn't register.

Suddenly, everything ahead turned brighter than a thousand suns, and she felt the front of her car lifting as it slewed to one side. The sound of two detonations within a fraction of a second of each other penetrated the car's thick armor, and the only thing she could think of at that moment was to brace herself.

The car tumbled once before landing upright again, sitting half on the road and half on the grass. All four inside, still held by harnesses that had tightened the moment the car lifted, looked at each other, stunned by the violence of the detonations and the heavy vehicle's spin around its long axis.

Guthren was the first to recover.

"Those were missiles, weren't they?"

"I don't think so, Chief," Dunmoore replied, nodding at the window, which showed a scene of utter devastation ahead of them. The second vehicle in their convoy was nothing more than twisted scrap metal, but there was twice as much debris as there should have been. "I think a vehicle packed with explosives hit car number two."

"Had to have been one of the two oncoming civilian jobs."

"The second car in the Grand Admiral's convoy seems to have been hit as well, sir," Captain Malfort said, pointing. "I'll call the immediate response team."

He fished his communicator from a tunic pocket.

"IRT, this is Navy One, incident on the main road leading to the base, approximately two kilometers from the main gate. I require emergency medical, aerial and ground security, and someone to close off the road. Over."

"Copy, Navy One. We saw the double flash. IRT has been alerted and is getting ready to go. Sit tight and don't move. Over."

"Ack. Navy One, out."

"Try to contact the Grand Admiral's car, Josh."

"Yes, sir. Armed Forces One, this is Navy One, over." When he didn't receive a reply, Malfort repeated his call. "Armed Forces One, Armed Forces One, this is Navy One, over."

Still nothing. Malfort turned in his seat toward Dunmoore and grimaced.

"Hopefully, it's nothing, sir."

"But they could still have been in the car that was hit."

Dunmoore craned her neck to look for it but saw only wreckage.

"If nothing else, the gomers aboard those civvie cars must be dead meat," Guthren said.

"Unless someone guided them remotely."

"RPVs don't work within two klicks of the base, sir. Military security feature. And if they were uncrewed, they'd have been under centralized traffic control and not left their lane. Someone was definitely aiming at you and the Grand Admiral. They simply miscalculated which car you were in."

"Let's hope they also miscalculated the one Kathryn was in."

Dunmoore, shaken by the sudden attack, felt her anxiety levels shoot up at the idea Kowalski might have been injured or worse. And Malfort still wasn't getting an answer from the latter's aide.

Sirens began to howl in the distance, and Dunmoore saw a shadow pass over them. Then, the IRT from the Terra Regiment appeared, surrounding the site. One of the armored figures approached her car, and the aide shoved his door open with difficulty, the frame having slightly bent when the vehicle rolled over.

"I'm Captain Malfort. Admiral Dunmoore, Chief Guthren, and our driver appear unhurt. How's the Grand Admiral?"

"Unknown, sir. If you would please come with me. We'll evacuate you to the base hospital aboard one of our armored cars." He made a hand signal, and one of the hulking personnel carriers stopped beside them, dropping its aft ramp.

Dunmoore considered insisting on being allowed to see if Kowalski was alright but then chose to obey the IRT commander. There was no point in making his life harder. He had orders to take them to the base hospital securely, and those orders were sensible. Although she merely felt bruised by the harness, she could have more severe injuries.

They climbed aboard the combat car, accompanied by two armored troopers, and sped off toward the base. Since the vehicle had no windows, Dunmoore couldn't see what was happening around the car in Kowalski's convoy that had been hit.

Upon arriving at the hospital, the staff immediately led all four of them to separate examination rooms, and a naval doctor joined Dunmoore moments after she had entered.

"How are you, Admiral?"

"I've been a lot worse. Some bruising around my shoulders and hips. That's it."

"Well, let's make sure, shall we?" He produced a medical scanner and slowly ran it over Dunmoore's body from top to bottom. "Nothing broken, no concussion. I'd say you're okay. Try to take a day or two off, but I doubt you'll do that. If the pain from the bruising worsens, come see me."

He smiled at her.

"And with that, you're free to go, Admiral."

As she left the examination room, there was a big fuss at the emergency doors, and four stretchers, one of them with the face covered, were pushed in.

Dunmoore stopped and watched as the attendants steered the three stretchers with live patients to the elevators, recognizing Kowalski, her senior aide, and the Armed Forces Chief Petty Officer. They were unconscious and had bloody faces, and she decided to follow them up to the intensive care unit to wait patiently while doctors carried out their examination. Guthren and Captain Malfort eventually found her and sat at her side.

After a while, a captain from the Terra Regiment appeared, wearing armor but with a beret bearing the badge of the Terra Regiment instead of his helmet — it hung from his utility belt in the small of his back. He stopped in front of Dunmoore and saluted. She recognized him as the man who'd evacuated her from the damaged car, the IRT's commanding officer.

"Sir, I thought you'd like to hear my report in person."

"You thought correctly, Captain. Please sit." She gestured at the chairs across from her.

"From what we can tell, two vehicles struck your convoy, the second and the fifth. Both drivers are dead. The vehicles were loaded with explosives, so it's pretty much a given they were on a suicide mission. The one that struck the vehicle in front of yours hit it head-on, which explains the wreckage. Its driver is dead, of course, as is the man who was sitting up front beside him."

"One of my protection detail from Fleet Security."

"The driver and presumably the other member of your protection detail who were in the fourth car are unhurt, and the car drove back to the base under its own power. Grand Admiral Kowalski was in the second car, and the only reason she, her aide, and her chief are still alive is that the assassin didn't strike them head-on but hit a glancing blow on the driver's side. And that's all I have for now, sir. More will come from Fleet Security, who've taken over the site of the attempt and are investigating in greater detail."

"Thank you, Captain."

He stood and drew himself to attention.

"With your permission, sir?"

"You're dismissed."

The officer saluted, turned smartly on his heels, and marched off.

"An assassination attempt, eh?" Guthren asked in a thoughtful tone. "Can't have been the SSB. They don't go for fireworks when trying to terminate someone."

Dunmoore nodded.

"Let's hope Zeke's agents can figure it out. And let's hope these people have shot their human ammunition and have no more suicide bombers to sacrifice."

"Somehow, I doubt that, sir. If they're determined, they'll have more lined up," Malfort said.

A doctor, the same one who'd examined Dunmoore, emerged from the ICU and headed for them.

"Admiral." He stopped in front of her. "You'll be glad to know they're out of immediate danger."

"When can I see the Grand Admiral?"

"Not today. Come back tomorrow morning. She should be up to a brief visit by then."

"What's wrong with her?"

The doctor grimaced.

"What isn't? Multiple fractures, concussion, internal organ damage, lacerations, and more. But now that she's in an ICU regen bed, she'll be okay. The other two as well."

"Thank you, Doctor." Dunmoore stood. "I guess I'd better get back to the office and notify everyone."

"You realize you're the acting commander-in-chief of the Armed Forces until Grand Admiral Kowalski is functional again," Malfort said. "General Nagato might be second-in-command, but the line of succession devolves to you as the senior naval flag officer, Marines being ineligible for the top job."

"No, I didn't. But I'm aware now."

"Let me call a car to take us to the HQ building. You're not allowed out where you can be seen anymore, sir."

Moments after Dunmoore entered her office, a grim-faced Holt appeared.

"I understand Kathryn is in serious but stable condition." He dropped into a chair across the desk from her. "Making you the acting Grand Admiral."

"Who did this, Zeke?"

"It wasn't the SSB. I'd stake my reputation on that. They're subtle assassins and not prone to suicidal action. I'm speaking with Axel Renouf once we're done here to confirm my supposition and see if he can help us find whoever did it. My folks are pulling out all the stops investigating this, but I doubt we'll get very far. There isn't much left of the suicide car drivers. Just enough for us to tell there was one in each. And that makes me believe there are more of them."

"Wonderful."

"I'll let you get on with sending out the notifications to the fleet commanders, General Nagato, and the SecGen." Holt climbed to his feet. "We'll figure it out, Siobhan. Have no fear. And we'll get our pound of flesh."

— Twenty-Six —

"Good afternoon, Madame." Dunmoore searched Lauzier's eyes for knowledge of the attempt on their lives but found nothing. Not even a soul. "I'm afraid Grand Admiral Kowalski is in the intensive care unit with multiple injuries resulting from an attack by persons unknown on our cars as we returned from the Palace earlier. I escaped largely unscathed and am now the acting commander-in-chief of the Armed Forces."

Did she see something in Lauzier's gaze? A flash of satisfaction, perhaps? Of course, it likely meant nothing more than pleasure at having an annoying adversary out of commission.

"I'm sorry to hear that, Admiral." Butter wouldn't have melted in her mouth. "Please give Grand Admiral Kowalski my wishes for a quick recovery."

"Yes, Madame."

"It seems like Kathryn will be unable to perform her duties for quite a while. That means you and I must meet as soon as possible to discuss our working relationship.

"I am at your disposal."

Lauzier's smile was as patently insincere as Dunmoore's.

"Shall we say tomorrow at ten in my office?"

"Certainly."

"Until then."

Lauzier's face vanished as she cut the link, leaving a thoughtful Dunmoore to stare at the spot where it had hovered.

The SecGen had nothing to do with the attack. Of that, she was almost certain. Her instincts were usually damned good, and they told her Lauzier was surprised by the news. Kowalski's junior aide stuck his head into the Grand Admiral's office.

"The message to all concerned about your temporary assumption of command and Admiral Pushkin becoming acting CNO is ready, sir. I've put it at the top of your queue."

"Thank you, Sam." She quickly reviewed it and signed off. "Get her out there."

The next morning at oh-eight hundred, Dunmoore, trailed by Guthren, who now openly carried a holstered blaster on his hip, showed up at the base hospital. The duty nurse gave her five minutes with Kowalski, who was awake and lucid. Dunmoore entered the room, leaving Guthren to stand guard outside.

The first thing Kowalski whispered when Dunmoore appeared in her field of view was, "Do I look as bad as I feel?"

"Worse, if anything, Kathryn. You're barely recognizable." Dunmoore smiled at her. "But you'll pull through."

"I suppose you took over?"

"Yes."

"Good. Stick to the plan and make sure things keep happening as they should. You know as much as I do about where we're going, so have at her."

"No worries. I'm meeting the SecGen at ten. She wants to discuss our working relationship."

"More like she wants to see if you're more amenable to her blandishments than I am."

"Then I wish her good luck. I'm even less likely to play nice than you are."

"And please don't hold back. It's time to bring things out into the open with her." Kowalski paused. "Any idea who did this to us?"

"No, but it wasn't the SSB. Zeke spoke with Renouf yesterday, and he was genuinely appalled. Besides, suicide attacks aren't the SSB's stock in trade. Zeke believes him, so that rules them out."

"Suicide attacks?"

"Each of the two vehicles that struck was under the control of a human being who didn't expect to survive. Not with the quantity of explosives involved. Our cars were heavily armored, and they literally shredded those they hit. Mine got only secondary damage, but it's out of commission, probably for good."

"I hope you're not returning to the Palace by ground."

"No fears. I'm flying aboard an armored shuttle placed at my disposal by 1st Fleet. Zeke wouldn't let me leave the base otherwise." Dunmoore chuckled. "You know, I pity the fools behind the attack. Zeke won't be nice to them at all."

She made a slicing gesture across her throat with an extended index finger.

"He still has to find them, though. Suicide attackers for hire are a new thing, and he won't even know where to start."

"Maybe not, but he has competent individuals working for him. I'm confident they will eventually find their origin."

The nurse entered Kowalski's room and gently touched Dunmoore's arm.

"It's time to go, Admiral. She needs her rest."

"Right. I'll be back tomorrow morning, Kathryn. If you need anything in the meantime, just let me know."

"Thanks, Siobhan. I will."

Dunmoore and Guthren returned to the main HQ building — via armored ground car — and she found Holt waiting for her in the Grand Admiral's office.

"Made any progress on finding the culprits, Zeke?" She asked when she spotted the smug look on his face.

"Yes. After speaking with Axel Renouf yesterday, I visited Marseille and saw Leon Pannetier again. He told me a fascinating tale. Apparently, there is a religious sect on Nabhka that hires out suicide mercenaries to assassinate people. We'd never heard of them. But Leon Pannetier had, and he gave Markus a subspace radio address to contact them."

"What will you do now?"

Holt's expression became grim.

"Terminate Markus with extreme prejudice. What else? We can't leave him alive after this. But before I put a round through his skull, we will interrogate him thoroughly."

"I feel like I should forbid you from executing a cabinet secretary in cold blood, Zeke."

"But you won't. You know what's at stake. If both you and Kathryn get killed, the plan will fail. I can't carry it through by myself. Neither can Gregor nor General Nagato. With Kathryn sidelined for the Almighty knows how long, you're it. And I will do whatever is necessary to protect you. Even execute a cabinet secretary."

"I know." Dunmoore took a deep breath and exhaled. "Do it, Zeke. You have my blessing as acting commander-in-chief."

"Thank you, sir." He jumped to his feet. "I've already put things in motion to abduct Markus and bring him to a safe house where we'll drain him of everything he knows before I personally end his life. This is not something I'm willing to delegate."

***

At a quarter to ten, Dunmoore went up to the rooftop landing pad where the shuttle provided by 1st Fleet waited to fly her to the Palace of the Stars. As always, Guthren was close behind her. The two Security operatives detailed to watch her back were already at the Palace's landing pad, making sure it was clear.

She and Guthren climbed aboard and strapped into jump seats behind the pilot rather than sit in the passenger compartment. Somehow, she felt less vulnerable on the flight deck, even though it was an illusion. If a surface-to-air missile struck the small spacecraft, it didn't matter where she sat. All she could hope was that by taking a shuttle rather than a ground car, she'd confuse the opposition long enough to make it there and back.

Dunmoore wished she were already on Caledonia, far from Earth, but she still had much to do before leaving.

The shuttle rose vertically until it was five hundred meters above the ground, then it changed from vertical to horizontal flight and covered the twenty kilometers within a few minutes, settling on the Palace's rooftop pad seven minutes before ten. Her two bodyguards were waiting by the door leading to the stairs and gave her a thumbs up, indicating everything was clear. She and Guthren climbed out, joined them and, with one leading the way and the other following behind the chief, they made their way down to the second floor and Lauzier's office.

When they entered the antechamber, Johan Holden, Lauzier's executive assistant, rose from behind his desk and dipped his head in greeting.

"Welcome, Admiral Dunmoore. The SecGen will see you right away. Your escort can wait here if they wish."

"Thank you."

Guthren cleared his throat and said, in a low voice, "I'll take your beret, sir."

Dunmoore immediately understood it was so she couldn't salute Lauzier, Guthren's way of ensuring she didn't visibly subordinate herself to the SecGen. She handed it to him, then followed Holden through the inner door.

Lauzier was sitting behind her immense desk and didn't rise as Dunmoore entered. She merely watched her approach with expressionless eyes.

"Good morning, Madame." Dunmoore stopped three paces in front of the desk and nodded politely.

"Good morning, Admiral. Please." Lauzier made a languid gesture toward the chairs across from her.

Dunmoore took a seat, then met Lauzier's steady gaze with her own. "What is it you wanted to discuss with me, Madame? I assure you I will carry on Grand Admiral Kowalski's work in its entirety."

"And that, Admiral, is what I'm afraid of. You see, Grand Admiral Kowalski has been directly opposing my administration's efforts in bringing the Fleet under greater civilian control."

"I'm well aware of that, Madame. And I intend to continue her efforts. The Fleet will not come under your direct control, so you can expand the Centralist effort and intimidate the OutWorlds into agreeing. On the contrary. We will continue to insulate ourselves from your politics so we can remain focused on our sacred calling — to defend and protect humanity against all enemies, alien and human." Dunmoore emphasized the last word, and her determined gaze dared Lauzier to deny the mission statement.

"I'm sorry to hear that, Admiral. Of course, Grand Admiral Kowalski's appointment during good behavior means I can't remove her unless she grossly abuses her position. You, not so much. Should you defy me, I can and will dismiss you as acting commander-in-chief of the Armed Forces."

"And replace me with who, Madame? Not a single admiral in the Fleet will accept the appointment."

Lauzier gave her an icy smile.

"I wouldn't be too sure about that."

Dunmoore returned the smile.

"Oh, let's be realistic here, Madame. You have no control over the Armed Forces. None whatsoever. We are our own entity now, just like a sovereign star system. In fact, we own one of those as well. Your administration may set a defense policy, and we might even accept it. But nothing more. We decide who becomes Grand Admiral, acting or substantive."

"Those are mutinous words, Dunmoore. Take care I don't have you arrested."

"For what? Stating the truth?"

"People faced arrest for speaking the truth long before humanity's first diaspora across the stars. And they will continue to be arrested long after we're both dead." Dunmoore saw a flash of anger in Lauzier's eyes and knew she was finally getting to her. "But that's beside the point. I am Secretary General of the Commonwealth, and thus, above everyone else, you and the Fleet included. You will obey me."

It was time to disabuse her of any notion she controlled the Fleet.

"No, Madame. I will not."

— Twenty-Seven —

"Neither I nor any other Fleet officer will obey you, Madame. You're a power-hungry sociopath who'll plunge the Commonwealth into a third Migration War if we let you. Your zeal for Centralism makes you the greatest danger to humanity in a long time."

The flash of anger Dunmoore had seen in Lauzier's eyes turned to full-fledged fury.

"I bed your pardon? How dare you sit here in my office, accusing me of being a sociopath and a threat to humanity?" Despite her controlled tone, Dunmoore could see she was on the verge of losing her temper. "You are insubordinate beyond belief, Admiral Dunmoore."

"A minute ago, I thought I was mutinous, and mutiny is a greater charge than insubordination. Which is it to be, Madame?"

Lauzier smacked the flat of her hand on the desk, sending a loud crack to echo off the office walls.

"That's it." She breathed in deeply through flared nostrils, staring balefully at Dunmoore. "I'm having you arrested on charges of mutiny, insubordination, and sedition."

Lauzier touched a control embedded in her desktop.

"SSB officers will take you into custody momentarily."

"Oh, I doubt that." Dunmoore smirked. "The SSB can't arrest me, and you can't charge me. You have no evidence."

"I've recorded this conversation, and it's all the proof I need."

Dunmoore reached into a tunic pocket and withdrew a thin rectangle no bigger than her palm.

"This is the most powerful personal jammer in existence, Madame. You have nothing."

Lauzier compressed her lips, fighting to retain what was left of her composure. No one had ever contradicted her in such a manner. All her life, she had been treated with the utmost respect due to a person of her pedigree and position. After a few deep breaths, Lauzier touched the intercom.

"Where are the SSB agents on duty, Johan? I summoned them via the emergency call."

A voice came on. Not that of Holden, but one of the Fleet Security men.

"Sorry, Madame Secretary General, but the SSB operatives have experienced a delay. They'll be free to enter your office once the admiral has left."

"What?" Lauzier's eyes narrowed as she speared Dunmoore with them.

"We figured you called them to arrest the admiral. They'll wake up in about fifteen to twenty minutes."

"This. Is. Intolerable." Lauzier glared at Dunmoore.

"This is the new reality, Sara. You and I, we're equals. Your responsibility is to govern the Commonwealth's civil society. Mine is to protect it, including from you and your ilk. Now, if there was nothing else, I'll leave you to contemplate things. I have a Fleet to run."

Lauzier made a dismissive hand gesture, not trusting herself to speak. Dunmoore stood and left her office without another word. She found two SSB agents lying on the floor with Guthren seated nearby and both Security operatives standing by the other door. Johan Holden was back at his desk, still looking a tad shaken by events.

"Time to head out, gentlemen," she said, taking her beret from Guthren and putting it back on her head. "By the way, what did you do to the SSB guys?"

One of the two bodyguards said, "We hit them with needlers when they refused to take no for an answer, sir. They'll wake up in fifteen or thereabouts."

"Is that what you carry? Needlers with non-lethal, short-acting ammo?" Dunmoore asked as they headed for the stairs.

"No, sir. We also carry blasters for the more complex problems."

Dunmoore chuckled.

"Is that what you call deadly use of force? Complex problems? Nice."

Within moments, they were aboard the shuttle and lifting off. Ten minutes later, Dunmoore was back in her temporary office calling up her work queue. She'd barely touched the first file when Holt showed up.

"Got a moment?" He asked.

"For you, always. What's on your mind?"

Dunmoore gestured at the chairs in front of her desk.

Holt sat and crossed his left ankle over his right knee.

"We need to send Kathryn to Caledonia. I spoke with the attending physician just now, and he says she'll not be fit for a few months. By then, it should be almost over. Best we see to her safety while she's vulnerable. She'll be stuck in an ICU bed for another two weeks or so, then be released with strict orders to stay home and rest. That will make her a sitting duck. I thought you might break it to her."

"Kathryn won't be happy. But I suppose you're right. Do we wait until she's out of the ICU or have her travel in a ship's intensive care unit?"

"I'd be a lot happier if she left as soon as possible."

"Okay. I'll determine which ship is nearest and can be redirected to Earth since I assume you'd prefer she doesn't travel in a 1st Fleet unit."

"That would be best since the policy for the last ten years has been to transfer the least politically reliable personnel from our point of view into 1st Fleet, where they can't harm the outlying sectors."

"That's what I thought. I'll speak with Kathryn tomorrow morning when I visit her."

The next day, at oh-eight hundred, Dunmoore entered Kowalski's hospital room and found her sitting up, though still heavily bandaged.

"And how are you today?"

Kowalski grimaced. "They're reducing the painkillers, so it feels like a combat car has repeatedly run over me."

"And it appears you'll be out of commission for a few months."

"Yeah. We'll see about that."

"You'll see about it on Caledonia, Kathryn. We're evacuating you aboard the cruiser *Cordoba*, which has ICU beds. It'll be here in four days."

"Now, wait just a minute—"

Dunmoore stilled her outburst with a raised hand.

"Zeke figures you're too vulnerable in your current state and will continue to be so for weeks, if not longer. I'll handle the rest of the plan and be the last flag officer to leave Earth aboard the last ship headed for Caledonia. It really is for the best. We need you to lead us through the next few years, and we can't risk an assassin getting lucky. Not in your enfeebled condition."

Kowalski tried to give Dunmoore a stern glare, but it barely registered, thanks to her puffy eyes, swollen cheeks, and bandaged skull.

"And you still look as bad as you feel," Dunmoore added. "Something that won't change for a while."

"Oh, all right. I can see you're bound and determined to have me away from here and know better than to balk."

"Good. We have four days to go over the plan one last time and fine-tune things. After that, I'll be flying solo."

***

Four days later, during which Dunmoore heard nothing from Lauzier or the SecDef, one of *Cordoba*'s shuttles configured as a medevac landed behind the base hospital. Three antigrav stretcher beds were quickly pushed through the hospital doors and up the shuttle's aft ramp — Kowalski, her aide, and the chief petty officer of the Armed Forces.

Dunmoore accompanied Kowalski into the craft's spacious passenger compartment, where the stretcher beds were secured to the deck.

"I've got this, Kathryn. Don't worry, and take the time to rest when you get there. You can work on the next steps while I'm finishing up here.

"I know you'll do just fine. See you on the other side." Kowalski reached out to take Dunmoore's hand and gave it a quick, if weak, squeeze. "And remember — when Zeke says duck, you damn well duck."

"Have no fear. Enjoy your trip to the Fleet's new home. Hopefully, it'll become our final shore."

Dunmoore walked down the aft ramp again and headed for the hospital along with the staff that had brought the stretchers out. Moments after they passed through the doors, she heard the shuttle's thrusters spool up. It lifted vertically under full emergency power and vanished into the low cloud cover within moments.

Suddenly, Dunmoore felt a great weight settle on her shoulders, as the full realization of having to carry out the plan's next phase by herself finally sank in.

Back in her office, she settled at the virtual workstation to review her notes one more time because tomorrow, Dunmoore would face the full Senate to trigger the next phase.

But before she could do so, an item in her work queue caught her attention. It was a terse note from MacKay-Sankuno's Waku Yutani informing her that his company would submit their bid for the naval targeting sensor upgrade to the Defense Department's Procurement Branch as requested by the SecDef.

Dunmoore let out a soft sigh. A shame MacKay-Sankuno had decided to go that way. Their solution was the best, technically speaking. But both Nostromo and Geiger-Cobb could come up with something similar. MacKay-Sankuno had just become the first object lesson to the defense contracting community that military procurement came under the Fleet, not the SecDef.

She wrote a quick reply telling him the Armed Forces would no longer consider his company for any bids and that the solution he presented to the SecDef would never be accepted by the Fleet. With any luck, MacKay-Sankuno's top leadership would have their heads handed to them by the board of directors or, better yet, the shareholders.

And now, it was time to prepare for the Senate.

— Twenty-Eight —

Paul Markus was not a happy man. He assumed the attempt on Kowalski and Dunmoore's lives was orchestrated by the mysterious mercenary sect since it had been a suicide attack. If so, it had failed. Kowalski was still alive, albeit in critical condition, while Dunmoore was walking around as if nothing had happened. Holt? He wasn't even there.

They'd blown their best chance and weren't likely to get another. At least Holt and his people couldn't trace the attack back to him, and since the three targets were still alive, the nine million in escrow wasn't going anywhere. Still, it had been five days, and nothing stirred in Fleet Security, at least nothing he or the SSB could see, which made him a tad nervous. Holt's sort were at their most dangerous when they appeared to be quiet.

He'd kept a low profile since hiring the assassins but decided to take one of his lady friends out to supper that evening. Markus chose a place in the old part of town, *Le Genevois*, which had the enviable reputation of being named one of the top fifty restaurants on Earth. Usually, reservations had to be made months in advance, but the Secretary of Public Safety needed only to call a few hours ahead, and a table would be waiting for him.

He and his friend, a chic, slender brunette half his age, arrived at the fashionable hour of nineteen thirty and enjoyed a five-course meal — consommé, smoked lake trout, wild boar tenderloin, cheese platter, and torte. The meal, exquisitely prepared, was well worth the extravagant cost.

They consumed two bottles of wine, one white and one red, and felt quite celebratory by the meal's conclusion. Markus tried to inveigle her into accompanying him home for a little after-dinner fun, but she demurred, and they separated at the restaurant's front door. He headed for his car while she walked to her nearby apartment. It was a clear night, stars shimmering overhead, the lights of the city reflecting off the lake's surface, and Markus felt pleased with himself as he walked to the underground garage.

Once there, he descended two levels, located his car, and unlocked it. He climbed aboard, but before he could start the power plant, he sensed a pinprick on his neck, and everything turned black.

The car drove out of the underground garage a few minutes later and headed northwest into the mountains and a secluded safe house used by Fleet Security.

Markus woke a little over two hours later and groggily looked around through unfocused eyes. He gradually became aware he was naked and attached to a bare metal chair, ankles fastened to its legs, arms tied together at the wrists behind the chair back. He was in a small pool of light, the rest of the space beyond it black as night. What little of the floor he could see appeared to be bare concrete. His mouth felt as if someone had filled it with cotton, and the aftertaste was horrible.

He feebly croaked out a "Hello?"

However, it remained without a response, and he concluded that no one else was present in the room.

As the minutes ticked by and he threw off the last of the knockout drug-induced disorientation, his anxiety rose to a fever pitch. He'd never been in a situation such as this, completely helpless and at the mercy of whoever had captured him.

After what seemed like an eternity, he heard a door open in the darkness, and footsteps moved toward him, though they stopped before reaching the pool of light.

"Paul Markus, Commonwealth Secretary of Public Safety," a disembodied voice said, coming from everywhere at once. "Welcome."

"Who are you?" Markus asked in a shaky voice. "What do you want?"

"First, I need to know if you've been conditioned against chemical interrogation."

"Yes."

"Then we'll do this the old-fashioned way. I want everything you have about the off-world religious mercenaries you hired to assassinate Grand Admiral Kowalski, Admiral Dunmoore, and Vice Admiral Holt."

"I did no such thing."

An electric shock, neither mild nor particularly strong, coursed through Markus' body.

"Hey!"

"Again, tell me about those mercenaries."

"You're torturing me. That's against the law."

The moment those words left his mouth, Markus knew how ridiculous he sounded.

"Yes, we are, and yes, it is." The voice seemed amused. "But that's neither here nor there. Tell me about the mercenaries."

Markus didn't immediately reply, and a second shock, stronger this time, made him gasp.

"I have nothing to say to you, whoever you are."

A third shock, even stronger, made Markus cry out in agony.

"Okay, okay. I'll tell you," he said once he'd recovered his breath.

The words tumbled from Markus' mouth, condemning him, though he didn't know it yet. He gave his interrogators everything, including the subspace address to initiate contact. When he fell silent, Markus looked around, trying to pierce the darkness, but in vain.

Then he heard footsteps again, and a figure appeared from the shadows.

"Holt!"

The vice admiral was in dark civilian clothes and had his hands in his pockets as he studied Markus.

"You're quite the psycho, aren't you, Paul? Putting a hit out on me and my bosses to please Sara Lauzier. A psycho who's infatuated with an even worse one. Well, you're about to merge with the Infinite Void, so you won't try again."

"What do you mean?" Markus's voice rose in pitch with alarm. "You're going to kill me in cold blood? I told you everything."

"And doomed yourself by doing so. You're guilty of arranging the attempted assassination of three of the highest-ranking officers in the Armed Forces. There's no way I can let you live, and believe me, you're not the first I've dispatched into the Great Unknown."

Holt's hand reached under his left arm, and a small-bore blaster appeared. He let it dangle loosely at his side.

"We'll make your body and your car disappear. You'll have been seen entering the underground garage, and your car has been spotted leaving it. Then you've dropped off the map because we switched off the central traffic control transponder and destroyed your communicator. No one knows where you ended up, and this place is far from Geneva. You'll simply have vanished into thin air. Oh, I'm sure Axel Renouf, your former permanent undersecretary, will figure we did it. Sara Lauzier will probably do so as well. But we're extremely good at leaving no evidence behind."

"No. Please." Markus' plea came out in a quivering tone. "Let's discuss this."

"You know, for a sociopathic bully, you sure caved fast. I guess it's true what they say about your sort. You always fold when confronted with a more powerful adversary." Holt raised his blaster and placed the tip of the barrel against Markus' forehead. "Goodbye, Paul."

Markus lost control of his bladder at that moment, and Holt stepped back in disgust before pulling the trigger. A small, neat hole appeared just above the bridge of Markus' nose as the blaster round flash fried his brain, killing him instantly, and he slumped as far as his restraints permitted.

Within moments, three men, also clad in dark civilian clothes, entered the room and undid the restraints holding Markus in the chair. They then picked him up and carried him away for disposal in a body composting box. Eventually, they would spread out what remained in the forest far from the safe house.

The car would be driven to Marseille and abandoned near the old port. There, scavengers were sure to strip it for parts within a few hours, leaving nothing behind.

This wasn't the first time Holt and his Fleet Security people had made dangerous humans disappear. But he sincerely hoped it was the last time. After all, law enforcement shouldn't carry out extra-judicial executions, no matter how warranted they were.

He climbed aboard his car and left the safe house for good. They wouldn't use it again, not in the brief time they had remaining on Earth. He made it back to his residence on the base shortly before oh-three-hundred and poured himself a large glass of whiskey, silently toasting his upcoming deliverance. Eliminating scum like Markus was doing humanity a favor, but he still didn't like it and hoped he never would.

Fortunately, he quickly fell into a dreamless sleep and was back in his office by oh-eight hundred as if nothing had happened during the night. Paul Markus wouldn't be missed for another twenty-four hours at least.

— Twenty-Nine —

Dunmoore looked up from the guest lectern and let her eyes roam over the Senate room while the senators filed in, chatting with each other. The four tiers of seats and small desks used by the senators were in a three-quarters circle, with the guest lectern and the President of the Senate's chair occupying the fourth quarter.

It was originally called the Assembly Hall and sat on the third floor of the Palace's main building. A vast, high-ceilinged space, it boasted an immense, latticed skylight providing natural illumination during the daytime. Frescos depicting scenes from distant antiquity covered three of the four walls, along with spectator galleries capable of accommodating hundreds. These were filled to capacity since a Grand Admiral rarely addressed the Senate in plenary session, and no one knew what subjects Dunmoore would raise.

At Kowalski's insistence, Dunmoore wore the five stripes of her acting rank on her service dress uniform cuffs — a broad one with four narrower stripes, the last topped by the Navy's executive curl. Later, when she changed back into working uniform, she'd wear the five stars on her collar.

The senators finally settled at their desks, and the myriad conversations died away as the President of the Senate entered and took his place in front of his chair.

"Honorable Senators," his voice filled the vast room, "I regret to inform you that Grand Admiral Kathryn Kowalski, who was supposed to address us today, cannot do so as she has been gravely injured in an attack by persons unknown. Appearing in her stead is Acting Grand Admiral Siobhan Dunmoore, who will speak about matters of grave import for the Commonwealth's future. In keeping with our traditions, save your questions and comments for the very end."

A brief fuss in one of the galleries attracted Dunmoore's attention, and she saw Sara Lauzier take a seat overlooking the hall directly in front and above her. Interesting. Lauzier wasn't hiding her interest in what Dunmoore had to say behind flunkies doing her bidding.

"Admiral." The President of the Senate sat. "The floor is yours."

"Thank you, Mister President. Honorable Senators, it is with great humility that I stand before you today."

Dunmoore felt a brief moment of pleasure at the strength and steadiness of her voice. If truth be told, she was a tad nervous at addressing humanity's top legislators, an audience of which she knew little to nothing. It was a far cry from speaking in front of a room filled with flag officers.

"What I am about to present will no doubt be controversial for some of you. Perhaps even many. But as the old saying goes, needs must when the devil drives. And the devil, in this case, is the future of the Commonwealth as a united human polity. I think everyone is aware of the increasing tensions permeating the body politic at the federal and sovereign star systems level. Of the battles fought between them because their visions differ radically, especially in the OutWorlds. And I'm here to tell you that left unchecked, these tensions and battles will lead to a third Migration War, possibly more murderous than the two previous ones put together."

Dunmoore paused to gauge the audience's reaction and saw sagacious nods from OutWorld senators, frowns on the faces of Home Worlders, and a growing rumble of conversation among the spectators.

The President of the Senate rapped his gavel twice and called for silence from the galleries lest he have them cleared.

"The Commonwealth Armed Forces, humanity's ultimate guardians, have watched the discord among star systems and with Earth grow at an alarming rate since the end of the Shrehari War. And we've concluded that we must not be used by any party to impose its will. Not the Commonwealth government, nor those of the various sovereign star systems and their groupings."

A fresh surge of muttering rose from the galleries, and the President of the Senate had to rap his gavel again.

"As a result, the Armed Forces will focus on their core mission — defend and protect humanity against all enemies, alien and human — to the exclusion of anything else. You may or may not be aware, but Armed Forces HQ has been quietly moving to Caledonia over the last few years. That move is almost complete. Grand Admiral Kowalski herself left for Caledonia yesterday, though she is still on the injured list. Within a few months, 1st Fleet, the 1st Marine Division, and the Terra Regiment will take over the headquarters here on Earth, forming the star system's sole garrison."

"By moving away from Earth, we are proclaiming our independence from the politics that permeate this world. The Armed Forces will exist alongside the Commonwealth's civilian administration and not subordinate to it. We will ensure said administration governs for the good of all humanity and quash any attempts at subverting the constitutional order established after the Second Migration War."

Dunmoore pointedly looked up at Lauzier and held her gaze for a few seconds. Several senators turned in their chairs to see where she was looking, and when they noticed the SecGen, they knew what Dunmoore meant.

"This is fact, not fancy, let alone aspiration, Honorable Senators. The Armed Forces are now equal to the administrative, legislative, and judicial branches. We are the fourth branch of what makes up the Commonwealth government writ large. Like the other branches, we will, of course, turn to you for funding. But that funding will be non-discretionary. Over the coming weeks, I intend to sit with the Budget Committee and hammer out the processes which will govern it, one which you will then turn into legislation adopted by a majority."

A few of the OutWorld senators were openly smiling while the known Centralists among the Home World senators increasingly fumed at her casual erasure of the gains they'd made in recent years.

"In effect, it means the Armed Forces will not take orders from any other branch of government. We will, of course, accept defense policy suggestions so long as they support our overriding mission. But that mission is the sole guide for the Armed Forces from now on. There will be no more interference in our operations by anyone."

Again, she scanned her audience's reactions and if anything, the Centralists appeared on the verge of apoplexy.

"However, the Armed Forces cannot continue to be engaged in interstellar law enforcement and the Special Security Bureau was never a proper law enforcement agency in any case. As a result, we are setting up an independent Constabulary that will fill the role of interstellar police and report to the Senate, not the administration. Members of the Fleet Security Branch will initially staff that Constabulary after they're transferred to the new organization, which will be commanded by the current Head of the Security Branch, who will become the first Chief Constable."

The OutWorld senators could contain themselves no longer and applauded loudly to the scowls of their Home World colleagues. Many shouted the traditional approval cry, "Hear, hear."

Dunmoore met Senator Bregman's eyes and saw they positively sparkled with merriment. She was giving the OutWorlds everything they'd dreamed of, most importantly of all, an end to Centralism — at least the threat it might be imposed by force. Sara Lauzier wouldn't give up easily and may well find other means to impose Earth's primacy.

When the applause died down, Dunmoore declared, "Caledonia is the Armed Forces home now, and the Colonial Office will no longer treat it as a Commonwealth dependency. It is a self-governing sovereign star system, albeit one that will not send any senators to Earth. We deliberately chose to remain unrepresented as a way of emphasizing our focus on our mission. Politics will have no role on Caledonia, and an elected star system government will not exist."

She looked up at Lauzier again and saw a tight-lipped face as if the latter was repressing fury at Dunmoore's announcements.

"That was what I came here to say, Honorable Senators. I am at your disposal for questions or comments."

Dunmoore knew Lauzier had some choice words she'd like to say to her, but the SecGen couldn't speak in the Senate unless its president invited her to the guest lectern.

Senator Bregman stood up, and the President of the Senate recognized him.

"Grand Admiral Dunmoore, thank you for that most illuminating speech. I'm sure I speak for many, if not most, of my honorable colleagues when I say it's about time the Armed Forces declared their independence."

Shouts of "Hear, hear" and "Shame" in almost equal numbers, illustrating the sharp divide in the Senate, greeted his comment. She suspected that he had carefully chosen his words to do just that.

When the shouts calmed down, he continued.

"I do not doubt that your actions will put a damper on the more excitable spirits seeking to bring about political change faster than they should. If they should at all. I would call for a vote of support in this august chamber, but I'm not sure I'd get a majority voting in favor. Besides, it doesn't matter. You've done what you set out to do. Nothing anyone here says or does will change that. Thank you, Grand Admiral."

Bregman sat, and the senior senator for Pacifica, an avowed Centralist, jumped to his feet. The President recognized him, and he immediately cast a baleful glare at Dunmoore.

"Admiral, contrary to my honorable colleague, I believe I speak for a majority of the Senate when I call your actions irresponsible and harmful to the Commonwealth. I would like a vote on the matter by this august chamber." He looked to the President. "I hereby formally demand a vote of confidence on Admiral Dunmoore's speech to be carried out forthwith."

About half of the senators nodded in agreement. The other half shook their heads.

"And to what effect?" The President of the Senate asked. "To show approval or disapproval? It's a bit late for that. Grand Admiral Dunmoore said the deal is done. Armed Forces HQ is now on Caledonia and conducts operations as a separate branch of the government."

"Still, I would like the Senate to vote on the matter."

"Do we have two-thirds approval to hold an unscheduled vote?" The President let his eyes roam over the assembled senators. "Please indicate whether you favor such a poll."

They busied themselves at their desks, voting electronically, and within moments, the results appeared on a large screen behind the President as well as on his desk.

"The proposal to hold a vote of confidence concerning Acting Grand Admiral Dunmoore's speech does not receive approval. Next question or comment."

The junior senator for Arcadia stood up and received recognition.

"Grand Admiral, I'm curious how you plan on handling the Armed Forces budget. The Senate could effectively starve you of funds should it wish to do so and make you submit to the administration once more. The same goes for your Constabulary."

Dunmoore let a half smile play on her lips.

"If the Senate starves us of funds so we're encouraged to submit to the administration, it will quickly find itself dissolved and replaced by a more reasonable legislature."

Her bald statement drew an eruption from the galleries and the senators themselves.

"That sounds very much like a threat," the senator said in a loud voice, to be heard over the hubbub.

"It wouldn't be the first time in human history that co-equal branches of a government threatened each other's existence over fundamental differences, sir. In some cases, they actually carried out those threats."

Shouts of "Shame" resounded from the Home World senators, accompanied by the pounding of fists on their desks, and the President of the Senate rapped his gavel repeatedly until the noise died down.

"But your question is purely theoretical, sir," Dunmoore continued. "The sovereign star systems you represent, including Arcadia, would never allow you to deprive the Navy of the funding it requires to protect the star lanes and the planetary high orbitals."

"The sovereign star systems could always field their own navies instead."

Dunmoore chuckled.

"The Commonwealth constitution, approved after the Second Migration War, forbids star systems from having any military beyond a ground forces national guard to prevent them from fighting each other as they did during the war. And this august chamber will not find a two-thirds vote to reopen that constitution."

She glanced up at Lauzier again and felt the urge to wink at her, something she barely suppressed.

The President of the Senate stood, effectively cutting off all other questions and comments.

"Thank you for coming today, Grand Admiral. It was a most illuminating speech, no matter what one's thoughts about it are."

Dunmoore nodded at him, turned on her heels, and left the Senate chamber, happy that the ordeal was over.

— Thirty —

Sara Lauzier, Secretary General of the Commonwealth, walked back to her office suite fulminating with fury, both at Dunmoore's outrageous declarations and the support shown by OutWorld senators. Apes, the lot of them, barking 'hear, hear' on command, with that vile Bregman leading their chants.

She wanted to slam her office door behind her to vent some of the anger she felt, but such a display wouldn't be proper for humanity's leader. Lauzier merely told her executive assistant she didn't wish to be disturbed for the next hour.

Once alone, she let the full course of her fury run free as she paced in front of the tall windows. How could Dunmoore stand in front of the entire Senate and declare the Armed Forces to be a fourth branch of government, independent of the other three?

Lauzier supposed she could bring the matter to the Commonwealth Supreme Court, but Dunmoore would reject any finding other than the one she wanted.

How did things escalate in this manner with no one noticing? The very notion was inconceivable, yet it had happened, shattering her Centralist dreams. Without a Fleet to enforce her will, she had only the SSB, yet it wasn't nearly enough. And with almost half the Senate firmly behind Dunmoore, she wouldn't get the two-thirds majority to ram through constitutional amendments voiding her actions.

Perhaps she should simply assume dictatorial powers and dissolve the Senate. She wouldn't be the first head of state to do so in human history. That way, she'd be much better placed to bring the Fleet back under her control.

Lauzier stopped to gaze out a window, smiling at her faint reflection in the pane of transparent aluminum. The notion was worth exploring.

***

"Paul Markus, Commonwealth Secretary of Public Safety, merged with the Infinite Void last night," Holt announced as he entered Dunmoore's office. He dropped into a chair across from Dunmoore's desk.

"I presume you took care of the merger?"

"Yes. I personally pulled the trigger. He confessed to hiring the mercenary sect from Nabhka after Leon Pannetier pulled out of the job. He paid them nine million creds for the three of us."

"The three of us? This means he targeted you as well. Interesting."

"Isn't it? I should have felt flattered, but it just annoyed me. The money Markus paid is in an escrow account pending successful completion, but my people are working on extracting it. In the meantime, I am looking at ways of calling the mercs off since Markus is dead. They're apparently persistent beyond belief. I expect Axel Renouf to call me about Markus' disappearance once word reaches him, by the way. He's smart enough to figure we might have had something to do with it. I'll probably tell him everything as a warning that no one is beyond our reach. How did your speech in front of the Senate go?"

Dunmoore gave him a quick summary, including Lauzier's reactions as seen from a distance.

Holt chuckled at that last bit.

"I'll bet she's still fuming, wishing she could break a kitchen's worth of crockery. If she didn't hate you before, she surely does now, and with the sort of passion only a true sociopath can muster."

Dunmoore let out an indelicate snort.

"I really don't care. There's nothing she can do to turn back the clock."

"But she can still decide to have you terminated, damn the consequences, and the SSB will carry out the hit if she forces them. We are uncertain of the exact number of their agents operating covertly at Fleet HQ, which is why the truce held such significance."

"You really think the SSB would have someone on the inside take a shot at me?"

Holt nodded.

"It's a possibility we can't discount. Then there are the people who tried to kill Ulli Radames."

"They're not on the inside."

"No, but with them, it makes potentially three different parties gunning for you."

"For us, Zeke. The mercs are already after you. If the SSB comes for me, they'll go for you at the same time, and that third party? They already targeted one three-star."

"I guess I might have to move up the timetable on Operation Night of the Long Knives."

"Not quite yet. Let's let things develop some more."

***

"Is anyone aware of Paul's whereabouts?" Lauzier looked around the table at her cabinet secretaries, who sat in their appointed spots save for Markus, conspicuous by his absence.

When they shook their heads, she turned to her executive assistant.

"Track him down for me, will you, Johan?"

"Yes, Madame." Holden rose from the small desk he occupied at the back of the cabinet room during meetings and left.

"In the meantime, let's proceed with business."

Eventually, Holden returned, bent over Lauzier's shoulder, and whispered, "No one knows where he is, Madame. He's not at home or the office, his car is nowhere to be found, nor is his communicator pinging a signal."

Lauzier's face hardened at the news.

"Thank you, Johan. Please inform Renouf and ask him to search for Paul."

Markus was her fiercest loyalist and the most useful of her cabinet members. If anything untoward had happened to him...

She turned to the Secretary for Transportation.

"Anything new on your proposal to create a Space Guard?"

"No, Madame. The Fleet isn't being cooperative, and we need its help if the scheme is to succeed."

When the cabinet meeting ended, Lauzier had Holden connect her with Renouf.

"What are your thoughts on Paul's unexpected disappearance, Axel?"

Renouf grimaced.

"I'm working on a theory based on Paul wanting to terminate Grand Admiral Kowalski for holding up your agenda. My predecessor shot down the idea of the SSB helping him do so."

"He always did look out for me."

"Indeed, Madame. The failed attempt on Kowalski and Admiral Dunmoore could well indicate he found someone to do it, and Fleet Security, in turn, traced the attack back to him. They can be extremely ruthless, which is why neither I nor my predecessors want to tangle with them."

"The Fleet might be responsible for making a Commonwealth cabinet secretary vanish? That's what you're saying?"

"Yes, Madame. And if they did it, we'll never find out. They will have disposed of his car, his communicator, and his body in a manner we cannot trace. His disappearance will most likely remain a mystery for all times."

"Can you speak with Fleet Security's head — Holt, was it? And find out."

"Certainly."

"Then, I want options on removing Holt and Dunmoore permanently. Kowalski is probably beyond your reach by now."

Renouf inclined his head, though he didn't relish telling her what would happen to him and the SSB should they make an attempt on the two admirals' lives.

"I'd better get on with it, then, Madame."

Once Lauzier had cut the link, Renouf sat back in his chair and sighed. His regret at taking the job of the SSB's director general was growing fast. He didn't want to die for Lauzier's sake, nor for anyone else's, yet that's what would happen if the SSB carried out Lauzier's wishes.

Renouf steeled himself and called Holt over a secure link. To his surprise, Holt picked up right away.

"I figured you'd be reaching out to me, Axel."

A frown creased Renouf's forehead.

"How come?"

"Your boy Paul Markus did a vanishing act, didn't he?"

"Yes."

"And you're curious about my potential involvement in it."

Renouf nodded.

"Well, your instincts are good, Axel. We made him disappear. Of course, he earned it. Do you want to understand the reason?"

"You know I do, Holt. Otherwise you and I wouldn't be speaking."

"That attempt on Grand Admiral Kowalski and Admiral Dunmoore — he commissioned it. It wasn't the first time he hired hitters to try and take them out, but the Marseille mob wised up when I spoke to them. The suicide attackers are a different story. In any case, we took Markus to one of our safe houses and interrogated him. He confessed to everything. And then," Holt grinned at Renouf, "it was exit stage left for poor old

Paul. As you might understand, no one will ever find a trace of him."

Renouf's eyes narrowed as he studied Holt.

"Why are you so gleefully telling me this?"

"Consider it a warning, Axel. If we can reach out and touch the most powerful member of Sara Lauzier's cabinet, we can reach out to anyone else in the Commonwealth, Madame Lauzier included. And we will if you or she makes it necessary."

"I really can't believe you're saying that, Holt. You and Dunmoore are utterly out of control and must be stopped."

"And who will stop us? We belong to the most powerful branch of government, the one that can actually impose conditions on the other branches by force."

Renouf shook his head.

"You've got to be having me on."

Holt grinned at him.

"Nope. It's a fact. Please give Sara my love when you report to her on Markus' demise. Cheerio."

The display blanked out as Holt cut the link. Renouf didn't even bother to see if the usual call recording had worked. He understood that Holt's words would be distorted beyond recognition and beyond an AI's capacity to reconstruct.

***

That evening, Holt and Dunmoore dined together in the latter's residence on autochef packs that had been carefully scrutinized by sensors to make sure nothing untoward was lurking inside them.

"You know," she said after swallowing the last chunk of chicken in pineapple sauce, "these pre-made meals are good. But I miss eating food prepared from scratch, even in the officer's mess, which, while not a fine dining establishment, compares favorably to the city's better restaurants."

"I just miss eating with my family." Holt let out a soft sigh.

"Did you hear from them recently? Are they adapting well to Caledonia?"

"Yes, and yes, even though my kiddos were uprooted after a long time here." A crooked smile appeared. "But there are no more mandatory so-called museum visits to drink in the splendor of ages past. Or at least that's what my eldest said in so many words."

"She's not much for studying the past, is she?"

"Up to a point, yes. But the school was pushing it a bit too much." Holt toyed with the stem of his wine glass, then tilted his head to one side. "Do you ever regret not having a family?"

Dunmoore considered the question for a bit, then shook her head.

"No. You, Gregor, Kathryn, Kurt, you're my family. Besides, I'm wedded to my career."

"Which will eventually end in a few years."

"Well," she gave him a mischievous look, "I did have the Fleet freeze a number of my ova so I could have a child once I was ready. Considering I still have decades ahead of me, making a kid or two after I retire isn't out of the question. Except I've found no one with whom I want to spend my life. One man during the war sparked my interest, but he died long ago on the mission that brought us together. We never did anything about it, of course.

I was *Stingray*'s captain at the time and couldn't afford romantic entanglements."

"A pity."

"Yes, it is." Dunmoore took a sip of wine. "But I'm married to the Navy. Can you imagine what a distraction a family would be right now? Even if they were on Caledonia? I'm probably Sara Lauzier's biggest target since my speech to the Senate. A spouse and children would be hostages to fortune. Still, with the miracle of modern medicine, I can have children in a few years from now. I just need to find a suitable father or at least a suitable sperm donor."

"You know, I think you will. I can feel it in my gut."

"And your gut is always right." Dunmoore raised her glass in salute, then drained it. "First, however, I need to survive the next few weeks. Time for dessert."

"One thing I wanted to mention. Since we have no way of contacting the suicide mercs, I think you should move out of this big, empty house and take one of the penthouse apartments on the top floor of my block. I understand they're empty with the move of most unattached senior officers to Caledonia. No need to tell anyone, and we'll have you picked up and returned in the underground garage. It'll only be for a few more weeks. That way, if they decide to attack your residence in the middle of the night, you won't be there."

"Do you really think they'd get on the base unseen?"

"Yes."

Holt's flat, single-word answer said more than an entire paragraph, and she nodded.

"Okay. I'll pack tonight."

— Thirty-One —

"Thank you for seeing me, Madame." Axel Renouf dipped his head as he entered Lauzier's office. "I'm afraid I come bearing bad news."

"Markus?" Lauzier gestured at the chairs in front of her desk, inviting Renouf to sit.

"Yes, Madame. Vice Admiral Ezekiel Holt confessed to interrogating and murdering him."

"Then you have him in custody?"

"No." Renouf shook his head. "We have no evidence. I tried recording our conversation, but he used a jammer, and there is nothing to connect Holt with Markus' disappearance other than his say-so. He told me Markus confessed to hiring the hitters who made the attempt on Kowalski and Dunmoore after his first set of assassins demurred."

"Damn it, Axel." Lauzier's eyes blazed with barely repressed rage. "I expect better of you."

"Holt said he told me about it as a warning to you and me that he could reach out and touch anyone in the Commonwealth. And he would, should we make it necessary."

"I want this damn nonsense to stop. Remove Holt and Dunmoore. I don't care how you do it or what the repercussions will be." Lauzier's harsh tone masked a growing fear that events beyond her control were happening at an alarming rate. "Just make sure they never bother us again."

"I'm not sure that's wise, Madame. Holt told me on the day of my appointment as director general that any attempt on their lives by the SSB would cause my death and those of my people. And I suppose he meant to include you in his most recent warning. I take his threats seriously, Madame. Armed Forces Security is larger than the SSB and more ruthless if its head personally terminated a senior cabinet secretary."

Lauzier speared Renouf with a stare so cold it sent a shiver down his spine. Then, a predatory smile appeared on her lips.

"If you won't do the job, I'll find someone else who will. You may go."

As he left her office, Renouf felt like someone had walked over his grave and wondered whether his time was up. After all, both of his predecessors had died suddenly of unexplained cardiac arrest when they'd disappointed Lauzier. And who would do the SecGen's dirty deeds if it wasn't the SSB? Could she have other assets? Perhaps someone in his organization should dig into Lauzier's communications, since the SSB could monitor even those she thought secure.

***

"Mikhail!" Holt smiled as Forenza's patrician face appeared on his office display. The director general of the Colonial Office's

Intelligence Service hadn't spoken to Holt since before Dunmoore took on the CNO's job, and he was glad to see him.

"Zeke, it's been a while."

"That it has, but then we're both busier than the proverbial one-armed paperhanger. What can I do for you?"

"It's more what I can do for you. But I'd rather we meet in person. How about your usual spot, by the Skanderbeg statue?"

"Considering the situation nowadays, I'd rather not leave the base unless I'm in an armored convoy or, better yet, flying from point to point in a heavy shuttle. How about you come by my place for supper tonight?"

"Sure. I can do that. What time?"

"Eighteen hundred? It'll be autochef packs, unfortunately. As you might know, my spouse and children are now on Caledonia."

"A wise move, my friend, getting them out of the line of fire. Eighteen hundred it is."

"I'll leave word at the main gate to admit you. We've locked down the base since the attempt on Kathryn and Siobhan. I'm in the senior officers' apartment block, unit two-oh-three."

"See you then."

The display went dark, though Holt stared at it for a few heartbeats longer, wondering what Forenza wanted. They weren't exactly friends. More colleagues who respected each other's intellect and abilities and found themselves consistently on the same side when fighting their secret battles. Holt had first met him on Toboso during the war, over twenty years ago, but still knew little about the man except that when he spoke, it was wise to pay attention.

Forenza showed up at the appointed time, and Holt welcomed him into his small bachelor apartment.

"You had no problems at the gate, I trust?"

"None whatsoever, but they scrutinized me and my credentials." Forenza wore casual attire - slacks, a jacket over an open-collared shirt, and loafers. "Though I'm not sure that level of security would stop a determined assassin."

"Perhaps not, but it's better than nothing. Drink?"

"Gin and tonic, if you have some." Forenza settled on the sofa in the living room while Holt busied himself in the open-plan kitchen.

"Coming right up."

Holt mixed two gins and tonic, handed one to Forenza, and sat across from him. He raised his glass.

"Skoal."

"Your health, Zeke."

Both took a sip, then settled back.

"How's business in the Colonial Office these days?"

Forenza grimaced.

"We're trying to push back against Sara Lauzier's attempts at reforming the relationship between Earth and the colonies into one of greater subservience with no independence in sight. It's a struggle. The Colonial Secretary is one of Lauzier's creatures, of course. He requires managing twenty-four-seven because he'll have flashes of genius late at night and wants to share them with everyone immediately. That they're the furthest thing from true genius doesn't faze him. I think this is the worst administration I've seen since the war. Lauzier has surrounded herself with sycophants, sociopaths, and the barely competent. It's as if she's consciously or unconsciously making sure none of her cabinet secretaries are more intelligent and more competent when it comes to public administration than she is. Or her loyalists are all sub-par, and she'll appoint no one who isn't beholden to her."

"Thankfully, the SecDef doesn't control the Armed Forces, so we're not in the same situation as you. We simply ignore him and his staff, especially the political cadre who are forbidden from entering Fleet HQ or speaking with anyone in uniform."

"Lucky you. Our secretary's political staff are an utter nuisance and think they can throw their weight around. The permanent undersecretary, a recent appointment by the secretary, lets them run rampant throughout the department. But not in my branch. I told the secretary's political chief of staff point blank that I'd shoot him if he or his pestilential gnomes interfered with the Intelligence Service. He seems to have taken me seriously." Forenza took another sip of his drink and shook his head. "It was never like this before Sara Lauzier became SecGen."

"You want to join us on Caledonia?" Holt asked with an impish grin.

Forenza let out a bark of laughter.

"It might not be a bad idea."

"I'm serious, Mikhail. You have access to assets we can only dream of. By joining forces, we'll both be that much stronger. And I can guarantee you'll have access to the Fleet's communications network."

A thoughtful expression settled on Forenza's face, and he was silent for a few moments.

"Okay. Let me think about it and speak with a few people. The Intelligence Service doesn't necessarily need to be co-located with head office."

The autochef chimed softly at that moment, and Holt drained his drink.

"Time to eat."

They traded gossip during their meal, Geneva being an inexhaustible source of scandal, scuttlebutt, and juicy rumors. But when Holt served coffee afterward, Forenza became serious.

"It's time to discuss the reason I asked to see you. Do you happen to have any sources close to Lauzier?"

Holt shook his head.

"No. Her accession took us by surprise. Do you?"

"Yes. A very close source, in fact. We infiltrated her political staff almost a decade ago." Forenza didn't mention this information was to be kept strictly confidential. He knew Holt would assume so. "My source has heard rather disturbing things from Lauzier in the last twenty-four hours. She's apparently researching legal ways to shut down the Senate and concentrate all power in her own hands."

Holt's eyebrows shot up.

"Really? Siobhan's address to the honorable senators must really have shaken her."

"Shaken? She's furious beyond anything my source has ever seen. Wonderful speech, by the way. I read the transcript with great interest. The Armed Forces as the fourth branch of government? Absolutely brilliant."

"So you approve?"

"I approve of anything that'll prevent another Migration War, and putting the Fleet beyond the administration's control will do it. Especially this feckless one."

"She wants to dissolve the Senate and take over the legislative branch herself, eh? I don't recall there being a constitutional mechanism to do it."

"There isn't. I checked. But I get the feeling that's unlikely to deter her, although I can't yet determine how she'll try." Forenza took a sip of his coffee. "I thought that if we both put our minds to it, we can figure out what she'll do and find a way of stopping her. Can you imagine the anger in the OutWorlds if she eliminates their only voices on Earth?"

"It doesn't bear thinking and might well trigger the civil war we're attempting to forestall. Why the hell does she believe dissolving the Senate is a good idea? Can't she see the consequences?"

Forenza gave Holt a half shrug.

"It's impossible to fathom the mind of a sociopath, Zeke. I don't believe she's quite sane if truth be told. She's so wedded to the Centralist ideals that it blinds her to everything else. This becoming a dictator in all but name seems like a not unexpected outgrowth."

"I'll put some of my best minds on the matter. If, between them and your people, we can't come up with something, I'll be surprised."

— Thirty-Two —

"Thank you for allowing me to join in virtually, sir." Dunmoore bowed her head at the chair of the Senate Finance Committee. "The security situation being what it is."

She was in her office but faced holograms of the committee members who, in turn, saw a life-size hologram of her sitting in front of them. The committee chair was Earth's senior senator and, therefore, a committed Centralist. He eyed her with a bitter expression on his face.

"Let us begin. You asked to meet the committee so you could expound on the way you wish us to handle the defense budget. Let me state I oppose your declaring the Armed Forces the fourth branch of government and dictating conditions, but it seems I have no choice. A majority of this committee's members want to hear what you have to say. So speak, Admiral."

"I appreciate your honesty, sir. Honorable senators, I think we agree humanity needs the Armed Forces and needs them strong and capable because the universe is filled with perils that only a well-equipped Fleet can tackle." She saw many committee members nodding. "That we declared ourselves the fourth branch of government does not change this fact, although it could be argued we are now in a better position to tackle those perils unconstrained by an administration that puts politics first. Since we agree that humanity needs the Armed Forces, what remains is discussing how the Senate will vote for funding."

"The same way we always do, Admiral," one of the other Home World senators said in a waspish tone.

"I'm sorry, Madame, but business as usual will no longer do." The senator glared at her, and Dunmoore suppressed a smile. Getting under the skin of Centralists was becoming rather enjoyable. Perhaps too much so.

"The Armed Forces are spread out far and wide and always expanding to keep pace with humanity's search for more worlds. We need long-term budgetary stability to plan effectively and carry out our mission in the most efficient manner possible. Plus, with Fleet HQ now being on Caledonia, annual budget negotiations will simply not be possible. Therefore, I propose the Senate move to a five-year cycle, with the Grand Admiral and his or her staff coming to Earth every five years to negotiate the next cycle. It balances out the need for our long-term stability with that of the Senate to exercise budgetary oversight."

"Five years?" The chair of the committee frowned. "That's rather presumptuous. Since time immemorial, the budgetary cycle has been on an annual basis."

"But why, sir? Why has it always been annual?"

Dunmoore's question stumped the senior senator from Earth because he merely sat there and stared at her. The junior senator for Dordogne chuckled.

"She's got you there, Karl. As far as I'm concerned, we don't need a one-year cycle, especially not for Defense, which has no choice but to take the long view."

"Furthermore," Dunmoore continued, "I would like an escalator clause to hike the budget year over year by a fixed percentage determined by the previous five years' increase in operating and capital costs because as the Commonwealth expands, so must the Armed Forces."

"Sounds reasonable," the Dordognais senator said before the committee chair could speak.

The chair glared at him.

"Let's not get ahead of ourselves."

"Look, Karl, she's right. We need the Fleet, and it needs stability. There's absolutely no reason we shouldn't agree to her requests. This isn't discretionary spending. Besides, there are plenty of examples during the pre-diaspora era where legislatures failed to vote annual budgets, and the world didn't end. The business of government just kept on ticking. I say we vote on whether we take Grand Admiral Dunmoore's proposals to the plenary."

"Does anyone else feel the same way?" The chair looked around at the committee's other members, his scowl deepening. "Very well. Let's vote. We have a motion on the table. Those in favor?"

Six of the committee's eleven members raised their hands.

"The motion is carried." He speared Dunmoore with his eyes. "Thank you, Admiral. That is all."

The holographic senators vanished just as her hologram disappeared at the other end, and she felt her body relax. There were surely enough Home World senators, especially those from the last few star systems colonized during the first migration wave, to vote with the OutWorlders and approve the new budget rules for the Armed Forces.

But another step in the plan was done.

***

The bells of Saint Pierre Cathedral of Geneva tolled three in the morning when two figures clad in a black so complete they were almost invisible emerged from the disused utility tunnel that ran beneath the base. They'd found it by perusing two-hundred-year-old public land surveys in the Geneva city archives, looking for a way in that bypassed the gates and the heavily guarded perimeter. Matching the survey to aerial photos of the base, they uncovered an overgrown access hatch behind the hospital, a little over a kilometer from their target.

The figures closed the hatch and rearranged the vegetation covering it to erase any trace of their passage, and, moving from dark patch to dark patch, they made their way to the residential sector, unseen by human eyes or video pickups. When they had their target in sight, one of them pulled out a sophisticated handheld sensor and aimed it.

Almost immediately, the display showed life signs in one of the bedrooms, a prone human adult breathing in and out slowly, fast asleep. He tapped his companion on the wrist in a disjointed rhythm, signaling that the target was indeed there, as expected.

They ran across the street, two black blurs, and vanished against the side of the large bungalow. A casual observer would have wondered whether he actually saw anything more than a play of shadows under the dim lights. The one with the sensor again aimed it at the house, confirming the life signs, then searching for active security measures. He found those as well — sensors embedded in the structure, live, and protecting the perimeter. Without a doubt, the sensors were linked to the base's guardhouse, which meant triggering them would bring a rapid reaction squad down on their heads.

After a few moments, he decided that Plan A was unworkable and tapped his comrade's wrist again, initiating Plan B. They moved to the back of the house, where the occupied bedroom lay, and dropped their backpacks on the ground to extract a dozen small shaped charges filled with high explosives. In quick succession, they attached those charges to the wall, level with the sleeping human form, and activated their detonators.

Then, they returned to the base hospital, still moving in the shadows, and uncovered the hatch. The first of them dropped into the tunnel while the second one pulled a small device from his pocket and switched it on. He then touched a control and followed his comrade.

Fifteen minutes later, the shaped charges blew, shredding the back of the CNO's house and extinguishing the life signs. Within moments, lights came on in the residential quarter, as the remaining inhabitants were woken by the multiple explosions that echoed over the base.

The house's sensors alerted the duty guards by reporting massive damage to its network, and a squad of military police was dispatched to the scene. At the same time, calls were made to activate the rapid reaction company from the Terra Regiment, which had moved onto the base in recent weeks.

One of those awakened was Ezekiel Holt, who immediately knew what had happened. Holt contacted the base duty officer, and he confirmed someone targeting the CNO's house. All buildings were non-flammable, so at least there was no risk of fire spreading, but when he got dressed and walked over, Holt saw the entire rear of the structure had been destroyed.

He watched the rapid reaction company form a perimeter while investigators from the base MP battalion secured the scene and lit it up with portable lamps. After a while, the lead investigator, an army major, walked over to where he stood and saluted.

"Good morning, sir. It seems that this was caused by powerful shaped charges, as evidenced by the inward direction of the explosion's force. We're going through every surveillance record to figure out how the doer or doers gained access. Fortunately, we found no human remains."

"That's because Admiral Dunmoore isn't living in these quarters anymore. I had a premonition something would eventually happen."

"Then why blow the place up if it was unoccupied? Surely, the doers ran a sensor scan before fitting the shaped charges."

A faint smile appeared on Holt's lips.

"We placed a replicant in her bed, a decoy that perfectly mimics human life signs. It gets switched on every evening and switched off every morning."

"Ah. Makes sense if you were expecting it. Well, your replicant isn't there anymore, neither is the bed or the master bedroom."

Holt's communicator buzzed for attention, and he fished it from his pocket. Siobhan. He thanked the lead investigator, who saluted again and turned on his heels.

"Yes, Admiral?"

"I imagine you've seen what there is to see at the site of the explosion by now. Care to share?"

"Your official residence suffered significant damage to its rear portion, and the replicant was disintegrated. Shaped charges, the lead investigator says. By the way, thanks for staying put. There was a time when you'd have been out here looking before I even got my shoes on."

"We all grow up one day, Zeke. When I heard the bang, I figured it was another attempt at getting me and two of those in a row makes one realize the wisdom of discretion. Do you think it was those mercs again?"

"Possibly, but hard to say. The perps ingressed and egressed without being seen, which shows a greater degree of planning and care than the previous attack, not to mention they didn't meet their deity while carrying out his holy work. It's possible that the same individuals who attempted to murder Ulli Radames were involved, given the unlikelihood of the SSB utilizing explosives. It's not their style."

"Well, at least the wannabe assassins are zero for two so far."

"Yes. But they only have to get lucky once. We have to be lucky all the time."

Dunmoore chuckled. "Trust you to pop my balloon."

— Thirty-Three —

"We found the escrow account, drained it, and left a note to the effect that the contract is null and void because the hiring party died, sir. If they check on the account regularly, as mercs would, they'll see it soon enough."

"Excellent, Peter." Holt nodded at his head of special operations, Major General Yuan. "Let's hope it'll stop the bastards from trying again."

"It almost certainly wasn't them who ripped the CNO's residence open, sir," the head of investigations said. "Different explosives entirely. The one used in the car attack was DMT-222 or a close derivative thereof, while the shaped charges were made with CCG-45, which is the standard for the Fleet. In fact, I'm willing to bet the charges were pre-made Fleet issue. We know a lot of stuff, explosives included, has gone walkabout from various armories and depots in the recent past with no clue as to where it went and who took it."

"Hmm." Holt frowned. "Could our doers be ex-Armed Forces or even currently serving?"

"The job on the CNO's residence was professional, that's for sure. The replicant was the sole target of the blast, and no surrounding houses suffered any collateral damage. Hell, there wasn't even any debris blown off the property. They kept it nicely contained. The mercs who drove their cars into the Admiral's convoy didn't appear to care about collaterals."

"Did the MPs find out how and where the doers came onto the base?"

"Yes. Since they didn't trigger any perimeter sensors and the grid is intact, the MPs figured they might have come via a disused underground passage that isn't on any modern plans. This area used to be industrial before we took it over a century ago, and it's a given we lost track of hidden infrastructure. Using ground penetrating radar, the MPs found a tunnel bisecting the base and followed it on the surface. There's an access hatch behind the hospital that was overgrown, but the vegetation covering it had been recently disturbed. The tunnel runs well beyond the fence with another hatch in the basement of an old warehouse. Traces indicate that's what the doers used. There's no video surveillance anywhere near that end, so it's impossible to track them. Video surveillance on this end shows nothing more than moving shadows, which shows we're dealing with pros wearing chameleon suits."

"I hope the MPs shut the tunnel down."

"Yes, sir. And they're looking for others on a priority basis."

Once the meeting was over and Holt alone in his office, he wandered over to the window and stared out at the sprawling base. If he hadn't listened to his instincts and convinced Dunmoore to move out of the house, she'd be dead. His best friend would have been ripped to shreds while she slept, relying on the safety of the base's perimeter, an illusory safety, as it turned out. How had the doers found out about the tunnel when it wasn't even registered on the base's plans? Holt shook his head and returned to his desk.

***

"Please tell me Dunmoore's dead." Sara Lauzier sat back in her chair, contemplating Axel Renouf, who'd just reported the mysterious middle-of-the-night explosion on Joint Base Geneva.

"Unfortunately, no. Even though the blast was directed at the Chief of Naval Operations' residence, she was no longer living there.

"Pity. Any idea where she's holed up?"

"No, but I assume it's somewhere on the base. No one saw her move, and she simply appears at the HQ building in the morning."

"And your operatives weren't responsible for the attack?"

Renouf shook his head. "We try to pinpoint a target before making an attempt and don't use explosives."

Lauzier groaned inwardly. It had to have been her assets. All she'd done was send them a message with a new target via an anonymous node and had no idea how they might strike, but they'd also failed this time. Perhaps they weren't as good as she was told. Yet if Dunmoore had changed her quarters with no one being aware, maybe failure was justifiable in this case. She wondered what they'd attempt next. If they could get close enough again, which didn't appear likely.

"And are you working on Dunmoore and Holt, Axel? I did ask you to take care of them."

"We're still looking at that, Madame."

Renouf was lying, of course. He had no intention of killing them but still hadn't found a way out of his predicament. However, he had gained additional information about those other assets she was utilizing. His people had identified her contact with something simply referred to as 'The Organization,' whose representative went by the name of the Paymaster. They were digging deep to find out more. Perhaps once they did, he would have enough leverage to resist her.

"Don't delay for too long."

"No, Madame."

***

"She's still alive." The tall, icy blond turned back toward her two operatives and speared them with cold blue eyes beneath brows so pale they almost appeared white.

They were in a safe house north of Geneva, a small, unremarkable structure on the outskirts of Versoix, one of many inhabited by anonymous bureaucrats working for the Commonwealth government. "How is that possible? You said you picked up the expected life signs in her bedroom."

"I did," the man, a dark-haired, burly veteran of many SOCOM missions, replied. "Either it wasn't her, or they set up something that mimicked a human being, boss."

"A replicant," his companion, equally dark-haired but less muscular, said in a flat voice. Her eyes, hooded like his, returned the blonde woman's stare without showing a shred of emotion.

She, too, was a SOCOM veteran and as deadly as the best of them. "It had to be."

"That won't please the Paymaster. And it's a given they found the tunnel we used by now. We won't get another chance."

The man shrugged.

"Shit happens. How could we have possibly been aware that they relocated her elsewhere and left a replicant to ensnare assassins?"

"We need to find another way of getting at her and Holt."

"If you have any ideas, I'm all ears, boss."

"I don't."

"Neither do we. He's a ghost, and she's rarely out in the open anymore. We assume both are in their offices during the day but could be in a bunker twenty meters below the ground. And now we don't know where she sleeps at night. I'd say her security situation is excellent."

"As is her damned luck," the blond, who went under the assumed name of Lilith Camus, growled. "Again."

Both operatives gave her a curious look.

"You got a past with Dunmoore?"

Camus nodded.

"During another lifetime, when she foiled some plans."

The man smirked.

"Do tell."

"No. What's past is past." Camus glowered at him for a moment, and then she paced the living room. "Our Paymaster wants Dunmoore and Holt dead. Fine. We tried infiltrating the base where they're both hiding and got skunked. No fault of ours. It was simply outdated intelligence."

"You know what, boss? I don't think we can touch either of them unless they make a mistake. At least they're unaware of who made the attempt. Otherwise we'd be in the clink by now. Fleet Security is scarily good when it wants to be."

Camus grimaced at him.

"Don't I know it."

"I think we should just tell the Paymaster we can't manage it and move on to our next job."

"No, not yet. Dunmoore is the most important target we've ever been given. Taking her out will do wonders for our reputation and the price we can command for a mission. Besides, we didn't quite put the deputy CNO down, so that's a point against us, and we don't need too many of those."

"But we did Gherson splendidly, so there's that. I just don't see a way at them. We used our best chance to get Dunmoore against a replicant. Holt? Like I said, he's a ghost. We need someone on the inside. That's what we need."

"Agreed. But we don't have anyone. We've been out of the Service too long. Let me think about it. If I can't come up with anything, I'll throw in the towel and ask that we go on to our next job."

"You sure you're not letting the past interfere with a business decision?"

"Yeah, I am. As much as I used to hate Dunmoore for what she did to me, I'm over it."

But judging by the expression in Camus' eyes, the man wasn't so sure.

***

"You want me to do what, Madame?" The President of the Senate eyed Sara Lauzier with suspicion as if he hadn't quite heard correctly.

"I want you to hand me emergency powers to deal with the Armed Forces under Paragraph 1252 of the Government Administration Act of 2398 and then furlough the Senate."

He frowned, trying to temporize while he caught up with her.

"I'm not familiar with that clause."

"The paragraph states the President of the Senate can grant temporary emergency powers to the Secretary General if he deems it necessary in order to handle a particular situation imperiling the integrity of the Commonwealth. Said powers to include passing temporary legislation, temporarily suspending federal civil rights, and imposing martial law."

"Surely, nobody has ever used it. Not even during the Shrehari War. I'd remember."

"It hasn't. In fact, the paragraph is so obscure and deeply hidden in the Act, I'll bet no one has heard about it."

"And why furlough the Senate? The Act doesn't mandate that action when invoking said paragraph, does it?"

"It doesn't. I merely want the senators out of the way when I enact certain things to rein in the Armed Forces. With the Senate furloughed, they have no official standing as representatives of their star systems."

"I've never heard of such a thing." The President of the Senate shook his head, eyes narrowed.

"Yet you can send them home for a defined period. Paragraph 537 of the Senate Act of 2388 gives you that power."

"I'll have to check both acts myself, of course, before I can pronounce myself on their application."

"Harmon, please remember who ensured your rise to the presidency despite the secrets lingering in your background, things only I am aware of." Lauzier's tone was even and pleasant, but he picked up a distinct undercurrent of menace in it. "We wouldn't want the senators to vote for your removal and replacement, now would we?"

"If I send them home, they might do that anyway."

"Not until the furlough is over, and many things can happen between now and then."

"Does the Senate vote on granting you emergency powers?"

"Of course, but I expect you to whip that vote in my favor. If all Home World senators agree, then the motion can easily pass. But I suggest you keep the furlough to yourself until the powers have been granted.

"What if I do?"

"Then your time as President of the Senate is over," she replied flatly, meeting his eyes with her soulless gaze. "You will carry this out exactly as I tell you."

A feeling of unease enveloped him, and he fancied she'd just threatened to kill him, something he wouldn't put past her. After all, Judy Chu died under mysterious circumstances, opening the SecGen's job. Besides, as President of the Senate, he was the head of the legislative branch and technically one of the three — no, make that four, now — most powerful people in the Commonwealth. And it paid exceptionally well.

"I'll try my best, Madame."

"There will be no try, Harmon. Do it my way, or you're out."

— Thirty-Four —

"I perceive no reason to authorize the SecGen emergency powers under the Government Administration Act. None whatsoever," Senator Bregman thundered after the President of the Senate introduced a resolution to that effect. "This august chamber would be mad to give her such extensive authority."

One of the Home World senators, the senior one for Meiji, rose.

"The Honorable Senator for Cascadia exaggerates. It merely allows her to constrain the Fleet in its quest to become the fourth branch of government. Or is my honorable colleague so in favor of an independent Armed Forces that he will throw caution to the wind?"

"I think I speak for OutWorld senators when I say the Armed Forces' independence from an administration so politicized, so slanted in favor of Centralism is a fine thing. Let the Fleet concentrate on protecting humanity across the stars in the best way possible and leave politics on Earth. We of the OutWorlds have the most to lose by not giving it the latitude it needs because we are the most vulnerable to threats, especially the frontier star systems. To reiterate, I find no basis for granting the SecGen emergency powers."

Bregman took his seat again.

"Does anyone else have something to add other than essentially repeating what our honorable colleagues from Cascadia and Meiji have already stated? If not, we will proceed with the vote."

The President glanced at the circle of senators and noticed that many were tight-lipped. They obviously wanted to speak their minds but wouldn't add anything new to the debate, and he'd not given the OutWorlders enough time to organize a filibuster.

Of course, he'd also not had the time to whip the Home World vote but was confident the bare majority they represented would carry it.

"We are voting on a motion to grant the SecGen emergency powers under Paragraph 1252 of the Government Administration Act for the prescribed period of ninety days. Please register your vote now."

He looked at his board as the votes came in and blanched. Would he receive the fifty percent plus one in favor? Initially, it didn't seem so, but then the count ended, and he breathed a sigh of relief. A majority of one was still a majority. That meant at least four Home World senators had voted against the motion, but since the vote was by secret ballot, he had no way of discovering who.

"Motion carried."

The President surveyed the assembly again, observed plenty of furious faces, and readied himself for the situation to worsen.

"And now, I am furloughing the Senate for the next three months under Paragraph 537 of the Senate Act. Return to your star systems and await my call."

He rapped his gavel once, stood, and walked out of the Assembly Hall to the growing hubbub of angry voices. To avoid being cornered by enraged senators, he grabbed his coat from his office and disappeared into the underground car park.

There, he took his private vehicle and left for parts unknown, determined to speak with no one for the foreseeable future. He didn't know what he'd just unleashed on an unsuspecting Commonwealth but figured it couldn't be good. Sara Lauzier with quasi-dictatorial powers for the next ninety days? He shivered, even though the inside of his car was nice and toasty. But he really didn't have a choice in the matter.

***

Sara Lauzier felt jubilant. The Senate had given her emergency powers and gone home. She was now the Commonwealth's sole supreme authority. The vote was closer than expected — by only one voice — but she didn't care.

The fact that the OutWorld senators were incensed by the President of the Senate's maneuvers was just more icing on the cake. Officially, she had a free hand for the next ninety days, but as long as the Senate didn't reconvene, she could run the Commonwealth by herself. The matter would probably end up in front of the Supreme Court, but by then, she'd have tightened her grip. And when the Senate met again, it would be in a much-diminished capacity.

Her first order of business was to bring about a constitutional crisis around the Armed Forces, resulting in their subjugation to her will. Once she had them under control, the rest of the Commonwealth would follow. Lauzier understood, in the same way Kowalski and Dunmoore did, that the Fleet was the ultimate arbiter of the relationship between Earth and the Sovereign Star Systems.

***

"She finally did it," Holt announced as he entered Dunmoore's office. "And the way Sara did it is quite ingenious. She got the Senate to give her ninety days worth of emergency powers, then had the President of the Senate send the senators home for the duration."

Dunmoore grimaced.

"And will she return those powers once the ninety days run out?"

Holt let out a bark of mirthless laughter.

"Not if she can help it. I figure she leaned hard on the President of the Senate and will continue leaning on him, so he doesn't recall the honorable senators to Earth. Without a functioning legislature, she's a dictator in all but name."

"What about the Supreme Court?"

"I'm sure Lauzier has something on more than a few of them. It's her modus operandi and a given that many have something in their past they'd rather not reveal. That being the case, the Justices either won't hear any cases related to her assumption of emergency power or sit on them until the heat death of the universe."

"I see. What should I expect next from her?"

"Her first order of business?" Holt made a face. "An attempt to bring the Fleet back under her control."

Dunmoore scoffed.

"Good luck with that."

"She'll pass emergency legislation annulling your declaration that the Armed Forces are a fourth branch of government, then have you, me, and anyone else she can get her hands on arrested when we tell her where to go."

"And who'll do the arresting?"

"She can federalize the star system police forces and use the SSB."

"But she can't touch Caledonia, and HQ is effectively there now."

"Yes, but Lauzier can cause much damage while she goes through every option she thinks of. Irreparable harm to the relationship with the OutWorlds, for instance. We can't simply sit back and watch her flail."

"No, I suppose we can't. How about we steal a march on her and activate Operation Night of the Long Knives?"

"Good idea. Everything is in place. I can trigger it to happen in forty-eight hours — we need that much for the subspace radio time lag to the furthest star systems."

"Then make it so, Zeke." Her office communicator chimed, and Dunmoore glanced at its display. "Well, speak of the devil. It's the Palace." She stroked the surface. "Dunmoore."

"It's Johan Holden, the Secretary General's executive assistant, Admiral. Madame Lauzier would like to have a conversation with you in her office in one hour.

"Tell Madame Lauzier I'll gladly speak with her over a comlink, but in person is a no-go. I've been targeted once too often recently and won't be leaving the base anymore."

"She insists, Admiral."

"She can insist all she wants, Johan. I'm not showing up at the Palace."

Dunmoore could almost see him suppress a sigh.

"Very well, Admiral. Let me speak with her about that. Holden, out."

Once his image had vanished, she winked at Holt.

"Might as well lay my marker right away."

"She won't like it. Oh, and by the way, when you do speak, use her first name. It'll drive Sara crazy. She's huge on respect. Toward her, not anybody else."

Dunmoore's eyes twinkled as she felt the old blood lust of battle return after so long.

"Noted. And stick around for my conversation with Sara. It might be amusing."

Moments later, the communicator chimed again.

"Dunmoore."

It was Holden again.

"Please stand by for Madame Lauzier."

"Certainly."

Lauzier's face replaced Holden's, and she did not look pleased.

"Admiral, I understand you're shy about leaving the base these days?"

"Two attempts on your life will do that. Now, what is it you wish to discuss?"

"I'm about to issue emergency legislation forbidding the Armed Forces from calling themselves the fourth branch of government and subordinating them to civilian authority — mine."

Dunmoore allowed herself a sarcastic smile.

"And you think it'll change a damn thing? Your legislation and a cred fifty will get you a cup of indifferent coffee in the Palace cafeteria."

"If you don't obey the law, I'll see you're arrested and tried for sedition."

One of Dunmoore's eyebrows crept up.

"And who'll do the arresting, let alone the trying?"

"Leave that to me, Dunmoore. But I'm sure you'll obey the law. Doing otherwise would invalidate your oath to the Commonwealth.

"I'll obey laws that keep me from doing my duty just like you obey those which prevent you from seizing absolute power. Meaning not at all. My oath is to protect humanity from enemies foreign and domestic, and I'm looking at a specimen of the latter sort right now, Sara."

Using her first name stung because Dunmoore saw Lauzier's eyes narrow with irritation.

"That's Madame to you, Admiral."

"No. I prefer being on a first-name basis with someone of your sort. That way, the nature of our relationship is crystal clear."

"Of my sort? Careful, Dunmoore, lest I lose patience with you."

"And then what? You'll scold me?"

Dunmoore made an effort to ignore Holt, who was silently doubled over with laughter beyond the video pickup.

"That's enough. You will show me the proper respect as Secretary General of the Commonwealth and your superior." Her tone had become harsher as she fought to control her anger.

"You're hardly my superior, Sara. We're equals at best, although my actions aren't for personal gain, while yours are."

"And you're dismissed as acting commander-in-chief of the Armed Forces, Dunmoore."

The latter shrugged.

"Fine. Then Grand Admiral Kowalski will have to take over before she's quite fit for duty again."

"If she doesn't submit, I'll also have her dismissed, even though she's been appointed during good behavior. Another piece of emergency legislation will ensure that."

"I was just kidding, Sara. You don't have the authority to relieve me of duty. Pass any legislation you want. It comes down to enforcing it, and you simply don't have the numbers on your side."

"You'd rebel against the lawful government of the Commonwealth?"

"No. Of course not. I am acting head of the government's fourth branch, so any lawful actions I take cannot be considered rebellion."

Lauzier reached up and squeezed both eyes with her right hand's thumb and index finger.

"You. Are. Ungovernable."

Dunmoore gave her a sweet smile.

"I try to be. And I'm glad it's working. So, do you want to try again, or are you dead set on passing legislation that'll try to reverse reality? Because we've effectively made it happen, and that's a genie you can't shove back into its bottle."

"We'll see about that. In the meantime, consider yourself under arrest."

"No." Dunmoore sketched a salute. "Goodbye, Sara."

Then, she cut the link and glanced at Holt, who was still grinning so broadly she thought he might swallow his entire face.

"You're pleased with my performance?"

"Pleased ain't the word, Skipper. Ecstatic would be closer to what I feel right now. That was a performance for the ages. You've enraged her beyond belief. It may not seem that way, but Sara was on the verge of losing her temper, and that's always a good thing because she'll do something utterly stupid we can take advantage of."

"So, what do I do for an encore?"

"Leave Earth and join Kathryn on Caledonia."

"Along with you and the rest of the headquarters staff."

"Of course."

— Thirty-Five —

The timer in the corner of Holt's office display was reaching zero, and he climbed to his feet, reluctantly, if truth be told, because he had a certain amount of respect for Axel Renouf, who'd shied away from targeting Dunmoore. But the operation had been planned years earlier and didn't depend on who the director general of the SSB was.

Major General Yuan arrived at that moment, dressed in a civilian suit like Holt. Both of them concealed deadly blasters beneath their jackets.

"Ready, sir?"

"As ready as I'll ever be."

"Everything is in place. As a matter of fact, our people should have already taken down the offices of the Bureau in the outlying sectors by now.

"Excellent, Peter."

A massive effort involving almost the entirety of Fleet Security and Special Operations Command, Operation Night of the Long Knives would put an end to the biggest thorn in the Armed Forces' side. Except for a privileged few, most participants didn't know the SSB was their target until the last minute to prevent leaks.

Because Holt considered the Terra Regiment and the 1st Marine Division politically unreliable, he'd ordered a squadron from the 1st Special Forces Regiment to help him seize SSB HQ days before Dunmoore gave the go-ahead. He knew the time was coming and had prepared. By now, those special forces operators would have left the undistinguished Q ship that had brought them to Earth and flown toward Geneva aboard unmarked shuttles.

As if he knew what Holt was thinking, Yuan said, "The squadron from the 1st SFR should almost be on final approach."

"In that case, we'd better go."

They met four dozen Fleet Security operatives in the underground parkade beneath the HQ building, all of them heavily armed and wearing civilian suits.

"Everyone ready?" Holt called out when he saw them.

"Yes, sir," they replied almost in unison.

"Then let's mount up and head out."

They climbed aboard eight identical, unmarked staff cars and filed out of the parkade, across the base, and out through the main gate, headed for Geneva. Yuan, who was in contact with the special forces squadron, controlled the convoy's speed, so it didn't get there ahead of time. Technically, Holt's presence wasn't required, but he preferred to be in at the kill and arrest Renouf himself. Or kill him if he resisted.

"Aerospace traffic control is furiously pinging the shuttles, sir," Yuan said. "They're warning them away from Geneva under penalty of imprisonment."

Holt snorted.

"A good thing they're not equipped with surface-to-air defenses."

The Terra Regiment's artillery battalion kept the air space above the capital secure, but Holt had explicitly ordered them to stand down because he'd be running an exercise just about now.

Soon, the SSB HQ building came into view, as did the shuttles carrying the special forces operators. Holt watched while one of them landed on the building's roof, disgorging armored troopers, and four more landed on the ground surrounding it. The convoy came to a halt in front of the main doors, and the Fleet Security operatives disembarked.

Immediately, the first four ran up the stairs and through the outer doors. They opened the inner ones and pointed their weapons at the two guards sitting behind a granite counter in the center of the lobby.

"Don't so much as twitch."

One of them tried to pull his weapon from its holster and both died instantly in a hail of blaster fire. The operatives placed explosive charges against the inside of the six scanner arches on either side of the counter and withdrew back to the inner doors. A few moments later, the charges blew, destroying the SSB HQ's first line of security.

An alarm came to life, echoing across the lobby, but the Fleet agents were already streaming in and spreading out, heading for their assigned targets. Holt and six of his people ascended the stairs toward Renouf's office, paying no attention to anyone they encountered.

He heard muffled explosions from below, indicating that the special forces troopers were penetrating the building's underground garage and cutting off any chance of escaping that way.

None of the astonished SSB staffers, drawn from their offices by the alarm, tried to stop them. In fact, most retreated the moment they saw the weapons carried by the Fleet Security officers, and Holt reached the antechamber to Renouf's office without breaking stride. He pointed his blaster at the executive assistant, who rose in protest, then threw the inner door open and entered.

Renouf was on his communicator, demanding to know the reason behind the alarm activation and the source of the dull thumps that had resonated a few moments earlier. When Renouf spotted Holt, he put the communicator down and stared at him.

"What is the meaning of this, Admiral?"

"The SSB is declaring bankruptcy and shutting down effective immediately."

Renouf rose from his chair.

"You can't do this."

"I've seized your HQ and every SSB station and outpost across the Commonwealth. It's over, Axel. The SSB no longer exists. Either your people surrender, go home, and find a new line of business, or they die. Your infrastructure is mine, and I will destroy it, not before draining your data banks, of course. We will arrest you and your senior staff and take you away from here to an undisclosed location until our operation is complete and you no longer present a threat."

Renouf, stunned by the events, could only gape at Holt. He tried to speak, but although his jaw muscles worked, no sound emerged.

Major General Yuan entered the office and came to stand beside Holt.

"The building is ours. We have everyone on the list in irons, ready to be transported, and our technical specialists are setting up to access the SSB's data."

Renouf's eyes shifted from Holt to Yuan and back.

"You bastard," he finally said.

"My parents were happily married when they conceived me, Axel. Now, be a good boy. Turn around and put your hands behind your back so I can shackle you." Holt pointed his blaster at Renouf's midriff. "Otherwise, I'll just shoot you, and I don't care which it is."

Renouf gave him a dirty look but complied, survival instincts besting his desire to be defiant and go down with the ship. After a pair of operatives took him away, Holt sat behind the former director general's desk and accessed his work queue.

"It's the same in every hierarchical organization, isn't it, Peter? The higher you get, the more of a burden administrivia becomes. I can't see a single operational folder waiting for his attention. Sad." Holt stood again and walked over to the windows. "Seems like the Geneva Police finally realized something is happening around here. One of them is having an animated conversation with a 1st SFR trooper who's obviously telling him it's none of his business, judging by the look on the cop's face."

"Should I go and see?"

"No. Let the police deal with faceless, armored guys who aren't wearing any insignia. Making ourselves visible won't help." He glanced down and saw a stream of civilians leave the building. "Ah, we're releasing the low-level folks. Excellent."

"After relieving them of their credentials, weapons, and anything else belonging to the SSB. They'll receive their official notification of dismissal via electronic means later today. That ought to be enough for unemployment benefits. And we'll get back the people we sent to infiltrate the Bureau after all this time."

Holt smirked at Yuan.

"Look at us, being humane with the former SSB employees."

Yuan shrugged.

"It was that or shoot them, and I'd rather we didn't stoop to their level. Besides, a few tried to resist, so it isn't like this was a bloodless coup. Will you call the SecGen from here and inform her that we've dispersed her pets to the four winds?

"I'd rather leave that pleasure to Admiral Dunmoore. She has an extraordinary way of verbally cutting someone to shreds and enjoys using it on Madame Lauzier."

"You're a prince among men, sir." Yuan grinned at his superior.

Holt inclined his head regally.

"I am that. And I shall now return to base and report success."

"I'll stay here until we finish draining the data and destroying the infrastructure."

"Enjoy."

"Thank you. That I will. I've always been interested in what the SSB were doing we didn't know about."

"And you're about to find out."

***

"It's over. A few of the SSB people died because they tried to resist, but the vast majority will be going to the employment office while the senior staff are heading up into orbit and the Q ship that brought the 1st SFR troopers. Holt dropped into a chair facing Dunmoore. "I'll start hearing about the off-world parts of the operation beginning in approximately twelve to sixteen hours from now. But I'm certain everything turned out fine. If not according to plan, then as well as can be. The HQ job certainly was slicker than I had any right to expect. We caught them completely by surprise, which is almost miraculous in a town like Geneva."

"It speaks to superb operational security, Zeke. Well done."

"Did you want to let Sara know her tame agency is no more? I thought you'd derive greater enjoyment from it than I would."

Dunmoore's eyes lit up.

"Thank you, Zeke."

She touched the controls embedded in her desk, and Johan Holden's face eventually appeared.

"Admiral. What can I do for you?"

"I'd like to speak with the SecGen."

"I'm sorry, Admiral, but she left orders that you not be put through to her."

"Tell dear old Sara I have important news concerning the Special Security Bureau. Or rather the former entity that was known as the SSB."

An air of curiosity entered Holden's eyes. "Former entity?"

"I'll discuss the matter with Sara. You can find out from her."

"One moment, please."

Holden's face disappeared when he suspended the link from his end.

Dunmoore glanced at Holt and shrugged.

"I guess he's off to hear his master's voice."

"Isn't that some ancient quote?

"No idea."

They waited in silence until Holden's face reappeared.

"Madame will speak with you now. Please stand by."

Lauzier's pinched features replaced him.

"What do you want, Dunmoore?"

"I'm calling to report the demise of the Special Security Bureau, Sara. Less than two hours ago, commandos under my orders assaulted its HQ on Earth and every SSB office throughout the Commonwealth. The SSB has been eliminated."

Dunmoore saw Lauzier's face blanch.

"You didn't."

"Try calling Axel Renouf. You'll get a 'this address is no longer in service' message. Poor old Axel is currently on his way to an undisclosed location, along with the entirety of his senior staff, under arrest for crimes against humanity. We've sent the rest of the SSB personnel home after dismissing them from federal service, but I retain the right to arrest any of them who are suspected of criminal activities.

"How dare you?"

Dunmoore let out a sigh.

"That seems to be a repetitive question, Sara. I don't dare, I do. And I do because I can. The SSB is no more. Fleet Security will take over the purely policing activities the SSB used to carry out until the Constabulary is established."

Lauzier simply stared at Dunmoore as if bereft of words.

"Cat got your tongue, Sara? Doesn't matter. You have no one and nothing to defend your regime now. You can federalize star system police forces, but they won't stand up against us. In the immortal terms of my favorite strategy game, consider this check and mate. Enjoy the rest of your life."

Dunmoore cut the link and smiled at Holt.

"Not my best, but it got the message across."

— Thirty-Six —

Sara Lauzier felt faint with rage. Thankfully, she was alone in her office, the door closed, and the soundproofing among the best money could buy because, after a few heartbeats, she screamed her hatred for Dunmoore, Kowalski, and the Fleet in general. They'd ruined twenty years of planning and work, twenty years during which she'd dissembled, smiled, and negotiated to get the top job.

And now that she was SecGen, it appeared she'd been steadily losing power to those ridiculous Navy officers whose earnestness and devotion to duty made her want to vomit. No, there had to be a way of regaining the upper hand.

Lauzier paced her office like a caged animal, and if anyone had entered it at that moment, she would have pounced and torn his or her throat out. It took a good half hour for her to calm down sufficiently so she could think about something more than tearing Dunmoore to shreds with her bare hands.

Dunmoore was an insubordinate scofflaw who opposed everything Lauzier stood for, and there was nothing she could do about it because Dunmoore held the sole remaining interstellar enforcement powers in her hands.

Appealing to the Supreme Court wouldn't do any good. Dunmoore would simply ignore the Justices as well. Lauzier could organize mass demonstrations against the Fleet, at least on the Home Worlds and Earth, but so what? The only leverage she might have was financial, and even then, the Armed Forces would simply buy what they needed and refer the invoices to the Defense Department. And should the SecDef refuse to pay, Lauzier had no doubt the OutWorlds would fund the Fleet directly, deducting the resulting sums from the tax remittance to Earth.

She dropped into the nearest chair, feeling faint from her lengthy outburst, emotions fluctuating between fury and despair. The flames of her anger eventually died to mere embers, leaving despondency at her helplessness behind. She'd suffered a thorough beating from lesser creatures.

But a Lauzier never gave up.

***

"The SSB have been naughty boys and girls, sir," Major General Yuan said as he walked into Holt's office. "They should never have documented some of the stuff we recovered from their database."

"It's the bane of every bureaucracy, Peter — the desire to keep complete records, no matter how dire the subject. There were a few twentieth-century nations that cataloged the worst atrocities they committed in clinical detail. One in particular stands out. But that's neither here nor there. What sort of stuff did our techs find?"

"The SSB was running quite the wet works department, with politically motivated assassinations being increasingly commonplace since the end of the war. We counted at least six thousand five hundred and fifty whose deaths from natural causes were anything but, and all OutWorlders or anti-Centralists, in the last five years. Then, there's the SSB's use of pirates, mercenaries, slavers, and everyone's favorite organized crime groups, such as the Confederacy of the Howling Stars. It doesn't matter how murderous or depraved they are, just that they're effective. Which explains a lot about the troubles we've been having in the Rim and other outer sectors, not to mention the Protectorate."

Holt made a face.

"Just when you thought the opposition might have had some redeeming features."

"None that I could see, sir. The universe is better off without them. And we have plenty of evidence to try many of the senior folks we've just sent off to Caledonia. Plenty of the more junior ones as well if you want to arrest and transport them."

"As much as I'd enjoy marooning the lot of them in a prison colony on Parth, I'll be content with those who gave the orders and leave those who took them to find new careers. Unless we find egregiously nasty characters while going through the files or interrogating the upper echelons. Then, I'll be more than happy to prosecute the truly deserving."

"Understood. And the first reports are coming in from the Home Worlds. Complete success so far. The SSB offices have been ransacked and shut down, the personnel relieved of their credentials and appointments and given a notice of dismissal.

The station chiefs and senior personnel are under arrest and waiting for transport to Caledonia."

"Excellent. Clearly, no one expected us to make this move. "It seems like we might achieve a clean sweep."

"Let's not jinx it, sir."

Holt chuckled at Yuan's somber tone.

"All right. We'll wait to hear from everyone before declaring anything."

"There's one interesting tidbit we found under several classification layers, and I'm unsure what to make of it. The SSB has been researching something called 'The Organization,' which is headed or whose point of contact is a certain Paymaster. It appears that the SecGen is using them to do the dirty work she won't give the Bureau, or the Bureau won't even look at."

"Like an assassination attempt on Admiral Dunmoore?"

Yuan nodded.

"The thought had crossed my mind. I figure they stumbled across this Organization somehow while probing the SecGen's communications and investigated. Not that they found much, save for a way of getting in touch with this Paymaster and transferring funds to him or her."

Holt thought for a few moments, forehead creased in a frown.

"That means this Organization is probably the player who attacked Admiral Radames and made the attempt on Admiral Dunmoore's official residence." Holt drummed his fingers on the desktop. "You know, maybe we can use or rather misuse it."

"How?"

A wolfish smile spread across Holt's face.

"Buy its services to remove the biggest thorn in the Fleet's side."

Yuan's eyebrows shot up.

"You wouldn't."

"In a nanosecond, Peter. She's been gunning for us. Call it self-defence."

***

"Sara has petitioned the Supreme Court to smack me down. Not quite in those words, but that's what she wants."

Dunmoore was recording a message for Kowalski and had already brought her up to date on Operation Night of the Long Knives.

"She asked them to rule my declaring the Armed Forces the fourth branch of government not only unconstitutional — which it is — but mutinous against the lawful authority of the SecGen. Which it is as well. I don't know what the Justices will say, but they're just as powerless to enforce any decree as Sara is. Of course, she's making a public spectacle of her petition to gain sympathy, and there have been so-called spontaneous demonstrations against me on Earth and the Home Worlds. Not that it'll do her a damn bit of good. I am preparing to leave with the remainder of HQ, so I'll not be close to the Palace of the Stars for long. In the meantime, I'm keeping my head down on the base, which I'll probably not leave again until I'm aboard a shuttle headed for one of our transports in orbit. And that's about it. Until my next report. Dunmoore, out."

She touched the controls, encrypting the message, and sent it to the communications center for subspace transmission to Caledonia. Then she stood and stretched. It had been another long day overseeing the preparations for departure, but the truth was she controlled nothing more than the personnel in Geneva now. Gregor was running the Navy in her stead, and she knew Kowalski had retaken the helm of the Fleet, even though she was on medical restrictions and officially still left command to Dunmoore.

She looked down the mezzanine at the now-empty operations center several stories below the surface. It seemed depressing, yet she knew its replacement, several dozen light years away, was buzzing with activity. After clearing the Executive Floor and leaving it empty, she'd taken one of the vacant duty offices as her own so that even a nuclear strike on the mostly abandoned HQ building wouldn't touch her. But it was time she left.

Dunmoore summoned Chief Petty Officer of the Navy Kurt Guthren and told him they were now on twenty-four hours' notice to move. Five naval transports were inbound and would take the remaining HQ staff off. Those with families were gone already, leaving nothing more than officers and noncoms with little baggage and ready to shift almost instantly.

"I won't be sorry to get the hell off Earth, Admiral. This place has a sulfurous stench to it."

"Neither will I."

Holt appeared at Dunmoore's office door.

"The Fleet Security folks remaining on Earth are ready to depart, sir. Everyone packed their last remaining containers. The household stuff already left for Caledonia long ago."

"Excellent. I want us to be the last ones off this world, in good order and leaving nothing behind. The 1st Fleet, 1st Marine

Division, and Terra Regiment are welcome to occupy Joint Base Geneva anytime now."

Holt smirked.

"They're well aware of it, and I've already encountered advance parties scoping out the premises."

"The admiral commanding 1st Fleet will sit in Kathryn's old office soon enough, wondering why we left him." Dunmoore stood and stretched. "I have nothing more to do here, which means I'll be hitting the gym to bleed off some of the tension that's been bothering me lately. Then, it'll be waiting for the ships. I am officially shutting down my office now."

"Mine isn't," Holt said. "And it won't be until the last of us climbs aboard the shuttles. But then, someone needs to be the rearguard, and I'm it."

Before Dunmoore could reply, her communicator chimed. She called up the message and groaned.

"I have received a summons to appear in front of the Supreme Court in three days to explain myself on the matter of declaring the Fleet the fourth branch of government. I guess Sara's gambit has legs, after all."

"Really short ones. You won't be here to appear, and even if you did, you'd tell the Justices to blow it out their collective rears."

"Not in so many words, Zeke. If there's one institution I still respect, it's the Supreme Court. At least the learned judges are trying hard not to get pulled into the Centralists versus sovereign star systems debate. But they have their duty to perform, and I have violated the constitution."

"In the best cause of all — preventing another civil war."

"That doesn't matter to jurists who sit in their own ivory tower and judge according to the letter of the law, not messy reality with all its dangling appendages."

Holt guffawed.

"I need to remember that — messy reality with dangling appendages. It sounds slightly dirty, slightly wrong, and all you."

"Feel free to use it in polite conversation," Dunmoore replied dryly. "Now, who's with me to the gym?"

— Thirty-Seven —

"Change of arrangements," Lilith Camus announced as she entered the living room of the little house in Versoix, where both operatives waited for her to return from the daily check-in with the Paymaster. Neither knew how it was done other than not in person. None of them even knew whether the Paymaster was a single individual or a collective acting under one name.

The man looked at her expectantly. "Do tell."

A wintry smile appeared on Camus' lips.

"We've been tasked with killing Sara Lauzier, Secretary General of the Commonwealth, as our first priority, ahead of Dunmoore and Holt. We pull this off, and we'll be set for life."

The woman whistled.

"You can't get any higher than that. Do we have a deadline?"

"We can take the time we need to complete the job."

"And the others?"

"We'll turn our attention back to them once we finish with Lauzier, who should actually be easier to target than Dunmoore. She can't hide in a bunker beneath the Fleet HQ building."

Camus didn't realize how closely she guessed Dunmoore's location but knew her enough to come up with a plausible assumption, considering her old foe would leave Earth for Caledonia any day now and avoid risking another attempt on her life.

"And," Camus continued, "once we're done with Lauzier, we'll return to Caledonia, where Dunmoore, Kowalski, and Holt will be easier to target than they are here."

The man frowned.

"Isn't Lauzier the one who commissioned the hit on the admirals? She's got the biggest beefs with them, especially since that speech Dunmoore made to the Senate."

Camus shrugged.

"It doesn't matter to us. If the contract to assassinate the admirals came from her, then it might be canceled once we take her down. Otherwise, we carry on."

He sketched a salute.

"You're the boss."

"Let's study our new target, shall we?"

***

"You what?" Dunmoore didn't know whether to cackle with maniacal laughter or call the fires of hell on Holt.

"If this Organization is any good, they'll get rid of Lauzier for us. The President of the Senate then temporarily steps into her shoes while the honorable senators elect a new SecGen. And he or she will be much more circumspect about openly pushing Centralism. As a bonus, we end the Lauzier dynasty."

"Her replacement might be even worse. Did you think of that?"

"Sure. But the example of Lauzier's fate will be forever in his or her thoughts."

"Still." Dunmoore finally settled on shaking her head in a dismay that wasn't entirely feigned.

"Look at it this way, as I told Peter Yuan, I acted in self-defence."

"And paid for the hit how? It must have cost a fortune."

Holt chuckled with delight.

"It's rather poetic. We covered most of the cost by using the money we took from Paul Markus' escrow account. A cool nine million, three for each of us. The rest comes from Fleet Security's black ops fund."

"Okay. I'll grant you that one," she said in a resigned tone. "Do you really expect this Paymaster's minions to succeed?"

"Does it matter?"

"I guess not. Even if they miss, the effect on Lauzier's psyche will be considerable."

"And in the meantime, someone other than us has become the focus of at least one team of assassins."

"Please tell me you're trying to track this Organization down so you can eliminate it in due course. We can't have that sort of outfit gallivanting across the galaxy, selling its skills to the highest bidder."

"We are, just as we're also looking for the religious mercenary zealots. But I'm not holding out much hope for finding either. They've evaded our sensors for the Almighty knows how long, and it's a big universe out there, one where their services will always be in demand."

Dunmoore sighed.

"I suppose."

Her communicator buzzed for attention, and she glanced at its display.

"Finally. The Starbase One operations center just announced that our five transports dropped out of FTL at Sol's heliopause. They'll be in orbit in fifteen hours."

Holt stood and grinned. "Excellent. I'll warn everyone."

As soon as he'd gone, Captain Malfort stuck his head into Dunmoore's borrowed office.

"Sir, I'll take care of moving your luggage to the spaceport." Since it'll be at least sixteen hours before the first shuttles land, may I suggest you get some rest?"

"You may. I'll head for my quarters. Please call the car." She shut down the workstation and climbed to her feet.

It was well past time to leave Earth. Especially before the Supreme Court decided whether Lauzier was right, and she had the feeling they would. Things would be much easier if she was light years away when the decision came.

Not that it mattered a whit. The Fleet had de facto become an entity separate from the administration and the legislature, even if de jure it violated the constitution. There was nothing anyone could do to change that.

"The car is waiting in the garage, sir."

"Thank you, Josh."

Once in her soon-to-be former apartment, Dunmoore removed her uniform tunic and poured herself a gin and tonic. It was past sixteen hundred hours, and she felt at a loose end. The place was bare, with nothing more than the furniture it came with, her bags packed and sitting by the entrance, save for one which was still open in her bedroom.

Her personal effects had left for Caledonia in containers a few weeks earlier. They would wait for her in the Joint Base Sanctum's Central Material Traffic Terminal's cavernous warehouse, along with those belonging to Holt, Guthren, her aides, and the over thousand personnel left behind as rearguard.

She glanced at the small collection of bottles, most of them half or more full, sitting on a sideboard and shrugged to herself. Whoever inherited the apartment was welcome to them.

Headquarters, 1st Fleet, was leaving Starbase One and relocating to Joint Base Geneva, and she knew some officer of middling rank would end up taking over the space. That the officer would likely be politically unreliable according to current Fleet views, if not an outright Centralist born on Earth or one of the Home Worlds, was neither here nor there.

The 1st Fleet had become the dumping ground for that sort over the last twenty years, being the least likely to find itself facing foes, be they pirates, reivers, or slavers, let alone Shrehari corsairs. They were already privately called the Palace Guards by the mostly OutWorld crewed Fleet, along with the 1st, 2nd, and 4th Marine Regiments, even though the Terra Regiment was the only unit actually providing ceremonial guards at the Palace of the Stars.

Dunmoore, unable to enjoy the balcony because of the threats against her, settled on the living room couch with a second serving of gin and tonic and called up a book on her tablet. She read until almost midnight, then stripped and slipped into bed for the last time.

The following day, bright and early, Dunmoore showered, put on a fresh uniform, and closed her last bag, leaving it with the others by the door. She ate an autochef breakfast, and once she'd disposed of the remains, there was a knock on the door.

"Good morning, sir," Commander Botha stood in the hallway, smiling as she usually did. An antigrav sled floated behind her. "I've come to take your luggage if it's ready."

"It is." Dunmoore stepped back and gestured at the bags.

Within a few moments, Botha had piled them on the sled.

"Captain Malfort will be by with the staff car to take you to the spaceport in one hour, sir. The first shuttles should land any moment now."

As if on cue, both heard the faint thunder of a dozen or more small spacecraft descending.

"And that's them. We'll be waiting for you to board the last one."

"Thank you, Liv."

An hour later, Dunmoore, ensconced in an unmarked staff car, left the apartment building's basement garage, heading for the spaceport on the other side of the base. When she arrived, she found the Commander, 1st Fleet, there to see her off.

"Hello, Walter. Nice of you to come say goodbye in person."

He saluted, smiling, and said, "I wish I were coming with you. Oh well, I'm retiring on Caledonia once my current gig is over and will join everyone there at that time."

"Glad to hear it." They chatted a bit more, then shook hands while Captain Malfort waited more or less impatiently to lead her to their shuttle and get out of the open air, where she remained vulnerable. "Take care."

"Have a pleasant trip, sir."

"Thank you."

He saluted again as the second to last shuttle thundered up on columns of pure energy, then remained at attention while Malfort and Dunmoore headed up her craft's aft ramp. Inside, she found Guthren waiting for her, along with Commander Botha and their piles of luggage.

"Admiral Holt went up just now. We're the last, sir, just as you wanted."

Dunmoore glanced out the aft ramp at the spaceport terminal, and the Jura Mountains looming in the distance and hoped she'd never be back.

"Let's go."

***

"Admiral Dunmoore and what remained of Fleet HQ have departed, Madame," Johan Holden reported. "The last shuttle carrying her lifted off fifteen minutes ago."

Sara Lauzier didn't know whether to be happy Dunmoore was finally gone or angry that she'd slipped through her fingers for the last time.

"Thank you, Johan."

Holden withdrew while Lauzier stood and walked to a window overlooking Lake Geneva. The damage Dunmoore and Kowalski had done to the Centralist cause was incalculable. At times, she felt such despair that suicide became an option, especially now, with the SSB gone, leaving her bereft of any enforcement arm. It would take years to build a new agency, more years than she had left as SecGen. Realistically, she couldn't keep the emergency powers beyond the ninety-day limit without the SSB looming in the shadows, intimidating her adversaries and forcing them into compliance with her wishes. And that meant they would allow her two terms, nothing more.

Lauzier unconsciously clenched her fists until her knuckles were white and her fingernails were biting into her palms. She felt rage building inside her again and fought it off with everything she had. These episodes were getting more frequent, and she might never regain control if she let the slightest bit come out. Once Lauzier had reasserted control over herself, she touched the intercom.

"Johan, please see if *Le Pied de Cochon* can accommodate me in one of their private rooms at nineteen hundred hours tonight. It's time I changed my surroundings, even if only for a few hours."

"Very well, Madame. Will you be inviting someone?"

She thought about it for a fraction of a second but realized that no one in her close circle was appealing enough to break bread with. Since the SSB's demise, she'd been isolating herself more and more, cutting off what few relationships she still enjoyed.

"No. I will dine alone."

— Thirty-Eight —

Per her instructions, Dunmoore was received without fuss aboard the Fleet transport *Carentan*. The captain welcomed her in person, but that was it, as far as ceremonial was concerned. He guided her to her quarters, the largest of the passenger accommodations, then returned to the bridge and oversaw the preparations for departure. Once her aides had dropped off her luggage, she dismissed them for the duration of the trip so they could take a few days off without worrying about her.

"Thank you, sir, we appreciate it," Captain Malfort said. "But if you need anything, please call on us. It'll be rather boring otherwise."

Dunmoore laughed at his mock-pitiful tone.

"Okay. I will. Still, boring once or twice a year isn't a bad thing. It reminds us to appreciate our active moments. Now go and enjoy."

Both aides came to attention and snapped off a salute.

"With your permission, sir."

"Dismissed."

Once they'd gone, Dunmoore unpacked the bag containing her toiletries and shipboard clothing, all she needed while aboard the transport. The remaining suitcases were neatly stacked in a little pile in an out-of-the-way corner.

No sooner was she done that the ship's public address system came to life.

"Now hear this, crew to sailing stations, I repeat, crew to sailing stations."

It was the signal they were about to break out of orbit, and Dunmoore turned her day cabin's primary display on, hunting for the channel that repeated the bridge view. She wanted a last look at Earth as they left humanity's cradle behind them.

Whether she'd ever be back remained an open question, but she doubted it. Now that she'd departed, Earth was nothing more than a sector capital for her, one with the usual subordinate Armed Forces Headquarters found on such a world. And the CNO rarely visited them other than those of the outlying sectors where the Navy existed in a state of higher readiness.

Once she'd found the bridge repeater channel, she pulled up a chair and sat, watching an arc of the planet filling half of the display with its shimmering atmosphere, looking so thin and vulnerable. Then, the aspect changed as *Carentan* pulled away, and the moon quickly filled the lower left quadrant. Dunmoore looked for a reverse view, but before she could find it, the bridge repeater changed to show Earth getting progressively smaller as the ship accelerated toward the hyperlimit.

After a few minutes, she sighed, stood, and shut off the display. It had been enough to begin the inevitable catharsis of leaving a place she'd grown to dislike immensely. But she suddenly realized she was as unemployed as her aides and chuckled to herself. Perhaps visiting the passenger's wardroom would be a good idea.

If nothing else, she'd find some officers with whom she could converse.

Dunmoore followed the signs to the compartment in question and found Holt seated with a younger, dark-haired man she recognized only too well. When she approached them, both looked up at her and grinned.

"Look who I found," Holt said, gesturing at his table mate.

Dunmoore smiled at them, especially the younger man, as she held out her hand.

"How about that? Lieutenant Commander Guido Vincenzo. It looks good on you." They shook as Holt grabbed another chair, and she sat. "When were you commissioned?"

"Shortly after we parted ways on Dordogne, sir. I became a lieutenant and earned my thin stripe a few months ago after the minimum time in rank. Someone must be looking out for me." He gave Holt a significant glance.

Holt held up both hands, palms facing outward.

"I just make sure talent gets recognized."

"You're still hunting corrupt Fleet personnel for counterintelligence?"

Vincenzo nodded.

"Yes. I just finished a job in 1st Fleet and was looking for a way back home to Caledonia when your transports arrived. One call to Admiral Holt and I got a berth in *Carentan*."

"Which is fortuitous because Vince and I have much to discuss over the coming days."

Dunmoore cocked a questioning eyebrow at him.

"Oh? Do tell. Last I heard, counterintelligence still belonged to the CNI, not the Chief of Security."

An air of mischief settled over Holt's features.

"Sure, but Vince is coming with me to the new Constabulary you announced in the Senate. He's setting up what I've decided to call the Professional Compliance Bureau, which will, in due course, become the Commonwealth's internal affairs branch, empowered to investigate malfeasance in the Fleet, the administration, the legislature, and the judiciary. He'll be going in initially as a commissioner, a one-star, but if everything goes well, and the PCB fills out as expected, he'll end up as a deputy chief constable, a three-star."

Dunmoore glanced at Vincenzo and inclined her head.

"Congratulations, Vince. That's quite a step up."

"Sure, it is," Holt said. "But he's the best internal affairs investigator in the entire Fleet. I can't think of anyone else for the job, and remember, I was in charge of counterintelligence for several years and know them all."

"No arguments here, Zeke."

"I just hope I'll meet the admiral's expectations," Vincenzo said.

"I'm sure you will. Zeke is an excellent judge of character. If he believes you are the most suitable for the job, then you are. Dunmoore looked around her. "Is there anything dispensing drinks? I'd like to wet Vince's upcoming appointment as a Constabulary commissioner in charge of the Professional Compliance Bureau."

"Coming right up."

Holt stood and walked over to discrete bartender machines set into one of the bulkheads, touched the display a few times, and held out his cred card. Moments later, three drinks appeared on the mobile tray — a gin and tonic for him, one for Dunmoore, and a beer for Vincenzo. He picked it up and returned to their table.

"The toast is to Vince, the soon-to-be first head of the Constabulary's Professional Compliance Bureau."

Holt raised his glass, imitated by Dunmoore.

"Who would have imagined my favorite bosun's mate would make commissioner?" Dunmoore beamed at Vincenzo. "Here's to you, Vince."

"Thank you, sirs." Vincenzo took a healthy sip of his drink, sighed, and put his mug on the table. "I still don't know how I went from being a petty officer at the end of the war to a lieutenant commander today, let alone a Constabulary commissioner in a few months."

"Perseverance, my friend." Holt slapped him on the shoulder. "And one of the keenest investigative minds I've ever encountered."

***

"So this is where our paths diverge, Zeke." Dunmoore stared into her glass of whiskey. She and Holt had just completed a best two out of three chess tournament, and she felt a little maudlin even though she'd won their first and third matches. "You're off to command this new Constabulary on Wyvern while I settle on Caledonia for good."

"It'll only be for a few years. Ten or twelve at most. Once I've set up a line of succession, I'll join you and the others on our new home world. What did you call it again? The final shore?"

"Yes. I believe it's from an ancient story. How difficult do you anticipate it will be to bring the idea of a Constabulary into existence?"

Holt grimaced.

"Probably a lot harder than I figure, but easier than I fear. The initial draft will take two-thirds of Fleet Security, and then we'll immediately begin recruiting. I see the initial training for new recruits to be modeled on that of the Marine Corps. Make them fighters first and cops second. The Constabulary won't be a civilian police force but a true paramilitary organization."

"Why?"

"Because there will always be a need for fighters on the outer colonies we'll be policing, people who can not only enforce the law but make it stick in the absence of Marine Corps units."

"Makes sense."

"Besides, I can envision no better way to instill the sort of discipline I want than by borrowing Marine Corps instructors to run our basic training for the first few years."

Dunmoore smiled at her former first officer.

"I'm sure you'll make it a stunning success."

"From your lips to the Almighty's ears. Though I confess I'm very much looking forward to the challenge of setting up humanity's first interstellar police service."

"Did you already plan out a rank structure, uniforms, tables of organization and equipment, and such?"

"Up to a point, but most of it remains incomplete. Mind you, my deputy, who's been on Caledonia for the last year, has laid the groundwork to get us up and running within a few months.

Once the Constabulary is formally activated, he'll be promoted to deputy chief constable for operations and receive a third star.

"Is that what you're calling the folks immediately below you?"

"Yes. The two stars will be assistant chief constables, and the one stars will be commissioners. Rank insignia for the officers will be the same as the Marine Corps and Army. The titles for O-1 to O-6 will also differ — sub-inspector, inspector, chief inspector, superintendent, chief superintendent, and assistant commissioner. The warrant officers and noncoms will also wear the same rank badges as the Marine Corps and have the same titles, save for command sergeant. There won't be any in the Constabulary. Oh, and the uniform will be gray with black trim. That's the straightforward part. The TO&E is a bit harder, especially since it'll evolve as the organization grows and fills more and more niches in the interstellar law enforcement universe."

A wistful look entered Dunmoore's eyes.

"You know, I'm just a tad jealous of your future. You'll be at the forefront of building something entirely new and spending a decade or more watching it grow under your capable supervision. Whereas I've got maybe five years left as CNO doing the same old job, and then it's retirement and a second career as a civilian."

"I could always use a deputy chief constable who doesn't require a law enforcement background. How'd you like to take personnel and training?"

Dunmoore smirked at his amused expression.

"No thanks."

"That's what I thought. You could always apply to become Grand Admiral."

"I don't have the right background for the job. Heck, I barely have it for the CNO appointment. Not enough time as a senior staff officer at Fleet HQ. The only reason I got this assignment was to help Kathryn execute the final stages of the plan."

"And you did a better job of it than Kathryn could have, something she'll be the first to admit once she hears the full story."

"Which you will tell her, no doubt?"

"Of course. Someone needs to toot your horn since you never do it yourself."

"I prefer to let my work speak for me."

"And that's been your problem all along. A bit more self-promotion would have helped you get to four stars faster."

"You figure?"

Holt gave her a solemn nod.

"I do."

"I don't. Without Kathryn, I'd have never made it back to flag rank, let alone pin four stars on my collar, and that's a fact." A wry smile appeared. "I pissed off too many influential people with my War College papers."

"Which are mandatory reading for all students nowadays. They're even talking about making them de rigueur for the Academy's third-year military history classes."

"Are they?" She pumped an ironic fist in the air. "Vindication at last."

"The passage of time often brings more nuanced perspectives to significant events. You simply published your papers too early after the war, when the most prominent actors were still around and could stop your career in its tracks by way of objection."

Dunmoore grimaced.

"I suppose there's a lot of truth to that. But I made it in the end." She raised her glass. "Here's to us."

"Because there's no one else like us."

They clinked glasses and drained them.

"A refill?"

— Thirty-Nine —

Dunmoore stepped off the first shuttle to land, followed by her two aides handling their luggage on a pair of antigrav sleds and looked around. Joint Base Sanctum had expanded enormously since the last time she'd set foot on Caledonia, over a decade earlier. And that was only what she could see from the spaceport, which had also grown exponentially.

"This place looks way bigger than Joint Base Geneva," Captain Malfort said as they made their way to the passenger terminal. "I still remember when it was a small station."

"So do I, Josh."

Holt and Guthren emerged from the second shuttle parked next to Dunmoore's and walked in her wake, but they handled their own luggage-laden antigrav sleds.

One of the terminal doors opened, and Gregor Pushkin stepped through. He drew himself to attention and saluted.

"Welcome home, sir, you too, Zeke, Chief. Everyone is in the Grand Admiral's office, ready to pop the bubbly as soon as you show up."

"Thank you, Gregor. It's nice to finally be here, light years away from Earth, where they're still spinning in circles, trying to figure out just what we did to the Commonwealth."

"You mean other than prolong its life until the OutWorlds are ready?" He gestured toward the open door. "I have a staff car and two vans waiting. The car is for us, one van for your aides and your luggage, and the second one for Zeke and the Chief's bags. The vans will take them to your residences so they can offload. Your containers are already there, albeit still packed."

"Excellent." Dunmoore gave Pushkin a broad smile. "But you could have sent your aide to orient us."

"I wanted to greet you ahead of everyone else, sir, and escort you to Kathryn's palatial digs."

They emerged on the other side of the terminal where the three vehicles waited, and the aides pushed the antigrav sleds aboard.

"No need to find me afterward," she told them. "I'll just be at a private celebration for the top brass. Get settled in, and I'll see you in our new offices tomorrow at oh-eight hundred."

"Yes, sir." Malfort and Botha both snapped off a salute, which Dunmoore returned.

Then, she climbed into the staff car with Pushkin, Holt, and Guthren, and they sped off to the main HQ building, a sprawling multi-story structure whose reflective cladding shone in the late afternoon sun. She knew there were as many levels below the surface as there were above, including the operations center at the heart of an armored box that could withstand a direct hit by a nuclear bomb.

"Nice," Dunmoore said as they climbed out of the car at the main entrance, where the road passed between the building and a stand of tall flagpoles bearing the flags of the Commonwealth, the Armed Forces, the Marine Corps, the Navy, and the Army. "Not nearly as depressing as our old HQ complex on Earth."

"Wait until you see the inside. Modern, clean, functional, everything one could wish for."

They entered, passed through security arches that scanned them and their credentials, and found themselves in an impressive lobby several stories high. The floor was white marble, or an artificial product that looked like it, and the largest Armed Forces crest Dunmoore had ever seen filled the far wall, framed by glass lifts on either side. Balconies, lush with hanging plants, radiated from the lifts on each floor, giving the lobby a pleasant, lived-in feel.

"Our offices are on the top floor, naturally." Pushkin led her to one of the lifts, which appeared to be waiting for them. "And they overlook the spaceport."

The lift's transparent door slid shut behind them, and it rose to the top, disgorging them through the door on the opposite side.

Dunmoore stepped out into a broad corridor with military art hanging on cream-colored walls. The floor was the same sort of marble as the lobby's, and the recessed lighting was pleasant for the eyes.

Pushkin briefly showed Dunmoore her office, next door to the Grand Admiral's, and Guthren his, before leading them into Kowalski's, where a good-natured crowd was already talking animatedly in a dozen separate conversations. They stilled when people noticed her, and applause started somewhere at the back.

While the chief petty officer of the Armed Forces intercepted Guthren, Dunmoore, trailed by Holt, marched up to Kowalski, saluted, and said, "Admiral Siobhan Dunmoore reporting with the remainder of Fleet HQ. And may I say you're looking a lot better than the last time I saw you."

Kowalski, who was bareheaded, nodded in return. She appeared to have fully recovered, or at least gave the impression of it.

"Welcome home, Siobhan. It's good to see you safe and sound. You too, Zeke."

"There were times when I thought I might not make it. But we carried out the plan and effectively neutralized Sara Lauzier and her successors.

"As I expected." Kowalski turned her head to one side and said in a louder voice. "Time to pop the champagne." Then, she glanced at Holt. "And how is the first Chief Constable of the Commonwealth Constabulary? I assume you'll be off to Wyvern soon."

"In a few weeks, sir. I still need an update from my deputy on where we stand."

"Firmly on the path to glory, Zeke. I received an update this morning, and they have cleared space for you on Joint Base Draconis so you can set up your new headquarters and school. As far as I'm concerned, you and your people can change uniforms immediately, although you'll still have to be tied to the Fleet for administration and logistics until you establish your own.

"That's good news. I'll let my folks know."

Kowalski's aide appeared with champagne glasses and passed them out. The Grand Admiral raised hers.

"Fellow officers and chiefs." When the crowd quieted, she said, "I propose a toast to the new Fleet. Long may it serve humanity across the stars."

Everyone raised a glass.

"To the Fleet! Long may it serve."

They took a sip, and Dunmoore let out a low whistle.

"You didn't stint on this, did you, Kathryn? It tastes like the finest from Dordogne."

"And yet it's Caledonian, the best in the star system, and is a fraction of what Dordogne champagne costs."

"Why did I never encounter this fine vintage when I was stationed here after the war?"

"Because it only started to be sold recently."

"Ah. And because I don't normally drink bubbly anyway."

"Shall we go up to the terrace and watch the shuttles with the last of our HQ personnel from Earth land?" Kowalski suggested.

Dunmoore couldn't help but laugh.

"You have a rooftop terrace?"

"Indeed. Follow me."

Kowalski took them through a side door and up a set of stairs. They emerged on the flat roof just as a shuttle was landing to the whine of thrusters. The terrace, surrounded by a glass railing, was made from a material designed to imitate wood, and there were chairs and tables scattered around.

"Nice." Dunmoore's eyes were drawn to the spaceport where another shuttle was on final approach. "You know, I still can't believe we pulled it off."

"But we did. However, I fear all we managed was to buy time."

Kowalski walked to one of the railings facing the spaceport and leaned against it. Dunmoore joined her, as did Pushkin, Holt, and Guthren, who'd finally detached himself from the Armed Forces Chief Petty Officer. Behind them, the other guests appeared, glasses in hand, and spread out as the sun reached for the western horizon, painting the underside of the few clouds marching toward it in a riot of colors.

"We've come a hell of a long way, haven't we?" Kowalski said in a wistful tone. "Who'd have imagined, back in our days aboard *Stingray*, that we'd end up forming the top leadership in the largest military force in the known galaxy?"

"I certainly didn't," Pushkin said. "Deputy CNO when I expected to retire as a commander, at best? I still pinch myself every morning when I put on my uniform."

"And we owe it to a person who pushed our careers at the critical moment," Holt said, "even though hers almost failed to take off at one point."

He raised his glass.

"To our Siobhan, without who none of us would be here today. This is as much her triumph as it is ours."

"To Siobhan."

Dunmoore accepted the kudos without blushing, then she raised her glass in reply.

"And to the Fleet's final shore, Caledonia. Long may it prosper as our home."

"Hear, hear."

"You realize we still have a lot of work ahead of us before we can sit back and call it mission accomplished? Moving the headquarters and declawing darling Sara was simply Phase Two."

Dunmoore nodded.

"Oh, yes."

Kowalski's senior aide approached them and handed her a tablet. As she read it, an air of astonishment replaced her relaxed look, and she asked him, "Are we sure about this?"

"It's on all the newsnets, sir. The signal reached Caledonia only a few minutes ago, sir."

Kowalski looked at her friends.

It appears that someone assassinated Sara Lauzier while she was dining at her favorite Geneva restaurant, a place she had visited a few times recently.

Dunmoore's gaze instinctively went to Holt, something Kowalski noticed, and she speared him with a stern gaze.

"Don't tell me this is your doing, Zeke?"

"Ah, it might be, sir." He briefly explained about the Organization, the Paymaster, and how he'd put a contract on the SecGen. "I hope you're not pissed off at me."

Kowalski studied Holt through narrowed eyes for a few heartbeats, then shook her head.

"No. If nothing else, the turmoil caused by her assassination on Earth will work in our favor, although people will point fingers at us."

"Let them point, sir. The Paymaster does not know who commissioned the hit, and it obviously happened after we left. Besides, it'll make her successor more circumspect in dealing with us."

"Well, I won't cry over her death, that's for sure. If anyone deserved a round through the back of the head, she was it." A faint smile replaced Kowalski's serious mien. "In fact, the more I think about it, the more your hiring this Organization strikes me as a piece of genius, Zeke. It removed our biggest foe and will certainly temper the Centralists' ambitions absent a driving force like Lauzier. She doesn't have a natural successor waiting in the wings."

"Would be dictators like her seldom do," Dunmoore said. "They'd rather not surround themselves with those who could replace them."

"And that's as good an epitaph as any for the late, unlamented Sara." Holt raised his glass. "To Sara Lauzier. She was a lousy SecGen and an even lousier human being."

The others silently followed suit, and they took a sip.

"Any idea who might be elected in her stead, Zeke?" Kowalski asked.

"Not a clue. The maneuvering for the position will be epic since there's no obvious choice among the senators. In the interim, the President of the Senate will head the administration, and he's a non-entity, politically speaking. He certainly won't continue Lauzier's push to centralize power on Earth."

"Which is all good. It buys us time to consolidate and let the sovereign star systems get habituated to the fact that the Fleet is its own entity, separate from the administration."

"The question I now have," Dunmoore said softly, "is whether the Organization's assassins are still coming after us."

— Forty —

Lilith Camus and her two operatives had gunned down Lauzier's security detail of ex-SSB agents and the SecGen herself in *Le Pied de Cochon* during an assault that lasted less than a minute, then they vanished into nighttime Geneva without a trace.

A few hours later, after ditching their car in the port of Marseille and taking a taxi to its spaceport, they climbed aboard a shuttle leaving for Earth's primary civilian orbital station, where they took berths on a liner headed to Wyvern.

They viewed the SecGen's assassination as just another job, and now that they had completed it, they would redirect their attention to their initial targets once more. But it would take time and travel. The ship they boarded was the first available and didn't count Caledonia among its many stops. Still, Wyvern was a hub, and they'd find something there. In the meantime, the Geneva Police would be looking for clues and not uncovering anything useful.

Yet Camus feared the Paymaster might cancel the hit on Dunmoore and the others now that Lauzier was dead, considering she suspected the latter had been their client. She rather fancied the idea of avenging herself for the slights she suffered and for the Navy career that was cut short. Camus had become a skilled assassin over the years since her last encounter with Dunmoore, and when the contract came up, she could hardly believe her luck. It would be a shame if the Paymaster canceled it.

She and her team breathed a sigh of relief when the liner went FTL at Earth's hyperlimit with no message from the planet about last-minute passengers who might have been involved in the SecGen's death, and they ventured into the second-class passenger lounge for a meal.

After a while, Camus had the uncomfortable feeling someone in the large, crowded compartment was looking at her. Still, whenever her eyes scanned the people surrounding their table, she saw no one paying her the slightest interest.

Until that is, Camus briefly met the gaze of an unremarkable man via one of the floor-to-deckhead mirrors covering the bulkheads. He wasn't directly visible, but his reflection quickly looked away when she noticed him.

She didn't recognize him and was sure he didn't recognize her, at least not entirely. Perhaps he thought she seemed familiar. Camus had undergone cosmetic surgery years earlier to change her appearance, but certain things remained — her hair color, the shape of her face, her eyes, her teeth, and, of course, her husky voice. Perhaps he was simply attracted to her, but her features had become unremarkable due to age and the surgery, even though she had been striking twenty years earlier. She certainly didn't consider herself attractive.

Yet the feeling of being observed remained throughout their meal until almost the end, but the man was gone when she and her two operatives finally rose. She shrugged it off and returned to her small cabin, where she slipped into bed and read for a while. Still, the man's interest bothered her, and after lights out, she compared his appearance to the memory of those she'd met over the years without result before falling into a dreamless sleep.

When the ship dropped out of FTL at the heliopause, they tensed again, waiting for a message from Earth to arrest them, but nothing came, and they jumped back to hyperspace at interstellar speeds, headed for Pacifica, the first stop.

Camus spotted the man again in the second-class lounge that evening, and he still gave her surreptitious glances as if trying to place her in his mind. She tired of it and, after dinner, walked over to where he sat and dropped into a vacant chair across from him.

"Take a good look at me and tell me who I remind you of." The man seemed startled by her brazenness and didn't immediately respond. "Clearly, I remind you of someone because this is the second supper in a row you've been eying me from afar."

He shrugged.

"You seem vaguely familiar, but I can't place you, and it's been bugging me to hell and back."

"My name is Lilith Camus. And yours?"

"Mike Georgopoulos."

The moment she heard the name, Camus remembered who he was, and the mental image of a man ten years younger appeared in front of her mind's eye. He'd been a crew member aboard *Mahigan*, the mercenary ship she'd commanded before Dunmoore destroyed it and the rest of her squadron. The aftermath hadn't been pretty, but Camus and her crews survived. Unfortunately, the mercenary consortium she worked for didn't, and Camus found herself a new line of business.

"And just who do you think I might resemble?"

He gave her a puzzled look as if his subconscious was trying to tell him something. Maybe her voice was triggering memories.

"An old acquaintance. Well, an old starship captain I once worked for. Lena Corto. But clearly, now that I'm looking at you from close up, you're not her, although there are resemblances."

"Then I hope I've satisfied your curiosity, Mister Georgopoulos." Camus stood. "Enjoy the rest of your evening."

She felt his eyes on her back as she left the lounge, not entirely convinced he'd accepted her identity as Lilith Camus, someone he'd never met. The more she thought about it, the more she remembered Georgopoulos as being perceptive. Best to stay away from him.

Lena Corto vanished a decade ago and would remain among the missing. Not that anyone cared about her. She was an only child whose parents had died shortly after she entered the Academy, and she'd lost touch with her few friends long ago.

"Problem with that guy?" The male operative asked as both caught up with her in the passageway.

"He thinks I resemble someone he knew back in the day."

"And is he right?" The operatives knew Lilith Camus once wore a different face and lived under a different name.

"Yes."

"Maybe he needs to disappear."

Camus shook her head.

"No. Leave him be. He's harmless. Besides, we still have a mission and can't endanger that by taking side trips into unsanctioned action."

"If you say so, boss."

***

Siobhan Dunmoore almost started whistling out of sheer joy as she walked across Joint Base Sanctum from her residence to the main HQ building rather than take the brand-new underground shuttle system. The weather was mild, the sun shining, a faint breeze brushed her cheeks, and the sight of the beautifully landscaped grounds combined to make her more cheerful than usual as she headed into work.

The last little while had been filled with bliss compared to her final six months on Earth. She could now concentrate on the job of CNO and ignore the distant politics entirely. Smiling as she returned the salutes of passing soldiers, spacers, and Marines, Dunmoore walked up the steps, through the main doors and the security arch, then headed for the lifts and the sprawling structure's top floor. As she got off, she spotted a tall, blond figure in a black-trimmed gray uniform wearing four stars at the collar.

"Zeke! Looking sharp in your Constabulary getup. And how is the Chief Constable on this fine morning?"

"You're sounding mighty chipper, Siobhan." Holt smiled warmly at her. "Did you get an extra ration of good spirits with your breakfast?"

"I'm just happy with life in general today."

"Ah, the old I've escaped Earth syndrome strikes again. Good."

"What are you up to?"

"Still working on the TO&Es with my staff. Actually, I'm on my way to see Kathryn so that we can discuss the final composition of the Constabulary Regiments that we'll establish on the federal and charter colonies."

Holt and the Fleet personnel transferred to the Constabulary had taken over a floor in the main building's north wing and dubbed it the Provisional Constabulary Headquarters, complete with a sign at the entrance. That sign prominently displayed the new Service's badge, the scales of justice balanced on a downward-pointing arrow surrounded by a stylized laurel wreath above a scroll with the motto *Fiat Justitia* — let justice be done — inscribed on it.

"Why just the federal and charter ones?"

"We can't really assert that the various independent star systems are sovereign and then impose policing by the Constabulary on their wholly owned colonies. But we will provide a unit if they ask."

"Makes sense. Then how will you deal with those sovereign worlds?"

"We're establishing groups that'll work alongside the local police to handle interstellar and federal business. Again, if a star system doesn't want us there, we won't go. But all the OutWorlds have signed on since they understand sharing the burden is in their interest. The Home Worlds, not so much — many of them are refusing our presence out of pique more than anything else."

They stopped in front of the door leading to the CNO's office suite.

"I may have said this before, but I envy you, Zeke. Building something completely new."

"You have, and I'd better get going. Kathryn still frowns on tardiness. How about you come over for supper tomorrow night?"

"With pleasure. Give Reyka my best."

"Will do."

He sketched a salute by waving his hand near his brow and headed down the corridor.

Dunmoore entered the antechamber where both of her aides sat at desks on either side of the inner door leading to her office. The one leading to Guthren's was open, and she saw him standing by the windows, sipping his coffee. When he heard her wish the aides a good morning, Guthren turned and raised his mug, one with *Iolanthe*'s furious faerie badge on it, in salute.

"Good morning, Admiral."

"And the same to you, Chief. It's a great day to be alive."

He gave her a grin.

"That it is."

She glanced at Malfort.

"What's on my agenda for today?"

— Forty-One —

Lilith Camus breathed a silent sigh of relief once she and her team had passed through Caledonia's strict entry controls on board the civilian orbital station. She'd been worried that the artificial intelligence handling inbound passengers might challenge them. But they sailed through without a problem, something she ascribed to the Organization having tentacles everywhere, including the Fleet's homeworld. They were using different identities from the last time they visited to take out the deputy CNO, and their appearances had changed, but it only took one out-of-place element to trigger the AI.

After crossing the station and taking the lifts down several levels, they emerged on the shuttle deck and settled on a bench to wait for one headed to Sanctum. With an uncanniness developed over many years, the three blended in with other passengers and were so unremarkable the eye simply passed over them. Eventually, they boarded the shuttle, and Camus took a window seat, intent on seeing Joint Base Sanctum from above as they made their final approach.

She was not disappointed. The sprawling complex shimmered in the afternoon sun, with little specks moving on the roads. But her scrutiny was too brief, and they landed in the civilian spaceport on the other side of Sanctum a few minutes later.

A quick walk through the terminal, a ride to the rundown part of the city in an autotaxi, and another, lengthier walk to cover their tracks, and they found themselves in front of a small, one-story house that had seen better days. It was not the same safe house they'd used during their previous visit but still belonged to the Organization, or so Camus concluded because the front door opened after an unseen sensor took a retinal scan of her right eye.

Contrary to its tired external appearance, the house's interior was clean, modern, and well-furnished. They explored it and selected a bedroom each, knowing they were here for a while. Camus checked the kitchen cupboards and found stacks of autochef meals, enough for at least a week. Since none of them drank anything more than water, she gave the cold compartment a cursory glance and saw it was empty.

Then, she stuck her head into the attached garage and saw an older model ground car that someone with limited funds would drive. She climbed aboard and started the power plant, which instantly came to life. Camus called up the car's ownership on the readout and noticed it was registered in her current assumed name. The Organization didn't skip any details when it paved the way for one of its teams.

"Satisfactory?" The man asked her when she entered the living room where both operatives waited.

"Yes. It'll do nicely."

"Found any weapons?"

Camus shook her head. "We'll have to buy them on the black market."

"No sweat. You can get pretty much anything around here — gear that's gone walkabout from Fleet armories, surplus that wasn't destroyed as it should have been, copies of military stuff, even perfectly legal guns. You only need to find the right people or a gunsmith's store."

"And you have connections?"

"From my time in spec ops. Just say the word, and I'll start looking."

"Not right away. First, we need to scout the targets and get a feel for their lives. Then, once we've decided on our approach, we'll know what sort of weapons we need."

"Right. And how will we get close enough to decide how we'll whack 'em?"

Camus allowed herself a faint smile.

"Apparently, Joint Base Sanctum is hiring civilian maintenance workers and groundskeepers. I noticed the job advertisement on my communicator while we were waiting for our shuttle back on the station. Our current identities and legends should be enough to get us in."

The man gave her an appreciative nod.

"Okay. I guess that's why you're the boss."

"Tomorrow morning, we'll apply."

***

"And finally, we received word that there's a new SecGen. The honorable senators went through twelve rounds of voting before they had a clear winner." Kowalski looked around the table at her direct reports and Chief Constable Holt, who still attended her weekly command conferences. "Which is a lot, and it means there clearly was no successor to Lauzier waiting in the wings. Elected by a bare majority of one vote is Andrew Patel, senior senator for Arcadia and a rabid Centralist."

"I guess Lauzier's assassination made little impression on the honorables. Or at least on Patel," Holt said. "However, I suspect he won't be killed any time soon. His security will be impenetrable because he's unlikely to ever leave the Palace of the Stars."

"Not that anyone would condone the assassination of a second SecGen." Kowalski's tone was as dry as the Great Caledonian Desert. "Of course, the first thing Patel did was summon me to Earth so he could stop this fourth branch of government nonsense. His demand came alongside the message he'd been appointed, proving he's impatient to regain control over the Fleet."

Dunmoore raised an amused eyebrow at her.

"I suppose you told him where to go?"

"I didn't respond at all. Nor will I. It should put him in his place, which is running the administration."

Maybe it would be more effective if you replied with a flat no, sir," Holt suggested. "That way, his blood pressure will rise, and he could end up beclowning himself. Patel has a reputation for not being discreet. On the contrary. I suspect he got the job mainly because he's such a blowhard he wore everyone down."

"Nice. We have a blowhard for SecGen. That's what the Commonwealth needs."

"But he's cunning and no dummy either."

"Not that it matters. All right, I'll send him a big no, and we'll see if he loses his mind."

"And on that note, this is my last command conference," Holt said. "As you know, I'm leaving for Wyvern in a few days to join the rest of my HQ group, which will be up and running by the time I get there. It's been a distinct honor and pleasure serving with all of you. If I may be so bold, you're probably the finest Armed Forces command team ever. What you accomplished in the last few years will enter history as Grand Admiral Kowalski's great reforms, but make no mistake, she couldn't have done it without you."

"And without you, Zeke," a visibly touched Kowalski said. "There were times over the years when I thought we wouldn't succeed, but you always bucked me up and forced me to refocus on the goal. Thank you for everything you've done for me and for the Fleet. I won't wish you luck with the Commonwealth Constabulary because I know you'll make your own. I'll simply wish you good hunting."

"Thank you, sir."

"I think from one Service chief to another, we can be on first-name terms, Zeke." She smiled at him.

"Your first name isn't Sir?" Holt gave her a mischievous grin. Then he held up both hands. "Okay, I'll admit it's a poor joke, Kathryn. Not up to my usual standards."

Kowalski shook her head.

"Never change, Chief Constable."

"Why mess with perfection, right?"

Holt's quip drew a few guffaws and a fond look from Dunmoore, who winked at him and said, "Exactly."

Eric Thomson

***

Finally.

Camus caught her first glimpse of Dunmoore and Holt strolling through the HQ gardens after over two weeks of working as a groundskeeper on Joint Base Sanctum. Strangely enough, Holt wore a gray uniform with four stars on his collar and a blue beret with the scales of justice balanced on a downward-pointing arrow badge.

Maybe he was a member of this new Constabulary she'd read about. Scratch that. A man of Holt's stature surely had to be the commanding officer of the organization.

She kept her face away from them, even though no one would have given her a second glance, not when she wore the ubiquitous maroon coveralls of the civilian outdoor staff. To senior officers, Camus, or Caerwen as she was known to her Fleet employers, belonged to the background, unnoticed.

Camus felt a jolt of her old anger at Dunmoore when she saw four stars at the collar and the left breast covered in ribbons and qualification badges. In a just universe, those stars and awards should have been hers and not the woman's who'd usurped everything she held dear.

Dunmoore laughed at something Holt said, and the anger became a rage so powerful a red curtain dropped in front of her eyes. Camus struggled to keep a semblance of control even as the impulse to close the distance between them and kill Dunmoore with her bare hands became almost overwhelming.

She hadn't realized her feelings were that powerful and almost gasped. But self-discipline, honed over the last decade to something almost monastic, quickly reasserted itself. The curtain vanished, and she could see clearly again, though she was still breathing hard.

Camus glanced at Dunmoore and Holt again, but this time, she felt an icy resolve settle over her. She'd get them, no matter how long it took. Her eyes followed the pair until they disappeared around a clump of bushes, and then she returned to her work, gently adding native flowers to an arrangement that, once finished, would mimic the Fleet's crest.

— Forty-Two —

Over the following weeks, Camus spotted Dunmoore walking through the base every second day or so but had no more red curtain rage moments. She even figured out where Dunmoore lived in Joint Base Sanctum's huge residential quarter, a city within a city. Her supervisors trusted her by now and assigned her more responsibilities, including landscaping work on official residences.

Base maintenance had hired her two companions — the man worked in the central repair shop, and the woman oversaw a section of cleaning droids — which limited their movements across the sprawling installation.

Yet she still wasn't closer to a solution. Holt vanished a few days after she first spotted them, and Kowalski didn't appear at all. She likely moved between the office and home either via the underground network, which was out of bounds to the three Organization operatives, or by unmarked staff car. And only a select few senior groundskeepers had permission to enter the perimeter of her residence.

Which left Dunmoore, who seemed the least security conscious of the two. But Camus considered her the prime target anyway because of their shared past.

And there she was again, this time walking home alongside Gregor Pushkin, who might well become a target of opportunity, although he hadn't directly contributed to killing her naval career. Anyone so closely associated with Dunmoore deserved the same fate as her.

***

"There it is again," Dunmoore muttered.

"What?"

She glanced sideways at Pushkin. "The sensation of being watched. I get it every two or three days as I'm walking either between buildings or to and from home. But when I look around, I don't see anyone giving me a shred of attention."

Dunmoore quickly peeked behind her but saw nothing more than a blond, nondescript female grounds worker bent over a flower patch. Pushkin followed her eyes and grunted.

"If it's her, you have to wonder why. Maybe she sneaked a peek out of sheer curiosity since you're the head of the Navy."

"Could be. But it's still eerie. That sensation began only recently, and you know I'm sensitive to such things. It saved my life a few times."

Pushkin grunted.

"In that case, stay on your toes. Changing the subject completely, have you heard from Zeke recently?"

"Yes. He sent me a quick note to say all is well. He's working twelve-hour days, which annoys Reyka to no end. The transition of Fleet Security personnel, equipment, and files is going as smoothly as he could have hoped. He's no further ahead with the suicide mercenaries or the mysterious Organization that Sara Lauzier hired to assassinate us."

"Hmm. Did you consider this sensation of being watched could well be from members of the Organization? It's quite possible Lauzier's death didn't cancel the contract."

"I have, but not seriously. It would take pretty good cover identities to make it onto the base, and I rarely leave it."

Pushkin glanced back at the groundskeeper. But she'd vanished.

"Even low-level civilian staff?"

When Dunmoore didn't immediately reply, his lips tightened, and he nodded.

"Take heed of your feelings, Siobhan. They might be telling you something. And it might be preferable if you took a staff car between work and home from now on and limited your noonday walks to the inside of the main HQ building."

Dunmoore stopped and faced him.

"All right, I'll do it if only because I know you'll nag me mercilessly and enlist Chief Guthren in the cause, making it two against one."

"Good."

"Then let's enjoy my last walk home under a beautiful summer sun."

They resumed their stroll, and Pushkin asked, "Did Kathryn hear anything from the new SecGen since she sent her big fat no, I'm not coming to Earth?"

"Not a peep. Which makes me wonder what Patel is up to."

"Hopefully, hauling in his sails now that he knows he can't order the Grand Admiral around like one of his lackeys."

"He's a politician, Gregor. They live in a universe of possibilities, not absolutes. Patel is still looking for ways of reasserting the SecGen's control over day-to-day Fleet business, even if you and I know that will never again happen."

"From your lips, Siobhan."

Dunmoore experienced that strange sensation of being observed once more and whirled around in time to see the same groundskeeper as before crossing the path twenty meters behind her. Though the woman's eyes looked strictly ahead, Dunmoore got the impression she'd been staring at her for a few seconds.

"Are you okay?"

"That woman, she's watching me from the corner of her eyes."

Pushkin looked in Camus' direction and exhaled loudly through his nostrils.

"Not that I can see, but I'll trust your instincts."

"I've committed her face to memory. If I see her again, I'll know who she is."

***

"So all we have is Dunmoore."

Camus nodded at the man.

"Yes. Holt is gone to Wyvern, where we might end up after completing the part of the contract here if the Paymaster wants to pursue him. But Kowalski has been invisible to us. She's moving around the base unseen, and we can't get into any of the main buildings or the underground passage network, let alone her residence."

"It's possible we'll work our way up and become trusted with access."

"Could be, but how much time will it take? We don't have years to complete this contract." Camus shook her head. "No, I think I'll figure out how to take down Dunmoore. We'll just have to leave Kowalski be and call it a partial success."

"You gonna do her at home?"

"That could be difficult, seeing as how we're tossed off the base at seventeen hundred hours and readmitted at oh-seven hundred the next day, among other problems, such as full body scanning before we go in. You have to admire the security measures."

The man chuckled as a thought came to him.

"You could always make it a suicide mission and choke Dunmoore with your bare hands when she walks out of the HQ building."

"Don't think it hasn't crossed my mind," Camus growled. "But I'd rather remain free and undetected and leave the suicide missions to the fanatics. We'll have to wait until she leaves the base for whatever reason."

"Easily said, but more difficult to carry out."

"We know her personal ground car's make, model, and registration number. I'm pretty sure we'll eventually get lucky with our surveillance of the main gate during non-working hours."

The woman sitting across from Camus in their safe house's living room groaned theatrically.

"And isn't that fun?"

"You got anything better to do?" Camus asked, cocking an eyebrow at her.

The three took turns monitoring the base's gate between seventeen hundred hours and twenty-three hundred hours on weeknights and full days on weekends, always parking their car in a different spot, always using a remote camera so it wasn't visible to the military police. Boring? Yes. But as Camus said, they had nothing else to do while on a mission.

She clapped her hands once and stood.

"Bedtime. Morning comes fast."

The man smirked at her.

"Yes, mother."

— Forty-Three —

"I've been meaning to ask for a while now. When was the last time you flew a fighter, Admiral?" The Director of Fighter Operations, Rear Admiral Kranger, nodded at the wings on Dunmoore's chest as he sidled in beside her at the officer's mess bar.

It was late Friday afternoon, and she'd made a habit of visiting the mess at least once a week to socialize with the other HQ officers and take the pulse of the community. Only for one drink and an hour or so, but everyone noticed her presence, and it made her seem more approachable.

She gave him a wry smile.

"Over thirty years ago, Grant, when I was but a callow ensign. I quickly gave up on the dream of being a gallant pilot when I realized it just wasn't right for me."

"Well, it does take a special mindset. Tell me, though, wouldn't you like to try your hand at it again, for old times' sake?"

Dunmoore laughed.

"Oh, dear. Those wings on my chest have been ornamental for over half my life. I'm not sure I could safely fly even a trainer."

"You have flown shuttles in more recent years."

She winked at him.

"Not that anyone would acknowledge giving me the controls. Still, even that was a long time ago."

"You may not know this, but I fly regularly with the 247th Defense Wing to keep my currency. A few hours per month, one orbital patrol, that sort of thing."

"And they happily let you take the controls of an F-303?"

Kranger nodded enthusiastically.

"Whenever I go up, the flight leaders always find it delightful to have a two-star under their orders. What did you fly again? F-301s?"

"Yes."

"I'll bet you can still picture the control panel, the cockpit configuration, pretty much everything about it. Well, the F-303 isn't that different. Merely an evolution of the F-301. You can probably spend a few hours in a simulator to scrape off the rust before taking the real thing up."

Dunmoore smiled at the younger man's enthusiasm.

"Keep going, and I might consider it — for a second or two."

The truth was Dunmoore had discovered that commissioned officers were wasting their skills at the controls of sublight fighters. It would be better if the Navy imitated the Marines and used noncoms.

After all, most shuttle pilots were petty officers, and the only difference between shuttles and fighters was the element of combat. Not that fighters had seen any since the early years of the last war. The carriers, except for *Terra*, had been decommissioned, and she was the flagship of the Fleet, a space control ship that no longer carried a fighter wing. Should any of the mothballed carriers be brought back into service, it wouldn't be in their former role. At least not under her command, and she doubted any of her successors would revive the concept. The last carrier admiral had retired years earlier, leaving no one to militate for them.

Then, obeying an impulse whose origin she couldn't fathom, Dunmoore nodded once. After all, she had competent subordinates who dealt with the minutia of running the Navy and she was getting antsy with less to occupy her mind.

"Why not? It might relieve the tedium of being stuck behind a desk."

A big grin spread across Kranger's face.

"Give the word, sir, and I'll set you up for your very own private simulator training."

She mentally reviewed her calendar and decided the sooner, the better, so she didn't find any reasons to back out.

"How about we start Monday, say, ten hundred hours?"

"Done and done, sir. You won't regret it. Swooping into orbit at the controls of an F-303 banishes the bureaucratic blues like nothing else."

The following Monday, Dunmoore found herself entering the 247th Defense Wing's unit lines on the far side of the Joint Base Sanctum's spaceport, received without pomp and circumstance by the wing commander, Captain Henk VanVliet.

"Good morning, sir. Welcome.

"Good morning, Henk. How are you?"

"Just grand, sir. It's another fine Monday on the Fleet's homeworld, and all is well. The F-303 simulator is ready for you, all set up by the team". He gestured to his right. "If you'll follow me."

They walked down a corridor decorated with images of fighters through the ages until they came to a door marked 'Simulators.' Upon entering, Dunmoore found herself in a control room with individual workstations and doors lining three of the four walls. One of them was occupied by a lieutenant who climbed to his feet with alacrity. He wore wings of gold on his left breast, the same sort that Dunmoore had.

"This is Drew Gaeta, one of our instructor-rated pilots. He'll be your controller during the workups."

Dunmoore nodded at him.

"Lieutenant Gaeta."

"Admiral, sir. I understand you haven't flown a fighter in quite a while."

She smiled at him.

"You could say that. But apparently, it's something you never really forget."

"Indeed, sir." He gestured at one of the inner doors. "Your simulator is right through there if you'd like to begin."

"Certainly." She turned to the wing commander. "You might as well get back to whatever you were doing before I showed up, Henk. I'll be in good hands."

"Enjoy, sir."

"That I will."

Gaeta handed her a helmet and said, "Of course, no AI assistance will be provided for any of the evolutions."

"Of course."

Dunmoore entered the simulator, a narrow room designed to mimic the cockpit of an F-303, donned the helmet, and strapped herself into the seat.

Almost immediately, the control panel and displays mirroring the outside lit up. She saw the HQ buildings in the distance across the vast tarmac and realized she was virtually sitting just outside the 247th's hangar.

"Navy two-three-one-zero, this is Control."

"Navy two-three-one-zero, go ahead," Dunmoore replied.

"I thought we'd start by taxiing and then shooting takeoffs and landings."

"Suits me fine."

"Navy two-three-one-zero, once you've completed your preflights, you are cleared to taxi to the main runway."

Dunmoore went through the preflight checks slowly, a bit clumsily, but things came back to her faster than she expected. She'd spent time studying the F-303 pilot manual over the weekend, which greatly helped.

Finally, happy that her fighter read green in all respects, she lit the power plant and let it settle. Then, she goosed the vertical thrusters just enough to raise the craft by a meter and oriented it toward the simulated taxiway.

"One-zero on the threshold of the active."

"You are number one in the pattern. Move onto the active, take off vertically to an altitude of five hundred, and hold there."

"Roger."

Dunmoore did as ordered and was pleased to see her steadiness at the controls while the simulated belly thrusters pushed her up.

"All right, time to land, one-zero. Straight down."

Again, she kept the craft steady and came to a hover one meter above the ground.

"Excellent, one-zero. Let's do it again."

By the time she stepped out of the simulator at noon, Dunmoore felt both fatigued and elated. Her old skills had returned with a vengeance, and even Lieutenant Gaeta declared himself genuinely impressed.

"Same time tomorrow, sir?" He asked.

"Yes." Dunmoore grinned at him as she nodded enthusiastically.

She was still smiling as she climbed aboard her personal ground car and drove back around the spaceport tarmac to the main HQ building. Dunmoore rarely took the vehicle, preferring to walk or use the underground network or now ride aboard a staff car, but she still had a reserved above-ground parking spot where she left it.

Once Dunmoore had disappeared inside, a blond groundskeeper slowly approached the car, working the flowerbed edging the lot, quietly jubilant at her immense stroke of luck. She knelt in front of the vehicle, slipped a tiny tracking device from her overall pocket, and stuck it beneath the front end. Then she kept moving along the edge, cleaning up dead vegetation between the flowers.

***

"How was it?" Pushkin asked as he fell in beside Dunmoore on the way to the cafeteria for lunch.

"Like riding a bicycle. It just came back to me, proving that the Navy's exclusively using commissioned officers as fighter pilots is a waste."

Pushkin cocked an eyebrow at her.

"One which the CNO will clean up, I hope."

"Eventually, although it's not high on my list of priorities right now. Besides, the Navy does need somewhere to dump Academy products who aren't quite capable of becoming starship officers and aren't quite smart enough for logistics or intelligence."

"True. Although I wish the selection criteria were tighter at the front end, so we don't end up with graduates who are of no use to the big ship Navy."

Dunmoore winked at him.

"If you can figure out how to make them foolproof, let me know."

"Nothing will ever be foolproof, and if by accident we make it so, the universe will simply invent a bigger fool," he replied in a gloomy tone.

Dunmoore let out a delighted peal of laughter.

"Now that sounds just like you, Gregor."

"Except I can't claim to have coined the phrase. If I'm not mistaken, it's a riff on one of Murphy's Laws of Combat. Are you at least enjoying yourself?"

"Surprisingly, yes. Very much so. It makes me feel thirty years younger, footloose, and worry-free. I can't wait to go up for real."

He grinned at her.

"Who'd have thought it? Admiral Dunmoore finding renewed enthusiasm in her old ensign's pursuits."

"More like I'm bored to tears some days and desperately need a distraction from the administrivia." She sighed. "I seem to recall being much happier as a rear admiral in command of the 101st Battle Group. Even commanding 3rd Fleet had its moments."

When Dunmoore returned to her office suite after lunch, she found a Marine Corps colonel waiting patiently for her in the anteroom. He jumped to his feet when she entered.

"Good day, Admiral. I'm Gert Jussel from Fleet Security. Your aide said you might have a few minutes?"

Dunmoore briefly glanced at Commander Botha, who gave her an almost imperceptible nod.

"Certainly, Colonel. Follow me."

Once in her office, she gestured at the chairs facing her desk and sat behind it with an expectant air.

"Sir, Chief Constable Holt has asked Fleet Security to investigate after the Constabulary found out the Organization — you've heard of them right?"

"Yes."

"Found out the Organization has at least one team on Caledonia, and he suspects they may be after you and the Grand Admiral."

"I see. And what has your investigation shown so far?"

"Nothing yet, sir. The notification from the Constabulary came in only yesterday evening."

"Did they say how they found out?"

"No." Jussel hesitated for a moment. "Sir, I recommend increasing your personal security precautions to the same level as those used by the Grand Admiral. And before you ask, we've been keeping an eye on both of you."

"I'll take your advice under consideration, Colonel. But I'd say things are much tighter here in Sanctum than in Geneva."

He nodded.

"That's a given, sir. Still, an assassin only needs to be lucky once."

"While I need to be lucky every single time. Okay. Agreed."

"Thank you, sir. That was all I had."

— Forty-Four —

Dunmoore could feel her heart beating faster as she taxied onto the tarmac behind Lieutenant Gaeta's F-303. This would be her first actual flight in a fighter in over thirty years, and she was more excited than she'd expected at wiping the tarnish of long disuse from her wings. Then, she breathed in and out a few times to calm herself, clamped down on her wayward thoughts, and focused on flying.

"Sanctum Control, this is Navy four-three-nine-five with one winger on the threshold of the active. Request permission for a local training flight up to fifty thousand meters." Gaeta sounded crisp and professional.

"Navy four-three-nine-five, this is Sanctum Control, you and your winger are number one for takeoff. Lift vertically for five hundred meters, then head two-seven-zero degrees, rising at a rate of three thousand per minute. Be aware of civilian traffic below thirty thousand meters heading to and coming from the Sanctum civilian spaceport. No military traffic at this time. Confirm with us when passing through thirty thousand." On the other hand, the controller sounded a little bored to Dunmoore's ears, but maybe it was just her interpreting his tone.

"Four-three-nine-five understands and will comply."

"Control, out."

"Alright, Admiral," Gaeta's voice came over the squadron channel. "Are you ready?"

"As ready as I'll ever be at this point. Let's do it."

"Nine-five, going up."

Gaeta's F-303 slowly rose on its thrusters, and Dunmoore followed, leaving thirty meters — the training distance — between them.

The sensation of lifting off under her own control rather than the AI's suddenly seemed indescribably exhilarating, and she forcibly restrained an impulse to waggle her wings.

"Passing through five hundred meters, changing to forward vector."

As Dunmoore hit five hundred, she switched from belly thrusters to aft thrusters. She pointed her fighter's nose sharply upward, keeping position thirty meters to the right and behind Gaeta, who accelerated sharply without warning. Dunmoore simply goosed her engines and caught up within seconds.

"Good form, Admiral."

"Thank you."

"Let's get above thirty thousand, then we'll try some maneuvers."

And maneuver they did — candles, Immelmanns, scissors, split S, cobras, pretty much every move in the book. Dunmoore not only kept up, she also thrived. This was soloing all over again, only better. Much better. She remembered everything, not just intellectually but deep down inside and to the tips of her fingers as they touched the controls. When she glanced at her airspeed, she was astonished to see she'd risen above Mach 5 and was continuing to accelerate.

At fifty thousand meters, they were halfway to space, and she admired the curvature of Caledonia beneath its seemingly fragile layer of atmosphere. Above her, the sky had turned black, while far beneath, puffy clouds obscured parts of the landscape. Still, Dunmoore could see a fair chunk of the planet's primary continent, from the tropical Middle Sea in the south to the Northern Alps high in the temperate zone.

Gaeta's voice broke the spell and called her back to reality.

"I think it's enough for your first real outing, Admiral. You did exceptionally well. I can't see the difference between your flying and that of most currently serving fighter pilots in the 247th."

"Kind of you to say so, Lieutenant."

"I think you can refer to me by my callsign now, Admiral, since I'm officially declaring you ready. It's Gator Five. And I believe yours used to be Redstar One, wasn't it?"

Dunmoore chuckled at that blast from the past.

"Yes, so it was. But the callsign has to be taken by now."

"Then how about I dub thee Redstar Niner? I'm pretty sure no commanding officer in the fighter groups is using Redstar."

"Sure, Gator."

"Let's go home, Redstar."

The words were barely out of Gaeta's mouth when he peeled off and headed downward at a steep angle. Dunmoore followed a fraction of a second later, closing the distance between them to twenty meters, the standard interval in active fighter squadrons.

When Dunmoore entered the antechamber to her office, her aides looked at each other with amusement, then Captain

Malfort said, "I gather it went well, sir. You seem rather pleased with yourself."

"I am, and yes, it was just fine. Make an entry in the personnel system — I'm back on casual flight status."

"Congratulations, sir. That was extremely fast."

Dunmoore winked at him.

"Flying fighters isn't difficult to learn and hard to forget."

"For some, perhaps. And what is your callsign, sir?"

"Redstar Niner." She raised a restraining hand. "Which is not to be used beyond the context of flying."

"At least not within your hearing." Malfort gave her a smug look. "But it will be useful for your protection detail if I take one example of many."

"I don't want to hear it," Dunmoore growled theatrically. "I believe I have a meeting with the Head of Naval Procurement next?"

"Indeed, you do, sir, in half an hour. The subject is the status of the next generation of frigates. The briefing note to prepare you is at the top of your queue."

"Thank you. You're both efficient and effective."

Dunmoore grinned at them before vanishing into her office, and the two aides exchanged another look. Malfort shook his head and smiled at her enthusiasm.

***

When Dunmoore showed up at the 247th Defense Wing a few days later for her first patrol, she was greeted by the commander of the 2472nd Squadron, who handed her a helmet with the inscription Redstar Niner on it.

"Welcome, sir. Are you looking forward to it?"

"I am, and thank you for the personalized helmet." She beamed at him.

"We couldn't have you fly alongside us without one. Everybody in the wing has their callsign stamped on their flight gear." He gave her a sly smile. "And after you finish the patrol, we have another present for you."

"Shall we?" He waved toward the hangar where a dozen F-303s were lined up, canopies open, and mechanics doing their final checks.

He led her to a locker marked Redstar Niner and opened it with a flourish, revealing a flight suit with her callsign beneath her name tape on the right breast. She slipped it on, donned the gloves, and made sure they were sealed, then put on her pilot's harness and helmet, leaving the faceplate raised. With it down and the oxygen feed from her harness connected, she'd effectively wear a fully autonomous spacesuit.

After getting dressed, she joined the rest of the squadron's pilots in the briefing room, where they greeted her with polite nods all around, nothing more, respecting her wishes to be treated like any of them.

The squadron commander gave out the assignments, making Dunmoore Green Four, the most junior of Green Flight and the element leader's winger. He then described the patrol, which was routine and would consist of a sweep out to the inner moon, looking for anything unusual lurking in the Lagrangians or in high orbit, hidden from long-range sensors.

They'd start the patrol in a tight squadron grouping but spread out once they reached space so they could cover as much as possible, do one loop around the moon, one orbit around Caledonia, and return to the surface.

Soon afterward, Dunmoore strapped into the cockpit of her assigned F-303 and closed the thick canopy before lighting her thrusters and keeping them idling until her element leader took them to the active runway. They would take off in pairs, seconds apart, and head straight up toward one hundred thousand meters, where the squadron would disperse into its extended patrol pattern.

And that's what they did, Dunmoore staying with her element leader all the way as if she'd never left fighters to become a naval warfare officer long ago. But she concentrated on her tasks instead of indulging in reminiscences and soon took her place in the dispersed patrol schema as the squadron headed to the inner moon.

Three hours later, having found nothing of interest, they returned to Caledonia and entered low orbit for one pass before descending. There, they reformed as a tight squadron and pointed their noses downward to enter a lazy spiral.

As Dunmoore passed through fifty thousand meters, her control panel suddenly lit up with danger red, and her thrusters cut out. She tried to restart them, but without success, as she left the formation and dropped rapidly.

"Green Leader, this is Redstar, I've lost all power, over."

"Redstar, Green Leader here. Did you try a restart?"

"Yes, but without success. I'm essentially in a steep glide and about to enter a tight helix so I can shed airspeed."

"Roger. Don't delay if you have to evacuate. That ship will turn into a brick rather quickly."

"Understood. I'll keep trying to relight thrusters until it's clear they won't come—"

Dunmoore suddenly noticed the power plant readout, which indicated an imminent overload. She had to eject. Now.

"Overloading power plant, Green Leader. I'm leaving the ship."

She turned on her portable oxygen supply, shut her helmet to seal herself in, and reached for the eject bar above and behind her head. She pulled it down but without result. After pulling it again and again, Dunmoore concluded it was inoperative.

"Ejection mechanism isn't working, Green Leader. I'm blowing the canopy."

But when she tried, it also refused to budge, and her anxiety, under control until then because she'd been going through the drills, made itself felt for the first time. She still had plenty of altitude, but it was decreasing quickly.

Her stricken craft passed through a layer of clouds, and she lost sight of the 2472nd Squadron, but moments later, three other fighters, keeping as close to her as they could, appeared. Green Flight, accompanying her.

"Canopy won't move, Green Leader. I'm officially out of ideas." She was pleased her tone remained matter of fact rather than show signs of her growing, though still mostly background fear. "And the power plant's overload indicator is in the red."

"Shit." Green Leader sounded more panicked than Dunmoore felt. "All those failures at once are not supposed to happen."

"I know. The chances are astronomical, given the proven safety record of the F-303. Any notions on how I get out of this, Green Leader?"

— Forty-Five —

Green Leader watched helplessly as Dunmoore's F-303 spiraled toward the waters of the Great Ocean, a vast, storm-riddled expanse covering almost half of the planet. Her impact point would be thousands of kilometers from the nearest land mass and several times that from the closest settlement.

He'd alerted Search and Rescue, and they were on their way, but it would be in vain if she didn't survive the crash. And even if she did, the conditions in the area were appalling, with seas the height of ten-story buildings, low cloud cover, driving rain, and gale-force winds.

In short, it was one of the worst places on this world for her to attempt an unpowered landing. Sure, her F-303 should resist the worst the storm could throw at it and keep bobbing at the surface, but since no one had attempted a crash into an ocean storm before, who knew what might really happen? If nothing else, the storm would toss her around like a rag doll, even with her seat harness tight, to the point where whiplash was the least of her worries.

And how would the SAR craft catch the wayward F-303 and lift it from the massive waves? Tractor beams didn't work well in an atmosphere.

He and the rest of Green Flight kept following Dunmoore's stricken craft as it spun in circles, prey to gravity and now the upper winds tossing it about, making it yaw and pitch with increasing violence.

Dunmoore had dumped her remaining fuel five minutes earlier, which had arrested the power plant's overload, although it meant she no longer had any hope to restart her engines. Stuck inside the cockpit, she was going down with her fighter, and there was nothing Green Leader or anyone else could do.

How did a routine peacetime patrol end with the Chief of Naval Operations possibly, perhaps even certainly, dying? And on his watch. Green Leader was responsible for the other three pilots in his flight, including the one who outranked him by six levels, because she was the junior in terms of recent flying time. He saw his career come to a grinding halt, never mind it wasn't his fault.

Green Leader glanced at Dunmoore's barely controlled descent once more on his sensor display and shook his head. She would hit the water hard even though she'd shed most of her speed, which, considering she was flying at Mach 5 before her engines cut out, said little for her terminal velocity.

The only thing he and the rest of Green Flight could do was accompany her down and remain above her until SAR arrived.

"How are you doing, Redstar?"

"About as well as you can imagine, Green Leader." Her voice still had that preternatural calmness he found both eerie and encouraging. "This is more fun than any rollercoaster I've ever been on."

He caught the sound of her chuckle.

"Not that I remember the last time I was on one. It had to have been before I even hit my teens. Whoops."

Green Leader noticed her F-303 exhibiting a more pronounced yaw as it descended into a lower band of wind, running in opposition to the upper band. She briefly vanished into a mass of gray clouds, and when she and the rest of Green Flight emerged from it, they saw the roiling ocean beneath them. Touchdown, and he fervently prayed the Almighty it would be no more than that, could come within a few short minutes now.

"I guess this is it, Green Leader. We're about to test how crash-worthy and sea-worthy the F-303 is."

And to his astonishment, she still sounded calm. He supposed that's why she was the CNO, and he'd retire as a commander at best.

"Remember to raise your nose at the last moment, Redstar."

"I will. Have no fear. I've survived this long against worse odds. There's no reason I shouldn't make it out alive. Battered and bruised, no doubt, but alive."

"Good luck, Redstar."

Green Leader watched Dunmoore's last moments on his cockpit display while his craft was bucking the low-level winds and saw her pull up the F-303's nose a fraction of a second before it struck the water in the trough between two giant waves. And then it vanished.

***

All light, what little there was in the storm, disappeared as Dunmoore's fighter plowed into the water, and the oncoming wave subsumed it. She felt the craft rise nose first until it was almost vertical, then it tumbled backward and kept tumbling until a thousand years later, or it might have only been a few moments, the fighter stabilized and slewed to the right as it fell back into the trough. Her harness had kept her body from moving, but her head had bobbed every which way, and she noticed twinges of pain in her neck.

Dunmoore was aware of being upright again, more by her inner ears than anything else. Gray waters boiled outside the F-303's canopy, making any visuals impossible. Then, she saw the sky for a brief moment before the fighter began another tumble, this one sideways, and fancied she'd spotted the rest of Green Flight hovering above.

"Ah, Green Leader, this is Redstar. I seem to have survived the initial impact."

Dunmoore knew her voice was less assured than before, that strain was evident in it, but after the breathtaking events of the last minute or two, she'd earned the right to sound like she did.

"Happy you're still with us." Green Leader sounded immensely relieved. "How's the integrity of your craft?"

"So far, so good. But it's a hell of a ride down here. I don't know how long before I succumb to whiplash."

"Try to keep a stiff neck, Redstar. SAR are on their way."

"How will they fish me or my F-303 out of this water?"

Dunmoore suppressed a gasp as she tumbled down the face of yet another tall wave. It was eerie to hear nothing, however. Not even the slosh of water over her canopy. It was as if she were in a soundless holodrama, one complete with movement.

"No idea. We've never had a fighter go down in an ocean storm before."

Just then, an unfamiliar voice came over the radio.

"2472 Squadron, this is SAR One Six. Come in, over."

"This is 2472 Squadron Green Flight Leader; we are circling above the downed craft. The pilot is alive and conscious, but being severely tossed, over."

"I have you on my sensors, Green Flight. Vectoring in on your position. Is the pilot of the downed fighter capable of communicating via these means?"

"This is Green Four, the pilot in question, SAR One Six. I get you five by five, though I'm on battery power only, so if you take more than a few hours, I might not be capable any longer."

"Excellent. That will make the recovery easier, and we hope to have you out within the hour."

"How will you proceed?"

"Let us look at your situation first, Green Four. Then we'll figure it out. Don't worry."

"I'm not. You'll pull me out of the drink. But I am getting a tad nauseous from the unexpected movement of the waves."

The SAR pilot chuckled.

"When they're this tall, you're lucky to only feel a bit like puking. We sometimes practice surface rescues, and even in a storm boat, most of the crew turn a lovely shade of green."

"You get a lot of actual business?"

"Enough to keep us busy, but it's almost all civilian. This is the first downed fighter we're chasing in living memory." A pause.

"And I have you on my sensors as well, Green Four. What's your callsign?"

"Redstar Nine."

With a flash of insight, Dunmoore realized the SAR pilot was keeping up a conversation to comfort and distract her, and she was oddly grateful. Another wave tossed her like a bathtub toy, and she barely suppressed a groan.

"Okay, Redstar, I think I have you on visual. Let's figure out how we'll do this."

As her canopy cleared of water for a few seconds, Dunmoore thought she could spot the large, yellow SAR craft hovering above her. It appeared boxy, with oversized outriggers on either side. Surely, it wouldn't try to set down.

Then, she noticed the spumes of water boiling beneath the outriggers as it descended and realized those came from thrusters, meaning its vertical drives were in them.

"Redstar, this is your friendly SAR pilot. We're going to grapple you with our giant claw. Now, we might catch a wing instead of your fuselage, so be prepared to ride home on your side."

"Um, giant claw?"

The pilot chuckled again.

"Yep. That's essentially what it is. A claw large enough to grasp something like a suborbital shuttle, which is much bigger than your F-303, and hang on to it until we can set it down somewhere safe. Mind you, it doesn't do much for the craft's exterior, but since we're in the business of saving lives, not paint jobs, who cares, right?"

"Right." Dunmoore found herself nodding emphatically even though no one could see, triggering a wave of pain from her neck muscles.

The fighter was swept up again and tumbled, disorienting her once more, and she didn't see the claw come down from the belly of the SAR craft. Her first inkling was when a shudder went through her F-303 as the claw gave it a glancing blow when the fighter rose faster than the operator expected.

Then she sensed a tremendous thud resonate through the craft, and she knew the claw had captured her. Only where remained a mystery. It certainly wasn't over the canopy, which seemed condemned to stare at the ocean's depths, even though she knew she was right side up.

But after a few seconds, that aspect changed, and she found herself on her side as the fighter broke through the surface and lifted away from the waves at an astonishing speed.

"Redstar, this is SAR One Six. We have you securely, but it seems we don't have you straight. If you like, I can deposit you on the nearest shore and then regrip for the trip back to Sanctum, or we can go straight there. Your call."

"Let's go home, SAR One Six. I'll survive a few hours sleeping on my side. Just as long as the ride is smooth."

"Oh, it'll be that. Okay. Home it is, Redstar."

"And we'll provide the escort," Green Leader said, breaking in for the first time since the SAR team arrived.

— Forty-Six —

Dunmoore had enjoyed more comfortable rides in her time, but this one still ranked among her preferred, simply because she was alive and headed for safety. The SAR craft gently deposited her F-303 on the edge of the 247th Wing's apron, and, after ensuring she was all right, it retracted the giant claw and returned to its station, a hundred kilometers north of the Middle Sea.

Half a dozen technicians in dark blue overalls approached her fighter. The lead tech gave her an interrogative thumbs up, which she returned.

"I understand your canopy won't open," a voice said over the radio, and she realized it was the lead tech speaking into a throat mike.

"No. Nor will the ejector work, and the power plant was overloading before I dumped my fuel."

"A lot of failures happened simultaneously, and we thoroughly checked this craft before clearing it for flight. Let's extract you from the cockpit first, though. We can discuss what happened later."

Dunmoore glimpsed Pushkin and Guthren climbing out of a staff car and hurrying toward her, looks of concern on both faces.

She gave them a wave and a smile, which relaxed their tense features as they stopped just beyond the technicians, two of whom were working on releasing the canopy.

"It appears to be seriously stuck," the lead tech eventually said. "We'll need to use major force. Admiral, could you please ensure that your helmet is sealed?

"Wilco."

"Thanks." He waved at one of the techs, who ran back to the hangar and returned soon afterward, dragging machinery on an antigrav sled.

The lead tech reached into the sled and pulled out a nozzle-like apparatus connected by a thick wire to a box.

"I'll cut through the canopy locks using this laser, Admiral. I requested you to seal yourself in because of the fumes once the laser punches through. I'll ask you to get out of the way, just in case, beginning by moving as far back as possible."

Dunmoore released the seat and slid it backward until it hit the aft bulkhead.

"Excellent. Stand by for the first cut."

She watched with fascination as the laser beam cut into the fighter's outer skin just below the canopy, where the first lock was.

After a few minutes, the lead tech said, "There. One down."

He moved to the other side of the craft and worked on the second of the forward locks. When he was done, he glanced at her. "Please move as far forward as you can, Admiral."

Dunmoore complied, but she couldn't watch him work this time and waited patiently until he said, "I've cut through the four locks. We'll try to push the canopy open now."

Mercifully, it slid back without too much of a fight, and Dunmoore climbed out, feeling battered and bruised, her left side numb but gloriously alive under Sanctum's late afternoon sun.

"We need to get you to the base hospital for a full physical, Admiral," Pushkin said as the techs parted in front of him.

"I'm fine, Gregor."

"I'd rather let a doctor make that determination if you don't mind, sir." He glanced at Guthren. "Or will the Chief and I have to carry you?"

"Let me at least get out of my flight suit." She nodded at the hangar. "I have a locker in there."

"Okay."

Dunmoore walked with enough dignity, Pushkin on one side, Guthren on the other, both ready to catch her if she stumbled, although she felt stiff and awkward.

"What the hell happened, sir?" Pushkin asked. "I understand you experienced three failures."

"Four, actually. The engines cut out, the power plant overloaded, the ejector didn't work, and the canopy froze shut. You know the old saying about once being happenstance, twice a coincidence and three times enemy action? What do you think about four times?"

"This wasn't accidental."

She glanced at him and grinned.

"You got that right. I'm sure it also occurred to the wing commander, and he'll be ordering a thorough investigation, but please remind him."

"Will do." Pushkin spotted the man coming toward them and peeled off for an intercept.

"How is the admiral?" Captain VanVliet asked.

"She's walking on her own two feet and can hold a conversation, Captain. I'd call that doing fine, considering the circumstances. You're aware her F-303 suffered four malfunctions?"

"Yes, sir. The squadron commander advised me. I'm about to secure the fighter pending a full inquiry."

"Good. Assassins targeted the admiral on Earth before she left, and they won't let up just because she's now on Caledonia. Make deliberate sabotage your primary focus. A properly maintained F-303 shouldn't have gone into the drink like that."

"Indeed not, sir."

"I'll let you carry on."

Pushkin rejoined Dunmoore and Guthren at the locker and watched her strip off the flight suit and don her uniform again, ready to intervene should she lose her balance and need assistance. But she managed.

Then he steered her toward their staff car and supervised her climbing aboard.

"Do you really think a checkup by the base surgeon is necessary?" She asked once Pushkin had joined her while Guthren took the controls.

"Yes. I could always call an ambulance and have you delivered via the emergency department doors, but you will subject yourself to a full medical examination. Otherwise, I'll relieve you of duty as temporarily unfit. You might remember it's my responsibility to do so as your second in command."

"Oh, very well." Dunmoore winced as she sat back.

"See." Pushkin gave her an accusatory look. "You don't know how your internals are doing. You took quite a beating in thirty-meter waves from what little we heard."

"More like thirty-five, but yeah. I did. Still, I'm fine." She raised a restraining hand. "And yes, I'll cooperate with the medical officer."

"Good."

They pulled up to the base hospital's main entrance, and before she could climb out of the car, a doctor wearing white with a single star at his collar and an orderly in blue pushing an antigrav chair came through the doors. Dunmoore recognized the doctor as the hospital's commanding officer and gave Pushkin a wry grin.

"Really, Gregor? Commodore Yee, the CO himself?"

"Don't look at me, sir. I merely warned the hospital we'd be bringing in the CNO after her fighter mishap. If Commodore Yee decided to examine you himself, that's his choice."

When she alit, Yee studied her with concerned eyes as he drew himself to attention.

"Good afternoon, sir. You're obviously in some pain."

"Minor, Commodore. The chair won't be necessary."

"I must insist, Admiral. Until I've scanned every cubic millimeter of your body, who knows what hidden damage could lurk, ready to worsen just by you walking? And it's not because you're the CNO. Every pilot who crashes and walks away gets the same treatment."

Dunmoore took the chair with reluctance to the satisfied looks of Pushkin and Guthren.

The orderly steered her through the doors and down a corridor until they reached a lift, which took them up two floors. There, the orderly escorted her into an examination room and instructed her to sit on a diagnostic bed. He left, and Yee shooed Pushkin and Guthren back into the hallway so he was alone with her.

"Please disrobe, Admiral. I'd like to examine your external condition as well as scan the internal one."

He tutted as he noted the amount of bruising developing on her shoulders, upper arms, hips, and lower legs, big splotches turning a deep shade of purple.

"The restraints keep you from breaking into a thousand pieces when your fighter goes out of control, but they leave their mark." He made a few notes on his tablet, then bade her to lie down. "Let's check what's beneath the skin."

A full-body scanner descended from the ceiling and stopped a few centimeters above Dunmoore.

"Lie very still now, Admiral. Try not to breathe for a few moments."

She did as she was told and stared up at the slick inner surface of the machine. Then it rose again, and she turned her head to see Yee sitting at a nearby workstation, staring at its display.

"The good news is no internal organ damage, although there is evidence of internal bruising. No concussion either, which is even better news, although your neck muscles show some tearing." He turned around in his chair and stood. "You can get dressed now. I'm prescribing three days of absolute rest — no going to the office, no strenuous activities, nothing more than shuffling between the bed and the sofa. Is that understood?"

"Yes, Doctor."

"And no bringing the office home. You're to hand the affairs of the Navy to Admiral Pushkin. I'll give you patches to deal with the pain. You'll no doubt feel a lot worse tomorrow morning and will be thankful for them. Normally, I'd give you five days of forced rest, but you have a reputation, Admiral, and I'd rather prescribe something you'll obey."

She gave him a crooked smile as she pulled on her trousers.

"Understood."

"You're lucky, all things told. Thundering in from fifty thousand meters and water landing in a major storm should have meant much more damage than you suffered. Other than the bruising and the muscular tears in the neck, you're essentially intact."

Dunmoore slipped on her tunic and winced again. Yee reached into a cabinet and pulled out a small box, which he handed to her.

"One patch every six hours should do. You have enough for the five days I'd normally recommend."

"Thank you, Doctor."

"If I may make a suggestion, sir. Leave the F-303s for the younger crowd. Like I said, you were lucky."

"I'll take it under advisement." She held out her hand, and they shook. "I'd have been glad for any of your doctors to examine me, Commodore. There was no need for you to personally take it on."

"Oh, but there was, Admiral." He smiled for the first time. "Some of my younger doctors believe I'm too long gone from the daily grind of being a diagnostician and belong in my office, administering the place. My seeing the CNO personally will shut them up."

She cocked an eyebrow at him and grinned.

"Sort of like my going up in an F-303, then?"

He gave her an amused look.

"Go get some rest, Admiral."

Once out in the hallway, she met Pushkin and Guthren, who eyed her with suspicion.

"So, what's the verdict?" The former asked.

"You're officially in charge of the Navy for three days while I'm on enforced rest. But other than bruising, I'm okay."

"In that case, we'll take you home and ensure you're comfortable. I'll let the Grand Admiral know."

***

"Did you hear about Dunmoore?" The man asked Camus when she climbed into the back of their car after a long day's work. "It was all over the base."

Camus nodded.

"She crashed an F-303 in the ocean during a major storm and is lucky to be alive. What the hell was she doing flying a fighter, anyway?"

The woman seated next to her companion in the front shrugged.

"Trying to recapture her youth, maybe? Who the hell knows what goes on in the minds of Admirals? They're clearly not like us."

"No, they aren't." Camus had already thought about how they could exploit the situation when she'd heard only half an hour earlier. "We need to find out if she was injured. Because if so, she's a sitting duck."

"If we can get at her. Isn't her home a fortress?"

"Not as much as you might think. I may even have an in with the team doing the groundskeeping at the residences of the senior brass."

"Really? Do tell," the man said.

Camus gave him a wintry smile.

"I've been the most diligent and talented worker in the wider team, and they're eyeing me for more select responsibilities, like the residences of the top leadership. It's possible that I can get the promotion in the next day or two and check if Dunmoore is at home, injured and defenseless.

"You know," the woman smirked, "I've always found it strange they use droids to do the indoor housekeeping but humans to work the outdoors."

"That's because the groundskeepers are artists rather than mechanical beings," Camus replied. "You can program a droid to set up a flowerbed, but it will never have the soul of human esthetics. Besides, the Fleet can not only afford the extra costs, it likes to think of itself as something that provides full employment on its own home planet."

— Forty-Seven —

When Dunmoore woke just after oh-five hundred the next morning and tried to get up, she gasped. Commodore Yee had been right. The night had worked against her, and now her body was in excruciating pain. She reached for the box of patches and slapped one on her neck, over her carotid artery, and slumped back into bed. It was going to be a few long days.

An hour later, with the pain masked, she finally climbed out of bed and showered before making herself breakfast, though it was a rather summary one — a few slices of fruit and a cup of coffee. She had no appetite for anything more.

But Dunmoore felt restless and activated a virtual workstation in her den. She burst out laughing when all it would display was a notice to the effect that she was on sick leave and not allowed to work.

"Okay, Gregor. Message received."

Dunmoore picked up a book and settled into what had become her favorite reading chair, facing the patio and the landscaped backyard of her bungalow, where she might slide the doors open and be both inside the den and outside at the same time. After an hour, she fell asleep, waking close to lunchtime and realizing her body might need more than three days to fully recover. She still wasn't yet middle-aged, as humans who routinely lived more than a hundred and twenty years went, but she was no longer young and capable of shrugging off injuries with nothing more than a few twinges.

Yet Dunmoore healed well. The next day, she felt better and moved without pain — once she wore a patch. Still, after a bigger breakfast, she settled into her reading chair. This time, since it was a cloudless, warm morning, she opened the patio doors and turned her den into an extension of the outdoors.

And fell asleep not long afterward.

She woke to the sound of voices and opened her eyes, batting the lids a few times as she cleared her vision.

A pair of humans wearing coveralls were working along the fence surrounding her residence, removing weeds, dead leaves, and flower heads past their prime. One was a middle-aged male with short gray hair and a gray beard. The other was female, also middle-aged but blond, and her face immediately struck Dunmoore as familiar. She was the one who Dunmoore thought had been watching her in front of the main HQ building.

Groundskeepers, evidently, doing their jobs keeping official residences spotless without the inhabitants having to lift a finger. One perk of being a four-star admiral.

Dunmoore observed them through narrowed eyes as if she were still asleep, but they eventually vanished from her sight as their route took them around the bungalow. They showed no indication if they'd become aware of her presence in the shadows of the covered patio and the den. In fact, neither of them so much as glanced in her direction, though with the distance and the sunshades they wore, they could have been looking at her sideways, and she'd not notice.

After a while, Dunmoore got up and wandered out onto the landscaped path leading from the patio around the residence among bushes, trees, and flowerbeds. But she didn't lay eyes on the groundskeepers again.

Still, something bothered her about the blonde woman. Dunmoore had gotten a longer look at her today, and she seemed both eerily familiar and a complete unknown at the same time. A shame Dunmoore couldn't catch a glimpse of her eyes. They were usually the biggest telltale of familiarity. Perhaps the two groundskeepers had intentionally worn shades, although the man evoked nothing like the woman did. Dunmoore was convinced she'd never seen him before. But the more she thought about the blond, the more it ate at her.

Dunmoore finally called the base maintenance section and asked to speak with the groundskeepers' supervisor.

"What can I do for you, Admiral," the thickset civilian employee asked politely.

"You had two of your staff work on my residence this morning. Could I please know their names?"

"Certainly. Let me check." A few moments passed, then, "Frank Mobutu and Lily Caerwen. Is there a problem?"

"No, not at all. It's simply that Caerwen seemed vaguely familiar, and I was wondering whether I knew her, but that doesn't appear to be the case. Thank you for your courtesy."

"No problems, Admiral. If anything on the grounds isn't up to your standards, please don't hesitate to inform me."

"I will. Dunmoore, out."

Lily Caerwen could well be a complete unknown. The name certainly rang no bells. And yet...

***

Lilith Camus had finally spotted her prey in her own home and felt a deep sense of satisfaction at seeing Dunmoore's vulnerability. Though in Joint Base Sanctum's residential quarter, the CNO's bungalow was sufficiently surrounded by trees, fences, and landscaping to be almost isolated. It had the sort of privacy only big money could usually buy. The Grand Admiral's house, next door, was even more isolated as it sat on a large piece of ground. But Camus had already decided she was too tough a nut to crack. Dunmoore would do for the purposes of the contract.

But how much time did she have before Dunmoore came off sick leave? And could she work her property alone? Mobutu was a good guy, an excellent worker, and honest as the day was long. He wouldn't countenance her making any move on Dunmoore. In fact, she suspected he'd be the sort to intervene forcefully, and she didn't want any collateral casualties. One hit on Dunmoore, then away from this world as fast as possible, headed to Wyvern so she could evaluate her chances of taking Holt.

When they reported to the section supervisor at the end of their shift, Camus casually let drop the fact she'd seen a few bushes near the CNO's patio that needed trimming. Maybe she could go there in the morning and take care of it before joining Mobutu at their next task.

The supervisor, impressed by her diligence, quickly agreed. Camus' way was now open, and she had until the morning to decide how she'd do the job. Since the security arch scanned them every time they came on base, bringing a weapon would be too risky. Camus would have to improvise with gardening equipment or use her bare hands.

She was strong and bet she was physically more powerful than Dunmoore since her job as a professional assassin demanded finely honed muscles. Whereas Dunmoore, well, she exercised regularly, almost religiously, but in the end, was nothing more than a sedentary flag officer on the cusp of middle age, not a trained killer.

That evening, to prepare for the coming assassination, Camus spent a lot of time meditating, visualizing her victim and the end she'd inflict. It helped center her and prepare her to deliver a swift, brutal kill.

Camus' two team members knew better than to make a single sound, but they prepared themselves for a swift departure, with alternate identities and faces at hand, the route to a second safe house mapped out. Since Camus would do this alone, their job was to support her in every way possible.

She retired to bed early and slipped into a deep, restorative sleep that would guarantee her preternatural alertness and awareness the following day. Camus had one chance of getting Dunmoore and avenging herself for the profound affronts she'd suffered at her hands years earlier. She intended to make the most of it.

***

"Your crash was definitely because of sabotage," Gregor Pushkin said when Dunmoore answered his call. "You passing through fifty thousand meters on the way down triggered the sequence. Whoever introduced the coding into the F-303's computer core didn't do a good job of having it self-erase."

"What?"

"The forensic investigators found enough bits to reconstruct it. They're assuming someone intended for you to self-destruct in a crash, which would have fried the core beyond saving. Interestingly enough, it was designed to activate when you were aboard the craft. If anyone else had been flying that tail number, they'd have been fine."

"Do they know how the code was slipped in?"

"No, but it gets better. Just for fun, they checked the programming of the other unassigned fighters in the wing, and guess what?"

"All of them had the same coding."

Pushkin gave her a fierce grin as he tapped the side of his nose with an extended index finger.

"Exactly."

"Any idea when someone put it in place?"

"No, but they're figuring not earlier than the date on which you decided to resume flying."

Dunmoore made a face.

"Now that's a safe assumption. I guess no one has a clue who did it, right?"

"Correct. But they're tracing every contact your craft and the others affected had over the last few weeks, whether it was maintenance, inspection, or use."

"I believe that someone skilled enough to manipulate an F-303's programming without detection would have taken steps to hide their actions."

Pushkin grimaced.

"You may be right on that count. But let's see what the investigators find out."

Movement outside caught the corner of Dunmoore's eyes, and she turned her gaze in time to observe the blonde woman walk past the patio carrying shears.

"Was that everything, Gregor? Because I just noticed the same groundskeeper I believe was keeping an eye on me outside the main building. She worked with another man on my residence grounds yesterday and is back this morning, seemingly alone."

"That was all, sir. If I may suggest, ensure that you have locked your doors. If she's paying you undue interest, she may be dangerous."

"Noted, Gregor. And thanks. Dunmoore, out."

She glanced through the open patio doors again but saw nothing. Curiosity got the better of her, and she passed through them, stopping just before the stonework underfoot gave way to aromatic native ground cover. She looked to the right, where the blond had gone, but in vain.

"Hello, Lily Caerwen?"

A sudden and prolonged cry of pain erupted from the direction she'd last seen Caerwen. Fearing the latter had hurt herself, Dunmoore stepped off the patio and carefully headed toward it.

As she came around the bungalow, she heard the cry again, a fraction of a second before the blonde woman erupted from a clump of bushes. She smashed something against Dunmoore's skull, and her universe turned black.

— Forty-Eight —

When Dunmoore's eyes fluttered open, she found herself staring at the ceiling in her living room. Someone had tied plastic restraints around her hands and ankles.

"Awake, are we?" A maddeningly familiar, throaty voice asked.

Dunmoore turned her head to one side and then the other, looking for its source, but in vain.

"I should have killed you straight off, like any other target. Yet I thought giving you a glimpse of your executioner would make carrying out this contract even more pleasant."

"Do I know you?"

"You were familiar with the person I used to be long ago." The face of the blond groundskeeper appeared in Dunmoore's field of view. "Can you guess?"

A humorless laugh burbled up.

"I have changed my appearance — permanently. It was part of reinventing myself after your bloody interference cost me both my naval career and subsequent civilian employment." Camus smirked at Dunmoore. "Still can't guess?"

She grabbed Dunmoore's wrists and hauled her up into a sitting position, then crouched beside her. "Maybe you'll get it if you're not looking up at me."

Dunmoore studied Camus through narrowed eyes.

"You must work for this Organization which took the former SecGen's contract to kill me, Kathryn Kowalski, and Ezekiel Holt. And you're the one who bombed my residence on Earth."

"Correct on both accounts, except I lacked certainty about Sara Lauzier's involvement. You see, we're not told who buys our services, only the targets and sometimes the desired manner of death. It's ironic because we killed her."

"You also made the attempt on my former second in command, Vice Admiral Radames."

"Yes, we did. And the fact he didn't die hurt my team's reputation."

"Well, he's still not out of the woods yet, so you may just tally him up in the success column after all. You keep saying we. Does it mean you're not operating alone?"

"That is a question I won't answer."

"Yet your reply tells me a lot." A bitter smile appeared. "Lena."

Camus gave her a silent round of applause.

"I figured you'd eventually suss it out, Siobhan."

"It took me a while to place your voice, but once I had, I could see the faint outline of Lena Corto behind Lily Caerwen's face — or whatever your identity is since you underwent plastic surgery. Probably something with the initials L C, right?"

Corto made a moue.

"Perhaps I am overly attached to them. But in a Commonwealth spanning countless light years, inhabited by countless billions of humans, I'm just another cipher, indistinguishable from the rest. I'll bet there are plenty of Lena Cortos running around, some of whom might even bear a passing resemblance to my former self. They say everyone has a double somewhere in the galaxy. But tell me, how does it feel knowing you're about to die at my hands after all we've been through together?"

Dunmoore cocked an eyebrow at Corto.

"Am I? Tell me, Lena, did you also somehow sabotage the F-303 I was piloting?"

"As much as I wish it was me, no." She shook her head. "I don't have a clue who might have done that. Are you sure it was sabotage?"

"Gregor called just now to tell me they found residual code in the fighter's core that set up cascading failures. In fact, I had to cut him off when I saw you walk by. He recommended I lock my doors. What would you have done if I hadn't come out?"

"Broken in." Corto shrugged. "There are few door locks that can resist me. It's one of the many skills I learned as part of the assassination game. That, and moving so quietly you'd have never heard me walking through your house. But I figured you might be curious to see me two days in a row, and I was right."

"Speaking of walking quietly, I don't think you'll move fast enough to avoid the blaster pointed at your back."

"Come now, Siobhan. Do you really think I'd fall for that?"

"No, but you'll stand up now and put your hands on the top of your head," Gregor Pushkin said from the living room door, pointing a nasty-looking weapon at Corto.

She rose and whirled around in one smooth movement, then suddenly stopped when she stared down the blaster's barrel.

"Lena Corto, eh?" Pushkin shook his head. "Turning up like a bad case of the runs. Hands on your head, Lena. I have complete confidence that I'll be exonerated even if my shot proves fatal."

Corto slowly obeyed, eyes fixed on Pushkin, whose aim was steady and whose facial expression was harder than granite.

"All right, now you'll take two steps to your left. Move it."

"What are you going to do, Pushkin? You're effectively alone with me since Siobhan can't help. Get close enough to secure my hands; it'll be over for you. I've had a decade to become a more efficient death dealer than you'll ever be. And you won't shoot me in cold blood."

"Are you sure about that, Lena? Step to your left."

She complied, moving away from Dunmoore.

"Okay, now drop to your knees, but keep your hands on your head." Corto did so, still watching Pushkin closely as if searching for a weakness she could exploit. "You know, I still have a hard time seeing good old Lena in your face, but your voice? That brings back memories. And now, lie down on your stomach and cross your ankles, always keeping your hands on your head."

When she was prone, Pushkin stepped into the living room and shouted, "Chief?"

Guthren's reassuring bulk filled the door leading to the den. "Nicely done, sir."

A knife appeared in his hands, and he walked over to where Dunmoore sat, careful to not place himself between Pushkin and Corto.

"I guess we arrived in the proverbial nick of time," he said, crouching to cut Dunmoore's restraints.

"You did, Chief. How did the two of you figure I might be in trouble?"

Guthren grinned at her.

"It's Admiral Pushkin, sir. He knew you'd disregard his recommendation to hunker down and grabbed me to come over here, stat, just in case the groundskeeper was more than she appeared. Which, as it turned out, she was."

"You're both staunch friends." Freed of the improvised plastic shackles, Dunmoore climbed to her feet, rubbing her wrists. "And as for you, Lena, what do you think of a lifetime on Parth? Because that's where you're going for attempted murder."

"You have no proof," Corto replied, turning her head sideways toward Dunmoore.

"Other than two eyewitnesses? Perhaps not, but they'll suffice to condemn you." Dunmoore glanced at Pushkin, then Guthren. "Has anyone summoned the military police? They're better equipped to handle a dangerously feral creature like Lena."

"No. We didn't want them out in force if there was no problem. Chief, how about you call them?"

"Will do." He pulled his communicator from a tunic pocket, touched the display, and briefly spoke into it. "They'll be here in a few minutes."

"Thanks. So, Lena, will the Paymaster disavow you now that you've failed spectacularly? The reason I ask is because criminal outfits like the Organization aren't likely to keep failures on the rolls, and they often terminate them with extreme prejudice. We can protect you if you'll cooperate with us."

A bitter bark of laughter escaped Corto's throat.

"Forget it, Siobhan. I can't tell you anything about the Organization or the Paymaster because I know nothing other than contact points. And I've been conditioned against interrogation, so good luck with that."

Dunmoore considered her for a few moments.

"Well, Lena, your perception of your abilities is far from accurate. You were a failure as a flag captain, a failure as a mercenary, and you're a failure as an assassin. If your superiors decide to terminate you, I won't stand in their way. The universe will be a better place without you."

She spoke without emotion, let alone the contempt Pushkin thought she might feel for Corto, and he gave her a glance only to see a bland face staring at their prisoner.

"You had an honorable if undistinguished career until you threw your lot in with that failure, Kell Petras, Lena. How the hell did you end up on my living room floor with a blaster pointed between your shoulder blades?"

A moment of silence passed between them, and then Corto said, "Luck. You always had it. I didn't."

"No. I don't think so. You were mean, Lena. Out for yourself and to hell with your crews, a character flaw that's rightly fatal in a Navy officer. Although considering the number of officers like you who prospered during the war, I suppose luck did have a role. Bad luck. But richly deserved nonetheless."

"Look, can we stop the forensic analysis of my supposed flaws, Dunmoore? It's already become tiresome beyond belief. I'm your prisoner. It doesn't mean I have to listen to you."

Dunmoore chuckled.

"Okay. Fair enough."

Chief Guthren, who'd vanished a few minutes earlier, returned with four MPs in light body armor behind him. He pointed at Corto.

"Be extremely careful. She says she can kill with a single glance."

"Don't you worry, Chief." The MP officer, a Marine Corps major, glanced at Dunmoore and stiffened. "Glad to see you're alright, sir."

"It takes more than a wannabe assassin to take me, Major. But like Chief Guthren said, be careful in handling her. All jokes aside, she is dangerous. Have her held incommunicado on a special warrant, no visitors, period. I'll make sure the warrant is confirmed within the requisite forty-eight hours. As far as anyone is concerned, she doesn't exist."

"Yes, sir." The major nodded at his people. Two of them held Corto, one by the legs, the other by the shoulders, while the third put heavy restraints around her wrists. They then placed the same sort of shackles on her ankles and hauled her to her feet before frog-marching her off to their waiting car.

Once they were gone, Dunmoore gave Pushkin an ironic look.

"So you thought I wouldn't listen when you recommended I lock my doors? I'm uncertain whether that reveals more about my shortcomings or your foresight."

"I have known you for twenty-five years. The chief's known you for even longer. We can pretty much figure out what goes on in your head by now, and sometimes that scares us."

But Pushkin's faint smile took the sting from his words.

— Forty-Nine —

"You wanted to see me?"

Dunmoore took a chair on one side of the transparent aluminum panel separating the maximum-security interview room into two completely secure compartments. Lena Corto, hands and feet manacled, wearing a bright orange jumpsuit, sat shackled to a chair on the other.

Though her icy blue eyes still smoldered with insolence, everything about her seemed to reek of defeat — the slumping posture, a face lined with fatigue, her hair unkempt — and Dunmoore wondered how she could have changed so rapidly in just twenty-four hours.

"I wanted to tell you I won't be spending a single minute on Parth." On the other hand, her throaty voice still had that mocking edge Dunmoore had heard the previous day.

"Oh?" Dunmoore cocked an eyebrow at her. "And how will that work?"

A cold smile briefly washed away the fatigue.

"Since I can't enjoy the pleasure of killing you, I'll simply deprive you of seeing me sent away for life, which amounts to a death sentence since I'm sure you'll arrange to have me deposited on Desolation Island. Call it my last act of defiance, if you like."

"Does that mean you're about to kill yourself?" Dunmoore chuckled. "How?"

"About to? No. I'm already a dead woman walking. I cracked the tooth carrying the poison just now, and it's spreading throughout my body as I speak. In a few moments, my heart will stop. There's no point in calling the guards. It's irreversible. At least I'm leaving this life on my own terms, not yours. And I'll take that as a victory."

A spasm contorted Corto's face.

"Goodbye, Siobhan."

Then, her head fell forward, and she was dead. Seconds later, a pair of military police guards entered Corto's side of the room, alerted by the diagnostic sensor affixed to the side of her neck. One of them felt for a pulse, then shook his head.

"Sorry, Admiral."

"She said she had a poison-filled tooth. How did they not detect that when they scanned her upon arrival in the detention facilities?"

"No idea, sir. But I'm sure our commanding officer will run a thorough inquiry. We're not used to losing detainees, especially by their own hands."

Dunmoore stood, eyes on Corto's corpse, wondering what had gone through her mind in those last minutes before she broke the poison-filled tooth. Calling her suicide a victory seemed bizarre, yet Lena Corto had always been a tad strange. Her ambitions had outweighed her competence, though she couldn't see it, and she'd twisted her failures into pale imitations of success. Like calling herself commodore and wearing a star when she was in command of a small mercenary flotilla after compulsory retirement from the Navy as a captain.

Suppressing a sigh, Dunmoore tugged at the lower hem of her tunic, reflexively straightening it, then turned on her heels and left the interview room. She'd receive a report in due course from the detention facility's commanding officer, but the Lena Corto chapter was over.

Technically, she was still on sick leave and returned home to change back into civilian clothes, but this time, she kept her bungalow tightly shut. If Corto had accomplices, they might well try to finish the job. Yet she needn't have worried.

When their leader didn't return, the two other assassins assumed she'd either been captured or killed. They vanished, leaving the safe house, then Caledonia's surface for the civilian orbital and the next starship out of the system.

The base maintenance service attempted to contact them after three days' absence but without success. As a result, they were struck off strength and replacements hired. Since they weren't the first employees to simply walk away from the job, their disappearance wasn't noted, let alone investigated.

When she returned to work the next day, her first stop was in Grand Admiral Kowalski's office.

"And how's the superannuated fighter pilot?" The latter asked with a wry smile.

"Doing remarkably well, considering everything that happened in the last four days." Dunmoore dropped into a chair facing Kowalski.

"You'll be glad to hear Senator Bregman strong-armed his colleagues into passing the Commonwealth Constabulary Act with only minor cosmetic changes from the draft we gave him. The Constabulary is now officially established as a separate entity from the Fleet and reporting to the Senate."

"That's excellent news, Kathryn. One down, a few more to go."

"It was the most important piece of legislation we needed. The rest," Kowalski shrugged, "whether or not they pass, the facts are what they are. I understand you had a run-in with an old colleague as well."

Dunmoore described her relationship with Lena Corto over the years, ending with her suicide the previous day.

"You know, how a respectable, if not universally respected, naval officer can become an assassin is beyond me."

Kowalski grimaced.

"From what I remember hearing about Corto way back then, her ambition wasn't backed by ability. Perhaps she finally found her niche."

"I'm not sure about that. She failed to kill me twice. Who knows how many other contracts she botched? Mind you, we have her to thank for Sara Lauzier's demise, so it's not like Corto was all bad."

A wince.

"You realize that on reflection, I'm not convinced Zeke putting out a contract on Lauzier was that good an idea. It makes me feel dirty."

"That's why you weren't involved in the decision-making. Remember, you named Zeke and me to our positions because you needed ruthless execution of the plan. We delivered. And for the record, I think hiring the Organization to assassinate Lauzier, using the money her minion, Paul Markus, intended to pay for ours, was a stroke of karmic retribution. Her replacement isn't nearly the sort of Centralist firebrand she was, and that's a good thing. It'll buy us a few extra years of civil peace."

"I guess you're right."

Dunmoore gave Kowalski a quick wink.

"I generally am."

"For things that aren't personal," the latter growled. "When it comes to personal matters, your judgment isn't quite as good."

"Granted."

"Will you be more careful from now on? We don't know who else might be gunning for us. You said once before you'd use the same security measures as I do, but obviously didn't follow up."

"Yes, I will. Promised." Dunmoore climbed to her feet. "And on that note, I'd better check what's in my queue. I'm sure Gregor took good care of the Navy during my brief absence, but he'll have dealt with the immediate issues, leaving the rest for me."

Kowalski waved toward her office door.

"Go and try to avoid saboteurs and assassins from now on. There are a lot of folks around here who are fond of you, me included."

Dunmoore gave her a mock salute and left. When she entered her office anteroom, she found Colonel Gert Jussel of Fleet Security sitting patiently in one of the visitors' chairs. He jumped to his feet the moment he spotted her.

"Admiral, your aides say you have a few spare minutes. I've got news concerning the investigation into the sabotage of your F-303."

"Then, by all means, follow me."

Once seated behind her desk, she gave Jussel an expectant look. "Go ahead, Colonel."

When Jussel finished speaking, a sober-looking Dunmoore leaned back in her chair and joined her hands.

"I have a hard time believing it, but since he's the only potential candidate, I suppose you're onto something. Leave it with me. I'll question him. That way, if you're wrong, no harm done."

"Yes, sir. Thank you for taking it on. Dealing with flag officers can always be dicey, especially when the evidence is circumstantial."

With Jussel gone, Dunmoore allowed herself a sigh.

"Why did you do it?" She asked in a muted voice. Then, louder, "Josh, please book thirty minutes with Rear Admiral Kranger as soon as possible. If you can rearrange my schedule to make it this morning, so much the better."

"Will do, sir," Captain Malfort replied through the open door.

A smiling Grant Kranger appeared fifteen minutes later and briefly stood at attention in front of Dunmoore's desk.

"You wanted to see me, sir?"

Dunmoore gestured at the chairs in front of her desk. "Grab a seat, Grant."

Something about her demeanor and tone must have registered because his smile vanished, replaced by a faint air of apprehension.

"Yes, sir."

Kranger sat cautiously, eyes on Dunmoore.

"You're looking good for someone who crash-landed a few days ago, sir."

"Maybe, but I can still feel it." She contemplated him for a few seconds in silence, aware his discomfort was growing. She could see it in his gaze. Perhaps he was a man consumed by guilt. "Tell me, Grant, why did you insist on flying every unassigned F-303 in the 247th Wing since I agreed to re-qualify as a pilot?"

"Because, as you well know, sir, idle fighters develop problems. I was simply using my status as supernumerary to take the unassigned craft out for a spin."

His answer was glib and believable, except for one thing.

"Yet you weren't doing it before I began."

He frowned.

"Really? I'm pretty sure they rotated me through the unassigned F-303s from the day I arrived. I simply formalized it. What's this about, sir?"

"You were one of the technical officers on the F-303 midlife upgrade project, weren't you?"

"Yes, when I was a commander."

"And your focus was on the primary programming of the core, correct?"

"Indeed. I have a master's degree in avionics information technology. I'm sorry, sir, but I don't see why we're having this conversation." A look of alarm had appeared in his eyes, though his voice remained steady.

"Humor me, Grant. How easy would it be for someone knowledgeable to introduce extra code into the F-303's core while sitting in the cockpit, going through the preflight checks?"

His frown returned.

"Difficult, sir. There are safeguards built into the programming."

"Could you do it?"

Kranger hesitated as if wondering whether answering honestly would incriminate him more than lying, then he nodded.

"Yes, I suppose. But it wouldn't be easy."

"Yet someone did so. The investigators found traces of introduced code that weren't properly wiped in my F-303. They reconstructed it and found it triggered the cascading failures that almost cost me my life. When they examined the other unassigned fighters in the 247th Wing, they uncovered the same code in each of them, and it was specifically keyed to me as the pilot. It means that no matter what F-303 I took, it would have suffered from the same failures." She studied the effect of her words on Kranger and noted incipient panic in his eyes. "Why did you do it, Grant?"

"I don't know what you're talking about, sir." His voice had lost its steadiness, though he tried to keep it even.

"Come now, you and I know you're the only one who could have introduced the code without anyone noticing, not even the maintenance people. Why, Grant?"

"You have no proof it was me."

"We'll get the proof we need in good time, but it would be easier if you simply told me why you did it."

His face had drained of all color by then, and he swallowed convulsively.

"I have nothing to say."

"What have I ever done to you that you'd try to kill me, Grant? We never even met until I became CNO."

Kranger's expression suddenly became stony.

"What have you done?" He asked in a harsh tone, leaning forward. "What have you done? You've destroyed humanity's last best hope with your evil machinations on Earth."

— Fifty —

An armed Captain Malfort entered Dunmoore's office, Commander Botha hard on his heels, both alerted by Kranger's shouting. Dunmoore glanced at her aides and raised her fingers, telling them not to intervene just yet.

Kranger, face red, breathing heavily, stared at Dunmoore, who simply gazed back, letting him talk, and talk he did.

"You're pure evil, Dunmoore." He now spoke in a conversational tone again, though his voice was shaky. "Thanks to you, humanity's fate will be dire. The Centralist plan to consolidate power on Earth was the only way of stopping the centrifugal forces threatening to split the Commonwealth apart. And for that, they needed the Fleet. Yet you declared us above politics and effectively destroyed the Centralists' hopes. A fourth branch of government? Who ever heard of such a thing? The military should be subordinate to the civilian power, not equal to it."

He paused and took a few breaths. Even so, Dunmoore didn't say a word.

"The damage is done, but I thought punishment was necessary. Especially after your cabal had Sara Lauzier, probably the greatest

Secretary General in history, assassinated. She was our best hope. Now, we face civil war, perhaps even total destruction."

"And yet you failed."

"More's the pity." Kranger glared daggers at her. "You have a knack for survival that's nothing short of remarkable. But others will take up the cause. I am far from alone in the Fleet looking in horror at what you've done."

"Do you realize that my actions on Earth were merely the culmination of a process twenty years in the making? If it hadn't been me, it would have been someone else. It should have been the Grand Admiral, but she was too badly injured."

"The Centralists, too, were working on a twenty-year plan after seeing what the war did to the Commonwealth. But their plan was the right one, not the nonsense you're peddling."

"We'll have to disagree on that, Grant. History will eventually prove us right, though. Centralism would have destroyed the Commonwealth. Now, do you admit to sabotaging my F-303?"

"Yes. And I'd do it again." He gave her a defiant look. "Except I'd have it explode in midair instead of crash. Your chances of survival would be nil instead of one in a thousand, and to hell with hiding the fact that it was sabotage."

Dunmoore glanced at her aides again and nodded once. Malfort and Botha, guns raised, surrounded Kranger.

"Please remain very still, Admiral," Malfort said. "Commander Botha has an itchy trigger finger she can't always control." He looked up at Dunmoore. "I called Security while Admiral Kranger was speaking. They'll be here momentarily."

Kranger looked at both aides, then back at Dunmoore. "You've won this one. But don't expect to win all of them."

"If I win the long game, I'm happy, Grant. And you're off to Parth for the rest of your life once a court martial pronounces its sentence."

***

"Wasn't that crazy, letting a man who tried to kill you into your office like nothing had happened?" Gregor Pushkin gave Dunmoore a significant frown once she finished telling him about Kranger, who was now in the detention facilities, facing charges of attempted murder.

"I figured he was low risk in person, considering the convoluted scheme he cooked up to put me out of business while protecting himself. Besides, I had Josh and Liv standing just outside my office door, ready to pounce." She smiled at him. "It worked out in the end. We have a confession, which means the court martial will be short and sweet, and Kranger will be off to Parth."

"But he said there were more who thought as he did in the Fleet."

"It's inevitable. We have plenty of Home Worlders, including in senior positions, who believe the Centralists are right. Yet I think Kranger is an extremist, a rarity. Ninety-nine-point nine percent of the Centralists in the Fleet would never consider assassinating one of us as retribution."

Pushkin grunted.

"But there's still that point one percent."

"Granted, yet no one ever said this job was one hundred percent safe. If it isn't Centralists, it'll be someone else with a grudge. And I promise I'll be more careful in the future. No more flying F-303s, for one thing."

"The crash cured you of reliving your misspent youth?" Pushkin raised skeptical eyebrows.

"You could say that. It turned out to be an affectation, nothing more. I'm retiring my wings again." Her face crinkled in a smile. "Even though the 247th Wing presented me with my very own leather pilot's jacket. Which I will wear."

"That's excellent news. Leave the flying to the youngsters."

She gave him a mock frown. "Hey, I'm not old. I'm merely on the cusp of middle age."

He raised his hands in surrender but grinned. "All right. Leave the flying to younger people, then."

"Marginally better."

At that moment, Kathryn Kowalski entered Dunmoore's office, saying, "I understand you've arrested the director of fighter operations for attempted murder, Siobhan."

"Yes." Dunmoore gave Kowalski a quick summary of Rear Admiral Grant Kranger's misdeeds.

Kowalski grinned when she finished. "Four attempts on your life in the last year. You must be doing the right things. I don't know whether to be jealous. But that's not what I came for. I just received word the Senate passed the remaining legislation to make the Fleet's new status official. It was close though — the ayes had it by a two vote majority with several notable abstentions."

Dunmoore felt a strange sense of euphoria come over her.

"It's over then. We won."

"Yes, we have. Now, we need to consolidate our victory and make sure it's never overturned. Or at least not until the Commonwealth evolves into something new." Kowalski took a chair beside Pushkin. "Which it will. Hopefully, the time we bought will be put to good use by our successors."

"Only if those successors aren't closet Centralists."

"No fear there. The highest a Centralist can hope to achieve with the safeguards we'll put in place is Flag Officer Commanding 1st Fleet. From now on, every Service chief and Grand Admiral will be an OutWorlder without a hint of Centralist taint."

"Do you think we'll live to witness a formal split between the OutWorlds and the Home Worlds?" Pushkin asked.

"I certainly hope so. Humanity's future lies with the former, not the increasingly fossilized older planets, and the only way they can find that destiny is by shedding Home World dominance. But if they delay too long, we might still face a third civil war, one which will almost certainly wreck any future our species may have. We bought time, but it is finite and ticking away every minute of every day."

"Then we can only pray that the time we bought will be enough."

— Afterword —

This, dear reader, completes Siobhan Dunmoore's saga.

She will still serve as Chief of Naval Operations on Caledonia for several years before finally retiring and raising twins while teaching at the War College as a civilian instructor. There, she will forever earn a reputation as one of the most formidable faculty members since she will no longer be constrained by wearing a uniform and treading carefully around certain subjects.

Once her children are fully grown, Dunmoore will retire a second time — from the War College — to her seaside villa in the south where she'll write her memoirs, occasionally lecture in Sanctum, and enjoy a well-deserved rest.

Gregor Pushkin and Kurt Guthren will follow Dunmoore into retirement from the Navy and take civilian posts with the Caledonian star system government, where their long experience will be put to good use. They, too, will retire a second time and join Dunmoore at the seaside.

Kathryn Kowalski, at the end of her tenure as Grand Admiral, will become Caledonia's governor general, followed by semi-retirement as she'll also occasionally lecture in Sanctum and sit on various boards of directors for enterprises providing material and services to the Fleet.

Mikhail Forenza ends up moving the Colonial Office's Intelligence Service to Caledonia, joining Naval Intelligence in a partnership that eventually sees both organizations merge.

Guido Vincenzo will become a deputy chief constable and run the Professional Compliance Bureau for almost twenty years before retiring.

And Ezekiel Holt? He will spend almost fifteen years as Chief Constable, building the Constabulary from nothing to an effective interstellar police force, before returning to Caledonia and a well-deserved retirement.

All are still alive, though elderly, at the beginning of Decker's War.

Thank you for reading this series. I hope you enjoyed it.

If you haven't yet done so, try my other series set in the same universe. You may find distant relations or descendants of some of your favorite characters.

About the Author

Eric Thomson is the pen name of a retired Canadian soldier who served more time in uniform than he expected, both in the Regular Army and the Army Reserve. He spent his Regular Army career in the Infantry and his Reserve service in the Armoured Corps. He worked as an information technology executive for several years before retiring to become a full-time author.

Eric has been a voracious reader of science fiction, military fiction, and history all his life. Several years ago, he put fingers to keyboard and started writing his own military sci-fi, with a definite space opera slant, using many of his own experiences as a soldier for inspiration.

When he is not writing fiction, Eric indulges in his other passions: photography, hiking, and scuba diving, all of which he shares with his wife.

Join Eric Thomson at www.thomsonfiction.ca

Where, you will find news about upcoming books and more information about the universe in which his heroes fight for humanity's survival.

Read his blog at www.blog.thomsonfiction.ca

If you enjoyed this book, please consider leaving a review with your favorite online retailer to help others discover it.

Also by Eric Thomson

Siobhan Dunmoore

No Honor in Death (Siobhan Dunmoore Book 1)
The Path of Duty (Siobhan Dunmoore Book 2)
Like Stars in Heaven (Siobhan Dunmoore Book 3)
Victory's Bright Dawn (Siobhan Dunmoore Book 4)
Without Mercy (Siobhan Dunmoore Book 5)
When the Guns Roar (Siobhan Dunmoore Book 6)
A Dark and Dirty War (Siobhan Dunmoore Book 7)
On Stormy Seas (Siobhan Dunmoore Book 8)
The Final Shore (Siobhan Dunmoore Book 9)

Decker's War

Death Comes But Once (Decker's War Book 1)
Cold Comfort (Decker's War Book 2)
Fatal Blade (Decker's War Book 3)
Howling Stars (Decker's War Book 4)
Black Sword (Decker's War Book 5)
No Remorse (Decker's War Book 6)
Hard Strike (Decker's War Book 7)

Constabulary Casefiles

The Warrior's Knife (Constabulary Casefiles #1)
A Colonial Murder (Constabulary Casefiles #2)
The Dirty and the Dead (Constabulary Casefiles #3)
A Peril So Dire (Constabulary Casefiles #4)

Ghost Squadron

We Dare (Ghost Squadron No. 1)
Deadly Intent (Ghost Squadron No. 2)
Die Like the Rest (Ghost Squadron No. 3)
Fear No Darkness (Ghost Squadron No. 4)

Ashes of Empire

Made in United States
North Haven, CT
28 July 2024

55544562R00220